A quiet hero and an i[...]

confront a ruthless planetary technocracy. The rest

is just adventure, romance, and high treason.

INTERSTELLAR BAG MAN

Something has been sending us signals.

Alan Root Robertson

This book is dedicated to people like me
who unsuccessfully search for something real
until we find that Real Himself
has always been standing right in front of us.

Emily is my encourager, C. S. Lewis my hero,
and Jesus Christ is both of those things
and everything else I've ever needed as well.

"And if there's life on other planets,
then I'm sure that He must know,
and He's been there once already
and has died to save their souls."

—the late great Larry Norman

PROLOGUE

In an age where the world seems to have gone crazy, or should I say, even *crazier*, we often turn to books to shut the noise off. Yes, they are an escape, yet books are more than just that. Books become friends. Patient. Dependable. Never complaining. Taking us as we are. Carrying on a conversation without our needing to do anything but supply a helpful imagination.

Science fiction is particularly appropriate for our time, because we live in an age where the possibilities have skyrocketed into semi-nightmarish regions. Nothing is allowed to be sacred. Normal got left behind. Welcome to the surreal jungle of a world we never dreamed would come to be, but the very place our forebears warned us about.

The future is a perfect setting for all science fiction because it's unknown and yet we can imagine living there anyway. Even better, we can make the truth anything we wish without harm of any kind to anyone. In other words, we can manufacture a world we hope for, or conversely, a world we fear.

And one last thing. Truth. There are those among us who say that truth is not an abstract, not a construct, not a cheat. That truth exists without the need of support or confirmation. Truth that was true long ago and will be true however far the future reaches. Truth that transforms our habits, but even more, truth that energizes our imagination and sense of place in the cosmos. What philosophers call *absolute* truth. I agree with those among us who say this. Your mileage may vary.

The Author

TABLE OF CONTENTS

JASON ON PLANET F3

"I like work: it fascinates me.
I can sit and look at it for hours."
— Jerome K. Jerome

Jason didn't like overstatement. Red-haired, tall, and thin, he was a simple, sensible man who preferred simple, sensible scenery. Because of that, Planet f3 of the Cadmium star system didn't appeal to him. Visually, it was overdone.

Oh sure, he was at the right location. The star map pinpointed his position with grim accuracy. But what greeted his eyes as he disembarked from his government vehicle, a seventy-foot-long silo, was a riot of color and odd geometric shapes. Cantilevered crystalline forms piled up on his left all the way to the horizon. Guessing he was looking at a barren globe, he was surprised to see a series of growths that were unmistakably organic. He sighed and shook his head. Work.

He returned to his silo and procured the regulation standard containment device for class-b organic material. The classification was nothing as interesting as form or composition or even apparent function. His mission did classification merely by mass displacement: the organic entities were medium-small. Reaching for the medium-small specimen jar, Jason began to hum a snatch of an old tune.

He was a little more than halfway through a two-year mission. Nothing glorious. Not a voyage of brave and exciting discovery. People like him were the second wave of human beings to visit new planets, sort of like cosmic pool water testers. Officially, a collector. Jason was supposed to bag and tag any life forms he discovered, and he had discovered a lot of life forms so far. Just nothing that spoke.

Nuclear acceleron particle pulse propulsion had been abandoned decades ago in order to more carefully study anomalies found on Earth's surface. Jason's voyage to this solar system had begun by precisely positioning his silo inside one of those anomalies, now known as tube portals, discovered in the mid-twenty-first century through extensive study of the location formerly known as the Bermuda Triangle.

Calibrating his travel coordinates within the anomaly was not difficult. It required minimal training, computer-assisted calculations, and a few important adjustments mid-journey. To get from Earth to his present star system had taken less than three weeks. Speed was not a consideration in the tube portal. It was thought to utilize an obscure law of physics that shrank distances, more like crystals dissolving than a ball being thrown with a linear trajectory. He didn't understand the principle, nor, he expected, did the pointy heads who claimed they could. Like electricity traveling down a conductor, it was something that people simply used without the need for even partial comprehension. And just as no one in their right mind grabbed a live electrical wire, Jason knew not to venture out of his shielded molybdenum silo while distance was being dissolved around him.

Once they knew what to look for, finding more tube portals had been relatively easy. One portal was just southwest of the capital city of Chaldea at the site from which Jason had been launched a little over a year ago. It was now standard practice: the first thing that space exploration required was to map out the available portals, kind of like someone with digestive problems locating the nearest available restroom just in case. The first team to visit this star system had mapped twenty of them on various planets within a few weeks of ordinary solar wind drive travel, two of them on this planet, one of which he had just used. Jason wasn't worried about getting back when the time came.

The government was putting the finishing touches on a new classroom series and needed some data to include. If Jason and his fellow collectors failed to provide what was needed, that was alright. The academic writers had already described what he was discovering. The illustrations were done by the best graphics people, and the textbooks were cutting-edge. Anything that they taught could be validated later, or not. The important thing was that the students were being taught and their resources were top-notch.

Students were entered into pod classes on their second birthday to begin the process of becoming productive members of society. Their young minds were introduced to the overarching life force of the universe, called the Plasm. The Plasm was the foundational truth of all scientific, religious, cultural, and commercial pursuits. It was crucial that young minds be made aware of this unifying principle early in their development before they became susceptible to the Sickness, which, if not diagnosed and treated early enough, would cause them to become a danger to themselves and those around them. Jason was proudly involved in that grand process, although not as one of its principals.

Maybe someday—if he kept his nose clean.

He descended the metal stairs from his silo with the medium-small jar in one hand. He appreciated the fact that this planet had a breathable atmosphere. Funny how small a zone on each planet could produce life. This planet probably only supported living things through a small zone, just as on Earth, where the organic layer was less than five miles thick on a planet about eight thousand miles from front to back. Not that there weren't always some crazy outliers that busted the rules and lived in glaciers or magma. But by and large, it seemed that the laws on his home planet were fairly universal. Gathering a sample of whatever the stuff was, he screwed the lid on and got out his labeling stylus. Then he froze.

Something was moving within the cluster of vegetation at his feet.

Taking an awkward step back, Jason clutched for his weapon. Able to produce bursts of energy that could reduce cold iron to a smoking puddle, it was equipped with a safety that Jason had modified to be quickly disengaged with a practiced thumb. Jason was no coward, but he had a healthy respect for the unknown. He steadied his aim with both hands.

First came a yellow-green head covered in feathers or fur or some combination of the two, then a short neck, a front foot, another, another, another, and six more feet. No tail. And no sign it had noticed Jason. It moved clumsily forward until it bumped into Jason's boot. He stiffened, and his trigger finger tensed, but the creature simply adjusted course on its way past him. Not a threat.

Breathing a deep sigh, Jason noticed his pulse was racing, and his upper lip was coated with sweat. No wonder they had assigned him to the second visitation crew. Rationalizing his reactions, he told himself that his nerves were still working properly.

He holstered his gun with clammy hands and tried to stop trembling.

Later, as he ate his lunch on an outcrop of purplish rock, he began to assess his life. I'm sure lucky to have landed this job, he thought. His pod mates were mostly in factories, welding together items like his silo. He thanked the Plasm for his good fortune and then unconsciously shook his head. The Plasm was not anything one thanked. He was glad his thoughts were inside his head. If his superiors knew he occasionally had this idea of being grateful to something, he might be under suspicion from the orthodoxy adjustors.

Another year and he would be on his way back for six months off, with the prospect of doing whatever he liked and going anywhere he wished. All on the government's dime. Fishing would figure prominently in his plans. He fished the old-fashioned way: with a worm and bobber. Nothing like the feeling of guessing where they were, executing the perfect cast, and seeing his bobber disappear as a hungry bluegill took his hook to the bottom and bent his light rig under the ensuing struggle!

As he went back for some more jars of various sizes, he imagined what else he might do. Seeing that girl was first on the list before grabbing his fishing gear. What was her name? Meg. Meg 4k6p2. Or was it 4k6p-3? It was 3. A fascinating girl. She worked in the lab as a chemist doing something or other with . . . what? Oh yeah. Artificial fruit. Dark hair, laughing eyes. They had only gone on one spin, but she had made an impression on Jason, wandering through his thoughts often over the last year. She'd been twenty-two and probably had paired several times since Jason had been gone. He hoped she hadn't made any lasting contractual agreements with any of her pairings.

Huh? What am I thinking? Imagine, drawing up a contract with her! Jason reminded himself that not only had they only met once, plenty of other girls were out there. He and Meg might not even have the necessary genetic capabilities to get government approval. Snap out of it, chump!

He'd like to hang with his old buddies too. Like Max, his pal who was already something or other in the government, the guy who had helped him become a collector. Jason and his pod mates had been together since they were two years old, undergoing the rearing and the preparation for usefulness to the population. He remembered his textbook, entitled Introduction to Our Enlightened Society. Good times.

His friends would be off all afternoon and evening if they had the morning shift, and there was all kinds of semi-legal stuff they could get into.

Jason nearly tripped on the green-yellow creature as it crisscrossed in front of him from under a low-lying canopy of larger-leafed growth. At least it looked like the same creature: plodding and stupid. He unscrewed a medium-large jar and bent over some foliage. He'd have to get a large freezer bag for the creature.

Then a thought struck him. His silo was nearly full. Maybe it wouldn't be much longer. He couldn't take much more aboard. Headquarters might even notice, and he'd get an early summons home. If he worked hard, this might be the last planet. He imagined what it would be like to head back home: rigging his sails one last time, watching them catch the solar wind, casting off his last planet on his first voyage. Maybe they'd let him train for a job exploring planets for the first time. That's where the real action was.

Jason didn't consider himself smart enough, or crazy enough, to be part of that group. Self-preservation was one consideration that had to be shoved aside for those who thought of signing up. They were at the very top of their pod class. He was just a collector, and that's all he might ever be. But just imagine! What would it be like to come back home after one of *those* trips . . . for those few that actually did make it home, anyway. Not many did, and they sort of served as a warning to any so brave. Or foolish. But still, to be part of that elite few and to be able to tell those stories...

He let his mind circumnavigate that happy scenario for a few minutes. When he returned to the present, he thought he could still hear the creature noisily making its way out of earshot.

Jason thought of all the bays in his silo that were already transmitting information on their cargo back to the research facility on the western slopes of the continent of Neotropa. Those mountains had been covered in a sheet of ice around one hundred years ago, before a gigantic comet had passed within an astronomical whisker of Earth, resulting in a new rotational axis and producing volcanoes, tidal waves, and hurricanes not seen in recorded history. Even the magnetic poles had slipped. The realignment had sent the new equator through Antarctica, now renamed Neotropa, and straight down the center of North and South America, now East and West America, narrowly missing Australia. Europe and parts of Africa and Asia had become arctic and subarctic and were developing continental glaciers.

It was apocalyptic. Many people had thought the world was ending, and the panic devolved into riots. Some people stopped working and gathered together for month-long religious services of all kinds.

It ended up not being the end of the world, but in the widespread chaos, national governments were unable to cope. If there had not been an emergency ceding of national sovereignty to a world alliance, humanity might have destroyed itself in bloody carnage. The temporary world government, dubbed the New Global Entente or just the Entente, quickly moved to eradicate elements of society that opposed progress and unity, especially old religions, the unpersuaded, and the uncommitted. Widespread apostasy, persuasion, and commitment followed. The process of bringing about unity and safety was called simply the Reorganization.

One strain of thought was especially virulent, believed to be a pathogen of some kind. The Entente labeled it the Sickness and, for the good of humanity, tried to eradicate it as best they could. It had become quite rare.

The newly liberated mountains of Neotropa, freed from their layers of ice and fortresses of subzero protection, were now sunny and warm with plenty of oceanfront and majestic mountains. They were fresh and unspoiled with seemingly inexhaustible deposits of titanium, iron, aluminum, vanadium, and molybdenum, all cheap and abundant and easily excavated. Gold and silver were no longer rare, and the monetary system of the world had fallen into irretrievable ruin. It was scrapped in exchange for power and privilege, and the Entente, having a monopoly on those, was established in supremacy. Mankind had turned from fighting over borders to sharing the whole world and looking for more beyond the solar system. The accidental discovery of the tube portals had goosed mankind from looking down to looking up and wondering if they might ever be able to plant their new wisdom in all the solar systems of the galaxy.

Jason shook his mind free from drifting, chuckled, and realized he was holding a medium jar with gently waving fronds of some grape or liver-colored plant and had been for several minutes. He didn't feel bad about living in his mind so much since he was the only human around for light years.

It's a lonely job, Jason thought as he clutched the jar and his mind drifted back to Meg 4k6p2. No, 4k6p *three* . . .

MEG, JILL, AND THE LAB

"There is nothing better than a friend,
unless it is a friend with chocolate."
— Linda Grayson

Back on Earth, as it happened, Meg 4k6p3 was thinking of Jason too. How much longer would he be gone? She sifted through the calendar on her wrist comm for the third time that week. Get a grip, girl! When he got back, he wouldn't have seen anyone for ages and wouldn't have time for just one person. She probably hadn't even crossed his mind. *A little much to expect from one spin, don't you think, Meg?*

She refocused on the bubbling mess in front of her in the control field. It was a fantastic failure. For years she had been in hot pursuit of producing anything vaguely resembling the texture and taste of a peach. The nutrients could be injected later from compounds produced by well-known processes, even though they didn't have quite the same effect as natural ones.

Why not just grow peach trees? What was all this about? What was the point of synthesizing easily raised food? Obviously, it would be convenient to have a perfect peach come out of a test tube any time one wished, but what if it never happened? What if the long natural process was more important to a satisfying result than the experts realized?

Glancing at the clock, she saw it was lunchtime. She dialed a few controls and pushed a couple of keys on the console, and the experiment was dumped, triggering the control field's fifteen-minute cleaning cycle. She reset the visual recorders, knowing there was a master file somewhere in the facility that recorded her work for her superiors to evaluate. That's one nice thing, she thought. They like me. They tell me I'm doing great work, even though I don't ever seem to get close to a solution.

One of her supervisors really seemed to go for her accomplishments, whatever the heck they were. He often stopped by to chat about the work, and Meg was only too happy to pass the time with him. After all, the boss couldn't chew her out for not working when it was the boss who was keeping her from work. Nice enough guy, but he still creeped her out a little.

Meg was dark-haired and slightly built with Oriental eyes. She was more than just a pretty face; she was a true scholastic prodigy, having had an easy time making top grades in her pod class in the sciences. Her curiosity drove her to observe and wonder at the world around her and kept her from the boredom that so many of her pod mates fought off with legal mind-altering substances. Being good-looking didn't matter to her, but her looks had opened doors on which others were still knocking.

Research was a top job in society, highly esteemed and usually awarded after a long internship under an insecure mentor who knew that if the researcher did his or her job well, the intern would replace the mentor. Meg had her own station upon graduation. Soon, her fellow researchers appreciated the mind behind her angelic face.

Meg removed her safety smock, strapped on her belt bag from her desk locker, quickly checked for splatters in the mirror on the one-way glass of her station door, and then headed for the cafeteria. The view today was supposed to be the Himalayas. It would be a nice change from the tropical 3D jungle projected through the "windows" for the last month or so.

Her friends Lauren and Jill were already at their regular table, waving to her as she started through the line. Lauren had bushy black hair, and Jill had long straight blond hair. What was Meg hungry for today? Coagulated nutrients could be disguised in only so many ways. Perhaps the higher-ups thought they were motivating their research teams by serving them their own experiments.

A thick, reddish-brown something was supposed to be meatloaf, according to the nameplate on the pan, a light-brown turkey something else, and a chocolate gelatin something else again. Hey, if they were getting their nutrition from modified plant proteins, why not enjoy it? She wryly doubted if she might ever be able to add a peach cobbler to the menu.

She selected the chocolate and moved on to discover there were real vegetables today. Raw but real. She preferred her sponsors' way of pan-searing them with butter and bacon and serving them with grated parmesan and tamari, but raw vegetables were still a treat.

The desserts were disgusting, using fake flour, fake sweetener, and fake frosting—and so adding no calories. She had a few sugar almond toffees in her bag that could cost her a notch in her belt, but they were worth it. For beverages, there was tea, coffee, water, and something red and carbonated. She chose the red stuff, then picked up her tray and headed for the table.

Jill smiled with a mouthful of "meatloaf" plainly visible between her white teeth. She was not just smart; she was also quite an athlete, holding most of the class records in almost every sport. She kept her hair tied up behind her as if to be ready for any game at any moment. Like Meg, her looks had opened doors. Lauren had also gone for the chocolate.

Her friends were happy and talkative. Good, Meg thought. With the two of them gabbing away, Meg could easily just eat her lunch and listen, occasionally getting a word in between her friends' rapid chatter.

Lauren and Meg were pod mates. Pod lots were large, and it was unusual to know many people outside the pod group in which one started .

Genetically, there was diversity within a pod grouping, but people, like everything else, were a crop. As such, the Entente selected for certain characteristics and kept some gene pools carefully under control. Hair, eye, and skin color, strength, intellect, creativity, hardiness, and athleticism were allowable variables within any population, but the scientists were close to hybridizing all of these.

The ability to make others laugh was still a genetic puzzle, elusive to the geneticists who could not seem to select for it. The attempt to isolate for humor was not going well, which, to Meg, was funny in itself.

Jill drove the conversation. Sometimes Meg wondered where Jill came up with some of her ideas, which seemed to come from somewhere out of place and time, but then she'd drop that thread and proceed to drag Meg and Lauren back into the shallow end of the conversation pool.

Their talk was mostly of other girls––their clothes and also their gossip, consisting of spins and pairing relationships observed throughout the day.

Pairings could last from a night to much longer, unless an agreement was allowed to be drawn up. Then the pair were allowed to share a livingspace. They might produce a single offspring if they wished or if one was needed from their genes, visit the genetic manipulation lab while pregnant to have their fetus adjusted, and finally to stay in touch for a time after the offspring was made part of a pod year.

Meg's sponsors, Mark and Hisako, had been exclusively paired for twenty-five years and were on a watchlist of possible carriers of the Sickness. They were the most wonderful people Meg knew, and she loved vacations when she could live with them in their space north of town and imagine she was living centuries earlier when society had been quite different and there were things called parents, families, and homes. She did not use those terms around anyone but her closest friends––they were no longer an accepted part of the lexicon of the Entente. But they interested Meg immensely.

The dress of a certain coworker had been discussed down to the last seam and Velcro fastening when it was time for the afternoon shift. Meg was glad she worked in research. Lab workers like her and her friends had longer workdays, but vacation time was longer too. She had no idea what this vacation time would be, probably just sleep for the first week.

Wouldn't that be heaven?

Heaven. Jason was up there somewhere. *What an odd thought,* Meg told herself.

DIRECTOR PHELPS

*"It is forbidden to kill; therefore all murderers
are punished unless they kill in large numbers
and to the sound of trumpets."*
— Voltaire

From a window high up in the Chaldean Office of Domestic Equilibrium, Director Phelps sat down in his chair and rotated away from his desk to see the city. His city, as he liked to imagine it. He was privileged, impressive, and important, as well as bald, handsome, muscular and in command of himself and whatever room he was in. High up in the food chain of the Entente, though no one knew exactly how high, what he did, or who he did it for. He didn't actually know himself. He just had some vague idea of preserving the status quo. He did know one thing though.

He enjoyed being himself.

He had a weakness for caramel popcorn from the section of the city called Old Town. He stayed in fastidious shape. He would often spend time on the streets in a hat, fake beard and sunglasses hiding his very recognizable face, just staying in touch with the people he had devoted his life to take care of. He would always wink at his secretary as he was leaving his office and upon his return regale the office with stories of his encounters and conversations. He believed himself to be universally loved.

He had paired many times but never drawn up a contract. His devotion was not to any person but rather to a vague idea he liked to call "the people." Especially the "little guy," as he referred to them in meetings. He had a marvelous sense of fairness and tolerance. Fairness could be defined any number of ways, and tolerance could be narrowly focused to include only those differences that didn't make any difference. Perfect.

This afternoon he was sitting in his office in the downtown government complex wrapping up the paperwork on a sting operation he had secretly conducted for months before moving in for the checkmate.

He had found that he didn't have to do many such operations if he made the takedown brutal and public enough. There had been some necessary eliminations. The pictures of their bodies stretched out in an orderly way at the scene were a work of art, inspiring a sense of well-being among the rest of the city's population. Of course, sometimes they were given trials before the Supreme Arbiter, which was great showmanship, attracting viewers and boosting network ratings. So reassuring! Their government was on the job, protecting, watching, and maintaining the peace of a well-ordered world.

The Director allowed himself a congratulatory smile.

He had a vague idea that at this point, most people took some time off, but the possibility horrified him. How could he take time off the most important work a man could do? How could the defender of the people, the champion of the little guy, just stop and take a vacation? Too much was at stake to think of cooling his heels on some beach in Greenland or jetting off to New Europe to camp on the slope of an active volcano.

He would call a meeting and assess the new field of miscreants. The Sickness never slept, so why should he?

He activated his communications implant, noticing that the charge was down halfway. Inserted into the nerve leading to his eye, the device had a virtual screen that seemed to be a foot in front of his face and was powered by his body's metabolism. He realized he needed to eat soon, so his device could catch up. He'd grab something after the meeting.

When his secretary answered, he instructed him to gather the analysts, the wonkish personality-challenged team that combed through numbers all day long to detect anything out of the ordinary. Possibilities were flagged, even though almost all of them were simple glitches, having nothing to do with an outbreak.

Vigilance: the key to population health. Such a fabulous thought that it was permanently inscribed on the bottom of every screen they used in the analytical segment, right below the Entente's motto: Fighting for You: Everything Is Unity.

As his team filed into the small meeting room and took their seats, set in theater style around his director's console, the Director smiled at each one. He knew them well—at least he knew everything in their files, though he seldom talked to any of them. The screen behind him, mirrored in his console, was blank, and his secretary, in an elevated station next to the screen, was poised for the flurry of probability mapping that was about to begin.

Each member of the team had a station with his or her name, an individual console, a beverage dock, and a large orange light that was the signal that Director Phelps had acknowledged their input as next in the flow. The seats were comfortable, and each team member looked forward to these meetings, knowing what a privilege it was to be working for the man who had pulled off more successful operations than anyone else in departmental history.

A great spirit of excitement and a sense of accomplishment permeated the team, not to mention the personal satisfaction of making a difference. They never wondered for a minute what that phrase actually meant.

The Director hit a few keystrokes, and the screens all across the room flashed to end the conversations no one was having. The hush deepened as the director spoke into his headset mic.

"With J.375 successfully completed, I was wondering if any of you believed you deserve some time off."

Smiles on faces. Hands went up all over the room. They were in on the joke and playing along.

"How many of you are planning on stockpiling those days and forging ahead while the opportunities to eradicate the Sickness continue to present themselves to us?"

All hands went up, and laughter was heard, the laughter of dedicated people who loved their work, enjoying their director's funny side. They were certainly not going to rest while there was work to be done and Director Phelps was there to lead them.

"Good! I knew you all felt that way. Besides being the best of your pods, I chose you also because of your attitude about time off —being something you can take when you're dead. Now let's see what's out there." Scattered chuckles continued before silence descended on the room.

Turning to his secretary, he nodded and pointed at the screen, which at once displayed a map of their conference room, displaying each team member, a small animated cartoon picture of their faces indicating their locations, and a double-walled orange dialog box below each face. These boxes could be moved about on the screen, but a flexible orange line would connect them back to the member from which they originated, a kind of organic tracking of the coalescing of purpose and direction in the team's collective mind.

The Director was quintessentially what his title implied, directing and channeling the vectors of information and thought into a unified determination.

There was no need for a lot of verbal interaction. During meetings, each person would work feverishly at his or her screen, watching policy take shape before their very eyes. Raw data was always connected to the individuals or files from which it came. The files could be stacked in 3D representations on the screen or opened and the papers within shuffled through by the virtual "gloves" each member wore on their hands.

Each set of gloves was connected to the screen directly in front of each member, but the director's gloves could operate any screen in the room.

The orange light came on in front of Stan cf56n. Thanking his lucky stars he had awakened yesterday in time to rummage through weeks of numbers to prepare for this meeting, Stan spun file turtle.376 into the director's grasp. It appeared on the main screen.

The Director spoke into each set of implanted ear plates. "Thirty minutes! Let's see what Stan may have dug up, boys and girls!"

Maybe it was nothing, but Stan had noticed several odd data sets. Data had to make sense; that's what data did. He had been looking at location information gathered by the observation clusters and noticed some funny-looking numbers. Maybe some of the clusters were malfunctioning, or possibly the data had been manipulated.

The director began throwing pages at different members, which appeared on their screens. Poring feverishly over these details, these people would send a bit of each assignment off to a colleague waiting nearby, and in this way, soon the whole room was buzzing with the dissection of turtle.376.

Ninety minutes later, no one had any suggestions. They all agreed that the data was nonsense. Several had even worked up nice charts to show normal data sets compared to these. When the charts appeared on the director's screen, it brought polite applause from the others who wished they had thought of doing that. But as far as the numbers Stan had found, it was clear that something was a little off—and suspicious.

In Chaldea, every citizen was tracked. It was an effective way to ensure everyone's safety. If a murder or robbery were committed or even attempted, it was easy to call up the numbers and show who was there when the crime went down. Once the population saw the precision with which mysteries were solved, crime dropped like a rock.

Exactly what was going on in this case was not clear, but the location sets were blurry, a bit smeared. Or maybe they weren't. Truth be told, they couldn't be sure. Even that was a red flag. Any possible outlier was worth investigating.

The Director dismissed them for the rest of the day. "We started late. You're tired. We'll begin fresh again tomorrow. This is a puzzle we will work together, like all the others. And we will prevail. The city's depending on us, and we've never failed them. Fighting for you!"

"Everything is unity!" There was a buzz of excitement as the team rose out of their seats, tidied their stations, and left the room. It was a little early; they were bound to get the best spots at the eateries.

As for the Director, he couldn't wait to send the afternoon's report up line to the Elders. Even if it turned out to have nothing to do with the Sickness, it would more than justify the allotment of new resources being assigned to his elite team.

He rubbed his hands together in grim happiness.

LIFE IN THE SILO

"We find that we live on an insignificant planet
of a humdrum star lost in a galaxy tucked away
in some forgotten corner of a universe in which
there are far more galaxies than people."
— Carl Sagan

Out in the colorful forests of Planet f3, Jason watched the fading light carefully. He was not worried about finding his way back to the silo, but he didn't want to fool with the temperature drop that was coincident with night. The thought of an early departure gave him new incentive to complete the loading of the specimen bays on the silo, and he had cut the remaining space in half in the last two days. He had visited seven eco sites and had only three more to go. He was hoping they were lush and well-stocked.

As he made his way back to the silo, he fired up his antigravity device along with his propulsion vents. Gliding over the landscape that he had painstakingly scoured that day, he was able to catch a little more of the sunset from his higher vantage. Once again, thoughts of gratitude to the Plasm arose inside, and once again, he was troubled.

What was happening to him? Was he exhibiting early stages of the Sickness? Had he contracted it through prolonged isolation?

He reminded himself to fire up a reorientation sequence that night while he was asleep. He needed to be re-centered, or he might crack up. Often when such disturbing ideas crept into his thinking, a sequence would help to refocus his mind and nip the pattern. Hopefully, this was just another such episode—short-lived and fixable.

Back aboard the silo, Jason let Harry out of his restraining field. Harry was a purebred mutt, a special combination of hardy genes that made him look a little odd maybe, but he was tough as nails and irrepressibly good natured. The closest breed descriptor would be Australian Shepherd, but Harry was taller, and his ears were longer. He danced around as Jason blopped his supper into a bowl and then set it on the floor.

It was little ceremonies like this that the behavioral shrinks back on Earth said were necessary to impose a sense of normality on an otherworldly and bizarre existence. Harry wagged his tail as Jason pounded on his side, but the dog did not remove his nose from the bowl.

Jason took off his work gear and got into his more comfortable evening attire––orange T-shirt, dark-green jeans, and cloth-and-rubber shoes.

Supper was nothing to brag about, just one of the hardships the collectors had to endure for the glory of their job. Pellets of a yielding, rubbery consistency with sprayed-on flavors. The ones that tasted like bacon or strawberry were long gone, so he had to make other selections.

He wished he didn't have to go through the process of chewing the stupid stuff, which was used to supply nutrition three times a day. It would be better if he could just inject it. But the space industry had long ago found—once again trying to normalize life in space as much as possible—that injecting foods had an adverse effect on creatures that had always ingested their meals.

Jason played around with the word ingest and the words in jest, but couldn't make any headway.

After supper he reached for the viewer and selected an ancient set of 2D images and sound. Of course, he could have made a selection from a thousand immersionfield titles, but he did not enjoy having his senses overloaded. He much preferred this outmoded audiovisual presentation which left him some idea of self.

This particular recreational file concerned a fictional character named Jason Bourne. The fact that they shared a first name was of course a bonus. It was pretty barbaric and primitive (not the subject, the technology), but it appealed to Jason. He liked the idea of a man who had been programmed by the government to be an assassin but, while recovering his memory from an attack of amnesia, rejected his programming and set out on a quest to right wrongs and stick it to "the man." Jason never stopped to consider why he liked the rebellious side of this movie hero, he just let the enjoyment wash over him.

How many times now have I seen this movie, he asked himself as he selected his homemade over-air speakers to broadcast the sound, bypassing his aural implants. You gotta watch the old stuff the old way if you're gonna get the same effect.

He reached the part where Bourne was buzzing through a whole detachment of military police with pinpoint precision, instinctive reactions, and no wasted movements. Never lethal except as required but always nullifying the assets sent against him. He thought it would be cool to be so in control of his surroundings, even while pitting himself against the entire system.

After swinging the viewer back into its storage dock, Jason opened the silo door and leaned against the bulkhead, sucking in the cold air gulp by delightful gulp. As he did, he was confronted by questions he didn't remember asking, wandering reflections he had not meant to have.

Mankind is odd, Jason thought. So is existence. What was everything all about? Was anything affected one way or another if he did his job well or just mailed it in like most of his fellow collectors? Would any of his paltry efforts and sacrifice allow the human species to continue another few steps into the future? Why was the future something we should struggle to arrive at?

Did it make any difference to care about this stuff? To care about anything? Did it make more sense to just live for each day's pleasures instead of wasting time giving life a second thought?

Remembering his classes in worldviews, he recalled how they had brushed past the early philosophers in the introduction. The course had focused on the rise of twenty-second-century consciousness, freed from the old restraints of myth and morality since the Reorganization.

Some real breakthroughs. A bunch of obviously bright and insightful theories had been hatched. One guy—Jason forgot his name—argued that existence was a noble end in itself, that continuing to breathe for as long as one could was worth robbery, lies, and even murder—if it came to that. No one in his class, not even his teacher, found anything troubling about this.

Jason understood what the guy was saying: live as long as you can, and then it doesn't matter about anything else beyond that. But Jason knew in his gut that something had to matter.

In such moments, when the day's work was done, all the maintenance on the silo and his own body had been performed, and he was killing an hour or so before enclosing himself in his sleep field, Jason's mind unconsciously took him down such roads.

He didn't like it, and he didn't appreciate it. Why should he have these thoughts at all? If the philosophers were right, such notions were a waste of time.

"Waste of time," he repeated out loud, surprising himself to hear a human voice, even if it was his own. Harry made a noise that sounded like "Gurf."

Jason reached for Harry's head and gave it a rough rub.

ALEX AT THE POD PARTY

"You have a grand gift for silence, Watson.
It makes you quite invaluable as a companion."
— Arthur Conan Doyle

Alex surveyed their surroundings carefully out of his peripheral vision but saw nothing but the pretty, slim, and unsmiling woman standing in front of him. She had dark sunglasses and a baseball cap, her blond hair pulled back into a ponytail. He handed the woman a privilege card and waited while she checked it with her belt scanner. He knew it was loaded, and once she confirmed it, she returned his card along with a small, flat package wrapped in brown paper. He handed her a similar package. Then they walked off in opposite directions.

Alex waited until he was safe inside his livingspace to unwrap his prize. As he tore the paper off, he felt the flimsy thickness of the paperback book and mouthed the title on the well-worn cover: The Great Divorce by C. S. Lewis.

It was one of the most dangerous of the forbidden books. The Entente believed that books had a great deal to do with the Sickness. Especially books written before the Reorganization which contained concepts and references and societal morays that had been shown to produce ignorance, disharmony, inequality, dogmas and other abnormalities. There were few books left to the populace. Most people preferred the total sensory stimulation of the immersionfield anyway.

Alex knew that the book he held was viewed by the state as a danger to himself and all those around him. He also knew that Lewis had a piercing mind and a wonderful way of writing, and

Alex hungrily read every one of his books he could rent from the underground.

Fighting for me. Alex chuckled to himself. Funny that little else would have preserved these old books as well as trying to eradicate them. Far from removing the books from circulation, the Entente's literary liquidation had done a perfect job of preserving them when they might otherwise have been ignored or forgotten.

Alex held an authentic blacklist book in his shaking hands. He turned to the copyright page and read the date of publication: 1945. Wow.

He drank in the first twenty-five pages as fast as he could absorb them. The bus stop, the gray town, the crabby passengers, each one hoping for something different to come from their trip to the strange place they were visiting.

Coming up for air, he walked over to his beverage dock, selected a malted milk protein drink, brought it back to his chair, and plunged back in.

Alex was off duty. As an enforcer, he could be called into service at any time, but it was unlikely. The populace were sheep. Under control. Sure, there were a few robberies and a handful of murders, but in Alex's mind, the Entente had pretty much taken over that industry—at least it seemed as if the state did most of the robbing and killing these days. If anyone was to be defrauded of property or life, the government would accomplish it without any help from the criminal classes.

What can I do about that? he thought. At least I get a good job out of it all.

He resubmerged his mind into his book.

Alex was an enforcer, not because he was big—he wasn't, though he wasn't undersized either. However, compared with some of the other officers, he was not physically imposing. Women and men considered him good looking, with black hair and black skin. He was nearly a legend, not only among the law enforcement community but also within the populace itself. He was always relaxed, even in tense situations, and never seemed in a hurry, although he could move quickly if necessary. His deceptive strength was seldom needed because he had a feel for talking people down from ledges, real or imagined. A gift for preventing fights that had moments before seemed inevitable. A knack for physically subduing even the largest and angriest people. He was a paradox: a thinking man in a muscle man's world.

And totally fearless.

When next he looked up from his reading, it was pitch black outside. He checked the clock. Oh gosh, he thought. Barely enough time to make the pod party. He should at least show up; he could sneak out later. No one would suspect him of anything if he was there at first and then found missing later, obviously taking a spin with someone he met. But if he didn't at least show up, the geeks who monitored citizen activity might wonder what else was taking up his evening.

With his privileges, Alex had been able to install an old woodstove inside his apartment. He had given some story about how his long working hours prevented him from indulging his love of camping, so he needed the smell of real wood burning in an old iron box to compensate. Secretly, he had rigged the stove to fire up unless a code was entered soon after entering his livingspace. He carefully put the book inside. Already inside was another book: Northwest Passage by Kenneth Roberts. He had just returned The Doorbell Rang by Rex Stout.

The black market was wonderful about finding the authors he liked. He had an order in for Treasure Island by Robert Louis Stevenson. No word on that one yet.

He caught a Public Vehicle, or PV, to the party, swiping his ID card as he boarded. Using public transportation left a better record of his participation than a bi or a quad. Alex laughed to himself that, although the names bi and quad designated the maximum legal numbers of occupants, very few people actually observed the limits.

Upon arrival, he checked his jacket, another marker for any watchful eyes.

The food bar was always his favorite hangout spot. He stood by it and nibbled while nodding to those who came by. No fried scallops but some nice steak bites.

The conversations were lively enough though pretty shallow, and Alex was bored. He almost wished an off-duty summons would call him back to work, so he could train his team, a bunch of rookies about ready to be passed along to another officer. They gave Alex the newbies because he could whip them into shape better than anyone.

He may have hoped for a summons, but he bitterly reminded himself that very seldom in all the years he'd been an enforcer had one come in. The officer on duty could usually handle anything that came up on his watch. He sighed and took another small bite of an interesting nutty cheesy something.

Half an hour later, some of his friends got him to leave the food bar and sit at their table. They were talking about a legal drug that everybody was trying and comparing the effects. Alex was only half paying attention.

A girl at the table was looking as bored as he was, and he hoped he knew why. When the person next to her got up to go to the bathroom, Alex moved to that seat and said hello. He suggested they leave for a quieter place to talk, but she looked him in the eye and said she wasn't interested. Alex assured her that he just wanted to talk.

After giving him an even more piercing look, she whispered something to the girl on her other side, folded her jacket over her arm, and stood up. Comments and hoots from around the table resulted, but Alex let them say and think whatever they wanted.

Picking up his jacket from the coat check station, he led the way outside. When they were clear of the lights and walking down a dark path in the gardens, Alex asked her how he hadn't seen her before. She told him she was visiting a friend, the girl she had whispered to. Alex asked why she hadn't visited before.

"Oh, I have."

"Not while I've been around."

"Come to every one of your pod parties, do you?"

"I try not to miss."

"Well, you must have missed the times I've been invited, or maybe you just didn't see me there. I don't call attention to myself."

Her voice registered somewhere. As a trained enforcer, he was supposed to connect voices to people he had met. "Are you sure we don't know each other?"

She gave him a darting glance, and Alex felt a sharp tingle in his spine. The truth dawned on him, and he shook his head. "Could I see you in sunglasses and a cap? I might be able to place you better."

"You knew all along."

"Actually, no. But I do now."

"You could arrest me, but I have evidence against you too. We have a dilemma."

"Not me. I have no desire whatsoever to arrest you. I've often wished we could talk. I had no idea when I saw you at the table that I might know you already. You just looked as fed up with everything as I was."

"Fed up?"

"With the shallowness, the rank sexuality, the 'rah rah our beloved leaders' attitude."

"You've gone from buying illegal books to talking subversion."

"Maybe I don't care."

"You're definitely strange. I'm Jill."

"Alex."

"What do you do with the books you buy from me?"

"I read them, of course! Aren't they wonderful?"

"You have no idea. Wonderful beyond words."

"Where do they come from?"

Jill looked hard at him for the third time. "You can't possibly expect me to tell you. This could be a setup. A sting."

"Didn't you say you had evidence against me?"

"Yes, but that could be part of the sting. How do you know I'm not ambushing you while you're trying to ambush me?"

"I like how your mind works. It could be exactly as you just said. I might be a trap, and you might be a trap too. But I know I'm not, whatever you may be. I'm frustrated with the emptiness, with the lightweight explanations and clever but unsatisfying philosophy. Frustrated enough to want to know more. Frustrated enough to be willing to risk everything, even my life, to get answers."

"You're seriously for real?"

"Serious as an arrest. Real as a loaded privilege card."

Jill smiled and for the first time allowed herself to really look into Alex's eyes. What she saw was a hunger for some kind of actuality, some kind of truth.

She recognized that look because she saw it in the mirror every day.

"So, what now?" she whispered.

"Come to my place, or let's go to yours. We've got to keep up the appearance of standard lust, or the surveillance team might flag us."

"I'm not doing that."

"Take it easy. I said, 'keep up the appearance.' We should at least go into one of our places and wait out enough time."

"I see. You're going to time us?"

"The average coupling takes three hours according to enforcement manual stats. We can shade that either way and still be convincing."

"I guess you're right. Let's go to my place. It's clean."

"My place is fine. You could eat off the floor."

"There are *plates* at my place. Come on."

They flagged a PV and hung closely together, making a masquerade of coupling preliminaries on the ride as well as upon disembarking. Alex found it easy to fake with Jill.

They got off at her block and made the short walk to her place with their arms around each other's waists. As soon as the front door closed behind them, they fell apart and burst into laughter, collapsing into two chairs around the kitchen table.

Their laughter came to a gradual stop as they looked into each other's eyes and saw that they might have found a true friend.

Alex smiled. Jill smiled back. They both looked away.

Then they both spoke the same words at the same time. "So, how did you like C. S. Lewis?"

MEG AND HER BOSS

I will not say that your mulberry trees are dead;
but I am afraid they're not alive."
—Jane Austen

I wonder what *he's* doing here, Meg thought as she saw Alex in the lunchroom line talking with Jill. Almost everyone knew Alex by sight, especially in the red uniform of a senior enforcer. She wondered if Jill was in trouble, but it was easy to see, judging by her face and body language, it was anything but. The two of them approached Meg's table.

"Do you guys know Alex?" Jill asked as she set her lunch down. "He and I have paired. Since everyone in surveillance knows about it, I thought my best friends should too, so I asked Alex if he could drop by."

Alex nodded to Meg and Lauren. "Hey. We met at—"

"At a party a few weeks ago," Lauren broke in. "We know. Though she didn't say you were . . . I mean that you're Alex the . . . the, um, enforcer guy . . . officer . . . person."

"We don't know many enforcers," Meg explained. "We try to not warrant that kind of attention. Of course we've heard about you though. I saw the footage of you with that behemoth druggie. I thought he was going to kill you, and the next moment he was on his back in pain, and you were crouching next to him, calmly talking to him as if nothing odd had happened."

"Sometimes people get the wrong idea about how to discuss things," Alex said. "I just suggested an alternative to the way he thought we might settle our differences. People can be reasonable if they understand their options."

Although Alex kept a straight face, the three girls burst into laughter. "Whatever you do, Jill, discuss things the way *he* wants to," Lauren warned. She got up. "Well, I'll see you guys around. I gotta get back to it." She gathered her tray and headed for the exit by the disposal slot. "We're supposed to serve my eggs Benedict next week," she called back over her shoulder, "and I can't get the runniness out without making them tough!"

Alex stood and said goodbye as well.

As soon as he left, Jill turned to Meg. "Wanna come over tonight? I'll make you some Russian tea, and we can hang out."

"I guess I don't have any other plans."

"Good. Around 7:30? You can come earlier if you get off. My tests are cooking, and I have the rest of the afternoon off, but I know you're in the middle of your peach thing. That is, if you can get anything done with your supervisor always dropping by to talk."

"He's just bored. But I can get off by five. Let me grab some Mongolian noodles for us."

"Great. Um . . . bring enough for three?"

"Who's the third? Oh, Alex?"

"Good guess, Einstein. I'll catch you later. We're going to take some unis up into the mountains for a couple of hours. See you at five then?"

"Right."

As Meg ditched her tray and headed back to her station, her mind was full of Jill's face. Meg liked her a lot, but it struck her that she really didn't know her that well. Certainly, they never usually talked about anything much outside of work. She suspected that she was about to find out a lot more about Jill 89k3g. Good, she thought, it's about time. She sat at her station and began preparations for the afternoon's exploration.

"Daydreaming, Meg?" her supervisor asked from beside Meg's chair.

"Oh! Hi, sir. Yes, but I'd be happy to show you the log from this morning's work. I nearly had a stable compound."

"Never mind that. I don't know if you've noticed that I frequent your desk more often than the others here."

"No, sir. I hadn't."

"Drop the sir, Meg. It's just Alphaeus."

"If it's all the same, Mr. Goff, I would feel more comfortable calling you sir, sir."

"As you wish. I don't care. I just thought we could have had lunch today, but you said you had to eat with your friends. How about tomorrow? Or maybe supper tonight?"

"Sir?"

"You obviously eat, so I thought you and I could do it at the same time."

"The same time as what?"

"That we could eat together and talk about things not related to work."

"Thank you, sir, but I would rather keep our relationship strictly professional if that's OK with you."

"It's not. You know I could order you to come to a meeting at any time day or night and specify the location and have no one there but you and me. Or order you to the play cabins up north of the city. It's been done before. In fact, I've done it myself."

"Sir, lunch is beginning to sound good. Tomorrow you say?"

"Tomorrow. I'll be at my table. Are you enjoying the mountain scenes or would you like something else?"

"I don't care, sir. Whatever. Would you like to see my work log?"

"No. Tomorrow then."

"As you wish, sir."

Meg's heart sank. She had tried to ignore the queasy feeling she always had when Mr. Goff came around and had attempted to keep the situation from getting personal. As a woman, she had a sense that Mr. Goff was watching for any interest from her, any interest at all, so she was always highly businesslike. But apparently, she had not been businesslike enough. Maybe Jill and Lauren would have some advice on how to nip this awful situation in the bud before she lost her job or worse. If she could produce a pairing mate . . .

Before she could stop them, her thoughts went to Jason.

As she refocused on her work, she began to wonder about peaches. Not so much why they wanted an artificial one—why did the government want most of the stuff they wanted?—but why a peach was so hard to replicate.

The chemicals were standard, and the shape was easy. She could produce fuzz on the outside and a pit on the inside. The stem was no problem: just leave it off. But at that point, the fake peach departed from the real one. The exact resistance of the peach skin to human teeth, breaking at the perfect pressure point to release just enough but not too much juice from a satisfying, yielding solid pulp inside. The pit of a peach was . . . well, cool. The plasticized pits she was using didn't have the coolness factor that a natural pit had. Continuing to mix chemicals, her mind wandered to a place she hadn't gone before.

What if a peach was more about process than anything else? What if the slow, gradual growth made more of a difference than could be artificially produced? What if somehow a peach was way more than compounds but instead a kind of journal, keeping a record of days of rain and sunshine, from pollination to fruition? What if the patient months it took were not an obstacle to be overcome but the key to the puzzle?

Why did people want control over other things? For that matter, why did they want control over other people? Why strive so hard for a fake peach instead of a . . . well, perhaps to cultivate and care for an old peach orchard?

She watched the compounds on the industrial table in front of her dissolve into a froth as her subsequent failure sputtered and smoked away. But her mind was working on a different problem than the synthesis of a fruit. It was weighing the differences in process between the natural versus the manufactured. She laughed to think of waiting for nature to magically produce a table and chair. But there was something about the slow, patient steps a peach tree took that produced a work of art through a persevering, gradual, unhurried progression.

If he were here, would Jason eat one of her fake peaches? What would she do if it killed him? What would he think about her if he knew she was thinking about him right now?

Stop thinking about him, you idiot.

Supper with Jill and Alex was fun, and they decided to schedule such dinners once a week. Though Meg knew that Jill and Alex spent a lot of time together, they didn't make her feel like a third wheel. They were simply three friends , not a couple and a spare.

Just as she thought, Jill had a lot more to her than one might guess, and Alex was a really good guy. Meg asked him for story after story about the calls he had taken on his job, and there were plenty. Alex downplayed his role in each episode, but Meg could fill in the blanks.

As they talked, Meg got the impression that she was being gently put through a test of some sort, though if she had to qualify why she felt that way, it would have been difficult. She didn't mind, and maybe she was reading it wrong.

Perhaps they were just really interested in what made her tick.

STAN'S ASSIGNMENT

*"I've searched all the parks in all the cities
and found no statues of committees."*
— *G.K. Chesterton*

D irector Phelps's team pored over the algorithms and tables in front of each of them. The observation clusters had given them a lot of hard data, but it didn't really help. Still, they thought they were beginning to form a hazy idea of some movements and patterns. They still had no clue as to the nature of what was going on, but they were painstakingly plotting graphs to try to get a sense of it. It was seldom easy to work through such irregularities.

The Director urged them on. "If some group is up to no good, we don't want to catch just a few of them, we want the whole bagful," he declared. "A couple of fish won't feed us. Hell, we've got to net the whole damn school."

The team was always impressed when the Director swore. It made them feel important, since regulations didn't permit it. They also saw the practicality of what he said.

But how to catch them if they didn't know where they were or who was involved?

The Director looked around the room with half-closed eyes. They all stopped, wondering what he was thinking. "We're not going to solve this one from a mile up. Someone's got to go underground," he said. "Undercover. Boots on the ground. Skin in the game. Be our eyes and ears. Infiltrate and destroy. It has to be someone who can look and sound the part. For instance . . . Stan."

All eyes swept over to Stan, who smiled sheepishly and shrugged. "What're you guys lookin' at?" he asked in one of his many comical voices. More laughter.

Everybody liked Stan. Brown hair, standard face, average build —the epitome of unremarkable. Charming, easy to be around, no principles to speak of. He often wore his baseball cap backward. Every person in the room was excitedly imagining being in his place, singled out for a dangerous assignment by the director. They all wished they might be the one selected, but only if it ended up that they didn't have to actually go.

Stan had been rescued from an outbreak of the Sickness in a section of the city. After they had eliminated the most virulent and carted the rest off, their search of the premises had found Stan in an inner room, somehow asleep. When awakened, Stan denied being a participant in the group; he had been curious and had hung around, that's all.

After taking him through extensive testing, the authorities agreed that he had been in the wrong place at the wrong time, perhaps even co-opted or coerced. They even wondered if he had a natural immunity, and he had participated in many tests to see if they could isolate his "antibodies." Stan proved useful in many ways and had become sort of the mascot for Office of Domestic Equilibrium, helping foil a few subsequent plots of the underground. He had great insight into the sickened mind.

The team lost no time in analyzing and recommending the safest and most effective insertion point for Stan and decided to have him escape from custody if they could make it look convincing. He was to use his status as a wanted man to draw the underground to him. Once accepted into their ranks, he could use his implant communicator on a coded channel to report his findings. The team calculated the process might take three months from infiltration to takedown. They provided Stan with a cover story and staged the drop.

Two enforcers chosen for their acting skills were brought into the operation and briefed by Director Phelps himself.

Later that same night, in a low-traffic section of the city, Stan stood on the street next to a prison transport, holding still long enough to receive a glancing shoulder shot from a stun gun. The enforcers grinned apologetically and waved him on, knowing they would wait a bit and then start after him. They'd "find" him at the predetermined location where the drama of the muffed recapture would play out as soon as they saw some citizens walking in the area.

Stan looked back and winked at the two officers who were about to (successfully) lose him and then (epically fail to) reacquire him.

They whispered back some standard insults, warning him to run fast enough to make it look good.

ALEX, JILL, AND STAN

*"Nothing in life is so exhilarating
as to be shot at without result."*
—Winston Churchill

After weeks of pretending to be a pairing, Alex and Jill had become best friends. They spent their off-hours at each other's places talking about books, philosophy, and truth. They would often read aloud to each other from the old books they pulled out of their hiding places.

Alex was amazed that he could simply enjoy Jill's company and was as contented as he ever remembered being. Jill was glad to be around a guy and not feel like her body was the underlying subject of every interaction. They both liked strong black coffee and vanilla wafers, Rex Stout, and George Orwell. They also liked to laugh.

There were all kinds of fabricated rumors, of course, but no one suspected they were up to anything as horrific as reading seditious books from illegal authors. At times, the thoughts and ideas the two discussed overwhelmed them. They talked about how the world used to be so different.

Few limitations were put on what people could think or where they could go. People back then unthinkingly assumed the risks that went along with that. It was a wild and woolly time.

The reporting of news used to be chaotic and unpredictable. Travel was dangerous. Crime was rampant and unchecked. There were abusive social units called families. There were elections where people showed up and pushed buttons next to the name of the candidate of their choice, believing they were participating in the affairs of state.

There were monogamous relationships and an emphasis on offspring. Nutrition was dangerously unscientific. People would wander about anywhere they liked and were allowed to say all kinds of things, whatever and whenever they liked. A kind of dangerous freedom that destroyed the process of building a worldwide society.

There were takeovers, wars, and rebellions, and there was never enough of anything. Scarcity was the fundamental axiom of economics in those days. So many facets of life they now took for granted were unknown or even frowned on back then.

But all that had been done away with. The Entente had mercifully seen to it.

Now society was protected, efficient, predictable, and under control. Everyone knew that loss of autonomy was a small price to pay for all the lives that were saved and enhanced. Whether those lives were worth living was not a thought that entered anyone's mind, though Jill and Alex seemed to be entertaining such notions these days.

They felt they could glimpse a pair of realities: the one that existed in their contraband books and private conversations and the other one they sadly returned to when their times together were over.

One night as Alex was walking Jill back to her place, they stopped to observe the strange behavior of a man across the street. He seemed to be trying desperately to be inconspicuous and failing totally. As he snuck off the sidewalk, dropping over a low rail into the darkness of the building's shadow, two uniformed officers sped past on antigravity boards, searching up and down the street. They recognized Alex as they approached where he stood watching and saluted. Alex asked them what was up.

"We had an escaped member of the underground in another sector, sir. Almost had him back there. He's around here somewhere. We'll get him."

"Need any help?"

"He's a slippery one, sir, but too important to let him get away. This is an agency priority."

"Well, carry on, boys. I'm busy, as you can see . . ."

Jill managed a convincing empty-headed giggle.

The officers smiled knowingly at Alex and Jill as they stepped back onto their boards.

The friends hadn't gone two blocks when they came upon the officers again, this time blocking an entryway where the man they had seen earlier stood at bay with his back to a door.

"Hold it right there," one of the officers said. "We don't want to hurt you."

"How did you find me?"

"Your implant is still transmitting."

"I turned it off hours ago."

"It still transmits whether it's on or off, genius. Down on your knees, and hold out your wrists. We can't miss from this close."

"I'd rather be dead than go back."

"That's OK with us. Your mass is the same to transport alive or dead."

"Can't you just leave a guy alone? I'm not hurting you."

"You carry the Sickness."

"No! I'm clean! I just wanna be left alone! I want out!"

"No one can leave. Everything is unity. Unity is safety. Your well-being is all we care about."

"Words! They have no meaning!"

"Surrender, citizen, or we'll be forced to hurt you. We've been authorized to eradicate you if necessary. You can come along quietly or come along even more quietly. Take your pick. But we order you to kneel and hold out your wrists. We won't ask again."

"Help me! Somebody help me!"

Something was off. Alex couldn't put his finger on it, but it was just wrong. Their responses were pretty much according to codes and protocols, but it didn't feel right.

Just then, Alex felt Jill squeeze his arm. "Do something!" she whispered.

Alex didn't hesitate. He told Jill to get behind the parked vehicle as he picked up a landscaping rock, hurled it at the window next to the officers, and then ducked down next to Jill.

Both enforcers turned to the shattered window, taking several steps toward it. The cornered man saw his chance and bolted past them into the dark. He raced past the vehicle where Alex and Jill crouched.

Alex grabbed his arm, and before the man could tear away, he clapped a hand over his mouth. "This way, stay low," Alex urged the other two as he crouched and ran into an alley between dwellings. They had to find cover. Alex knew that if he couldn't disable the man's implant, it was only a matter of minutes until the enforcers found him. He grabbed the man by the shoulder.

"Do you really want to shake those guys?" Alex whispered.

"Yes, I . . . Alex cx94b? You?"

"Yeah. I've never seen you before."

"But you're a . . . I'm . . . I'm sorry. I'm not doing well. I'm confused. Is this a trick?"

"You've got to trust me."

"Why should I? Let me go."

"Those guys will just track your implant. You have to let me disable it."

"You heard 'em. We can't do it."

"I can, and I will, but it'll hurt."

"What are you going to do?"

"Follow me. There's not a second to lose."

The man nodded. Initially running bent over but standing up after a block, the three of them made it around several corners before halting behind a trash station out of the light of the street.

"Hold still, and don't cry out," Alex whispered. "Concentrate on suppressing your impulse to scream."

The man had gone stiff when Alex first took his arm, but now he let his shoulders sag, nodded, and closed his eyes. Alex felt for the place where his ribcage came together under the sternum. With a complicated maneuver, he pushed up underneath and lifted the man into the air and then brought him down hard on his back. The man groaned but did not cry out.

"You OK?" Alex asked.

"Ughnnn . . . you were right, that . . . Ah! That hurt like hell. What did you do?"

"I'll bet you're not transmitting anymore."

"I don't see how I couldn't be. The transmitter's part of our arm bones from when we were babies. You'd have to cut my arm off to stop it."

"I disabled the power to your transmitter. The electrical impulses jump off the nerves that make your heart beat. We still don't have much time. Get up, stuff your hat in your shirt around your belly, and walk with us."

Alex helped the man to his feet, reversed his jacket, and relocated Jill's ball cap to the man's head, letting her ponytail loose to create a whole different hairstyle.

The three of them listened for a moment, and then Alex led them across the street. They walked slowly and casually down the sidewalk in front of the well-lit stores.

Alex reasoned that the enforcers were looking for a runaway, not a trio of sightseers. Hiding in plain sight was beyond any fugitive's emotional ability to pull off. The enforcers would know the signal on the implant plates had been severed but that the man still had to be in the area. Their problem was that they were looking for a man in hiding, not three people strolling down the sidewalk.

Alex said the only danger now was that they might be brought in for questioning as possible witnesses.

"We've got to get off the street," Jill urged. "We're close to Meg's space. She won't ask questions." Alex agreed, and the man shrugged as if to say, I'm game. A few minutes' walk brought them to the door.

Momentary surprise did not keep Meg from drawing them quickly inside. Jill turned to look at their fugitive; her head cocked to one side.

"Stan?"

Stan had trouble focusing. He was jerkily shaking his head like he was trying to clear the cobwebs, but he looked up quickly. "Jill? It's you! I . . . Oh wow. I thought that was your voice earlier. It's been a while."

"Whatever are you doing?"

"I'm . . . yeah, good question. What am I doing? I think I'm trying like hell to un-enlist and walk away, and it's not working."

"Un-enlist? I don't understand?"

"Well, I'm not sure I do either. One minute I was on a team of geeks working for a guy named Phelps . . ."

"We know of him."

"Yeah? And the next minute, I had a full-fledged panic attack. It felt like I was being strangled by the stench of the Entente constantly banging away with their clutches on everything. Everything I did. Everything I thought. A claustrophobic fear was clogging my mind, and I just . . . freaked. I was gasping, choking. I had to get somewhere and breathe. Just draw a breath. I made some excuse and walked out, and before I knew it, I was walking and walking, and I never slowed down. I knew I couldn't go back. I knew I had to just . . . stop."

He winced when Meg put a hand on his shoulder. "Stop? Stop what?"

Stan stared at her, "I knew I had to, well, stop. Stop being. I was gonna commit suicide. I figured the only way out was to do away with myself. But I thought I could maybe take some of those clowns with me when I blew myself up or something. But I guess I'm not as smart as I think. I got caught, the Supreme Arbiter sentenced me, and I was scheduled to go to the labs for . . ." He gulped. "Experimentation. Something went wrong during my transport. I'm not exactly sure how I got away, but all of a sudden, I was free."

Alex had been looking him over and had seen Stan wince. "You've got some stun marks on your left shoulder here. Looks like you were grazed. We've got to get you someplace safe."

Stan hadn't stopped staring at Meg. "You're beautiful. But you probably know that already. Um, thanks for, um . . . Thanks for opening the door just now."

Meg blushed.

"Oh KAY!" Jill said. "I think we're all starting to feel better!" She turned to Alex. "I'll keep him with me tonight if Meg will put us up. I can get him to another friend's livingspace tomorrow. They're away for a while on work assignment. I don't think he'll be noticed there for a while anyway."

Alex nodded. "Sounds like a plan. I'll be leaving. Call me for any reason. Anything."

Alex felt himself clutched and smothered in an intense hug from Stan, followed by sounds of sobbing. "I mean thanks, man, just, oh wow, thanks."

Alex extricated himself with difficulty. "Happy to do it."

Meg and Jill gave Alex hugs too, though much less dramatic, said goodnight, and then closed and locked the door. Turning, they saw Stan had already stumbled to the couch and fallen fast asleep. Jill got a blanket and covered him up.

The enforcers reported back to the Director that Stan was now officially loose.

They did not report that they could no longer track him, nor that they had lost him well before their theatrical stunt called for.

JASON FINDS SENTIENT LIFE

*"In chess, one cannot control everything. Sometimes
a game takes an unexpected turn, in which
beauty begins to emerge. Both players are
always instrumental in this."*
—Vladimir Kramnik

For Jason, it was a great couple of days on Planet F3. He had filled the rest of the specimen slots in his lab and was hoping to receive a directive—the summons that signaled the end of a mission. If that came, he could make his way to a tube portal and head home.

"Whaddya think of that, Harry?" he asked, beaming as he stood outside the silo one day. "They'll tell us we did a great job. They'll say they seldom get a full silo back and that we may have set some kind of record. I owe it to your sage barks of advice and encouraging slobber. By the way, buddy, you've occasionally been facing the wrong way when you use your waste management unit for your tinkle, and from time to time, I've had some cleanup to do. We can work on your aim on our way home. Home! If you hear an incoming message, bark!" He gave Harry's ears a good rough scratch.

Jason was used to being by himself, outdoors, and this life suited him just fine. He was pretty skilled in the art of wilderness exploration and survival, which had landed him this gig. He had no desire to be one of the factory workers or city dwellers, confined each day for 8 hours in those crowded buildings with everything controlled: light, air, humidity, temperature, noise... what was the point of all that? He much preferred his nomadic profession, where he was his own boss. And he could spend all day outside, no matter which planet was providing that.

And now his occupation kept him in his element all day long, and the next morning, he woke up to another day of the same. It was a great source of happiness for him. Harry was a bonus, and the two had grown quite close since they were teamed up for this mission.

Still, he missed the companionship of his pod mates and the times they would go hunting or biking sailing or fishing or exploring the newly liberated caves or mountains or coastlines of Neotropa, or at least as much of Neotropa as they could reach from Chaldea in an afternoon or weekend. Ehh. There'd be time for that when he got back, a lot of time for that.

The final setting of the solar sails was a ritual that every collector looked forward to. A fine cigar, a box of matches, and a small bottle of bourbon had been included in his equipment for just this moment. The portal he had sailed from when he had arrived on Planet f3 was about five hours away from his present location. Jason had loved the part of his training where he had practiced this skill. Hey, maybe Meg would like a ride . . .

Oh great. Back to Meg. She couldn't possibly still be available. Even if she were, she wouldn't be interested in a collector who had to be gone a lot of the time. Get a grip, old boy. Until you maybe get promoted to dispatcher, you're never going to get to pair with anyone. And since politics are your worst suit, you're never going to make dispatcher. You'll probably die on some planet or other trying to stuff hot-pink vegetation into a jar . . .

"What the . . .?" Something had bumped him. It was the furry, feathered, yellow-green thing again. "Scared the bejeebers out of me, man!" he said to the creature, but it ignored him, just like the other one had. "I don't have any more bags, and I don't have any more room . . . hey! Where do you think you're going?"

The creature had wandered into the silo. Jason waited for Harry to go nuts, but there was silence. "Harry?" No response.

"Harry, you OK, buddy?"

The faithful dog's head appeared at the silo entrance and disappeared again. "Harry! Stop! Don't get near that thing. I'll get him out of there. We don't need another one of 'em. We already have one of his friends in a bag." Harry's head appeared again with a loud and excited bark.

Jason knew there wasn't a lot of stuff down low that the creature could mess with. All the same, he had to evict the little guy before he got into anything higher up. Feathers on some creatures were for flight or at least gliding. There *were* controls and items at waist level and above that the creature might possibly damage. Jason dropped his tools and climbed into the silo.

"Where are you, you multi-legged something or other?" Jason squinted in the silo's artificial light. Max was watching something at the food storage bin, blocking Jason's line of sight, his tail wagging madly back and forth. "Harry, you sorry ball of fur, you're supposed to keep him out, not welcome him in and show him where the food is." He gently kneed Harry aside and stood next to him, looking at the creature. Harry's food was scattered around the bin, and the creature turned to look at them.

"Hey! Get out of there!" Jason said, waving his arms above his head. "Who invited you anyway?"

"I invited myself," the creature said in unhurried, perfectly understandable English.

UNWANTED ATTENTION

"Some cause happiness wherever they go;
others, whenever they go."
—Oscar Wilde

In the lunch space, Meg tried not to look at Mr. Goff. She knew the eyes of her friends constantly wandered over to the separate glass room where the supervisors ate their privileged meals. The supervisors were allowed foods that were reported to have far superior taste and texture, many of them imported and expensive. Meg could now confirm the reports were true.

"How do you like your food, Meg?" Mr. Goff asked.

"It's a lot better than what we get out there, sir."

"I've asked you to drop the 'sir,' Meg."

"And I've told you I'm not comfortable with that, sir."

"Tell me about yourself."

Meg pondered her response. She hoped she could paint a boring picture and then realized it wouldn't be hard. "Well, sir, there's not a lot to tell. You know I came to work here immediately after my specialized training. My pod class has a lot of people working here. We're genetically inclined to this kind of work. I have some good friends, and we're very happy together."

"Sponsors?"

"I . . . yes, I know who they are."

"Do you ever see them?"

"See them? Not to speak of."

"Have you ever paired?"

"Sir?"

"I think you heard me, Meg."

"I did hear you, and I don't think you should be asking me that."

"Meg, it's my job to ask you that."

"Not over lunch it's not, sir."

"This is a working lunch. Do I need to remind you what I could do if I chose to?"

"No, sir. I have had many spins."

"I didn't ask you about those."

"I have never paired."

"Why not?"

Meg thought fast. "I'm more attracted to other women." She blushed.

"Have you spun with other women?"

"Sure, lots of times."

"Names?"

"I'd rather not say, sir."

"Because you're lying. I know you spend every vacation with your sponsors and that you're very attached. I have the names of the people you've spun with, and they all belong to men. I know you've never paired. That is one of the reasons you interest me."

"I interest you? Sir, there's a code that protects me from aggressive, sexually suggestive conversation."

"That code does not apply to your supervisor. You know that."

Meg stood up. "Well, it was a delicious lunch, and thank you for inviting me. Sir, you need to know that I have no interest in pursuing a relationship with you."

"Of course I know it. That's one of the reasons why I find you intriguing."

"Goodbye, sir."

"See you this afternoon, Meg."

Meg left the room in alarm. What could she do? What could anyone do? She thought Mr. Goff, though very good-looking, was odious in many ways, not the least in terms of his persistence and his obvious intent. She caught Jill's eye, and they left the cafeteria together.

"Well, Meg, lunch with the supervisor! What a move you could make here at our little chemical complex!"

"Shut up. It's abhorrent. The man is a pig."

"He's very handsome, don't you think?"

"His physical features are not objectionable."

"I think he's cute."

"It doesn't matter how unobjectionable a toilet is; I still don't want to kiss one."

"Keep your voice down," Jill muttered. "The halls record all conversations, and a computer checks them."

Meg recovered quickly. "It was good food," she said in a moderately loud voice, "but I don't think I want to eat with Mr. Goff anymore. I prefer my friends."

Jill winked and scribbled something on a piece of illegal flash paper. After handing it to Meg, the two talked about the standard office gossip as they took the long way back to their stations through the arbor plaza. Meg glanced down at the note which read, *Desperate, my friend?*

Eyes wide, she glanced at Jill, who was nonchalantly grabbing soft fir branches as they passed. Meg reached for her hand, and Jill returned her squeeze. "Could you believe the skirt Sandra was almost wearing today at lunch?" Meg said. "Any shorter and it would have been a belt!" On the flash paper, she wrote, *I am BEYOND desperate.* Jill nodded as she read the message and wrote something as she rejoined. "And the heck of it is that her legs aren't that great. Unless you like chubby ankles!" Meg grabbed the note and read it. *Angelo's. 8:30.*

As they passed a garbage can, Meg crumpled it, and it burned to ash in a cool moment in her hand before she dropped it into the receptacle.

The afternoon dragged by. The clock had never moved so slowly.

Mr. Goff dropped by, as promised. Meg was politely vague. After what seemed like forever, he told her to have a good night's sleep and then left.

2:00. 3:00. 3:30. 3:40. 3:45. 3:48 . . . Meg forced herself to concentrate on her work. Just when she felt she couldn't putter around her station a moment longer, 4:30 arrived with a pleasing tone emanating over the intercom. From various locations in the lab, she heard exclamations of "Finally!" and "What a day!" and several other unprintable declarations.

Meg dumped her work and filled out her log while the control field cycled. That day's entry was short. She grabbed her uni slot pass and bolted out to the pad lot. The handlebars recognized her handprints, and the uni came to life. It was one of the new hydros. A small amount of steam was all it left behind as Meg rolled down the industrial park roads and into the city. She stopped for a cow bread to go at the waterstation as she filled the tank.

She made it to her livingspace and flopped on the couch, realizing as she unwrapped and bit into the cheese-infused bun that she was famished—she had not eaten a lot at lunch. Her mind was already going through her closet, picking out a pair of khakis and a light natural-fiber shirt. She tucked her hair up in a ballcap and, with her slim figure, erased most of the gender evidence she possessed. Glancing at the clock, she was frustrated to find it was only 6:00. Two and a half hours still! What could she possibly do? She watered her plants. She clipped her nails. She checked her breakfast machine to make sure it was loaded to deliver fried eggs with firm yokes and a buttered English muffin in the morning. She sat in her chair and drummed her fingers. The clock said 7:55. If she left now and walked slowly, she would only be a little early.

Just as she was about to leave, her livingspace monitor chimed, and a robotic voice announced that a Mr. Alphaeus Goff was standing at her entryway.

IZGAD INTRODUCES HIMSELF

*"The meeting of two personalities is like
the contact of two chemical substances:
if there is any reaction, both are transformed."*
— Carl Gustav Jung

J ason stared at the creature, frozen. In all the worlds where his job had taken him, this was the first time anything had spoken. None of the other planetary life forms had ever done that, and truthfully, he didn't expect them to. For sure, whatever spoke had better not have more than two legs. This one had, well, a whole bunch of them. He became aware that he was not breathing and involuntarily gasped for air.

For a moment, nothing happened.

"How about that?" the creature finally remarked. "I just now used the word cluster 'I invited myself.' Judging from your pulse and your eyes, not to mention your respiration rate, I have done something unexpected. Was it being able to open your container? It *was* tricky. Although I hate to admit it, I did not get it on my first try. I am still getting used to this creature's abilities. Absolutely intriguing."

Jason was still incapable of speech, but he nodded slowly. The creature turned back to the food storage unit and continued speaking amid moist noises. "Hunger is an interesting state of being. This creature is telling me that the cure for it lies in putting some of these substances in his mouth, masticating it, and then . . . never mind. I will just let the creature handle this."

"What are you?" Jason blurted.

"The age-old question. Many answers, none of them satisfactory. I believe the one that amuses me the most was from one of your earthly poets who said we are but a dream! Imagine! No sense of . . . well actually, no sense at all. The least dreamlike things in the world are the sentients. The Maker has let them echo himself in ways great and small, and nothing is so wide awake as the Maker. So, Jason, if you would close your open mouth, I can tell you I am not a dream." His pronouncement was followed by ripping noises and a loud munching.

"Um. Who are you?" Jason managed.

"Not entirely sure," came the soggy voice of someone talking with his mouth full. "That's part of what life is about, my friend. Not inventing who we are but discovering it. Ever noticed how consistent your personality has been from the start of your present existence?"

"Present existence?"

"Existence is complicated. You think you began about twenty-two years ago, but actually . . . well, never mind. I'm being told to stick to the point. I am . . . I am a heteroclite. That is the word, I guess."

"A heteroclite?"

"That is the word I heard."

"What is it?"

"I am not sure. I am catching up on your language. I will get better; I always do. Have you got a word index?"

"A dictionary?"

"Yes."

Jason wheeled, still a little unsteady on his feet, and pulled a monitor to him, speaking distinctly at the screen. "Heh-terr-oh-clight."

The screen asked in a monotone, "Did you mean chedarim, hedonist, hematite, hepatocyte, heterocyst?"

"Heteroclite," Jason repeated.

The screen responded. "Heteroclite: noun. An abnormal person."

"I could guess that," Jason mumbled.

"But you did not, did you?" the creature mumbled from inside the bin.

Jason moved to the storage bin door and looked inside. "Take it easy, huh? I had those organized by date. You're eating a couple of days' worth of grub."

"You will not need them. You have been recalled, have you not?"

"It's the first I've heard of it."

"Give me a minute. I will be right with you. We need to talk. I bear a message for you. And then we need to make plans."

"Look, whoever and whatever you are, the only plan we need to make is finding stuff on this planet for you to eat, so you can leave my food bin alone."

"You will be more comfortable in a chair, and I would like a nice soft rug if you have one."

Jason looked at Harry, who stood intently watching the creature, his tail wagging excitedly.

Jason shrugged. "Well, if you're any judge of character, Harry, I guess the guy's OK. I can see the entry in my logbook now: met talking dragon bird. Dog approved with appropriate discernment and rear-end movement."

"No entries in your logbook until we have conversed extensively, if you do not mind," the creature said, its mouth full. Glancing back at the food storage bin one more time, Jason grabbed one of the telescoping chairs and set it in the space by the open door.

"How many of your kind are there?" he called over his shoulder as he pulled a rug around.

The reply came amidst chewing sounds. "Just me at the moment. This yellow guy is part of a community of yellow guys, but . . . Just give me a minute, if you please? This is my first meal ever, and I am trying to figure out a bunch of sensations . . . Absolutely intriguing."

Jason sat and stared out the door. This was the very thing he had dreamed about when he became a collector, having conversations with extraterrestrial life forms. He had imagined it differently, though. He had thought he would be walking into a village of some description, not talking to a lizard-centipede thing wolfing down his supplies. Oh well, you can't have everything . . .

When the creature had finished eating and made its way outside for a moment, it came back in and settled on the rug.

"Do all of your people look like you?" Jason asked.

"This is not our form. I am . . . well, hitching a ride, so to speak. Your idioms make no sense, but I appear to be using them anyway."

"Hitching a ride? In that creature?"

"Yes, of course."

"How do you do that?"

"I am disabused of the idea that you would understand my explanation, and it would take too long."

"What do you look like when you don't look like that?"

"We look like whatever the need is. I might take a visible form. I might manipulate the matter around me to appear solid. But I am a different creature than you material beings. That again is about as much as I think you can understand from any explanation I could give."

"And you took over this creature's body?"

"Did you take over this silo?"

"Huh? What are you talking about?"

"I am in this creature as you are in this silo. Neither of us took over anything. I asked the creature if I could come in, and the creature gladly received me."

Jason was silent for a moment.

"OK, I guess. Um . . . Where are you from?"

"The Maker, just like you."

"What planet, smart guy?"

"My kind does not come from planets."

"Everyone comes from a planet."

"Have you ever been wrong before?"

"Are you saying you float around in space?"

"I do not float. And space is simply a boundary, so why would anything live in a boundary?"

"It's a big boundary, buddy."

"Oh, I see. It is coming into my mind what you consider to be big. No, space is not a small place in that way, but you are three-dimensional in your thoughts, locomotion, and reference point. I suppose, to put it in your manner, where I am from, nothing is dimensional. You do not have words for the conditions and structural composition that would explain the place from which I come. The space around planets seems big to you because you have a dimensional reference. But dimension is merely a constructed thing; it is neither universal nor eternal. You should know that from your mode of travel in this metal tube. And the important thing about a boundary is not that it is what you call 'big,' but it is an ending point as well as a beginning point and, therefore, a kind of demarcation of change. Size is a barrier to you, so you consider space to be of great size. Size is not a barrier to me, so I only see a limit for certain parameters to be in play, nothing more."

Jason thought about that. "So if you don't live on planets or in space, what's left?"

"The stars."

"You live in the stars?"

"I suppose it would not be incorrect to say it that way. The stars seem to you to have dimensions in this world, but from my reference point, a star is a torn place in your reality through which the glory of my world streams through."

"Isn't it hot?"

"I am learning so much by talking to you. You must know that I am taking a crash course in this form of communication at this very moment. The more I talk, the more I learn to use your language. Intriguing. The Maker is letting me know about temperature now. You may have guessed that temperature is another dimensional phenomenon, and as I have been laboring to tell you, I do not exist in a dimension. The stars are not hot; they are . . . to me they are like the tube portals are to you: doors."

Jason caught his breath. He had been prepared for an alien entity that was friendly or hostile, but at least it would be a fellow traveler through the universe. To find that this particular alien had a completely different "reference point," as the creature called it, was something he hadn't imagined. "Are you from another universe then?"

"There is but this one universe. I am with you from another reference. You could not live where I live unless you were made differently."

"But you can live here, where I live."

"Yes, but this yellow creature is not me; he is just letting me ride in him. I told him I needed to talk to you, and his 'hotel had a vacancy.' These idioms are fascinating me as the Maker gives them to me. I say them, and he puts meaning in them for me. This is the greatest adventure I have had yet. Absolutely intriguing. I am even learning as I speak to use idioms! An idiom is . . ."

"Excuse me, I know what an idiom is. So, you're not a yellow feather fur thing?"

"No, this is . . . well, he does not have a name. Not even sure he is a he. But he was friendly enough and had the proper vocal capabilities, though I do not think he has ever done more than grunt or warble a song."

"You've possessed him?"

"Do you possess your body?"

"No! My body is me."

"That is not at all correct. Your body will wear out, but *you* will keep going."

"How can I keep going without a . . . are you telling me you believe in ghosts?"

"I do, but they are not what you think they are. However, you will not continue without a body. You were designed to inhabit one."

"But you said my body will wear out."

"And you will get a new one. Or you will not."

Jason didn't know what to do with these ideas. "Sounds kooky to me. So what, did your body wear out?"

"I do not need a body; it's not how I was designed. You live in a body that also lives in a space. The word you use for that space is 'home.' But that other place, that home, is not where you can always be found."

"Oh, so you're telling me you're not at home right now?"

"Perhaps that is part of it. Is your body always to be found in your silo?"

"No, I live near the capital city of Chaldea when I'm home. When I'm on a mission, I live in this silo."

"Same here. I am just living in this good beast while I am on a mission. Speaking of which, question-and-answer time has to pause for a while. We need to make plans."

"I see. You mentioned a message."

"Yes. I will wait while you prepare to record."

"I need to record it?"

"It is pretty long. And you will need it later. For the others."

"You may not know it, pal, but there are no others. Just you, me, and Harry here."

"There will be others. Seven others, to be exact. Ten including you, me and Harry. If you do not mind, turn on a recorder?"

Jason shrugged and then turned to the monitor. "Record function, private storage, indefinite length. Begin on voice activation." He turned back to the creature and shrugged. "Ready. I think. If what I've been doing these last few moments can be called thinking . . ."

The creature sat bolt upright and stared out the doorway. "The message is this: *"The moment of the Maker is a threshold event: a terrifying time with fierce anger and retribution to wipe out evil from the land. The windows of the heavens will no longer give the earth their light. The sun and the moon will go black. The Maker will repay the rebellious for their wickedness, the lawless for their evil acts. The Maker will bring to nothing the arrogance of those who think only of themselves and will humble the prideful boasts of those who have no remorse. The Maker will release the heavens from his order and control. The earth will shake violently within its orbit at the fierce wrath of the Maker Most Powerful in the hour of his fiery righteousness. But those who are sorry for what they have done, he will pardon them, protect them, and from the moment of their turning, he will embrace them as his own children forever. For his children, he will form new realities more exciting and full of wonder than before. They will be his family, and he will give himself to them."*

There was silence after that. The creature spoke no more, and Jason clicked his recorder off and hit "save offline." His mind was a jumble of confused thoughts.

Presently, the creature stirred. "My gracious host is sleepy, so I will wander off with him and experience the sensation of sleep in a sunny, protected spot. I think I know just the place. My order has longed to look into your phenomena, and I am excited about this 'unconscious mode.' While we are sleeping, think about the message. I have a proposition to make, but it can wait until my host has slept and you have gotten some, oh what a delightfully meaningless phrase, 'space!' As if you did not have space now! These idiomatic vocalizations the Maker gives me are absolutely intriguing. I will be back in a few hours. Until then, my friend."

With that, the yellow creature wandered out the door and ambled off into the outside world.

Jason sat motionless. Harry came and rested his chin on Jason's knee. Absent-mindedly, Jason scratched him behind one ear and smiled at the automatic back-leg-thump response.

"OK then, Harry, alrighty. How 'bout that…you sure this guy is someone we should be hanging around with?"

He looked at the recording log on his screen and transferred the recording to the ghost drive on his wrist comm. He ran the recording back and hit "play." "*. . . release the heavens from his order and control, and the earth will violently shake within its orbit at the fierce wrath of the Maker Most Powerful . . .*"

Jason frowned. The Maker? Was that the Plasm? The Plasm had emotions . . . of anger? Expectations?

No one had ever taught him that the Plasm was like that. The Plasm was more like a chemical reaction, not an emotional being. The message implied that there was something or somebody who had expectations of people on Earth, and they had woefully fallen short. And a price would be paid.

It didn't sound happy. He thought of Meg. She was back on the Earth, perhaps in harm's way. Was this a warning? Could anything be done?

Jason had daydreams of enjoying a life with Meg where they had fun and ate and talked and kissed and knocked around with their friends. He hadn't thought that maybe there was not much time, if any, left for their planet.

His head hurt. I'm hungry too, he thought. Just then, a message blinked on all four screens.

DITCH GOFF, MEET JILL

"A slave is someone who sits down,
and waits for someone to free them."
—Frederick Douglass

The robotic voice of the monitor informed Meg that Mr. Goff was waiting outside her door. She had to think fast. He knew she was in. She couldn't ignore him and hope he would go away.

Why me? she wondered. She had to make that meeting with Jill, so she had to get rid of this guy.

She was scared, but even more than that, she was ticked. The nerve! The conceit! The sadistic bully. He had tangled with the wrong female this time. If anyone was going to lose something over this, it wouldn't be her; it would be him. There wasn't time for anything elaborate. She just had to change the dynamics.

We'll see what happens later, she thought grimly.

She grabbed a tube of ketchup and, using the mirror, smeared it artfully on the side of her head. Throwing a lamp against the wall and being careful of the shards, she went to her ID pad on the wall and sent an alert to the first responders. She guessed she had two and a half minutes before they arrived. *Just enough time!* she thought.

She put the finishing touches on the scene and opened the door, looking him up and down with her eyes not entirely focusing on his face. "Why, Mr. Goff, sir!" she purred. "Good to see you! Come in, come in!"

Leading the way to the chaotic scene in the center of the room, she turned to him in better lighting, and it was only then that he saw the red streaks on her face and surveyed the room.

"What's going on here, Meg?"

Meg laughed in the silliest way she could muster and came close to Goff, slurring her words. "Has anyone told you how handsome you are, Mister Sir Goff. Goffey Goff? Coffee Goff! Your name rhymes with coffee, Mister Goffey!" Meg added more convincingly idiotic laughter.

Goff reached his hands to her head and, puzzled, pulled them back quickly when he encountered the red paste. "Are you hurt?"

Meg screamed and backed away. Pointing an accusing finger at him. "You killed me!" she shrieked. "You killed me! You heartless, cruel man, you killed me! Murderer!" Then she burst into tears and fell to the floor.

Goff was entirely taken off guard, half reaching for her and half frozen where he stood—which was precisely the tableau the emergency response team saw when they used their override cards and burst into the room. Meg raised herself on one elbow, whimpering slightly, and brought a forearm up to cover her face. "Don't hit me again! Not again! I'll do anything you want, just don't hit me anymore!" Then she collapsed. The health workers stepped between her and Goff.

"I'm afraid we're going to have to ask you for identification and then request that you go to your livingspace and await an enforcer." They got out their ID scanners.

Goff held up his palms and backed out of Meg's livingspace.

"Wait!" one of the workers called, but he was gone. "We got him on the subsector scan," the senior worker said. "We'll call it in later."

They turned to Meg, who had stood up and was wiping the ketchup off with a towel. Before they could speak, she smiled. "Sorry, guys. I had a date with a hot guy, and this loser was bothering me. I would really appreciate it if you could just dress up your report a little by saying you found broken furniture and minor injuries. That you suspect a violent offender, although I was too scared to press charges. I really need a favor. This guy has been a pain in the rear end for a while now."

The younger worker frowned, but the senior worker, a woman, looked sympathetic and nodded reassuringly. "I know just the type, dear. They think they own all the women in the sector just because they're big and powerful. Don't you worry about the report. It will be just what it ought to be. I doubt if that guy will bother you anymore after this. He'll be flagged. Come on, Mort, let's get out of here. Unless, Miss 4k6p3, you want us to help you vacuum up that broken glass or stop the blood from oozing . . . out of the ketchup tube!" She touched Meg's shoulder with an understanding smile.

Meg was prepared to try to fake a tear, but the tears were welling up for real due to the kind worker's touch. "No, this space comes with a bot that cleans. But . . . I don't know how to thank you. I can't tell you how grateful I am."

Meg noticed her eyes weren't the only eyes tearing up. The woman waved it away and made some verbal notes in her reporter. Turning to her companion, she grinned. "Let's go, Mort," she said gruffly. "Somebody somewhere in the subsector may be needing us right now—to get spaghetti sauce off their elbows." Mort smiled kindly and touched his hat as he closed the door on their way out.

Meg pushed a button and made a circle on the screen to instruct the bot what she wanted taken care of. As she grabbed her coat, the bot was already retrieving the wreckage and removing all evidence of the spill.

She never could keep herself from saying, "Thanks, little fellow," to it, which cracked her up.

As she reached for the door, she had a wild thought. What if Mr. Goff hadn't gone to his space? What if he was waiting somewhere outside? She couldn't lead him to Jill and get her in trouble.

She spoke the number code to turn off the lights inside. The bot didn't require light to do its job. Thank the stars, she thought, my porch light hasn't worked for days.

She stepped through her front door and closed it quietly behind her. She moved to the left behind the landscaping, using a path the neighborhood kids had made. She hadn't gone more than a dozen steps before she saw, through the shrubs, a shadowy form standing behind the PV station wall.

So, he expected me to try to get to a friend's house, she thought. And he would have had me. She turned his number in anonymously for suspicion of loitering and deviancy out of sector. Added to the sweet little report from the emergency health workers, that would make two offenses in one night. Being brought before the Supreme Arbiter for disciplinary action might be the happiest possible outcome for him.

She hurried to the next PV station. It looked like a bad storm was coming. She had forgotten her jacket, but she wasn't going back for anything. Angelo's was a twenty-minute ride, and it was already 8:15. She found the first vacant seat halfway back and messaged Jill that she was en route. Before she sent it, she stopped and reworded it: *I'm doing what we talked about, thanks.* No need to leave a signpost that might raise any kind of extra scrutiny.

Angelo's was packed when she got there. Not only was the food great, the lights were low, the latest diversions were everywhere, and the atmosphere was super relaxed. Meg stopped by the host desk and fluttered a hand at the girl who asked if she had a jacket to check and inquired if she would like a seat in the elevated section or on the floor.

"Neither yet. I'm looking for a friend."

"Name please?"

"Oh! There she is . . ." Meg started off toward Jill, who had stood up from her floor booth. The elevated booths were spinning slowly and floating overhead in what seemed to be a random pattern. If someone opted for one of those, it would be an hour at least before he or she could step off at the starting dock, unless the person wanted to make a small scene. While elevated, the person not only got a fun ride, he or she saw the most interesting people, not just looking down but also in the air with them.

Meg made her way over to her friend. They hugged. Lauren was not there, but Meg hadn't expected her to be. One didn't use flashpaper for a public announcement.

"Sorry I'm late, Jill. Mr. Goff picked tonight to show up at my space."

"Oh, Jill, that's terrible. Of course I've noticed him getting more persistent lately; everyone has. There've been some awful things said––horrible stories from some of the other girls. The things he wants to do before he gets around to what he came for. How did you get away?"

"I'll tell you later. Your note asked if I was desperate. I am." More tears.

"Keep smiling, dear girl. If someone thinks we're talking about anything interesting, they'll tune in and listen. Ha ha! And so then what did she wear with it?"

"That's just it, she had to go shopping the very next day!" Meg laughed loudly.

The two friends kept it up. Meg had a sausage and green olive calzone, and Jill had a house salad. After they had eaten, Jill passed her another flashpaper note. It read, *Leave and head for the PV. Slowly.* "Well, big day tomorrow," she said. "Usual time?"

"Yeah," Meg replied as she read the note. "Think they'll change the view in the cafeteria soon?"

"Not until they run out of the thematic placemats that go with it."

SECRET INDUCTION

*"Please accept my resignation. I don't want to belong
to any club that will accept me as a member."*
— *Groucho Marx*

A s they parted company, Meg and Jill acted their
parts well. Meg left the eateria and stopped a few
paces out, pretending to be intently checking her
messages, though her eyes never actually focused on her implant.
Pretending to nod and dictate a few responses, she slowly walked
forward. Before she had passed the trash receptacle by more than
a few feet, someone handed her a bundle. "I think you dropped
this," the person said. "You're gonna need it."

"Um . . . thanks!" Meg replied, taking the parcel as well as a
local transmitter. She stuck the latter in her pocket and
immediately heard Jill's voice in her implant.

"Amazing what people will do for a privilege ticket. I don't
have a clue who that was."

"Jill! This is illegal! How did you get a local transmitter?
They were all collected years ago!"

"Who do you think wires 'em up? My friends! Don't worry,
Meg dear. And don't squeeze the thing too tight. It's rigged to
melt and would make a mess in your pants, looking like gum that
had gone through the renewer. Actually, it has roughly the same
chemical composition, if you want to check it at your workstation
sometime."

"I can't believe I'm talking to you on one of these!" Meg whispered sharply.

"Believe it. And relax. This is the side of me that I've never been able to show you. But that's about to change. Wait at the substation for the PV, but when it arrives, pretend to have forgotten something at Angelo's and start back, pulling on the raincoat in the crowd that's boarding the vehicle, and make sure the hood is over your head. The jumble of people ought to make ID difficult if anyone is scanning. Walk to the corner and wait. I'll be there in a green duo."

"Right."

"You scared?"

"Actually, I'm excited. Which feels stupid because I have no idea what I'm excited about, do I?"

"Patience, patience. I see you now. Turn around. Pretend you recognize me."

"But I don't. All I see is a hooded figure in a duo. Is that you?"

"Yeah. That's why I said pretend you know me. Wave. Good. I'm stopping. Walk up. Excellent. Climb on."

Meg's heart pounding, she did as Jill instructed. Soon the two of them were in parts of the sector that Meg was not familiar with, but Jill said their destination was not far from Meg's livingspace.

Meg was impressed with Jill's espionage talent. "It's like you're a brainy lab scientist by day and a secret enforcer by night!"

Jill laughed. "Who do you think taught me all this stuff? My own personal secret enforcer."

"Of course! But why the secrecy?"

"Because what we're doing and where we're going is super off the grid."

"Is Alex there?"

"We go there a lot, though never at exactly the same time. Shut up for a while. I don't want you accidentally guessing what's coming."

They approached a set of older livingspaces, and Jill parked. Meg followed her to the door of one of them on the lowest level, and the two of them went inside.

Two people at a table stood when they entered. "Nando and Madeline, this is Meg."

"So, this is your friend," Nando said. "We've been discussing you, Meg. Good to finally meet you."

"Why, thanks," Meg replied. Inwardly she added, I think. But she liked Nando and Madeline immediately. Woman's intuition.

"We've got some questions, if you don't mind, Meg," Madeline said, leading them into an area where they could all sit down.

"What kind of questions?" Meg replied as she took the chair she was shown.

"The standard kind. But you need to know that we've got a short-term memory wipe hypo there." Nando pointed to a drawer in the coffee table. My partner and I have worked in electronics for the state for many years. If we need to hit the panic button on this conversation, the three of us will administer the necessary dosage to you. We wouldn't think of hurting you, but you understand we've got to be cautious."

Meg glanced at Jill, who smiled encouragingly. "Don't worry. I wouldn't have brought you here if I thought there was any problem at all. I couldn't tell you more at work, and even here, we can only jam the space for a little while before anyone listening might wonder how long we were going to run the vacuum bot."

"The vacuum bot?"

Madelyn touched her arm. "That's the sound effect we add to our jammer. Just dropping off the information grid needs an explanation. If anyone wants to investigate, we actually *do* have a vacuum bot over there, modified to produce a frequency of a similar type as those used to jam a government monitor. By accident, of course!"

"But you don't run it?"

"Hard to talk over a vacuum bot, Meg," Jill said. "We have another jammer running right now, one with a little more power. We can't be overheard."

"Well, you've got my interest piqued. What on earth is going on? Why am I here?"

"First approach. We're looking you over for admission to our secret society," Nando said, smiling.

"Oh, I see. What sort of thing am I being looked over for?"

Jill looked Meg in the eye. "Illegal stuff, the kind that would get you a visit from the state and a couple of months in an isolation facility with a bunch of government shrinks, followed by a blind date with a reorientation sequence or two. I should also warn you that we've heard of terminations for this activity. Of course, you might say this is reckless and dangerous, and you'd be half right. You can see that we're not reckless by the precautions you've already navigated. But it is dangerous, both for you and for us to bring you into it. I have no doubts about you, but we're a community. We're about to take you through the questions, ones we all answered to each other once. You said you were desperate. We all are, my dear. That's why we guard this society so carefully. It's our lifeline out of the distorted and pointless world we live in and into another that's halfway sane. Are you ready, or should we get out the syringe?"

Meg didn't hesitate. "It's all so sudden, but I'll let you know when to get that syringe out. I promise not to struggle when and if it comes time to use it. Let's get to it. I'm so ready."

The other three looked at one other and smiled, satisfied with what they saw and heard. They settled back in their chairs. Meg did the same, realizing as she felt the supporting back of the chair that she had been holding herself stiffly for a while, almost without breathing.

Nando spoke into a beverage dock, ordering a pot of hot tea. When it appeared, he poured the steaming tea into cups and passed them around. The aroma calmed Meg. When the tea was poured, Madelyn began.

"Are you now or have you ever been or plan to be a member of any other society, open or secret?"

"Why . . . no. Never."

"Have you any aversion to doing things that the Entente finds to be unlawful?"

"Of course I do, within loose parameters. I have a great regard for the governing authorities, but my blind obedience has limits."

"Would you be averse to us checking through your messages and logs to see the kinds of activities in which you've been involved?"

"Well, no, I guess not. You understand that some of the stuff I did a few years ago would be embarrassing if it was made known, but you don't seem likely to make any of this public. I guess that would be fine."

The questions went on for some time. Meg was impressed not only by what they asked directly but what she realized they could infer. Government authorities couldn't have done a more thorough job.

After about thirty minutes, Nando took over, but he didn't have many more questions to pose. Finally, Meg saw the others look from face to face, taking a silent vote. Each one nodded to the others.

Even though she still didn't quite understand what she was a candidate for, it was an affirming thing to be approved by these people she instinctually recognized as worthy of her trust. Meg discovered that her tea cup was still full and stone cold. She took a sip of it. It was wonderfully flavored. Bergamot, orange, vanilla, lime. Even cold, the tea was refreshingly good.

"My genetic line once lived in this apartment many years ago," Nando said. "The man who sponsored my sponsor lived here. When I'm among friends, I call him my grandfather. You told us you're familiar with nouns like that."

Meg nodded.

"When I got out of school and met Madeline, we were looking for a place, and I saw this space was available. We moved in and accidentally discovered something: my grandfather had a special collection of artifacts preserved in a secret room. My grandparents were some of the first citizens of Chaldea, and these apartments are some of the oldest still being used. I think they have charm, though they don't have some of the fancy amenities the newer ones have. But Meg, I assure you, none of the new spaces have a room like this! I think the time has come to show you his collection."

The others stood up, and Meg quickly gulped the remainder of her tea. Jill laughed.

"There's one more thing," Nando said. "We must modify your tracker, the electronics in your skull that were put there with all your vaccinations. It will take several passes. If you will hold still a minute." He held something that looked like a remote control and moved it around her head. Meg felt odd sensations, some painful. But she did not cry out. Nando pulled out another device and read the screen. "Your location when you come here has now been randomized. If there is a plausible alternate location, our software will dig that out of the Entente's database, and you will read as if you were there instead. You will, of course, read accurately in all other locations."

Madeline smiled. "Welcome, Meg! You've just stepped off the grid."

The other two went back to their table, and Jill motioned Meg to follow her down the hallway opposite the door through which they had entered. They proceeded to the roof lift. Once inside the lift bay, Jill showed her wrist comm to the controls, and Meg's stomach jumped into her throat for a moment because instead of going up, the lift descended. The interval told Jill that they had gone at least ten levels below the street. Probably more. The door opened, revealing Nando and Madeline again, standing in the doorway. Meg recognized them as projections and smiled. Nando and Madeline smiled too.

"We're the sentries who monitor all activity here," Nando said. "We've got our eye on you two. You better behave."

Meg was on pins and needles. She knew this was it. The projections stepped aside and Meg caught her breath. The room was perhaps twenty by twenty with a fifteen-foot ceiling. All natural rock, possibly the result of mining. She saw a two couches and three armchairs and lamps to light each. Behind one couch was an insta-tree, configured for easy climbing and comfortable sitting. The walls were lined with shelves four feet high, and on the shelves were . . .

Books!

Books of every color and size. More books than Meg had ever seen. Old books, well-thumbed books, hardback books, paperback books, books with no cover at all. Precious books that Nando's grandfather had hidden there despite all attempts to rid the planet of them.

Jill turned to her. "Have you ever seen anything as glorious as a room full of books that the Entente decided you should never read?"

"I don't know, Jill! It's wonderful, but . . ." Her eyes traveled around the room. "What's in them that's so . . . glorious, as you say?"

"It's now 9 p.m. I should probably have you home by 11:30 if we're going to make the first shift with halfway clear eyes in the morning. Sit down in that chair, and I'll bring you a treat."

Meg did as her friend suggested. Moments later, Jill returned with one of the books. "Close your eyes," she commanded. Meg felt a cloth-bound book, the edges and corners smooth with wear, as it was placed in her outstretched hands. It felt good, smooth from loving use, like the handles on the tools that her sponsor, Mark, had, each with its own place on the pegboard over his workbench.

"Open," Jill said.

When Meg opened her eyes, she saw a book by A. A. Milne. The title read, When We Were Very Young. She shrugged. "I don't get it. This doesn't look dangerous."

"You have no idea what these books can do. But the Entente does, and that's why we're not allowed to read them. This series was written for kids. Pretend I'm a kid. Read it to me."

Frowning a smile, Meg opened to a random spot and began. Here is what she read.

"Little boy kneels at the foot of the bed,
Droops on the little hands little gold head."

Meg finished reading the whole delightfully magical poem and then looked up, puzzled. "I really liked it, but it's so different. Who is this god person the child is talking to? What an odd little poem. It gives me the strangest feeling."

"You're time traveling, Meg—experiencing a time from long past when the poems in this book were written. Before the Shift, before the discovery of space travel and the Plasm, there were primitive beliefs in personal deities, often simply referred to as god or an almighty or something. There were odd arrangements called families where people stayed with their sponsors until they went through a ritual called marriage."

"Yeah, I know. I didn't know *you* did."

"Yeah, what a concept, huh? A kind of pairing. For life. A permanent arrangement made in order for the progeny to stay with the sponsors and be brought up by them instead of by the state. I think I'd like that. I think I'd like a world where that happened."

Meg closed the book and turned it over. "My sponsors have a stash of books like this too. They don't know that I even know it, but I've accidentally run across them on vacation at their livingspace. I never picked one up before. If they didn't want me to know they had books, I didn't want to burst their bubble. These things are supposed to be dangerous. But I don't get it. What's in them that's so dangerous?"

Jill smiled. "Ideas, Meg 4k6p3. Extremely dangerous ideas!"

FACTORIES AND SCHOOLS

*"From each according to his abilities,
to each according to his needs."*
—Karl Marx

Director Phelps was in his element in front of a pod class of young students. Well, he wasn't exactly in front of them, he was instead in the theater-styled meeting room in his own building, and the pod class was somewhere else, he didn't really even know or care. *As long as they're not underfoot,* he thought to himself.

He was a born showman. Selling his department and the society it helped to maintain came naturally to him, not surprisingly since he was completely sold on it himself. His pride in the world he sought to preserve showed through in every word.

For their part, the pod class was mesmerized by him. This was the face they saw in governmental feeds, the signature they often saw on directive notices, the personality they enjoyed knowing was fighting for them. Some of them even had action figures of him that spoke the motto as their mouths moved and a fist came up to their chest. As they lay back in their dark classroom, engulfed by their immersionfields, they felt as if they were right there in the room with him.

His first stop was to take them to one of the many production facilities on the outskirts of the city, with a feed provided by a remote drone he controlled. Often the workers would spot the drone, smile and wave. Productive citizens are happy citizens.

The students could switch between Director Phelp's face and the drone feed or superimpose one on the other, depending often on their gender. The young girls kept a large shot of the handsome man while the boys tended to want to do close-ups of the machinery used. Either way, the Director's magnificent deep voice narrated their view...

"One day you may be tasked with jobs as factory workers, making products for everyone to enjoy. This is your duty and privilege as part of a happy, well-functioning society. Your lives are much improved over the lives of factory workers in times past.

"In those days, there was a terrible burden on those who had to take their meager wages and then turn around and allocate that money for food, housing, transportation, healthcare, insurance, repairs . . . the list was endless and the money always ran out before the expenses did. Sure, the bosses might try to help, but they were in the same boat as their workers, and by and large, the workers were on their own to access the essentials of life.

"Not that long ago, there were units of people housed together based solely on the results of procreation, forced to live in situations with no thought to who they might or might not be compatible with. The eldest were obligated to provide for the youngest, a crushing burden. Contrast that with our society where everyone's needs are met in a community that values fairness and equality. Those forced and repressive procreational associations have now been superseded by a strong circle of like minds, that functions with efficiency and strives for the advancement of the collective, not merely the individual. With basic needs foreseen and met, each person can now use his or her income for entertainment, extra food items, and recreation.

"Income is now equalized because nothing's more demoralizing and destructive within a production facility like this––indeed, to a contented citizenry of the planet––than ugly, unchecked personal ambition. Transportation and housing are standardized too. Anyone can take a factory tran to work and return to the factory housing assigned to them. They can buy magazines, beer, candy and legal diversions at the factory waterstation where the tran often stops or somewhere near the factory eateria where they meet their friends for delicious meals. Of course, if their shift is on duty, it's no problem at all; they may eat in the factory cafeteria, free of charge.

"In times past, we gathered the sick in giant buildings, great sanctuaries of germs and disease, where admission was nearly the same as a death sentence. Not so anymore, I'm happy to say! Anyone who feels sick is now afforded the comfort of their own livingspace for the duration while government healthcare providers visit and treat those patients. Oftentimes, we can simply send a drone-bot!"

The students laughed out loud as cartoon footage of a bot interacting with someone in a room was shown. The bot dropped a syringe on the floor and as the patient and bot reached for it, they became tangled up and both fell over. The Director's chuckle was heard as he resumed.

"The bots we send out are true miracles of science, containing patient and disease information and diagnostic equipment a human health worker could never hope to attain. Myself, I actually *prefer* a visit from one of our mechanical friends!"

More footage, this time of a real bot saving the life of a patient with timely recognition of the problem and the correct remedy. Ending with the patient weakly smiling with two thumbs up. Applause from the pod class... the Director, with the timing of a professional actor, waited for the correct moment and resumed...

"Now this is very important, and a great advantage over times long ago. If the patient does not, for some unknown reason, show signs of recovery within a reasonable period, they may opt to become candidates for scientific experimentation at the government labs. Any worker I know would be proud to have his or her declining health used to help others! Our citizens are the most forward-thinking people the world has ever known!"

Once again, applause was given as young hearts stirred to the incredible joy of being a citizen of the Entente. Along with a stirring soundtrack (and the appropriate accompanying drugs), beautifully crafted and animated banners appeared that read, *Your Sacrifice Keeps Us Fighting For Everyone!* Interestingly enough, that was the motto most often seen on the walls of those labs. People seldom returned from there, and when they did, it appeared something had happened to their personality, and they didn't seem to be very bright.

Director Phelps' voice brought them back to a new scene as he smoothly switched drone feeds to show a school in the outskirts of Chaldea. The camera flew over dark images of students in their recliners. All of a sudden, they realized it was they themselves that were appearing in their immersionfields and different students, unable to see the drone, would see themselves and wave, with the other students giggling. Director Phelps particularly loved this part of the presentation. Any chance to engage the students with laughter he considered a plus.

"My young friends, education back at the turn of the millennium was hit or miss, something the students could refuse like an immunity shot. The students themselves decided what they would and would not learn, often ending up totally unprepared in their later lives. They sat in uncomfortable desks beside distracting windows. The educators were overwhelmed with the size and scope of the task, and it was hard work. They had to try to persuade their uninterested class to do the necessary work in order to gain the knowledge society deemed necessary. Shameful remedial classes were provided for students who fell behind. Students who did not pass were punished by being held back a grade."

The students were treated to black-and-white images of lonely young people in tears and anguish. The Director's voice cheered them all up as he continued with his reassuring words.

"Like factories and everything else, education has now also turned a corner, thanks to advancements in understanding the human organism. Modern schools are now bursting with cheerful students, all in the same pod class, and all of them leaning back in their reclining chairs in control fields" (more waving on screen and more laughter) "which supplies them with purified air, dim light and beverages of their choice."

He did not add that the beverages of their choice all included a mild sedative...

"No longer are our wonderful, bright students engaged with a dusty blackboard or a boring book. Each one of them is relaxed, often your eyes are even closed and your minds fed through brain implants received in utero when your cerebral functions were the highest of your lives." (Gasps of delighted amazement...)

"Our new education model is a modern wonder in applied efficiency and comfort!"

As more visuals crowded the pod students' sight, the Director shook his head in admiration of how education was now a matter of feeding the mind, infusing the ideas into the subject the state had shown to be most beneficial for society. No need for any volitional help from the subjects themselves. How simple and elegant! The rows of students looked like they were asleep, but in reality, they were being gently bombarded with images, sounds, smells, vibrations and other sensory inputs.

These young, empty minds were like dough being conditioned, fields being plowed and planted, metal blanks being heated, softened, and hammered into shape.

Now at the end of each day, education experts could take pride that not a single student had any objections or problems or needed to be shamefully evaluated or make any choices or ask any questions. It was all done for their benefit. And when they became productive members of the collective, they could appreciate the methodical, systematic, meticulous, and disciplined education that had given them the outlook and attitude needed to function within the collective for the good of all.

Without a doubt, safety and happiness were at the core of what human beings craved. History had shown that any society that began in bloody revolution for the elusive concept of freedom had eventually gladly traded their freedom for security and a promise that all bad things that happened to people would be eliminated.

And what good was freedom, anyway? What an archaic triviality! To demonstrate the superiority of safety/happiness over freedom/independence to a community, one had only to look at the grid of citizenry that resulted. Anywhere one looked in a society where safety and happiness were the prime values, one would see people working productively, enjoying their well-earned recreational opportunities. No wars. No conflict. No competition for limited resources.

Take sex education, for example. In times past, sex was poorly understood and because of that, misused. Rape, adultery, and promiscuity were said to be immoral, as if sex had a moral component! New insights had shown it to be merely a physical activity, like eating, exercising, or defecating. It should always be expressed naturally and without all the baggage of monogamy, offspring, obligations, responsibilities, and all the other outmoded nuisances of the past. The old, Puritanistic spoilsports had twisted sex into a semi-sacred act instead of the diversionary release it obviously was. Sex just needed to be safe. And now it was—safe from disease, fertilization, and especially old-fashioned guilt.

Miseducation about sex was just one area where homo sapiens' growth had been stunted. In the old days, people had the misery of owning their own businesses, attempting to amass wealth, wanting things called "careers" where they were forced to choose their own occupations. They had the anguish of participating in their own governance, being constrained to produce offspring they would be solely responsible to feed and clothe in a socio-economic legality they were stuck with for the rest of their lives.

Once again, thought the Director, these antiquated ideas revolved around the lie that the human heart yearned for freedom. That deluded notion produced chaos in which everybody felt entitled to live almost any way they wanted. There was conflict over mates, property both physical and intellectual, and borders, disputes with neighbors next door and in the next country. There was unexpected death. There were spiritual beliefs that isolated and terrorized the population.

Worst of all, people were sometimes unsure of what to think, tossed here and there by every new revelation, left alone to try to find their own fearful path through the maelstrom of life.

Education used to be offered. Now it was achieved.

It used to be classical. Now it was scientific.

It used to be hit-and-miss. Now it was 99 percent effective.

The myriad mistakes of the past had been corrected. Yes. Thankfully, these students would grow up to be productive workers. Healthy. Happy. Clean. Without any symptoms of the Sickness.

And very safe. His visit with these students was at an end, and the time had come to say goodbye for now.

"Well my young friends, this is where I leave you. I wish you luck as you become productive members of the Entente, and make your way into this delightful world!"

More applause amid the surreptitious and entirely appropriate chemical stimulants.

HARRY TAKES ON A PASSENGER

"Some day you will be old enough
to start reading fairy tales again."
—C. S. Lewis

Jason followed the appropriate protocol for incoming messages, logging the galactic time and position of receipt. His codes were months old, but he knew they'd be fine. He didn't know why they even used codes for messages. Who the heck was going to intercept them?

Upon hitting the final sequence, the screen brought up the visual of his immediate superior, a guy his age: his friend and pod mate, Max. Max's face and the upper part of his uniform filled the viewing area, and his voice was stern and without inflection.

"This is a coded message from the command center for Jason t43p7. If you are not Jason t43p7, viewing this message is a punishable offense covered by book 5 section 24, book 7 section 9, and book 12 section 67 of the regulations. Violators will be arrested and charged upon discovery."

Yeah, yeah, Jason thought. Like there are hordes of people here who shouldn't see this.

"This is a time-sensitive message. Jason t43p7, you are hereby recalled from active duty. Return to your launch site with your cargo and upon completion of processing of both you and your silo, receive your new instructions." Max broke into a wide grin, and his voice sped up a little and sounded much more natural. "You will begin your well-earned furlough. Well, sort of. We're all proud of you and your work here at base. Newsblurbs of you and your herculean efforts have already been sent around the fleet as an inspiration. The high-ups have sent out the word. We're gonna make you a hero, and you, my friend, will be the poster boy of a new wave of signups for the collector squads. Immediately transmit a few shots of you and your collection bins, so we can begin our PR blitz. You'll become a worldwide symbol. We'll use your face and your public appearances will even be used to promote the image of our space academy."

Max looked sideways, giving a throat-slashing motion to cut the official feed, and then leaned into the camera with a relaxed smile. "Well done, Jase! You've just got us an additional ten years of top-level funding. Everyone wants an autograph! We've become a little light on our recruiting, just between you and me, so I think the big dogs have decided to bring you back to a ticker-tape parade and sorta romanticize the 'brave collector.' And of course, his faithful pooch. Hiya, Harry!" Max straightened up, nodded off-camera, and put a clenched fist to his chest. "Communication ended. We're fighting for you!"

Jason waved the salute back at the screen halfheartedly. "You're frightening me too," he muttered. Then he remembered that his response was being documented and gave the correct salute and response. "Unity is safety. Sorry about the temporary loss of signal. I think I just got it fixed." He retrieved and altered the disorderly portion of the transmission, expertly producing the "loss of signal" for which he had just apologized. The communication was ended.

"Nice," The creature said from right next to him, nearly causing Jason to jump out of his skin.

"Whoa! Don't do that!"

"Do what, exactly?"

"Look . . . pal. Uh . . . what's your name?"

"Is that necessary?"

"Yeah. We humans kind of like to use names. What is it?"

"Call me Izgad."

"Iz . . . Izgad? What kind of name—"

"You think my name is humorous? Absolutely intriguing."

"No, no, I . . ."

"It means messenger. I have been sent to you. Not only to give you messages but also to help you."

"*Help* me? Sure. Thanks. Now I forgot what I was steamed with you about. Oh, that's right. I remember," said Jason with all the sarcasm he could muster and then, getting close to Harry's face and waving his hands, he half shouted, "Don't just start speaking to me when it's been over a year since I've heard a live voice other than my own! Scared the bejeebers out of me, chief!"

"So instead of speaking, shall I just give you a prod?"

"No, that would be way worse!"

"Intriguing. What then?"

"You could . . . I don't know, probably nothing. You're just going to take some getting used to."

Izgad looked up at him. "You are one to talk."

"Was that a joke? You can joke?"

"It was an accurate assessment, but if you find it amusing I am all right with that."

Jason now had the news for which he had been hoping. Time to set sail! By using a combination of antigravity levitation and solar wind, a silo could be moved almost anywhere on a planet with ease and without a lot of bulky fuel or equipment. Beyond the boyish joy of rigging the silo for its last flight, a solemn celebration was involved, with the celebratory victory cigar and the offering of a toast to the fact that Jason was pointing his ship toward home once more. He was keenly aware of the symbolism involved and relished each moment. He lost no time in beginning the ceremony. Not the sails just yet. The smoking and drinking part.

He looked up from his glass to address Izgad through the haze of his cigar. "Are you, like, all-powerful? Could you just kind of 'poof' us home?"

Not moving a muscle from his coiled position on the rug, the feathered creature spoke. "I could, but I cannot."

"What do you mean?"

"I mean we are not allowed to just go around poofing people, as you call it. We have strict orders about the purpose and timing and extent of the power we can bring to bear in any given mission. You will still have to sail to the portal."

"And you're going to bum a ride?"

"I have been sent to you. I am not bumming a ride; I am your new best friend."

"Just my luck. I'd ask you to help me rig the ship, but I enjoy it too much to share. It's kind of a ritual we collectors dream about that marks the end of a deployment."

Izgad raised his head. "There is no rush. We have to talk, and it is going to take several days or so."

"What?"

"You heard me. Let me know when you have finished everything. I never knew about sleep before. It is wonderful, like drifting on stellar gasses. I have got to try it when I get back home. Dreams are like freeform associations. You never know what is going to happen next, and anything can change in an instant. I wonder what my beast will dream this time. Goodnight."

"Good night," Jason echoed, to himself, using the mildly exclamatory connotation of the phrase.

The rigging took a little longer than strictly necessary. Jason wanted to savor the experience, plus he wasn't all that excited about beginning the session with Izgad. Finally, the task was completed and the silo ready for flight. Jason woke Izgad, who stretched luxuriously and then waddled into the silo. Jason followed.

"First of all, it is nearly time for the broadcast," Izgad announced.

"What broadcast?" Jason asked.

"The one Harry sends from his cranium every two weeks."

"What are you talking about?"

"It will take some getting used to, your habit of pretending you did not hear what I just said. Do I need to repeat it?"

"No, I heard you. But Harry isn't broadcasting. Never. Not even once a year."

"One day you will trust me since I am as incapable of lying as you are practiced at it. Look at the screen on your left, and I'll access Harry's last transmission."

Jason turned to his left and saw a low-level camera shot of the inside of the silo. Suddenly, his own figure opened the silo door, and the viewpoint jumped up and circled his legs. Jason's voice came from the screen, "Hey, boy, good to see you too. We got a good haul today, Harry old boy . . ." His voice continued as the viewpoint tilted up and remained motionless, fixed on Jason's hand, which had just grabbed a treat. As the treat was lofted high into the air, the screen kept it dead center until it disappeared with a snap right below the view. Jason's voice continued. "I had those weird thoughts again, Harry, the thought that I should be grateful to something, something that's not the Plasm. I even found myself talking to whatever it was, and I had a sense there was something or someone there. I ought to be afraid that I've got the Sickness, but it's the healthiest feeling I've ever experienced." Jason's voice stopped, and his hand grew larger and shook the camera back and forth from above.

The transmission stopped. Jason couldn't move. No one told him the Entente had implanted a camera in his canine buddy, let alone with broadcast capability. Harry was a sneak. A spy. His own dumb dog. No, not a dog, a rat. Ratting him out.

What kind of trouble was he in? Didn't Max know what was on this latest tape? Sure he did. Unquestionably he did. So, why hadn't Jason picked up anything in Max's attitude? The other collectors must be truly lousy for me to be up for hero status, he thought. Though I shouldn't worry how they'll handle it, I'm sure they'll do a complete reboot on my mind during processing. They won't cure me. They'll just wipe my brain. Then they'll have a vegetable who can smile and do photo ops for PR. Maybe I've got the Sickness, and no one with the Sickness ever skates. I just signed my conviction papers. And beyond everything, *they used Harry!*

Harry was his friend, and the Entente had weaponized him and turned him into an unwitting snoop. Anger rose up in Jason against the inhumanity of the Entente.

"Penny for your thoughts," Izgad hummed.

"They'll lobotomize me when I get home."

"Probably. If we let them."

"How can we stop it? I'm cooked." He turned to Harry. "How could you, boy?"

Izgad's creature walked over to Harry and stood beside him, looking up at Jason. "Easy. Harry had no idea. He still does not really understand, but he knows you are upset. Just look at him."

Harry's ears were back and his head lowered.

"Sorry, Harry," Jason said. "Good dog. It's not your fault. I mean, how could you know. . ." Harry stood up and pushed his head into Jason's leg. Jason squatted down and rubbed Harry's ears with both hands. Harry thumped his tail in reply. "So, Izgad old man. What now?"

"Thank you for asking. I believe you have overestimated the efficiency of your department. They have not received this. Before we do anything else, we need to erase and retake some of Harry's recordings from the last couple of days. I made note of the position numbers, and you can drop in new footage after you reshoot a couple of moments. At the same time, it is of paramount importance to get rid of the segments where I am speaking and you are reacting. There must be no record of our meeting. We should be OK because, as I am given to understand, Harry's spy cam—absolutely intriguing, what an astounding amalgamation of slang!—is programmed to upload to your home link every three weeks, so we should be able to intercept all the objectionable footage." Izgad paused and then spoke into the air, using a different tone. "Oh . . . Sure, I will ask . . . I wouldn't worry . . ." Then he looked up at Jason. "And my creature asks that you not load him in a freezer bag."

"It's OK with me. We've got one of his kind already anyway. It would have been a squeeze."

"Next, you and I need to spend some serious time talking. There's a lot I need to convey, and it is important that you listen with an open mind. I will tell you nothing but the truth."

"Sure. While I was rigging the sails, I had time to think. If you're hostile, you sure don't show it."

"I assure you I am your friend. We can proceed to our next task after you've heard all I have to say and I have answered many of your questions. I will not answer them all because part of my mission is opaque to me as well. More on that later. But now we reach the part where I transfer to Harry, and we leave this lovely creature to his wandering about the planet again."

"Transfer? To . . . to Harry? You . . . are you . . . Is this OK with Harry?"

"To tell you the truth, he was the one who offered. I was going to bring it up, but he invited me over before I could. If I remained in this creature, there would be disadvantages that Harry does not present."

"Oh. Sure." Jason was trying to catch up. A moment later, he watched as the green lizard dragon thing waddled out of the silo and into the underbrush, clueless again. Behind him, Harry suddenly began running around in circles, barking with joy.

"So this is what is meant by 'dizzy?'" Izgad asked. "Whoa, Harry! Whoa! I am also glad!"

"Are you in there?" Jason asked, peering at Harry.

"I believe I must be because my observational abilities are rotating at great speed."

"So do I still call you Izgad, or are you Harry?"

"As you like," Izgad said over his spinning shoulder, "but Harry might get confused."

"So you're still the heter-which-ish thing person?"

"Heteroclite. Yes. My nature, like yours, is permanent in whatever physical conveyance it finds itself. Even in whatever diminutive orbit! Whoa, Harry! Easy! Easy!"

"Your syntax is odd."

"I've only been speaking your language a short while, and it is outrageously primitive. Give me some time to adapt to your sentence construction."

"So, you said you want to talk?"

"In a bit." Harry had not slowed down. "First, we shall shoot the new footage we need for the broadcast. The light is a little off, but I doubt they are sharp enough to catch a couple of degrees difference in azimuth."

Harry completed his seventeenth rotation and attempted to stick the landing on the rug, which slid with him and Izgad out the portal door. The last thing Jason heard was Izgad yelling. "Watch out, Harry!"

THE DIRECTOR GETS A HUNCH

"The nine most terrifying words in the English language
are, 'I'm from the government
and I'm here to help."
—Ronald Reagan

As usual, late in the evening, the Director was alone in his office. His staff was also there late with him. Those who didn't like the hours were winnowed out as dead weight. Each of them was busily finishing up the day's tasks so as to be ready to hit the ground running in the morning.

The Director poured a little more Scotch into his coffee and lifted his cup in symbolic salute to the progress of mankind. The progress, he told himself with only a tiny amount of pride, that he, the Director, was helping to effect. The progress that was moving mankind from bloody-clawed animals to transcendent gods.

A forward-thinking man, he was in a rare mood of looking back.

Society had begun with tribal leaders. Those leaders got the best caves, the best cuts of meat, and the best women. They promised to take care of their people, but they never quite delivered.

Over time, those leaders became kings and continued to take the best, still promising to take care of their people and still not giving a rat's rear end.

Eventually, the kings were usurped by the rabble of ordinary people, both in ancient England and in revolutionary America and France, the collective still devolving into just a few despots and still having no concern for anyone but themselves.

Hunger, disease, exposure, fear, and war all persisted to trouble a frightened world. A large and inefficient population—the sick, the aged, the deformed, the incurable, and the insane—were allowed to weigh down the rest of society. Darwinian philosophy had shown what to do with such people, but it was not until the formation of the Entente that the state had the proper moral and military tools to accomplish the necessary cuts in demographics.

Especially problematic were carriers of the Sickness. But no longer would the Entente allow such a drag on their progress. It had been necessary to round up these outliers and isolate them from the general population. Some had been cured. The rest, those who resisted reconditioning and persisted in their delusions, had been delivered into the hands of the very gods they would not renounce. Their removal was both necessary and justified.

With the coming of the absolute state, mankind was put on an enlightened footing for the first time in history. Pragmatism and utility replaced superstition and tradition. Given the rotational shift and the geological cataclysms that were daily occurrences, the panic in the population and the disillusionment with whatever "god" people had once created to cherish, it was the perfect storm of a crisis to bring forth the supremacy of the benevolent intelligentsia overriding all aspects of living and thinking.

With the abolition of all objections, morality could now be reworked and improved. With the new tools of practical ethics, the construction of the "new person" could proceed at breakneck pace. And with the establishment of the Entente, mankind had finally taken the last great step toward true spirituality.

The old religions were mistaken in their approach but not in their needfulness. Psychology loudly proclaimed that the general population had to know that something bigger than themselves existed. The state could provide the lion's share of that component, but there was still a small unmet cry for a great purpose or impelling force of some sort. Though science might grant great understanding and wisdom, phenomena still existed on the frontiers of knowledge that had no scientific rationale.

Something to explain the edges of understanding where the explanations fell off the edges of the map . . .

The Director sat up. What? He felt a chill in the room. One of those episodes was happening. He had been thinking about spirituality and phenomena that had no rational justification.

Though he would not describe himself as tuned in to the metaphysical, he was feeling something odd, something that was happening more and more often.

It was a presence in the room, like an odor. He had sensed it a couple of times before. He found that if he just went with it, something interesting happened. He closed his eyes and paused. The presence seemed to leap toward him. Unflinchingly, he allowed his hand to go to the comm button. "Hello?"

"Yes, Director Phelps," his secretary replied. "May I help you?"

The Director concentrated. "Send an interception team to . . . Sixty-third and Tyler. Have them . . . take an enforcer. Make it an officer. That's all."

"Yes, Director Phelps, right away."

He leaned back with his eyes still closed. That was all. As if the door had opened and closed, which it hadn't. But unquestionably the presence, whatever it was, was gone.

He looked at the time. Eleven minutes until nine. This should be interesting. I wonder what's up? Whatever this is, it's time I got back to work. Vigilance.

Looking out over his city, it appeared it was going to be a heckuva stormy night...

ALEX ON THE JOB

"Life is not a matter of holding good cards,
but sometimes, playing a poor hand well."
—Jack London

Having just finished A Tale Of Two Cities, Alex was reading Robinson Crusoe to Jill when the call came.

"Sir?" an apologetic voice said. "Sorry to bother you, sir, but there's an interception on, and you're the officer on call."

"Do you need an officer on this intercept?"

"Apparently, sir. It was part of the instructions."

"Very well. Send me what you have. I'll be on the move in five."

"Excellent, sir, and again, I apologize."

"We all have our duty."

"Fighting for you."

"Everything is unity. Officer cx94b out."

"Yes, sir."

Jill looked at him. "So, I'll see you tomorrow. Robinson Crusoe is allegedly the very first novel. You can tell Defoe was still working the kinks out. Dickens seems to have reached the pinnacle of the format."

Alex smiled. "There are parts of Defoe's story that drag, but he launched so much of what the landscape of the novel would become. It seems as if Crusoe's worldview, like ours, was informed by books."

"Wasn't there a particular book that was especially transformative?"

"Uh-huh," Alex said as he stood up and grabbed his gear. "It was called the Bible. A religious history of some sort."

"Everyone has a soft spot for something that offers some kind of big explanation. You'd better go."

"Right."

Alex dropped Robinson Crusoe in Jill's lap as he grabbed his jacket.

Outside, he checked his pocket for his identifier and then climbed aboard his cycle. One of the perks of the job was having a vehicle that was flat-out fun to drive. The special modifications made this machine superior to anything else on the road. For one thing, there were no regulators, correctors, surveillance, or auto conductors on his wheels, just the freedom of being able to make any turn, go any speed. Even to have the chance of a wreck was such a kick. None of the vehicles on the road could catch him.

Arriving at the coordinates, he noticed a standard contingent was already there. "What's up, people? What are we doing here tonight?" he asked as he braked to a halt. The dark sky showed no stars above.

"Nice wheels, sir!" a young female enforcer said.

"You have no idea. And my question?"

"Of course, sir. You know as much as we do. We were just ordered to this spot. No other information supplied."

"Nothing more specific? Is that odd?"

A heavy-set cadet cleared his throat and spoke up. "Sir, I've been on two of these interceptions where we had no idea what we were doing. We just waited where we were told and, sure enough, we were in the right place at the right time. I got this star for the first one." He pointed to his chest.

"So we wait, huh?"

"Yes, sir."

"Anybody bring along a pack of cards?"

"Sir?"

"Cards. Ever been down in the original parts of the city and seen the old men playing cards?"

"No, sir. But I've seen an implant diversion that was called 'pack of cards.'"

"Yeah, that's it, except these aren't implants, they're fifty-two rectangular plastic-coated tickets about this big with symbols on them. Spades is one of the games you can play with them. I once spent a whole vacation playing Spades with three friends in a cabin up north."

The cadets laughed. Mainly because their superior had finished a story, and they were conditioned to believe officers expected laughter to follow their stories. Alex noticed the wind was picking up.

"I'll bring some cards next time, sir," a cadet said, smiling. "If they're available at the waterstation."

"Don't worry about it. It's just . . . hold it." Alex switched on reception for his communicator. His dispatcher's burly face appeared.

"Alex, that you?"

"Hey, Johan. Can you tell me anything?"

"Not exactly sure, but I'm seeing two people running toward you on my monitor. One seems to be injured. Maybe you're supposed to detain and question."

"Roger that," Alex replied, wheeling to scan the dark street. He saw them approaching, keeping to the shadows, suddenly aware of the waiting enforcers. They froze, knowing they couldn't run from an interception team. There would be no need to chase them down.

"Hold it!" Alex called to the two figures, then turned to the tech. "Jam 'em."

"Aye, aye, sir. Almost have their tags. Got 'em."

"Nice work," Alex said as the two newcomers grabbed their heads and went down. "Get 'em to the command vehicle, and we'll see if they can tell us why we're out here working instead of somewhere else having fun." He felt the heavy humidity of the warm wind. It's gonna be some storm. Alex's mind went to Robinson Crusoe on his tropical beach.

Inside the vehicle, the intercepted men were placed in hovering containment frames, allowing the enforcers to move them around the room with the push of a finger. Alex herded the older of the two over to a stool where he sat down, read through the man's file, and then fixed the man with a steady, friendly gaze. For a moment, he said nothing, just looked at him. Then he addressed the man in a quiet, unthreatening voice.

"Hey, Jimmy. You're hurt. I'm sorry. A little simple cooperation from you, and we'll get you fixed up. I see here your profile says you're not a citizen of Chaldea. Your little fishing town is a couple thousand miles from here on the northwest coast. What are you doing with your buddy here? You don't have a permission packet for travel."

Jimmy said nothing. Fear was the primary emotion Alex read, but he detected an inexplicable anger component as well. Alex tilted his head. "Not talking? You know you can tell me what you know about this, or I can dial a frequency into your implant that will give me a window into your whole mind. I'm an officer of the enforcers, given unlimited legal and physical empowerment to protect our fellow citizens. I just need to know you're not a threat."

Jimmy's eyes closed tight. Alex was going to count to twenty, but Jimmy opened his eyes at eighteen. "I'll talk."

"No!" the other prisoner cried.

Alex turned to address the outcry. "What, Fenton?" His tone remained friendly. "Not wanting to cooperate? You know we can get anything we want out of you. Why make this harder than necessary?"

"Listen, Jimmy," Fenton pleaded, "don't go mushy. Think of what you promised the others."

Alex smiled. "Others, huh?"

Jimmy glared at Fenton. "Quiet!"

"He knows there are always others," Fenton mumbled. "That's all they know unless we blab."

Wind and rain suddenly lashed against the walls. The storm had arrived. The thunder sounded close but muted inside their vehicle.

"It's over, Fen," Jimmy said.

"Maybe for us, but if you don't blab, it's only over for us," Fenton replied earnestly.

Alex nodded at him.

"Jimmy's right, Fenton. You know what we can do with you. You'll be glad to tell us everything you know, but we might break some stuff while we're thrashing around inside if you don't just give us the answers we need. What were you guys doing?"

Fenton seemed to have made his point. Jimmy looked down and bit his upper lip. Silence fell.

"I don't want to use force to compel you to cooperate, fellas. It's a little messy—the science isn't quite perfected yet. I wish you'd just talk. That way nobody gets hurt."

Jimmy looked up. "Just let us go home, for the love of God! We're not hurting anyone! We promise never to be caught at large in your jurisdiction again!"

Alex shook his head, amused at his archaic reference to a deity. "Doesn't matter whose love you invoke; you know we can't do that. We've all got our responsibilities to each other. You got flagged this evening. It's your turn to fight for the rest of us. Fight for us against the anarchy. Against the destabilization. Against the Sickness. By telling us what you know, you'll be doing your part in the fight. For the love of god," he added.

"Do you have any friends, Officer cx94b?" Jimmy asked in a scared tone.

"Sure, Jimmy. Everyone has friends. You have friends too. Believe it or not, I'm one of your friends."

"Then if you are, let us go. We're not gonna betray our friends."

"Can't do it, Jimmy. I've got to do the right thing. You do the right thing too, and just give me the information I need to do my job."

One of the cadets fidgeted. "Sir? Do you want me to generate the frequency?" Alex's eyes did not leave Jimmy, but he patted the air toward the tech cadet as if to say, not yet.

"I know you; you're famous," Fenton said, staring straight ahead but addressing Alex. "You're Alex cx94b. Sir, please believe me that it's precisely because of our friends that we can't tell you anything for your report. If you truly do have friends, as you say, you know you'd do anything for them. You'd never make their lives harder."

Alex nodded, "You're right, Fenton. And not talking to me is making their lives harder. We need all of us to make all of us safe. Every person has to do the right thing and fight for one another. Our unity is based on everyone doing their part. Your friends don't want you to do anything that would jeopardize all of us. Your friends—and I am your friend, Fenton—would want you to cooperate with recognized authorities. That's who I am. I'm the officer in charge of this interception, and I officially represent your friends and fellow citizens. Come on. For the sake of your friends, what were you guys up to just now? Why are you out of sector? Why are you traveling on foot at night in secret when everyone should be asleep, preparing for another productive day in Chaldea?"

The two men stared at their feet. Alex turned to his tech. "OK, I guess they've left us with no choice. Give me a little less than .01 amperes, but be careful, brother. We just want our friends, Jimmy and Fenton, to remember what they'll force us to do if they refuse to fight for all of us."

"You got it, sir. A little less than .01. Coming up." His fingers worked the tactile surface of the delivery system, loaded the required amplitude, and then, after looking at Alex and getting a nod, pushed and held the yellow lever.

"Aaaaaaaaaaaaaah! Stop! Stop!" the two men screamed. Alex's hand went up, and so did the lever in the tech's hand.

"I'm sorry," Alex said to the two prisoners, who were still moaning, "but you were the ones who brought that on. Take your time. As soon as you can focus, I want you to look at me. I have something I want to say." Neither one of them moved for a full minute. Then they slowly raised their heads to look at Alex: first Fenton and then Jimmy.

"Again, I'm genuinely sorry we had to do that. It's never my intention to hurt people, but that includes all the citizens in my sector. I can't let anyone else hurt people either. That's why I have to know what's going on and why you have to tell me what you were doing. It's because none of us want anyone to get hurt—not you and not the people of this sector. Come on now. You see that you may as well just talk to me. I'm going to find out one way or the other. The next frequency I use will cause you not only a lot of pain but will also rip some holes in your ability to string thoughts together. I'll be able to ask you questions knowing you're gonna give me all the answers I could ever want. But your minds will be damaged, in some ways permanently. For the sake of—"

Alex's attempt at persuasion was cut short by a lightning strike that sent 200,000 amps through the vehicle's specialized equipment, arcing through the tiny space in a spectacular display of light and heat. A fire sprang up on the central console and spread rapidly.

Though knocked out of his chair, Alex was up immediately. He jammed the stabilization lever all the way down and brought his fist down on the red fire extinguisher button, which released jets of foam targeted at the flames. The fumes were too noxious to remain inside.

A cadet had already thrown the door open and was dragging some of his stunned companions out of the vehicle. The restraining field around the detainees was cut, and they slumped to the floor. As Jimmy hit the rug, an object flopped out of his jacket.

In one smooth motion, Alex reached to pick him up and used his foot to shove the object forward, his right hand grabbing it and holding it firmly to Jimmy's chest. In a practiced lift, he expertly rolled Jimmy and hoisted him over his shoulder, the object pinned between them.

Ordering the nearest officer to grab Fenton, Alex stepped out into the pounding rain. Flashes of lightning alternately revealed and concealed their surroundings.

Turning to a cadet, Alex told him to alert HQ that they had been hit. The cadet looked up, wide-eyed, and then reported that all the electronics had been fried, including their wrist comms.

Alex was unfazed. "The nearest station is an easy thirty-minute walk from here. In the meantime, let's head for that PV stop over there for shelter and to get some air—no need for anyone to stay with the vehicle. Everyone follow me. Jimmy and Fenton secure? Here we go."

Despite the blinding rain and the thunderous light show all around them, Alex was pleased to see how sharply the team operated. They were efficient, well-trained, and disciplined. The group he usually worked with were raw recruits, specifically assigned to him because of his well-earned reputation as a teacher. Like him, tonight's group was not a standing team but the representatives of several teams, the ones who were on call that night.

"Nice work, people," he said.

Reaching the stop, he set Jimmy down, palming the object back into the jacket pocket out of which it had fallen. With any luck, Jimmy probably didn't even know Alex had seen it, but it changed Alex's approach.

Now he had to figure out what to do and quickly. The object was a book.

A book that was definitely on the forbidden list.

It was The Book of Esaias.

❖

CONTACT WITH THE SICKNESS

*"Do I not destroy my enemies
when I make them my friends?"*
— Abraham Lincoln

The lightning strike had been an unforeseen event, but Alex and the others simply fell back on their excellent training. Alex issued a few directives, but largely, the team knew what to do. They had moved quickly from their sparking vehicle to the shelter of the nearby PV stop, and in no time, the area was secure.

The storm not only created a visual barrier, but the loud, opaque noise all around them presented an acoustic barrier as well. They were all soaked to the skin. Lightning was still pounding away in spectacular and alarming fashion.

Alex knew about The Book of Esaias. It was often associated with the Sickness, the correlation being made relatively early in the quest for a cure. Alex had no qualms about touching the book, since he did not hold the superstitious view of most that the book itself was contagious. But he knew that not only did these two men endanger society at large, the book presented a danger to these two men. His heart went out to them.

His team proved highly efficient in setting up a perimeter. Then they placed battery-powered bracelets and anklets on the prisoners. Three of the five cadets had been injured to some extent and were in no condition to walk. Alex and the others had administered regulation first aid to them and to the prisoners. Alex then did a visual inspection of the area and a ran through a mental checklist of their situation.

In the absence of communications, Alex continued to follow the operative rules for such an eventuality. They were protected by the glass enclosure of the PV stop. Ashe sensed the storm letting up, he spoke to the two enforcers who were uninjured.

"Brynn? Nate? Well, how about this? I've seen worse. Communication still down? Fine. We're OK. Brynn. I want you to return to our vehicle and begin preparing it for towing. Nate. You remain with our three injured cadets and see to their comfort. The worst of the storm is over, and I'm going for help, escorting the prisoners to the nearest station, which is less than a mile or two back along this connector here. Once there, I'll send a rescue squad quickly back to this location. Questions?"

"No, sir!" the cadets replied.

"Good. Then I'll see you all back at sector dispatch in a couple of hours. You've done your jobs well to this point and under these circumstances. It will be so noted."

Alex knew he could have simply stayed with his unit until they were eventually found by scanners, but he wanted to get his wounded seen to as quickly as possible and he had no idea how extensive the blackout was. Plus, the book he had seen had triggered something in his mind, and he wanted to follow up.

Jimmy and Fenton walked ahead of Alex, following his instructions. Their hands were cuffed behind their backs, and they were tied to each other at one elbow and one knee. They could still walk easily, but an escape from a senior enforcer was out of the question. As far as Alex knew, there would be no visual record of their trip. Their implants would show their positions, but there would be no audio either.

When they had proceeded about a half mile from the unit, Alex spoke to them.

"Jimmy, you're carrying a book on the forbidden list."

Silence. Then a determined answer. "I am."

"You know the consequences for that crime?"

Another short silence. "Yes."

"Fenton, I'm just guessing that you have books too."

"I'm carrying two books, and the one Jimmy has is mine, I'm not sure how he got it from me."

Before Jimmy could protest, Alex broke in. "Stop here."

Neither stopped. "Are you going to kill us?" Fenton asked.

"Stop and turn around."

With difficulty, the two men did as Alex told them. Alex looked at their faces, their rain-soaked hair sending rivulets of water into their blinking eyes.

"Give the books to me."

"What?"

"Just do it. And listen. When I take you into the station, I want you to tell them you were here to set up a drug connection. They'll be lenient and probably only hold you for a couple of days before sending you back to your sector. If they find out you were carrying forbidden books, it's doubtful anyone will ever hear from you again."

Alex took the books from their shaking hands. He had noticed a loose brick in a wall they were passing. He reached out and tugged the brick out, jammed the three books into the hollow, and then replaced the brick. He turned back to the two men.

"Let's get you to the station and processed."

They stood in the rain.

Fenton looked Alex in the face. "I don't understand. Why would you risk anything for us?"

"You know what? I'm not sure. All I know is that of the six officials who processed you tonight, I'm the only one who knows what was actually going on with you two. I'm following a hunch, my friends. You could rat me out, but then we would all fry. Or you could do exactly as I say and promise me you will never bring one of those books into my sector again."

"We can't promise you that."

"Why not?"

"Because we want everyone to be able to read that book and others like it."

"Do you have the Sickness?"

"Yes."

"Both of you?"

"Yes."

Alex had never before encountered the Sickness in citizens outside of his training simulations.

The diseased citizens in the simulations were clinically insane. These two weren't.

The diseased citizens in the simulations were violent. These two weren't.

The diseased citizens in the simulations would not admit to having the Sickness because they were unaware of it. These two just had.

Apparently, the simulations were dead wrong.

Alex's experience with books let him recognize that outside of their fanaticism and foolhardiness, these men had found the same joy that he had found. As he well knew, their own library did not have a copy of The Book of Esaias. Alex was trying to figure out how to stage a faked escape when a bolt of lightning hit a power coupling twenty yards ahead, nearly blinding them. He laughed. Perfect.

Reaching into the wall and pulling out two of the books, Alex returned them to the men and told them to walk straight toward the sparking electronic debris of the coupling. When they began to question the safety of this idea, he interrupted them. "Just do it, please."

As they obeyed, he spoke again. "I've left one book where I stashed the others. I've had a similar encounter with books that you both seem to have had. I've never experienced anything remotely like it. I know I might be caught someday, arrested, and tried, but to me, it's already been worth it. So . . . I think I get you guys. And I'm sure you won't mind paying for your escape with one of your remaining books, since you probably had ten each when you came."

Fenton smiled. "Seven each, actually. These particular books are rare. And we never dared hope we could position a book so high up in the enforcers."

"Well, that one back there in the wall will be well cared for. Let's move. Hurry!"

Alex took them in among the glowing fragments that were all that was left of the power coupling. He marked his clothes with black marks from the burned and charred fragments of materials. Carefully picking up hot wires, Alex used them to burn through their restraints, even though his knife would have done the job easier. He knew his badge would show that their path had taken them into the field of this power coupling and wouldn't be able to distinguish that they had not arrived until a few moments after the strike. Picking up a broken crossbar, he gave them their final instructions.

"I'm going to be knocked on the head by this 'falling' bar. Your burnt restraints will remain on the spot. You are to get out of here:

disappear. The large culvert under the city highway has cameras at both ends, so don't go that way. Your best bet is to lift a bi and leave it at a waterstation or an eateria somewhere in the sector next to yours after wiping it down and removing its memory. Get going!"

The freed prisoners looked at each other. Was this actually happening? They turned back to face Alex.

"Go!" Alex shouted.

The next moment, he saw them running off into the darkness. I hope they get home alright, he thought as he raised the crossbar. Then he swung it. Hard.

The last thing Alex remembered before he felt the pain of the crossbar shrinking his head was the smiles of true friendship on the faces of Jimmy and Fenton.

MEG VS. GOFF, ROUND TWO

*"Offensive operations, oftentimes, is
the surest means of defense."*
—George Washington

Meg had barely made it to her space the next morning
when Mr. Goff opened the door.

"Good morning, sir," Meg said. "I had the weirdest
dream last night. I think I was a little juiced. I've been trying out a
new diversionary drug. In the dream, I seem to remember you
coming to my door. But that can't be right—you at my door? Crazy
about dreams, huh?"

Mr. Goff stopped, his mouth open as if to speak. Meg's
question had thrown him off his approach. As he was considering
how to react, Meg turned to her station. "If you want to see what
happened yesterday, I can call up the logs. As usual, the results had
to be cleaned up. I think I'm making headway though. As some
twentieth-century inventor said, at least now we know another way
not to make a peach! Pretty good, huh, sir?"

Mr. Goff smiled. "Meg, you . . . you went somewhere last night.
You're right, I stopped by your livingspace, and you know you
didn't have a dream. But you did have an accident that I had
nothing whatever to do with. You looked pretty bad, and I wanted
to stay and help, but the medical workers told me to scram. I guess
I didn't like their tone, and things got a little testy. Who knows
what they'll put in their report? So, I went and got something to eat
and came back later. You weren't in your space, according to the
door log."

He left a space for her to deny or explain. She didn't take the
bait. "As I said, sir, last night is a little fuzzy. Now that you mention

it, there did seem to be health workers in my space last night, but I couldn't tell you why. They can get in anywhere. It's a little creepy."

Mr. Goff was about to say something when his wrist comm interrupted. "Yes? Speaking," he replied into thin air with his eyes focused on nothing a long way off. "Oh, really? What can they be wanting? They didn't? How many of them? No, I haven't the slightest idea either. OK. Tell them I'm just making the rounds, and I'll be there in twenty minutes. They said my ID was discovered to have been where? OK . . . Yes . . . OK. No, I'll just . . . I'll come right now then. Of course . . . of course . . . right . . . alright." His eyes refocused on Meg. "I've got to go. Lunch?"

"A couple of us are eating at Sparky's today. I'll get my logs to you if you'd like to see them."

"No, that won't be necessary. I'll see you later."

"Of course, sir. I expect to see my boss while I'm at work every day during regular hours."

"That isn't what I meant, Meg."

"I've got a new approach to the peach texture. It came to me on the way in. I think I'm fighting for us on this." Meg executed a semi-circular punch in the air to highlight her use of the well-worn phrase.

Mr. Goff turned and left. Meg collapsed in her chair, her eyes closed and every muscle tense. A headache was coming on.

At that moment, Jill dropped by and poked her head in Meg's station. "He's getting an early start today, huh?"

"I didn't tell you what happened with him last night. I don't really want to anyway. Ready for another day?"

Jill winked. "As always. Oh, FYI. You'll get a flashmail this afternoon. You'll have about two minutes to retrieve it and view it, so be on your toes."

"Roger that. Lunch at Sparky's today."

"Since when?"

"Since the boss asked me, and I told him we were going there."

"Oh, OK. But they don't have good salads there. The greens are kinda fake and greasy. I guess I'll try one of their omelets."

"For lunch?"

"Breakfast is the best meal of the day, sweetheart. When are we grabbing a PV?"

"Eleven thirty. Bring a jacket. They dial down the temp there."

"See you then," Jill said, and then the door closed.

As Meg turned back to her work, she wondered what would break down first with Goff: his will or her luck.

MEG AND HER BOOKS

"Outside of a dog, a book is man's best friend.
Inside of a dog it's too dark to read."
— Groucho Marx

Meg turned a page, absorbed in her reading, surrounded by the delightful silence of the library. She was as high up in the insta-tree as she could be, her legs kicking back and forth as if she were five years old again. Her right hand held an apple that she was halfway through, unlike the book that she had almost finished: Captains Courageous by Rudyard Kipling. She was in bliss.

Her main problem with her newfound admission to the library was figuring out how to cover for her frequent absences from her former lifestyle patterns.

Alex had taught her how to check to see if she was being followed and how to vary her frequency and visiting hours so as not to trigger a routine summons and investigation. The software of her tracking implant had been overwritten so that she could "ghost" somewhere else while she was at the library. Ways of remaining part of the background noise in a population that was being monitored were as simple as pairing up, as Jill and Alex had done, or as complicated as using one of the library's algorithms to leave a false trail of bus rides.

Nando and Madeline were old hands at this game, having worked in the very department they were now bamboozling, and Alex knew some tricks they didn't. Occasionally, Meg would leave the library to deposit a handprint at a shop and then return to read more. She dreamed of vacation time when she might be even more opaque to the grid.

But avoiding detection was a small hurdle compared to tearing herself away from the treasure trove of books at the end of each visit. The time seemed to fly by. By now she had her favorite sections in the shelves: history, biography, and fiction, both youth and adult.

She loved talking with Jill, Alex, Nando, and Madeline about what they were reading. They wore the same starry-eyed smile as she did, and each would share excitedly about the discoveries they were making in the books they were devouring as fast as they could.

The experience was as if someone had been eating unseasoned food all their lives and had just discovered herbs, salts, curries, and peppers. Suddenly, life opened up, blossoming from the narrow existence she had lived until now.

She discovered a short period in American history called the Wild West. She read anxiously about the French, Spanish, and English expeditions of discovery in the sixteen and seventeen hundreds. She loved the tactics of great commanders like Genghis Kahn, Alexander, Napoleon, and Pontiac. She devoured the fiction of the mid-1800s and early 1900s: Journey to the Center of the Earth, Treasure Island, Watership Down, That Hideous Strength, Anne of Green Gables, Lord of the Rings, The Count of Monte Cristo, Tarzan, The Time Machine, A Christmas Carol, and A Connecticut Yankee in King Arthur's Court. She loved the poems of Hilaire Belloc, Shel Silverstein, Robert Frost, and A. A. Milne and became absorbed in the mysteries of Rex Stout, Agatha Christie, and Arthur Conan Doyle. She would spend hours scanning the picture books. She was Marco Polo, Christopher Columbus, Ferdinand Magellan, Henry Hudson, Daniel Boone, George Washington Carver, Thomas Alva Edison, and Neil Armstrong, launching into the unexplored, the unknown, and the undiscovered territory. She longed with all her heart to experience what they did, to set out on a quest with unimagined dangers and otherworldly rewards.

But each day there came a moment when her adventures ran out of time, and she returned to her hyper-protective, oppressively uneventful, shallow, drab life; nearly tasteless by comparison. Only now she brought those other places and times with her in her imagination. She lived more in her daydreams these days. She was happy, having tasted something more extraordinary than her former routine could provide.

She finally had hold of something no one could ever take from her.

THE BOOK OF ESAIAS

*"A great book should leave you with many experiences,
and slightly exhausted at the end. You live
several lives while reading."*
— William Styron

The report Alex filed on the capture of the two men out of sector was clean and in order. His account was easily verified by the tracking system, a couple of battery operated surveillance cameras that had caught disjointed moments of their passage, and a cursory visit to the scene after the storm.

He had regained consciousness shortly after being found and brought in to the station and reported the circumstantially accidental loss of the two prisoners. It was the first black mark on his record, and it vanished into his years of exemplary service without even triggering a supervisor's examination. It had been a simple case of bad luck, and it could have happened to anyone.

Oddly enough, the Director himself, a man with a penchant for meticulous detail, had for some reason not launched much of an inquiry into the botched job he himself had instigated. His hunch had become a confused memory and nothing from what he called "higher up" was forthcoming on the operation.

It was as if the lightning had hit more than a couple of circuits that night.

Within a week, Alex made a clandestine visit to the brick wall, and their underground collection had a new celebrity: The Book of Esaias. It was a little water-soaked, but with tender care, it was restored and given a marquee spot all by itself.

Alex had not had time to do more than glance at it so far. Besides, he was going through the Aubrey-Maturin series by Patrick O'Brian. The others had gathered around it admiringly when he brought it in. It was definitely the crown jewel of their collection so far.

With its arrival, they all noticed a change. The library had always felt like hallowed ground, but now the Book of Esaias gave off a palpable vibe. It was not like the other books they cherished and delighted in. This particular book didn't seem to care if they liked it or not. It was somehow above and beyond their approval or disapproval.

Meg could sense the phenomenon, curiously drawn. The Entente had it on a short list of items that automatically constituted a capital offense. With its addition, the library was thus made both more dangerous and more exciting.

Sitting in the library, Meg and Jill were discussing the new addition with Nando.

Madeline was only a projection since she was actually upstairs in their little apartment in case someone knocked at the door. "They say the Book of Esaias is one of the books in a collection that were usually bound and sold as a unit," Madeline said. "Sixty or more books. All together in one cover."

Meg wondered at that. "Strange! Why that many? Were they something like an anthology written by one prolific author?"

Madeline shrugged. "I don't know. Great question."

Jill shook her head. "No. I've read that those books spanned more than fifteen hundred years, so if it was one author, he'd have to have been eating right and exercising!"

Nando chuckled. "Very funny, Jill. A real comedian. My understanding is that Esaias is part of a mythological tradition."

"Whose mythology?" Meg asked.

"They're stories told by an ancient nomadic people called the Habiru," Nando replied. "Jill, sounds like you've done a little research on this particular book."

She nodded excitedly. "Some say the Book of Esaias was written around 700 BCE. Others say it couldn't have been because it accurately predicted events in scary detail centuries and sometimes millennia before they came true and that some of the predictions still haven't happened yet."

Madeline raised her eyebrows. "I have a hard time with prophecy, but I find the book itself curiously enchanting."

Meg nodded. "Ditto. I can feel the pull myself, though I don't know why. Is it true that this one book was transcribed into thousands of different languages before the great unification took place?"

"I understand that they've discovered nearly two thousand re-renderings so far," Nando replied. "That far outdistances any other book by a magnitude of ten to twenty times. Curious, huh? It was perhaps the most widely read book of the old world system."

"What do you make of how we're each drawn to the book as if the book has its own personality?" Meg asked.

Nando smiled. "Yeah. I don't know. It's crazy. Something spooky's going on with that book."

Jill leaned forward. "I wonder if it's extraterrestrial. Some sort of revelation from beyond. Could that be?"

Nando shrugged. "Not likely. Because if so, why would our government have wanted it destroyed when they've been trying like crazy to find clues of life out there? If this is from space, why ignore it or try to protect us from it?"

Meg looked at him in surprise. "Some really do say it could be from aliens?"

Jill leaned back. "Lots of books pretend to be, you know. They claim that mere humans didn't write them. Societies who have these so-called holy books give them unusual reverence because they're supposed to be unfiltered truth from the great beyond. Truth that could only come from outside our world. Truth from whatever's waiting for us in space."

Meg nodded. "I know a guy, a collector, who's out there. Among the stars and planets. He says there's nothing we've run across yet that can form sentences, let alone write a book." She didn't add that she spent an inordinate amount of time wondering what this particular collector was doing.

Nando nodded. "Probably so, but when I say beyond, I mean truly beyond. Not just beyond our moon or our solar system or even our galaxy. Outside the circle of our universe."

"What's beyond the circle of our universe?" Meg asked. "I've never heard of anything."

Nando looked at her. "Maybe nothing. Maybe there is no such thing as outside, beyond. But it's the type of idea that's persisted in human thought ever since the beginning of time."

Their time was up. Jill and Meg left, staggering their departures, carrying with them the joy of dealing with something more real than the world to which they were returning.

The friends knew a lot of people, including themselves, who were seeking truth. As they continued to exchange their discoveries, they came upon a disturbing possibility...

That truth itself might be seeking them.

FIGHTING FOR YOU

"We must be prepared to make the same heroic sacrifices for the cause of peace that we make ungrudgingly for the cause of war."
— *Albert Einstein*

In his office downtown, Director Phelps looked over his team's findings of the day. Connections among people they had under surveillance were beginning to take shape. Stan's report would be added soon. No need to move prematurely on any of the names who were possible suspects. Citizens weren't going anywhere, he thought, smiling to himself.

Everyone knew that all crimes were committed, so to speak, in a finite system. The offenders had no prospects of evading detection, so apprehension was entirely at the discretion of the authorities. Whether he moved immediately or a decade from now, he knew that these perps would be pie to pick up at any moment of the day.

And he did not want to move too soon. In these matters, timing was everything. A sting that was closed up too early often missed the key players and only caught the underlings. There was no such thing as waiting too long.

He re-encrypted the files and sent them to the storage server marked "turtle.376, Director's eyes only." Then he spoke into his wrist comm. "Get me agent .257 . . . Yes? Hello? 257? Yes, it's me. Fine. Been watching our boy, Stan? Fine . . . fine . . . yes. Let me know of anything that looks odd to you. Good job . . . fine. Fine. You may soon be reinstated if you keep this up. Stay sober, or there's not much I can do for you. Continue as you were. Fighting for you. Yes...yes...Out."

The Director leaned back in his chair and swiveled away from his desk to gaze out his high window overlooking the beautiful cityscape. His lofty view of Chaldea symbolized the great work he was doing for the people. The people who needed him. Needed his unsleeping watchfulness and rare mind. What satisfaction he gained from his work. His high ideals, his elite skills, his intimidating intellect, his . . . he might as well acknowledge it, since it was absolutely true, and even his own modesty could not deny it —his unquestionable superiority to those very citizens. It was not his fault that he was better than they. Even his humility was on a higher plane.

Given his evident primacy, it had to be.

He had no time to know any of them or to spend time in the places where they lived, but he didn't have to. He knew what they needed: a common purpose, a sense of security, and order. All those things that he, Director Phelps, was already providing for them, albeit un-thanked and unappreciated. Making the decisions they were unequipped to make. Bringing in the future they were too unimaginative to foresee. Providing the common purpose that they were incapable of discovering for themselves.

Everything is unity, and he was both unity and everything to these dear people.

In the Director's mind, humans were, for the most part, nothing more than highly developed animals, most secure in packs where they could be controlled and herded toward a better end that only people like him could understand. He was their benevolent overseer. They could not be expected to share in the decisions he made constantly for them. They did not have the ability to meet life head-on as he must do for them all.

Fighting for you! What a wonderful truth some bright mind had fashioned one day in the past. It encapsulated the one thing simple people truly desired, giving them the good news that they need do nothing beyond being thankful for their wise and brave leaders. Taking from the people the heavy burden of actually engaging the world around them, leaving them to enjoy lives that were carefully and diligently engineered to be safe and efficient. Free from fear for the most part, as long as they stayed in their place within their designated boundaries, liberated from worry and stress.

Perhaps that was what the Director loved most about his work, the sense that he was at the post that only his unique and elevated mind could occupy: that of caring for a people who, over history, had shown they yearned desperately to be managed. They required a firm hand to guide and to guard.

The vast majority who owed him everything knew nothing of him, but that was just fine.

For being so aware of his own exceptional qualities, the Director was still a humble man. To anyone who saw him when he left his quarters in the central building of Chaldea to wander around among the public, he must have seemed like any other handsome, overly intelligent man they might meet. He wore no insignia except for his old special forces belt, a grey woven composite strip fastened with the buckle of the Guard, the military force that was both army and secret police.

Though largely no longer needed, the Guard continued to assist in the eradication of pockets of ignorant resistance in the far-flung corners of the globe. It gave the planet a functioning military in case of invasion from interplanetary species yet unknown, or in case our planet needed to effect such an invasion on another world. It served as an elite and quasi-secret society in which it's members floated above any accountability to the lower classes of citizens, giving and receiving favors and prerogatives.

Plus, it was just fun. The military got to play with high-tech toys and rearrange mountains with experimental explosives in subarctic Africa.

The Director's career in the Guard was something in which he took immense pride. Being channeled into the Guard marked him early on as someone possibly destined for leadership. It was the first winnowing of the wheat and the chaff, so to speak. Of course, few of the Guard ended up as The Director had, for it was only the beginning of a process that provided Earth with the cream of the cream, the best of the best, who could hold and carry forward the mantle of power and authority.

The Director was aware that in the distant past, some societies had chosen their leaders by popularity contests, by promises made, or even by mere height. No more. Now it was the special ones, the ones with the mark of greatness—those who knew how to coax efficiency out of the jumble of disarray.

Efficiency and pragmatism were the hallmarks of the new order, which was showing the way toward the future, recognizing that people had always been and would always be sheep and that the Plasm had gifted a few among them to dominate for the good of the others. It was ultimately for the best. What might be resented by more primitive societies was now universally accepted by the masses of human beings, content to live in pleasure and security, cared for by the wise and the vigilant. It was no longer a goal, an ideology, or a dream. It had become reality.

Ultimately, power rested with the Elders—the shadowy elite who were opaque even to those who answered directly to them. The Director did not know the faces of those whose orders he obeyed, only their voices. He had no doubt that one day he would gain admission into this final fraternity consisting of those, it was rumored, who did not die, who communed with the Plasm in a sort of oneness that a parched man had with an ice-cold beer.

Checking his communications again, he saw that all his charges were well in hand for the moment. The Director changed into his exercise gear right there beside his desk.

IZGAD RATTLES JASON

"We must love them both, those whose opinions
we share and those whose opinions we reject,
for both have labored in the search for truth,
and both have helped us in finding it."
— *St. Thomas Aquinas*

J ason was having a difficult time accepting that his dog knew more than he did. At that moment, he and Izgad, newly settled in Harry's furry body, were sitting outside the silo on the landing above the aluminum drop stairs leading down to the planet—Jason in a floating anti-gravity chair, Harry on the thickest rug in the silo. Izgad was doing most of the talking, but Jason wanted to clear some things up.

"So you're telling me to forget enzymes and proteins built from elements leached out of the substrate rock that formed themselves into tiny creatures over billions of years. That instead of the settled science, this law of protochemtrophy, you want me to believe that life was spontaneously called into being by some magician? Isn't that sort of . . . silly anthropomorphic nonsense? You want me to swallow that life had no inorganic roots, to believe that all the physical laws of the universe could be suspended while this imaginative event took place?"

"I am not asking you to believe anything at all. I am just telling you what happened. As far as suspending the physical laws, those laws were created right along with the rest of your universe. Why should that be so hard to comprehend, or, as you say, swallow? You get along fine believing a lot of crazy things. For example, you believe that blue mold on cheese means you throw it away unless you spell the "blue" with the e and the u swapped. You believe that time is linear when it is truly multidimensional, actually nondimensional. You believe that your brain can process vast quantities of input signals because of chemical reactions when the actuality is closer to what you would consider to be, again using your terminology, magic. All these incorrect assumptions do not appear to handicap you severely. So, I repeat, I am not asking you to believe anything. I am just showing you reality. What is. If you can store it in your mind for later retrieval and evaluation, that is all we are attempting here."

"But if the entire universe came from the workings of this person you speak of, wouldn't our scientists have found that out?"

"Absolutely intriguing. You are convinced that scientists, unlike all other people, search for truth?"

"Um . . . is that another erroneous assumption?"

"Scientists are human beings, not automatons. They are subject to the same temptations and imperfections as others."

"And as human beings, scientists might accept what they know to be false?"

"I should not put it that way, but that is probably what it boils down to. I am hearing myself use your idiomatic phrases. Listen to me say an idea can boil. I would say, rather, that human beings are complex in the way they process informational input. They are able to rationalize irrational thought to the point where they no longer see it as unthinkably absurd."

"The Plasm producing life from inorganic compounds using the natural physical laws of protochemtrophy is unthinkably farcical?"

"I am surprised you have to ask. Have you discovered any process by which life could be produced from inorganic compounds?"

"Maybe you don't know about the Neo-Darwinian theory of evolution."

"And what laws of physics does it utilize?"

Jason was silent. His education had assured him that there was nothing to consider or question. Simple, natural, inevitable processes were all that was required to produce...well, to produce any number of functioning universes. Universes with spectacular displays of light and color, interwoven symbiosis, miraculous orbits, and gravitational constants. Universes with order and rhythms, intimacy and secrets, wonders and vastness waiting to be discovered, none of it predictable, all of it astounding. He did not so much doubt all that he had been taught about protochemtrophy as much as he began to recognize its limits and to begin to acknowledge the possibility of an alternative explanation.

But that didn't necessarily mean Izgad was right. Wasn't his story laughably childish? Wanting Jason to believe—no he said he didn't care if Jason believed it or not—*telling* him that somewhere there existed an enormous intellect that had waved a wizard's wand and called forth the space-time continuum? Ridiculous!

And yet, Jason couldn't shake this invasive idea. Could it really be that simple? That obvious? That the interconnectedness he could see existing within the universe mirrored the interconnectedness existing in the mind of a single intelligence who was the First Cause?

Perhaps even the being to which Izgad was referring?

Suddenly, Jason's schooling fought back. "You're trying to tell me that a frightened child's nursery tale is the truth and that the accepted and time-tested scientific explanation mankind has known for centuries is absurd? What's so absurd about it? Science is the most rational pursuit of all. There's no such thing as a rational absurdity."

"You are correct."

"So how can you say science can produce a rational absurdity?"

"Science has done no such thing."

"You said it has!"

"I said nothing about science. I was talking about scientists. Scientists are human beings, and as such, rational absurdities make up a lot of what passes for thought among them."

"I need another beer."

"Would you get me one too?"

"You drink beer? Harry never did."

"Only because you never offered him any."

"Oh. Um . . . sure. Be right back."

Jason just needed to step away for a moment. He was amazed at the idea that science could be less than objective truth. Wait, no. Izgad had not said science was lying; he said scientists were—or at least they were mistaken. How did he put it exactly? He said that because scientists were human beings, error was not only possible but probable.

Jason knew from experience that many people were easily pressured into parroting beliefs just to get along, unthinkingly regurgitating and ardently defending ideas they had never spent a moment seriously considering. He knew that few had the brains to challenge accepted norms in science, and those who did were finally won over not by reason but by fear of losing reputations and jobs.

He knew he didn't have the brains to challenge scientific norms. I don't know how solar sails operate or how my proton watch works or how time can be dissolved, but I still operate in the world that contains those phenomena, and it doesn't seem to bother me! No one had to grasp any of the principles of physics in order to have fun on a uni, enjoy alcohol, or turn on a light, for that matter. Though if asked about such things, they'd still try to explain them and get frustrated, not with their lack of ability to explain but with the listener's lack of ability to follow!

A question formed in his head, and he shouted it to Izgad from inside the silo. "So, Mr. Smarty Pants, how come every single intelligent person believes that the Plasm came up with life through natural chemical reactions over time?" He grabbed a beer and turned to head for the door.

"You coming with that beer? If you remember, I am not wearing pants, and anyway pants do not exhibit intellectual capabilities. You said every single intelligent person believes the Plasm produced life? Are you telling me you have checked with every single intelligent person?"

Jason emerged and sat down. He poured some of his beer into a dish and set it next to Harry. "No, I don't know all the intelligent people who have ever lived, but I've never heard anyone disagree with it."

Izgad's voice came wetly between slurps of beer. "No one in your science classes objected to the idea that life is a series of undirected chemical processes?"

"Nope. As far as I remember, just me. But the textbooks all said that the production of living matter was nothing more than a naturally occurring and inevitable production of protein sequences given the proximity of the needed elements and the enormous length of time available."

"Oh, well, if the textbooks said it . . ."

"Smart people write the textbooks."

"You see how we have gone from every smart person in the world to just the subset of smart people who write textbooks? Our sample size is shrinking."

"What's your point?"

"The point is, the things that 'everybody knows' change over time. At one time 'everybody knew' that if you were sick, you had too much blood. At one time, 'everybody knew' that salt and coffee were bad for you. And at one time, 'everybody knew' that the sun was a deity. You think the Plasm is axiomatic since everybody knows it. You think that because everybody knows the Plasm produced the fantastic life forms you see on all these planets that it must be so. Don't you realize that the reason everyone believes in the Plasm is because they have been told that everyone believes in the Plasm?"

"Uh, I . . ." Jason paused as he digested Izgad's last sentence. "Mmmm . . . I see your point. It does seem amazing that one of the foundations of our society seems to be more a matter of faith than science. To tell you the truth, that's a little unnerving."

"I am not close to revealing any trade secrets here. The first step to being able to think clearly about the rest of what I have been authorized to tell you is to know that you are a created being living in a created world. That the One who did the creating is a Person, and that you belong to and must answer to this Person. Are you following me on that much?"

"I guess so. Not saying I buy it, but I'm interested and curious."

"Excellent! All I could reasonably expect from you is your interest and curiosity. I am delighted." Harry licked his lips. "Could you spare a little more of that beer? I find it . . ."

"Right: absolutely intriguing."

"I believe you are mocking me. The beer?"

Jason suddenly realized he had not even taken a sip from his bottle. As he absentmindedly poured a little more into Harry's bowl, he went back over this new paradigm. Not undirected. Not accidental. Not impersonal. Calculated. Purposeful. Personal. It was amazing how this simple shift in perspective was sending shockwaves through a life of assumptions. Everywhere he turned in the piles of things he took for granted, he could see the rearranging going on. It was as if the pattern of his life was being ripped apart at the elemental level.

Nothing was being reassembled. Not yet anyway. It was total deconstruction.

Although this idea was new, he recognized it as a possibility that had been lurking in the background of his thinking ever since he was a kid. This was nothing shocking really; this was a curious closed room he'd been standing in front of for a long time. The room had always been there. Now the door was open a crack.

"I guess somewhere inside I knew that what you just told me might be true. I didn't know it consciously. I knew it down deep. I've always mistrusted the explanations of the Plasm and thought the people who were teaching us that stuff were, well, trying too hard. One of my favorite movies has the following line: 'Pay no attention to that man behind the curtain!' The man behind the curtain pretended to be all-powerful and all-knowing, but he was a fraud. When the curtain was pulled back, he was just a carnival barker. That's how I'm processing your words. The Plasm has seemed to me for a long time to be like that man behind the curtain. A lot of bluster. A lot of pressure to accept the concept, but it's a cheat. All hat and no cattle. No there there. No substance to the dogma they indoctrinated us with. I guess I've always suspected it, but it was all I had, all I knew, so I didn't question it. I guess I feel like I'm . . . I don't know, cresting a hill, tasting a new food, discovering a new planet. Waking up."

"Good. Excellent, actually. Ironically, Harry says he feels like he is doing the opposite: getting sleepy. Would you mind splicing in the new footage we made for your reports while we close our eyes for a bit?"

Before Jason could answer, his new friend had circled a spot on the rug three times and curled into a tight ball, obviously assuming what Jason's reply would be.

GOFF BUT NOT GOFF

*"I'm not strange, weird, off, nor crazy,
my reality is just different from yours."
— Lewis Carroll*

The Director's team was gathering in great anticipation. Turtle.376 was heating up. The clusters continued to map an unusual pattern of activity outside some fairly unremarkable older buildings in a northeast sector. Over the last several months, the movements had been random, but even so, the observation clusters's software was able to produce a hazy graph out of all the electronic clutter. Clearly, something was happening somewhere near that location. Stan's latest report had informed the Director that the activity probably involved black market books, but the Director wasn't going to pass this on to his team. Yet. If they discovered it, fine, but until then, books made this operation extremely dangerous.

Dangerous, that is, to himself if the operation were somehow botched. He needed to chest his cards until he could claim another brilliant victory. For the people.

"We've heard from our eyes inside!" the Director's voice boomed through the meeting room. The room was instantly quiet as people focused on their leader. "He reports that our hard work is bearing fruit!" he said triumphantly. "Along with the evidence of the emitter, we have a good idea from our infiltrator that there is a big target in the old city. Some kind of criminal cache. Weapons, contraband, seditious underground items of some sort. He's getting closer by the day. I'm sending you the set of buildings that he thinks might be the center of the activity. Vigilance, my young friends, vigilance."

Smiles all around the room. There was nothing as good for team spirit as getting a project near to the point of calling in the enforcers for a raid. "Let's make sure we wrap turtle.376 up in a neat package, everybody. If we do this right, I'll give you geniuses another six weeks of paid vacation for you to turn down!"

Laughter. Director Phelps was so funny and great to work for. And what a cause— protecting society from the Sickness. How could any job be more fulfilling? They couldn't wait to go back to sifting through unsuspecting citizens' lives as if they were nothing more than entertaining TV shows. It didn't matter that they would never want anyone invading their own privacy this way, it was their job to compile data on everyone who lived in or around the city. Plus, it was great to gather around and laugh at what people did when they forgot that someone might be watching.

After dismissing the team, the Director strode back to his office in high spirits. When his secretary told him that he had someone in his office, he half expected to find a member of the Elders waiting to commend him, but his secretary said it was a Mr. Goff. Who is this guy? he wondered.

As he stepped into his office, he saw an older man, handsome and dark-haired, slightly built, eyes a little vacant and unfocused, sitting in his chair behind his desk with some of the drawers open.

"What the hell do you think you're doing, Mister . . ."

"Goff," the man said, continuing to rummage through a drawer without looking up. "My name is Goff. I'm not surprised you don't know me, Director. I'm a supervisor at the nearby research plant. That's not the limit of my responsibilities."

"What do you mean? Are you with the Elders?"

"The Elders? No. They have only existed for decades. I've been around a lot longer."

"Yeah, right."

"The age of this body is forty-three, but I wasn't talking about this body."

"Whose body exactly were you talking about?"

"Bodies are like vehicles. You ride them until they stop going where you want to go."

"You say you what? You 'ride' bodies?"

"I've been in twenty-four bodies. This one is my latest. I'll be looking for another one soon."

The Director's hands dropped off his hips. He cocked his head. "So you're nuts. Suppose you close all the drawers and move away from my desk, so I can call to have you restrained. If I have to move you myself, it'll take you some time to recuperate, though there probably won't be any permanent damage."

Goff continued to search, unimpressed by the threat. "In your hand-to-hand combat training, you were second in your class and spent some time as an instructor. When you were a boy, you would protect the weaker kids on the playground, one time taking on five boys larger than you. With a little luck and one of them being slow, you put two of them in the hospital, gave one a permanent scar, and sent the other two running away."

"You couldn't possibly know that unless..."

"I am an emissary of a mind that existed before the stars."

"Nothing existed before the stars."

"I and my kind did."

The Director was uneasy. He knew crazy people. He knew people who talked big to make themselves appear important. He knew carriers of the Sickness. But this was new. This was not any of that. The man was obviously not crazy, talking big, or a carrier. This guy was looking straight at him unblinking from the Director's own chair with no sense of guilt or embarrassment. And how did this weirdo get in? He tried one more time.

"I'm going to say it once more. Get. Out. Of. My. Chair."

"I'm here to bring you news."

"Are you getting out of my chair?"

"There's a threat to the collective. The Sickness has spread."

"I'm not even going to count. Last chance."

Goff did not move, but the voice that the Director heard come out of him next made his blood freeze. The change was not just audible but visceral. The new voice was harsh, lifeless, cruel. Inhuman.

"I am not to be trifled with, puny being." Goff's eyes were glazed over, windows into emptiness, and he laughed in a way that made the Director unable to think clearly. Goff picked up a heavy iron bar on the Director's desk, and while his eyes looked deeply into the director's white face, easily bent it in half.

"What the hell are you?" the Director heard himself mumble.

"I am not one you may order out of your chair. I am not one who answers to you or the Elders. My order is ancient and powerful beyond your imagination. We have held this planet under our domination throughout human history. I have watched kings and kingdoms rise and fall. I have shouted with mobs, and I have terrified children in their beds. I have done things that would make you unable to sleep quietly ever again. Listen closely. I said I have a message for you. There is a threat to the collective. This business involving Stan cf56n and turtle.376 is of more importance than you could possibly know. Even we cannot see or understand why yet. But you must concentrate on it and be willing to spend all your resources on seeing this mission brought to a successful close. We are disturbed by something about all this. Do as we say, and there will be great reward. Fail, and you will wish you had never been spawned."

With that, Goff's body rose unnaturally from the chair as if he were a malfunctioning AI robot and, brushing past with an unearthly snarl and an odor of decay, left the room.

The Director stood rooted to the spot as the world spun around him. As he became aware of himself again, he gradually stopped shaking and began to turn the scene over in his mind. Something about the man's voice reminded him of the way his intuitions sounded, but there was a terrorizing thrill in it that was beyond his waking experience.

He made a mental note to reinforce security around the building and then pulled up the visuals on turtle.376. How the devil had Goff, or whoever he was, known about turtle.376? That was impossible. The Director knew his team, and they had never leaked a whisper.

Not just security on the building, but firewalls around his operational data needed reinforcing. Should he contact the Elders? No, there was no scenario in which his encounter with Goff would reflect favorably upon him. He vetoed it.

Sometimes the thing to do when all choices could be wrong was to do nothing. If this man answered to the Elders, then the Director just had to keep his head down and pour his energy into Stan's investigation. If this man were higher up . . .

There was nothing higher up than the Elders.

The Director scoured the visuals on turtle.376. What was it about this case that had alerted that godforsaken voice?

Wait, he thought. Maybe looking for large gatherings of people was not the key to this case. Grabbing several files and grouping them on his screen, he realigned the search parameters to check for traffic over a broader period of time. Perhaps he could correlate movement to a location that had eluded the emitter. He checked random dates and times, but this time he broadened the time frame to include single visits over a twelve-hour period. Nothing. Slamming the keyboard, he spun around to look out the window. Get a grip, Phelps.

He had already painted the grim picture to his team about moving too early. Now he began to worry about moving too late. Maybe he had been too careful.

What the hell? If he pulled the trigger on the raid soon, he felt like any criticism of his timing would be minimal. And he knew enough to know he was going to get something at that location. He pulled up his date finder on his implant and surveyed the possibilities. Yes, soon. Very soon. After all, he was the director. This would simply be another triumph. Phelpsie, you son of a bitch. This'll be one more notch on your gun.

Goff stopped in the hall, his pupils beginning to return to normal size. He looked around him. Where was he? What place was this? Looking at his watch, he realized he had no memory of the last couple of hours. When he got back to his office, he would do a quick study of the phenomena of sleepwalking. He pushed the "down" button on the lift tube.

Had he been doing *that thing* again?

UNDERSTANDING STAN

"Everyone is a moon, and has a dark side
which he never shows to anybody."
—Mark Twain

S tan was a puzzle to Jill. She had known him growing up—
not in her pod class but through her studies and at parties.
Stan had a wonderful knack of saying crazy things that
broke the tension, and he was easy to be around. He was the
comedian of his class. Everyone liked him.

After Jill and Meg's makeover, they swore he was impossible to
recognize. They shaved a large bald spot on his head, buzzed the
rest, and gave him some convincing freckles and a pair of heavy
black glasses. Nail polish gave him a gold-leaf tooth. His heavy
brown beard was coming in nicely. His wardrobe took on a goth
look. Without his tracking device, he could not be discovered by
surveillance. He was careful to stay away from eye scanners and
facial-recognition lenses, keeping a low profile.

It was no problem for Jill to get her friends' OK to install Stan
in their vacant livingspace. She would occasionally drop in on him
to make sure he was OK. She had lost track of him for a few years,
and it was good to sit with him on the secluded back porch of the
house where he was laying low and catch up.

"I hear you made it into the Guard a few years back," she said.

He laughed. "No, not the Guard. Nothing that cool. I was part
of a governmental watchdog agency under a man named Phelps."

"I've seen his name in the papers."

"I'll bet you have. He is in the Guard. He's the real deal. Conrad
Marion Phelps. The Director. Handpicked by The Elders for
leadership."

"The Elders? They actually exist? No one knows who they are or what they do."

"Yeah, they exist alright, though I've never seen or heard from them. Phelps talks with them though; he's a direct downline. Like I said, I've never seen them myself, but I have no doubt they're everything we grew up hearing about: super smart, genetically superior, and directing everything from a mile high. Don't ask me where to go to find them though. They're real, but I sure couldn't produce one of 'em."

"What were you doing for them? I mean him?"

"I was on Phelps's team. We kept an eye on radicals and fanatics. We thought we were keeping peace and order. I honestly believed we were doing good stuff."

"You changed your mind?"

Stan glanced over his shoulder. "Boy did I ever," he said softly.

"Why?"

"Listen, Jill," he said, growing serious. "I don't know what you've been up to for the last couple of years, but I've been getting deeper and deeper into the tall weeds of the Entente. Suddenly, I thought, what the hell? Who do these people think they are telling us where we can go, who we can pair with, what we should work at, and micro-manage us like a science experiment?"

Jill raised her eyebrows. "Aren't these thoughts seditious?"

"Who cares? I'm tired of being used. I'm done with being a pawn in somebody else's chess game. I want my life back."

"And you made the mistake of letting someone know you felt that way."

"Naw. Nobody knew I had the first problem with anything until the day I showed up missing. I know you're wondering why I'm telling you this, and honestly, I don't know. I've just always had this idea that you were different, that I could tell you things. That you understood."

"How do you know I won't betray you?"

"I don't. Not really. But the truth is, it wouldn't matter if you did. I'm not afraid of 'em because they don't own me. Ever since I got away from them—with help from your friend, Alex—I just know I'm never doing that again. If they want me, they'll have to kill me 'cause as long as I'm alive, they'll never get me to go back."

"It's just a job."

"No, it's not! Don't you see? You work at that lab. You have something that could be called just a job. But me? I worked for the government. They think of people as pets, cattle, slaves. They make up the catchphrases that substitute emotional flimflam for actual thought. It's amazing how easily people can be manipulated."

"Unity is safety. Fighting for you. Everything is everything." Jill almost laughed as she said them.

"Exactly! I've said those things all my life. What do they mean anyway?"

They kept talking, reminiscing about their childhood and sharing about what had happened to their pod mates. It felt like old times.

The friends held their breath wondering what would happen next with Stan. They didn't expect any news coverage since, obviously, his escape would be an embarrassment to the government. And there was none. Stan seemed to have a magical ability to avoid the authorities. Alex wondered how he was doing it and knew he had to check on his suspicions.

One day when the friends were together at Jill's, suddenly and without warning, Alex locked Stan in a submission grip. Stan went down like a rock, crumpled and helpless, to the gasping protests of the others. Ignoring them all, Alex clicked wrist and ankle restraints on Stan and snapped a control collar around his neck. Stan's eyes and mouth were all that he could move.

Alex dragged him over to the wall by his feet and stood towering over him. Resting the tip of a termination rod on Stan's chest, Alex looked him coolly in the eye. "It's over, Stan," he said in a low, steady voice. "I overheard some lunch chatter from Phelps's team about you. We can't afford to let you go free, and we can't afford to imprison you."

Meg cried out in confusion. Jill looked in bewilderment from Alex to Stan and then back to Alex. "What do you mean?"

Alex looked at Stan but spoke to Jill. "This guy is your friend? Some friend. I heard enough to know we're all in danger as long as he's alive." He bore down on the termination rod.

"Alex, no! You can't!" Jill cried, wide-eyed.

Alex smiled grimly. "I've never used one of these, but I've seen them used. It's a little slow and apparently very painful, but the coroner reads it as a heart attack. We'll dump your body on the other side of the city."

"Go ahead," Stan said bitterly. "I might as well be dead as go back to that dehumanizing mess Phelps calls his team. If you won't take me in, I'd just as soon check out altogether. You'd be doing me a favor, and I mean it. I'd rather you knew that I'd never betray you, but I guess once I'm dead I could care less what you think. Seriously, Alex. Go ahead. I'd do the same thing if I were you."

"Any last words?" Alex asked.

Stan looked him in the eye and smiled. "Just this," he said, his voice steady. "The night you found me, I'd been on the run for twelve hours. I just left work that day and bolted. I was trying to get out of the city. I had no idea what to do or where to go after that. I wasn't gonna let 'em take me alive, so you executing me now will just mean I got a little extra time to see and appreciate what real friends are, what trust among friends feels like, and what like-minded friends can build. I can die now a better man. For that, I am deeply in your debt." He squeezed his eyes shut and took a deep breath as if to say goodbye to the world.

Alex raised his brows and looked at Jill. They both nodded. Alex slid the termination stick back into its holster. The restraints and the collar were removed and returned to Alex's belt. Feeling a strong hand on his arm, Stan was helped to his feet. Bewildered, he opened his eyes and looked from smiling face to smiling face.

"Either you're the best liar I've ever seen, or you're for real," Alex explained. "There's actually no chatter about you beyond quiet admiration that you seem to have eluded detection for so long. They say they're confident they'll find you, and if not, they'll do a story about your death or capture. But everything I gather says your story is straight. Jill and I just had to do one last test."

Meg blurted, "A *test*? A little warning next time?"

Stan looked at his wrists. "This is the second time I've been set free recently. I'm starting to hope I might have a chance. If you could show me the best way out of town, I wouldn't know how to thank you."

"You want to leave?"

"Don't you want me to?"

Alex frowned. "Well, you could be useful. Plus . . ." He allowed a corner of his mouth to twitch. "We might start to like you the more we get to know you." Alex turned to Jill. She nodded and then looked at Stan.

"It's your choice, Stan," she stated. "It will be dangerous to stay in the city, but I'm not sure what 'safe' looks like for you anymore."

"I left safe in my Sunday pants," Stan said, grinning. "I have nothing to lose anymore. But I would dearly love to stay and learn more about fellowship and trust. I guess if you don't mind, I'm asking you to let me experience those things I just found—things I'd hate to lose."

The four of them would often eat together, and it was natural to introduce Stan to some of their black-market books. O course Stan asked them where they came from, but the three friends told him that it would be best if he didn't know. Then he wouldn't have to try to cover if he were ever reacquired by the authorities who might still be looking for him. On several occasions, they divulged that they might one day need a getaway vehicle and driver. Stan gladly volunteered and tried unsuccessfully to find where they might be leaving from. And though he tried to follow them discretely to discover the source of the books, he could not. He actually didn't   know whether he was happy or frustrated about that.

He had to send something back to Director Phelps, but there wasn't much yet to report. *Just keep your eyes and ears open*, he told himself.

FLOUNDERING IN PHILOSOPHY

"Two things are infinite:
the universe and human stupidity;
and I'm not sure about the universe."
— Albert Einstein

With the sails rigged and the silo flying above the forests, the trip back to the portal was exhilarating. Jason left the door open and the wind whistled through the main compartment as the scenery flashed by. He imagined himself as Cortez or Columbus in the great age of tiny wooden ships. The sails operated by gathering energy from the sun around which Planet f3 raced, but it wasn't radiation as much as it was a kind of current. Jason remembered that ancient people had long wondered why the tails of comets always pointed away from the sun. Recently, it had intrigued some people so much so that they had investigated and discovered that solar wind was real and invented a way to take advantage of it.

Jason hovered over the controls making minor adjustments, not because many adjustments were needed once the portal's coordinates were entered but because he did not want to cede his authority to the auto-nav. The tube portal was dead ahead, about three days away. He squinted at Izgad. "I imagine you could do some freaky stuff if you wanted to. I wonder. Just for fun, could you . . . maybe . . ." He spotted a roll of tape on the console near his hand, "Maybe pick up that roll of tape over there without touching it and set it on the other side of me? I'd love to see you suspend a couple of the laws of physics, just for laughs."

"Your concept of the laws of physics is backward. You believe that nature is constrained by laws just as your government constrains the people on your planet through laws and their enforcement. But those kind of laws are arbitrary. The natural world is not constrained by laws in that way. A better way to look at the relationship between nature and your so-called 'laws' of physics is that the behavior of nature announces the laws. There are general patterns in physical actions, and those actions infer laws, but nature does not obey any laws."

"Well, yeah, of course. I wasn't saying . . . I mean, I know that. Everyone knows that. I think you're just trying to tell me that the universe is complicated and that even things we think are laws may not always hold. Is that it?"

"Yes, partially. The laws of nature are not constraints; they are conveniences but only partial descriptors of the world around us. Trends. Probabilities."

"Oh."

"Oh what?"

"I just mean . . . I was thinking about parallel universes, which each have their own timelines and physical laws. Are we right in thinking there are an infinite number of universes?"

"There are not an infinite number of anything that has been created. The number is always known. Not by you or me, but the number is known."

"But space is infinite! The people of Eastern Europe during the time of the great trans-oceanic voyages on Earth believed the world came to an end and the oceans ran off the edges. They believed it was balanced on the back of a giant turtle. Now we know that space goes on and on as far as we can see."

"Repeat your last six words."

Jason mumbled to himself for a moment then looked at Izgad. "As far as we can see. Are you telling me that at some point as we travel, we come to a place where there are no more stars?"

"No, you come to a place where there is nothing at all. And you're wrong that the people believed in a flat earth. Some may have, but Eratosthenes accurately measured the circumference of the earth in around 200 BC, fifteen hundred years before the Europeans you are talking about."

"How can there be nothing?"

"Well, there cannot be nothing anymore, but before the universe was brought into being, there was a lot of nothing."

"How can nothing exist?"

"I didn't say nothing existed. Someone has always existed. But everything that is not that Someone was once nothing at all."

Jason blinked, "Whoa. You're saying . . . I don't know what you're saying. I can't follow you. It's like trying to breathe under water . . ."

"I am sorry to have frustrated you. What we have just talked about is inconsequential."

"What?"

"The things that we have been discussing are wonderful, but they have no bearing on my mission. I got sidetracked into talking about them. Forget what we have been saying and listen to me, Jason. When we arrive at the portal and begin our homeward voyage, we will need to be ready for what you find."

"And what will we find?"

"A collection of people, some of whom you used to know, in a situation that is dire. We will not have a lot of time."

"Tell me more."

"That is all I know at present. You may have noticed that the Maker keeps us from knowing more than is good for us. I have faith that, when we need to know more, we will."

"I don't know what good it is for us to know that something is screwy back on Earth but not to know enough to prepare to be of some help."

"How do you know we are not preparing right now?"

"Because all we're doing is flapping our gums."

"Absolutely intriguing. Flapping our . . . oh! Conversing. Well, there is much you need to know before you arrive."

"Yeah, for one thing, how I'm now traveling around with a talking dog."

"That should not present insurmountable difficulties for the hero of the Intergalactic Collection Program. Not that you are traveling with your dog; that will be easy. But it should not become known that I am traveling with Harry."

"Where did you come up with the name Intergalactic Collection Program?"

"I just made it up. Harry says it should be called 'bag, tag, snoop, and poop in outer space.' He is actually an accomplished comedian, if you have not previously noticed. What is poop? Oh, wait, is that a colloquialism for when you get tired?"

Jason didn't answer, just fiddled with the controls. "You say there's stuff I need to know. What kind of stuff?"

"You need to hear the great Story, the Primal Story."

"What primal story, and what's so great about it?"

"The source from which all other stories rise. It is an ancient story that can be identified in almost all the old world cultures. All truly good stories contain something of it. If not, our hearts sense it. You might say you didn't like the book, or if you were looking for a dark thrill, you might say you liked it because it pushed the envelope. How under heaven can you push an envelope? Never mind; I don't need to know. What I am saying is that all stories are either derivative of or antagonistic to the Primal Story. Does that make sense?"

"Um, yeah, but are you saying that just like there's a maker, there's a story? An original something before all other somethings?"

"Very good. Yes, that is exactly what I am saying because the writer of this particular story, and its central character, is the Maker."

"I kinda figured."

"Don't get smart with me, my two-legged friend. The Primal Story is different from all other stories because it is real, not made up. We might take flour and eggs and milk and baking soda and make a pancake. My, how much information is streaming through my head! Whatever is a pancake, and how soon can we try one? But making a pancake is not an act of creation. It does not involve the fabrication of matter ex nihilo; it is merely the rearranging of stuff that is already here. Similarly, when you and I tell stories, we do not create new ones; we just rearrange the Primal Story. We take this bit of imagination and put it with another bit of invention and then add some ingenuity, and there is your story. But it is nothing new. It is merely a recombination of what was always there. The Primal Story is special because it is not a retelling of another story; it is the one that started every other one. It exists on its own whether it is told or not, whether it's believed or not, because it represents an eternal truth about the eternal one who is telling it. It has substance. You can cut it with a knife and fork, measure it on a set of scales. You can swim in it, and you can die in it. It is being told through space and time forever, and because the Maker has always been, so has the Primal Story always existed."

"Uh-huh. I think I see what you mean," Jason said, staring vacantly into space. "I sort of get that all stories we enjoy have similar patterns. Well, I guess not all stories do. But those other stories that ignore the pattern, they seem like someone smashed a beautiful sculpture on the ground and ruined it for everyone just to get a reaction. The writers of such stories want people to look at them and not necessarily the story. They hope people will see them as troubled geniuses and they'll be famous. But it doesn't take a genius to destroy something."

Harry began to contort his body to get his head around to reach his tail. "You surprise me sometimes by voicing things for which I assumed you did not possess the capacity," Izgad said. "You are exactly right to . . . excuse me a second. Harry says he wants a 'sniff and lick.' I don't understand, but he says it's important. So we're . . . I think I'm disgusted. Does Harry always accomplish personal hygiene using his own mouth? I thought that is where . . . it _is_. Harry, why are we sniffing and licking there? No, Harry . . . Jason, could you tell him to stop?"

Jason was too absorbed in thinking about the Primal Story. He liked stories, especially the kind where the situation was desperate, and a group of friends found themselves up against a bunch of bad guys. Like Jason Bourne. Stories where it looked like everything was lost, but it turned out OK in the end. Better than OK even. Stories where the friends found that the most important thing in life was teamwork with people of different skills and temperaments, that they were better and stronger together than they were separately. He would love to be caught up in a story like that.

But he was just a collector, a cosmic vacuum cleaner picking up flotsam and jetsam, putting it in jars and sacks, and carrying it all back home to be combed through by the truly valuable people.

ENTROPY AND OLD LADIES

"The mind, once stretched by a new idea,
never returns to its original dimensions."
—Ralph Waldo Emerson

Izgad broke into Jason's thoughts, "You have a faraway look in your eyes, Jason."

Jason decided to ask a question that had been bugging him. "I guess you know what I'm thinking. You can read my thoughts, right?"

"Read your thoughts? What in the grand heavens gave you the idea I could do that?"

"I mean you can mess with time and space. I thought being able to read minds was easy for a creature that can do that kind of creepy stuff."

"No, no, no. First, why would I want to immerse myself in the cesspool of your mind and swim around in the muck of your thoughts? Second, I am a creature just like you, though more powerful, far older, and seemingly with less divided loyalties."

"You don't live forever?"

"I will now, but I had a start date, just like you."

"Well, that makes you sort of a god then."

"Nonsense! If the Maker stopped thinking about me for a moment, I would cease to exist. My powers and age are superior to yours, just as yours are to a butterfly, but being superior to a butterfly doesn't make you a god, does it?"

"I guess not, but I would seem like a god to the butterfly, right?"

"The butterfly barely knows you exist. Most people never know my kind exists, or if they suspect it, they have the wrong impression. But we were talking about the Primal Story, weren't we?"

"Yeah, sorry. Are you going to tell it to me now?"

"In a way, I have been telling it to you ever since we first met. You have heard it all your life. You remember that the creature I met you in was hungry? That we entered your silo to get into Harry's food bin? Well, that physical hunger is a type of the hunger every created thing has for the Maker."

"Hunger?"

"Hunger, thirst, yearning, longing. All point to a quintessential lack that must be satisfied and filled. You have experienced this kind of hunger that has nothing to do with your mouth, stomach, or intestinal tract."

"I'm lost, Izgad. I have no idea what you're talking about."

"Can you define 'hunger'?"

"Sure."

"Tell me."

"It's a feeling of emptiness in your stomach."

"In your stomach only?"

"Yes, in my stomach only."

"Are you not hungry to see your friends?"

"Well . . . I guess so. Yeah, sure. I didn't realize we were going to get weird with words."

"It is not weird. I said I had been telling you the Primal Story ever since we met. Hunger is a basic proof of it. Let me ask you this: do you wish the world were a place where little old ladies got beat up or where they were taken care of?"

"Stupid question."

"Answer it."

"I wish it were a place where little old ladies were taken care of."

"Why?"

"Why?"

"Yes, why? Why would you like the world to be that way instead of another way?"

"Because it would be wrong to beat up old ladies."

"Why, Jason?"

143

Jason thought for a moment. He recognized the question from his philosophy classes. Not that the teachers had taught him anything remotely like this, but he and his friend had found a book—of course, a contraband book—on logic and rational thinking. The problem of the haunting existence of a conscience, of the persistent and dreadful possibility that absolute morality was something everyone already knew about.

Of course, the Plasm didn't care which kind of world it was for old ladies because the Plasm was an impersonal force, like gravity. Gravity was not concerned with the rightness or wrongness of a choice.

Was Izgad suggesting that a world where old ladies had value was better?

Was the high value of an old lady true whether he agreed or not?

He ducked the question. "You tell me why it's wrong to beat up old ladies."

Harry had an itch, causing Izgad to speak in staccato. "Because the . . . Maker has . . . preferences . . . when it . . . comes to . . . this kind of thing."

"OK. How many makers are there?"

"There are three but actually only one."

"That makes no sense."

"Not to you, but why should you have the final decision on whether anything makes sense?"

"How does the Maker relate to the Plasm?"

"There is no Plasm. The Plasm is a fairytale fabricated as a substitute for truth. A lie to inoculate you against the real. There is, always has been, and always will be, the Maker."

"So, why do all the smart people in our world say there is a Plasm?"

"I seriously doubt they all do, but even if they did, that does not change the truth."

Again, Jason paused. Was Izgad saying that everyone could believe in something, strongly believe it, and still be wrong? Was it as simple as peer pressure? Jason knew that kind of influence was powerful.

He looked at Izgad and let out a lungful of air through vibrating lips. "I can't pack any more of this in right now. You hungry?"

"I was thinking you might never ask. You want some of *my* really great chewy rubber food, or shall we have some of *your* really great chewy rubber food?"

After eating, they sailed along in silence, partly because Jason needed time to think, or maybe to stop thinking, and partly because Harry was ready to find a corner and take a good nap. "Bark if you need me to throw a rug somewhere!" Jason called out from the controls.

"I do no bark." Izgad replied.

"I wasn't talking to you!"

Harry found the perfect spot behind a chair in a corner where Jason kept his dog bed. Harry scratched it into giant folds in the middle, circled three times, and then dropped; asleep before he hit.

As Jason continued to fiddle with the navigation panel, his thoughts were assaulted by the law of entropy. It said every system tended toward disorder unless acted upon by an outside force, if he remembered it correctly. If that were right, the Plasm couldn't possibly have constructed the universe because, by definition, it was not an outside force. It was contained within the system, since the people who thought it up didn't want anything to exist outside the system. They didn't want anything to which they might have to one day give account.

So, he thought with a laugh, they were forced by logic to submarine their own story! If the Plasm were inside, it could not prevent entropy. And if it were outside, it was no different than the celestial deities it claimed to replace.

Jason's understanding of the universe was now up for grabs. *What was the Plasm?* he wondered. A thought struck him, from within or from without he did not stop to consider. If the Plasm was nothing more than an impersonal force, logic demanded that it needed a cause and would be subservient to that cause. So if not the Plasm, then what?

Jason reflected on the purpose of his mission—to find sentient life. In all the planets he had visited on his journey so far, the only beings that used a dictionary were Earth's humans. It wasn't that the worlds beyond the solar system were bare rock; they were wonderfully dressed in plant and animal life of varieties and abilities that assaulted the imagination. Neither were they silent. The eerie calls of the fantastic creatures on Planet f3 haunted his dreams at times.

But language?

Civilization?

Global awareness?

Technology?

Inventions?

Extensive use of tools?

Nope. Nada. And perhaps this was the most remarkable aspect of the entire remarkable universe. Why on only one planet in all the galaxies was there a creature who planned years in advance, who wrote poetry, who cultivated flowers with no nutritional value, who used machines to build other machines and bombs and bridges, who composed symphonies, who invented endless ways of cooking shrimp? Why was mankind such a lonely species with no counterpart?

But wait. Was Izgad that counterpart?

No, not really, Jason thought. Izgad had no need for machinery, vehicles, or food. Izgad was vehement about not being a god, but what more would one want from a god than what Izgad could do?

Maybe Izgad was actually the one who started the Primal Story and the universe.

No, Izgad himself was being instructed by some power or other greater than him. That much was evident from their conversations. Izgad could not be the Maker.

Izgad was just an oddity, an anomaly, a fly in the soup of facts about the universe. Jason had never heard anyone talk about a creature that resembled Izgad. Jason decided to leave Izgad out of the picture until he found a place for him to fit in.

So, back to the universe itself. Just like the ocean and the atom, space had turned out to have more and more to discover and to be increasingly complex and beautiful the higher and farther and deeper he went. But just as there were no talking trees or beasts, no jabbering molecules in the subatomic, all the exploration so far had failed to turn up anything like mankind. This was odd.

What were humans, and why were they so exceptional? Why were there not space aliens with fantastic technology that far outpaced what humans had been able to accomplish on planets much closer to the center of the universe, worlds that had cooled faster and begun to evolve life earlier? If such sentient beings existed, why were they not getting in touch with us? Were they hiding?

Was it possible that humans were unique in all the cosmos? Like all the dumb creatures and yet totally unlike them?

Dolphins, apes and birds could communicate, otters used tools, and insects had social structures. But none of that stuff was anywhere close to being on par with humanity. The ability to dream, laugh, cry, organize wars and bingo nights, invent apple peelers and tree houses, admire pretty women . . .

Jason winced inwardly. *Just when I've almost solved the mystery of the existential world, I wonder about pretty women, and here comes thoughts of Meg . . .*

They arrived at the tube portal without incident. Jason waved goodbye to Planet f3, and looked one last time on the bright sun of the Cadmium system. For some odd reason which he quickly passed off, he felt a twinge of nostalgia for this place.

He closed the door. Inputting the x, y and z axis positions, the numbers for which he pulled off the nav comp, he positioned the silo at the correct angle within the field of the portal and finished inputting the rest of the calculations to make the trip back to Earth. The launch would produce no motion whatsoever, and there would be no sound from outside the silo.

He initiated the sequence and then settled back. There was nothing more to do but wait as the algorithms did their distance-dissolving thing.

They were on their way home.

THE PRIMAL STORY

"There's always room for a story that can transport people to another place."
—J. K. Rowling

Inside the silo, all was peaceful and calm. After all, they weren't hurtling through space, they were doing something much more like effervescing or melting through it. Jason rooted around in the fridge for the bottle of champagne he had been cooling for this moment.

Popping the cork and without waiting for the foam to bubble off, Jason poured himself a healthy glass and then gave Harry a generous bowlful.

"To us! To our return! And to getting to see our friends soon!" Jason cried, remembering just in time to look the recording camera in the eye and add, "Everything is unity!" in jubilant tones.

Jason reached over and clicked off the recorder. "We don't have to worry about Harry's spy cam on the trip. We sort of lose contact with everyone during the time we're traveling. That last message should get there about the same time we do." He found a comfortable chair and poured some more champagne.

Harry closed his eyes and began spasmodically shaking his head from side to side and wiping the back of his paw across his snout as Izgad spoke. "Harry agrees with me that champagne is not very good. Intriguing. Why that liquid is universally considered the prime beverage for celebratory purposes is beyond me."

Jason looked at his glass and nodded, laughing.

Harry left his bowl, walked across the room and stood directly front of Jason's chair, ears up, alert and focused. "I think the time has come for me to relate the Primal Story," came Izgad's voice.

Jason, on his third glass of champaign, was feeling relaxed and agreeable. "Absolutely. Fire away, my man."

"The story I am about to tell you began long ago. I need you to listen as if your life depended on it, which it does. Are you ready?"

Jason leaned back in his chair and smiled at the dog containing the heteroclite who had recently become his best friend. "Let 'er rip, mister."

Harry sat on his rump and tilted his head to one side as Izgad began.

"Imagine we can go back to the beginning. There is a prosperous, unspoiled kingdom, a spotless paradise, healthy and happy. The king rules his beloved subjects in righteousness, peace, and joy.

"One day he announces that he will depart his kingdom for a time to go on a journey. In his absence, he entrusts his kingdom into the hands of stewards. But while he is gone, the stewards rebel and decide they will each be their own master. They take over the king's castle, polluting and wrecking the beautiful kingdom until it is nearly unrecognizable.

"From far off, the king hears news of his kingdom in shambles and of the people's hearts, which are dark and afraid. He hears that his subjects no longer look for his return but instead follow clever but empty sayings, shiny new inventions, and dark, demented priests. They do whatever they want as long as they can justify it in their wicked hearts.

"The king is furious with them, but he does not return immediately to destroy them in his righteous wrath. Instead, he begins a long siege in which he limits his own power so as not to utterly snuff out any spark of repentance, giving them every opportunity to recant their depravity.

"Over time and with great patience, he sends various emissaries to the rebels, pleading with them to return to their true king. But those ambassadors are mocked and many of them treacherously murdered.

"Finally, out of mercy, the king sends his only son, the prince. Disguised as a commoner, the prince goes to the rebels and announces the king's gracious offer to grant clemency to any who will renounce their insurrection and return. Many of the rebels are ashamed of their lawless ways and receive the prince.

"But others see the prince and say to themselves, 'If we kill him to whom the kingdom rightfully belongs, then the kingdom will be ours.'

"The prince knows what they are thinking. Indeed, he knows them all too well. He informs his faithful followers that he will soon be falsely accused, sentenced, and murdered just like the emissaries sent before. The difference, the prince tells them, is that while the emissaries had been rebels themselves, he has never turned away from his father, the king. Therefore, he is the only one who has never taken part in the revolt. As such, by the king's own law, he is the only one who, by his unique innocence, can assume the death sentence for treason against the king. He alone has the purity to take another's place to have that terrifying judgment fall upon himself. He tells them that he will surrender his life to accomplish clemency for any who wish it, and he tells them that by his dying he will fatally wound the rebellion and even death itself.

"His followers don't understand. They become confused and fearful.

"But as it turns out, everything happens precisely as the prince said it would. He allows the vicious leaders of the insurrection to believe they have ambushed him, and in a fraudulent trial, they falsely accuse him of heinous wrongdoing. He offers not a single word in his own defense except, when asked if he is, in fact, the prince, the son of the king, to answer truthfully in the affirmative.

"Condemned for the crime of impersonating himself, he is led off to heinous torture and a cruel execution, absorbing all the hateful violence that their fiendish, deviant minds can think to heap upon him. The prince sacrifices himself, takes his final breath, and dies, his last words a plea for forgiveness for the very rebels who have despised and done away with him.

"When the prince gives up his life, his followers go into hiding. As darkness and lawlessness are celebrated throughout the realm, the evil stewards throw a celebration to congratulate themselves. They go from party to party, indulging to their hearts' desire whatever depraved acts they can devise to demonstrate their contempt for the king.

"Three hopeless days go by, but on the dawning of the third day, a few of the faithful report that they have seen the prince alive, that he has appeared to them risen from death! Not resuscitated and not revived. He has defeated death itself. It is now powerless to hold him!

"Many believe the testimony of those witnesses and are restored to the king's graces.

"When they do, something extraordinary happens inside them. They are transformed by the knowledge that they have been redeemed and restored to the king's favor, having done nothing to deserve his love and mercy. They know the love of the king and prince and come into fellowship with the great counselor, an infinitely powerful, mysterious, and wise guide who represents the king and the prince in the midst of the faithful and draws the hearts of the unfaithful to repent and return to him.

"The wicked stewards care little for these rumors of the king's mercy, the prince who took their punishment, or the arrival of the great counselor. They go about their shallow lives giving them not a thought, accumulating for themselves, thinking of themselves, hoarding for themselves, living for themselves, and in the end, dying alone and afraid. They laugh to each other, saying that the prince died in vain, singing in their drunken revelry, 'Everything continues as it has from the beginning. He has changed nothing. Life is a dream. Let us believe in ourselves and be merry while we can.'

"But the faithful spread the news far and wide, and many rebels turn their hearts back to the king.

"One day, unexpectedly, the prince himself returns in fearsome power and glorious light to the shock and dismay of the rebels. They attempt one last battle, but they are quickly crushed, and the faithful followers of the prince are given a great reward. The prince takes his place on his father's throne, and his followers gather before him in wonder and delight. The dark world is destroyed to its very foundations, and the prince begins a brand new kingdom with his father, the king, and the great counselor, more magnificent than the last. And so they live: happily ever after."

When Izgad finished, there was a long pause. Jason was spellbound. And then he heard himself speak. "Wow."

"Wow what?"

"I . . . that was quite a story."

"Every word of it is true."

"Huh. I've never heard that story before. But . . . actually, I think I have. I've heard it all my life. May I ask you a question?"

"Ask away."

"Is this king someone whose handiwork I see in the world around me?"

"Yes. Absolutely."

"Did this king begin the space-time continuum as you have told me?"

"Yes."

"Does the prince still have followers?"

"Yes. You call them dangerous and believe they carry a Sickness."

"If I follow the prince, do I have to change how I live?"

"That is not the way to think of it. Just as the fluid in a bottle conforms to the shape of that bottle, whoever follows the prince will discover that they are being conformed to the shape of his life."

"Will I lose my identity to this prince?"

"On the contrary, you will discover your identity and find the purpose for which you exist."

"But by choosing to believe this story, I become an enemy of the state."

"Definitely."

"But I work for the state."

"Do you?"

"Sure. At least I did. Do I not?"

"Whatever your previous situation, your allegiance will have shifted."

"Yeah, I suppose so. Will I be in danger?"

"Yes."

"Really? They said that back on Earth I'm a hero."

"A fortunate designation that we can use to great good. You have been in danger from the moment of your birth. It is simply the nature and the source of the danger that ever changes. And I can tell you this: others of my order have been at work on your planet, some to mar and some to mend. An ongoing battle is centered in this universe on that tiny bit of rock you call Earth. Those like me, whose allegiance is to the Maker, will fight to protect your friends. And Jason, once again I tell you it will be best not to alert your government to my presence."

"You mean the Entente will destroy me if I tell them about you?"

"No," Izgad said as Harry got up and walked toward his bed.

"I mean they will destroy you if you tell them about *you*."

THE FOG OF WAR

"So what do we do? Anything. Something. So long as we just don't sit there. If we wait until we've satisfied all the uncertainties, it may be too late."
—Lee Iacocca

Alex was the one on duty when the call came in announcing a raid on the address he knew by heart. What triggered their interest in this particular location? They knew something was going on there! How?

But Alex knew all that could wait. The urgent question was; how could he save his friends and the books? He was glad they had planned several emergency scenarios early on in case of a crisis like this.

He was a past master at managing his face, but he must have reacted because his junior officer noted a change. "Everything OK, sir?"

Alex grinned. "More than OK. We've got some real action here. You ever been on a payoff mission?"

"No sir!" the officer replied with a slight crack in his voice.

"Come look at this. I want your best shot at how to accomplish it. Go in heavy and risk detection but have enough firepower to deal with whatever we find, or go in light and risk some of the rats jumping off the ship?"

"Sir, I would go in heavy. If we close the net, none of the rats are going anywhere."

"Is that your final answer?"

The junior officer hesitated. "No, sir," came his faltering response. "With all due respect, sir, what would you do?"

"I would take all the time I had been given and weigh the options. There are more decisions to make than simply light or heavy. This may be nothing more than a sex club, or it might be something as big as a group of insurgents armed to the teeth and desperate to sell their lives dearly. We want to decide if we should block outgoing transmissions so that no warning makes it out. That would require an electronics team. We need to know about tunnels: a sonic team. We need to know if there are contraband weapons involved and, if so, how powerful: an imaging team. Most of all, we need to know if there are any carriers of the Sickness involved, something nearly impossible to know without interrogation by a psych team. You follow me?"

The junior officer looked like he felt: overwhelmed. "Um . . . sir? Could you go over that again?"

Alex smiled. His team was raw and unseasoned. Thankfully. He knew it was the slimmest of chances that he would be actively serving when this day came. He had often wondered about the mounting travel signatures that the library was amassing, however careful they had been to disguise their trails. There was the barest chance that they could not only get everyone away but also save the essence of the library itself.

And what a gift it was that the team under him was not full of experienced veterans who would make this raid quickly and efficiently. His team was raw—Alex was considered one of the top trainers. Having a team of rookies under him would make his desperate plan go a lot easier.

He told the junior officer to make notes and then fired off a series of rapid instructions to burden the team with preparation that would give him time to alert his friends. With a great sense of self-importance, the junior officer began to relay orders to prep teams, requisition equipment, clear the area of uninvolved civilians, and alert the news to take advantage of maximum coverage of how the Guard was "fighting for you." The officer didn't think there would be much fighting as he confidently assessed the military muscle he had been instructed to assemble.

Jill got the coded message from Alex: *Abandon ship*. She wrote a message to Meg that read, *You look sick. You should get checked.* After she deliberately contaminated her workspace and alerted the decontamination crew, she walked to Meg's office and knocked.

"You OK?" Meg asked in a worried voice as she opened the door to find her friend outside.

"I'm fine, but my workspace is going to be out of commission the rest of the day," Meg said a little louder than normal. "Small accident. See you tomorrow!"

Meg closed the door, her heart pounding and read the flash paper that Jill had stuffed in her hand. She knew what the message meant. Something terrible had happened!

Two contaminations in the same afternoon might look fishy, so she used three times the cesium 55 she needed in the following experiment and ran out of supplies for the day. Punching out and grabbing her bag, she hurried to her uni, climbed on, and raced to the prearranged rendezvous point: a waterstation with a back lot that had no surveillance, a standard rendezvous for supervisors with workers who wanted to move up in privileges.

Jill was already there. Meg left her uni to climb into Jill's quad. Meg looked into her friend's face. "Tell me what's happening!"

Jill hit the accelerator as she replied. "All I know is that the authorities are getting ready to raid Nando and Madeline's place. Alex doesn't think they know what's there, that it's a library, or they might just bomb it and then sort through the rubble. He thinks they detected our routine signatures appearing in the area, and it tripped an algorithm in one of the watchdog servers. He says it's a huge operation, but because the call came in on his watch, he's using all the stall tactics he can. At least we'll have a window, however small, to salvage some books and destroy the rest."

"Destroy the library? We've got to move it!"

"We've prioritized the books that are oldest, rarest, or most beloved. The four of us will carry those out in backpacks, but the rest of the library will be left behind. We assembled it over years. We couldn't possibly move it all in one trip, and one trip is all we'll have time for. Madeline is alerted and is loading up the packs already. Nando has scanned every one of our books, and we have the whole library on several compressed data files in belt packs. But Meg, if one of us is caught carrying a physical book, it'll be bad. If we're closely followed, we can drop the packs and hope to escape with the backups. This is the real thing, the event we hoped would never happen."

"Please tell me we don't have to destroy anything!"

"I'm sorry. A raging hot fire is the only thing that gets rid of fingerprints and other DNA trackers that all of us have left in there."

"A fire . . ."

"More like a small atomic fusion reactor. We'll detonate it once we're all clear. But Meg, we'll at least have those static backups of every book."

"It won't be anything like holding the actual books, but it's still comforting. Where are the data files?"

"In the library. Too dangerous and too precious to store anywhere else. I'm afraid we've put you in danger, my friend."

"No apology necessary. The library and my sponsors are the two things I would gladly die for!"

"Yeah, but dying is less of an option than the extensive psych experiments they'll perform on us for years. Death would be preferable to being caught."

As they approached the library location, Jill gave some final instructions. "Madeline will assign you a pack for books and a belt bag for the static backups. If we're caught with either one . . . well, just don't get caught with either one. We may have to ditch the bigger packs, but with any luck we'll get to safety with our whole cargo."

"Have you heard from Stan?"

"Yes. He's got a multitran waiting to take us to the safe house. At least, that was the plan. But we've lost track of him. Pretty sure he'll be there. Unless something has happened, anyway."

Meg swallowed. "I've never done anything like this."

"Never snitched a cream pop from a waterstation?"

"Well, yeah, actually it was an orange drench. I was four years old."

"This will be like that, only scarier."

Meg laughed, "Thanks. At least you can run like a deer. I can protect you by running at my top speed and being caught first. I've dreamed about being part of this kind of thing. 'Fighting for you,' as they say. I honestly feel like I am! I feel like I'm part of something that's really important, something that could change the world."

"Listen to you! A high-brow philosophical ideologue, and I never knew it!"

They parked close to the doors.

Nando and Madeline quickly let them in and took the lift down with them to the books. Once there, Madeline helped them shoulder the overloaded backpacks as Jill and Meg buckled on their belt packs that carried the data files. Madeline and Nando had already done the same. Nando had wiped the whole computer system, first erasing the directory and then overwriting and scrambling the rest of the data. Madeline hurriedly double-checked the incendiary charges, tears flowing down her face. They had debated this step for a long time and finally decided that on the slimmest of chances they would ever be allowed back into society, it was the books or them. If the library itself were discovered, they would probably lose their lives, or worse, be sent to the laboratories. Not to experiment but to be the experiments in what was loosely and inaccurately termed rehabilitation.

The operation took very little time, but everyone was eager to be gone. Meg and Jill could not help but pause and look back as the lift doors closed on their paradise, the land of waking dreams, soon to be obliterated.

"Oh, Meg, I wish I had a picture of how big your eyes got the first time you stepped into this room! Well, let's hope we can build another library soon."

"Bigger and better, Jill."

Meg ran her sleeve across her eyes. Jill put the back of her hand under her nose. The friends watched the room as the door closed and the lift ascended until there was no more to be seen.

"Goodbye, old friend," Meg whispered in a shaky voice.

STALL AND STALL SOME MORE

Alex told his junior officer to carry on while he headed for a separate part of the building to, so he claimed, get some guidance from an old superior he knew. He was the most difficult man to get in to see, and Alex was hoping that today it would be especially time-consuming.

Delay was the tactic of the hour. He hoped his delays appeared to be simple caution and wouldn't be flagged, but he had no choice. The books and his friends needed time.

The chief's pretty little secretary was flustered but maintained a show of competence. "I'm sorry, Alex, but the chief is in a meeting and asked that he not be interrupted."

Alex leaned forward, placed his hands on her desk, and smiled. "Well, could you check with him again when he wakes up?"

"How did you. . . as I said, he's in an important meeting. Not to be disturbed."

"Well, this delay is inevitable, I suppose. Might as well make the most of it. Do you have any of that dark, oily coffee? Last time I was here, officers were allowed some of the chief's supply if they had to wait for any reason."

"Sure, but making it takes time."

"Looks like I'm going to be here for a while, so I might as well get something out of it. And one of those crullers?"

The secretary smiled back. "You know all our dirty little secrets don't you?"

After two cups of coffee and 4 crullers, he was shown into the chief's office.

The chief eyed Alex with interest. "Alex cx94b it says here on my screen. Haven't changed much. Course I remember you from class. We flagged you way back then. A lot of old duffs like me have followed your career with a little more than idle curiosity. You're something of an item, young man. Who knows how far you're going to go with us? What brings you here today, Alex?"

The chief was grey-haired, grey-eyed and heavy-set, looking as if he could still pass the physical requirements test except for the substantial paunch that was evident even behind his desk. Standing at attention, Alex invited the chief to review his orders onscreen. The chief scrolled down slowly, repeatedly pushing his thick glasses back in place that kept sliding down his nose and reading with his mouth moving. He had done many such raids back in the day and wished he could come along on this one. "Those were great times. Oh, I could tell you stories of things we'd do that would never show up in our reports! Come to think of it, you've prob'ly already heard a lot of 'em. Have you done many of these raids?"

"Yes, sir. This will be my seventieth."

"And you're still young. Hey, sit down. At ease. My friend, don't let them promote you out of all this too soon. I'm stuck behind this desk now, and nothing seems to interrupt my days except *inspecting* the occasional illicit merchandise from these raids. We say we destroy it all, of course, but what ends up being the official record is not always what actually happens. You understand this if you've done as many raids as you say you have. My, what I wouldn't give to be going with you on this one . . ."

It took Alex some minutes to bring the chief back to the point, though he was in no hurry. Alex asked him some tactical questions to be sure there was a record of the necessity of this delay. He figured he had bought an extra hour. He hoped it would be enough. He saluted the chief on his way out of his office. "Fighting for you!"

"What? Oh. Yes. Yes, um, unity is . . . well, it certainly is something, young man . . ."

As the door closed, Alex heard the chief warn his secretary that he did not want to be interrupted again, if she liked her job. . .

❖

Back with his team, Alex was hoping for more delays in assembling the squad, but he had trained his rookies too well. Of course, he did not let his disappointment show. "Brilliant work, everyone! It's an honor to be leading you on this assignment. Raise your hand if you're a first-timer. All but two of you? Any appropriate words from you two? Give us a final bit of encouragement..."

He bought a few more precious minutes of delay and then, finally, gave the okay for the team to man their vehicles and proceeded to the coordinates in their instructions.

As standard procedure, Alex first sent his junior officer alone to the front door to assess the situation and pretend to be checking on something unrelated. In this case, they would say they were working a mugging in the area and checking for eyewitnesses, but for Alex, it was just one more precious delay. If his companions were still inside, they were cooked, but if they had made it out, this would give them a chance to put more distance between them and any identification or pursuit.

The junior officer knocked on the door, which was answered. It was Nando and Madeline.

"Hello," Madeline said, her face beaming as she showed no signs of surprise. "Unity is safety! Here's hoping you're having a safe, productive, and happy day. Is there something we can help you with?"

"We don't mean to alarm you, citizen, but there has been a petty robbery in this area, and we're checking for a fugitive who has gone off-grid. Mind if I come in for a minute?"

"Oh! You're a . . . a . . . law person thingy? A reformer?" Madeline queried in her ditziest impersonation.

Nando winked at the officer. "Enforcer, dear," he said in a patronizing tone.

Madeline turned and put her hand on Nando's shoulder. "No, this is not an enforcer. Enforcers have badges and uniforms."

"He's plainly wearing a uniform."

"Oh. So he is. But no badge," she clucked.

The officer pulled out his badge and displayed it. "Stand aside, please. I need to ask you some questions about a local mugging, if you don't mind."

Madeline gave a squeal of delight. "Oh, honey pie, isn't this exciting? A real live reinforcer and he's going to torture us!"

"I told you, lovekin, the word is enforcer, and he's going to just ask us some questions."

"But you said he would have a badge."

"That thing he showed us was his badge."

"Oh no, my love, badges are worn on the chest. People don't keep them in their wallets."

"You've been watching too many movies, pet."

"Oh, I think he's very stylish. Nothing as cute as a young man in a smart uniform. Is that genuine artificial cloth? Shouldn't we ask this young, handsome man to come in?"

"He already told us he's coming in whether we like it or not."

"They need someone to design a uniform that doesn't look quite so...quite so uniformy. I'll just bet he dresses a lot nicer when he's not on duty. And speaking of clothes, dear, I think we need to update your wardrobe. Wouldn't you like that? To at least modernize your shirts so it looks like you've been paying attention the last couple of years?"

"You were fine with the way I dressed when we first met!"

"But back then I was coming off a bad relationship with that man, oh what was his name . . ."

The officer put up his hand. "Please stand aside now!"

Madeline began to cry. "He yelled at me, Nando. He yelled at me . . ."

Nando turned to the officer. "My wife is very high-strung. Easily upset. Do you suppose you could come back another time? I'll call and let you know when she's calmed down. Maybe you can check on some of the other buildings first. We don't care about you searching our place since you won't find your mugger here, but if she gets upset like this, it could last days. Are you married, young man?"

The junior officer was having a hard time exercising self-control. "Stand aside this instant, or I will report that you were uncooperative and have you taken down to the station for questioning. You think she's hysterical now, wait until she's spent some time with the kind of questioning they can do down there! Out of my way!"

"But you're not being fair," Madeline said. "We don't know why you want to come in!"

"I'm checking on a mugging!"

"But you haven't told us what you want in your mug," Madeline wailed. "Beer? Seltzer? Coffee? Leave room for cream and sugar?"

The officer tilted his head to one side. There was a moment where Madeline paused and seemed to skip a beat. He reached to grab Nando and went right through a projected image. Madeline and Nando continued to talk, but he was no longer listening. "Holograms!" he shouted into his communicator. "I'm so sorry, sir. They were incredibly lifelike!"

"Say again?" Alex replied over the comm.

"Encountered countermeasures, sir! Advise we begin right away!"

Alex sent the whole team in, knowing that if the hologram welcoming program had been activated, his friends would have been clear of the building.

When he stepped into the space, there was general chaos, as he had hoped. More delay as people tried to do their various jobs in a crowded room. But so far, no one had discovered anything unusual about the room besides the presence of the hologram generator and a jammer.

"Nothing! Why were we sent here?" one of the officers shouted.

Alex knew exactly where the concealed lift was, but until the building was scoped, his initial crew would not suspect its presence. "The clusters seem to indicate this as an unsanctioned meeting place," he said. "People from all over the city have regularly frequented this space, and we want to know why. Our orders are to search this place down to the crumbs on the floor to discover what attraction this space has for all those people, and that's exactly what we're going to do! Make it count!"

"Get your rears in gear, people!" the junior officer shouted.

Expensive equipment was brought in and set up. Sensors, detectors, scanners, analyzers, mappers, and even dog teams to sniff for heavy traffic patterns in the space. Alex was impressed with the amount of toys that could be brought to bear on a big search-and-grab mission.

Alex clocked it at an hour and thirty minutes on his wrist comm from the time his junior officer knocked on the door to the time they discovered the shaft down to the library. He knew from the moment he saw his orders that the library could not stand up to the full weight of an enforcement team search, but he had a sense of pride in his own contributions to making it a hard nut to crack.

The four friends were barely out of the library before Alex arrived. Looking back from the shadows between buildings, they were amazed at the size of the government's response. According to plan, they now split up to make their separate ways to their next destination: a multitran that Stan was supposed to have waiting for them on the other side of the park. They still had gotten no response from him, but there was nothing to do but head for the site and hope for the best. With a smile for good luck, they slipped away, keeping to dead spots previously mapped out by Alex, staying below the radar.

As she made her way to the rendezvous, Jill checked her pocket for the trigger device, waiting for the signal from Alex to blow the library.

The Director was behind his desk when the enforcers brought their captive into his office. With the latest iteration of control band on his neck, the man could not struggle. The band emitted frequencies that interfered with his voluntary movements. The enforcers asked Director Phelps for orders.

"Good job, each of you. Leave the remote control on my desk. You will find the Crab Hat has been booked exclusively for your team, and I believe they have perfected their dark stout to taste exactly like the Guinness black beers from the early twenty-first century. It's all paid for by your grateful collective. That's all for tonight." He stood up next to his chair and held a clenched fist tightly: "Fighting for you!"

"Unity is safety!" came the mechanically staccato responses as fists slammed into chests. They moved swiftly out of the room with the same precision they would have used on a field operation. It never hurt to impress the boss.

With the click of the door, the Director turned to his prisoner and released the confining current. The man slumped as his head dropped, and then he jerked himself upright. There was silence for several seconds as they eyed each other. The Director was relaxed and in control. The prisoner's face was unreadable.

"I believe I've seen you before. Without the beard. Tell me everything you know. And what the living *hell* happened to your hair?"

Stan smiled. "They're meeting up at a multitran I left for them where we can grab 'em all."

The Director quickly fed some instructions into his wrist comm.

IT ALL BLOWS UP

"In the midst of chaos,
there is also opportunity"
— Sun-Tzu

Alex saw the latest video communication from Director Phelps: "Target is cache of contraband. Upon discovery and documentation of cache by DODX, send a microBIO team to gather evidence and sonic team to make sure of all entrances and exits. Grab all fleeing suspects, and get news teams to report on capture and confiscation of contraband. Fighting for you."

Alex's face was impassive. But something was off here. On impulse, he ran the message back and viewed it one more time. His quick eye spotted a familiar face. Behind the desk was a civilian. Was that? It was . . .

Stan. Had he been arrested? Was he a captive?

Nope. No restrictive devices. Not drugged. Looking at home and self-satisfied. Look at that smug grin. *He had been in on the raid!* No, worse, he probably *triggered* it! The stinking' cockroach. Lying to their faces all along. Betraying the very people who had befriended him.

Alex asked himself how he could have fooled them so easily. The guy had passed all the tests! *Never mind*, he told himself. It's done. You can't change the past. Now you've got a job to do. You've got to help your friends escape.

But wait. Something else made no sense. If this were a brilliantly coordinated take-down, why was he the senior enforcer on this mission? If Stan had betrayed them, naming names, why was he still operational? Why had he not been arrested? Alex realized he didn't have time to figure that one out either. The reason was probably that they were watching him closely to find out who he was in touch with.

Wasting no time, he turned to the nearest technician. While talking quietly to him about the assignment, he put his arm behind the man and, with a touch that would have made any pickpocket proud, lifted the technician's communicator and typed a coded message to Jill. He punched "send," then erased the message and returned the communicator, all with one hand and within seconds.

Meg and the others had joined up again, still under cover but within sight of the waiting tran. It looked deserted. Nando stepped toward it. Suddenly, Jill frowned at her implant and blinked at the code she saw. "Everyone, stop," she whispered sharply. "Change of plan."

Meg, in mid-step, bumped into Madeline, who had stopped immediately. Nando turned back. "What's up, Jill?"

"Message from Alex. He sent two images: a firecracker and a wrench."

"Code?"

"Yes, his and mine. It's time to blow the library."

No, whispered Meg as Madeline reached out to hold her. Jill grimly held the detonator up to her chest and, holding back tears, pushed the button with all her might. Even from far away, they could feel the tremor and hear a muffled roar. Their heads were bowed in grief. For a while, no one spoke.

Madeline was the first to regain her voice, "And the other icon?"

Jill nodded, "It means someone or something has thrown a monkey wrench into our plans. We need to improvise because we've somehow been compromised."

Nando spoke, "And Stan is not inside that tran, as far as I can see. Have any of you heard from him?"

Heads shook. Madeline agreed, "There's no one in the tran, I'm sure of it. And look at where it's parked. We could never get to it undetected. It looks oddly suspicious, doesn't it?"

Meg stared at it, "So what does improvise mean?"

Nando turned to her, "It means we have now got to be doubly and triply careful. No way are we going to use that tran. We're on our own to get to the safe house. If the safe house is even still safe."

Madeline nodded. "There's no way to know."

"Sir! We've discovered a shaft leading up to the roof!"

Alex looked at the junior officer with raised brows. "We've known all along this building comes equipped with a lift."

"But sir, I meant to say we've discovered that this shaft also goes *down*. We're preparing to send an imaging team into the shaft to find out more. This is the break, sir! This is the key to the mission!"

"Good work! My report will show that you and the others have been a credit to the training you've been given. Stay here just a moment while I—"

Alex didn't have to come up with one last stall tactic because, at that moment, every last member of the raid team was knocked off their feet by the impact of a deep explosion from below. The structure of the building held but just barely. There were still cave-ins in multiple locations and in the surrounding buildings as well. Alex heaved an involuntary sigh of relief as he knocked a piece of ceiling off his junior officer and helped him to his feet.

Racing toward the shaft, he yelled, "Come on!" He didn't need to get very close to feel the heat or see the fire and the column of choking, boiling smoke, which was quickly emptying the room of those who did not have gas masks. Alex whipped his mask out and noted that the junior officer had not packed his. "Come back when you can breathe in here. I'll check on the others."

"Yes, sir. Sorry, sir." The junior officer raced off.

Alex made his way to the few members of the raid who were still functioning. He touched the shoulder of one young imaging technician. "Was anyone in the shaft when the explosion occurred?"

"No, sir. We were awaiting your order. It's a good thing you're a careful man. A bunch of us wouldn't be here if you'd rushed that decision, sir. Thank you."

"No thanks are necessary. Charging into a situation where we don't know what we're up against is asking for trouble."

"Yes, sir. I don't imagine you need an imaging team anymore."

"No. But if you see the sonic team out there, send them in. I want to get a picture of what's down there, even if it's just chaos and rubble."

"Fighting for you, sir!"

"Right. Everything is unity...oh and do me a favor, go out and give my junior officer your mask, would you? Then send him back in. I'm giving him the joy of his first personal report to our superiors . . ."

The progress report was on his screen. The Director hated to show any deep frustration or anger. It was not part of the image he had diligently built, but his hands had unconsciously become fists. Stan's report about the illegal books had not included the fact that they were rigged to explode, and although the team was remaining on site and trying to salvage any intel they could, there was no escaping that the mission had netted exactly zip along those lines.

He and Stan were the only ones who knew exactly what the contraband on site actually had been. Stan wouldn't be a problem––he'd let Stan know in graphic detail how highly dangerous it would be to blab what he knew around town.

But if it became known that he, the Director, had let a cache of books slip through his fingers, it would be highly dangerous to himself as well.

The Guard was not overly fond of failure. He must act and act decisively.

He sat behind his desk to receive Alex's junior officer, who had just been rushed in for a face-to-face. He loved these moments where he could take the eager look on a young officer's face and wipe it off. No hurry. Let the man think he was making a good impression.

He motioned for the man to speak and listened to his preliminary report without interruption, nodding at various points. Then he calmly questioned the junior officer, a hint of sharpness in his tone. "You say you have no idea what was down that shaft? And that now the place down there is nothing more than glowing embers? No way of tracing DNA identifiers? No clue as to what was attracting them to that location? No indication of how large a gathering it was? Nothing?"

The junior officer blinked rapidly while maintaining an impassive face. Staring straight ahead, he tried to keep his voice from cracking, which made it crack even more. "Sir, we had no way of knowing the place was rigged to blow sky high. Our sonic teams were just arriving along with imaging and electronics. This was obviously a highly organized—"

The Director cut him off, "You've not been tasked or asked to make evaluations, only to carry out the simple orders you were given. You appear to have bollixed and botched the operation."

"Sir! If I may! These were pros. They knew what they were doing. We didn't stand a chance against the setup we encountered. It's in the report, sir. We followed all procedures, prerequisites, and protocols."

"I don't give a damn about that. You had a job to do and you were not up to it. I'm exceedingly disappointed in the way you handled, or should I say *mishandled*, this mission. Your superiors will be hearing from me later tonight. You may have some disagreeable times ahead, both for your career and your personal well-being. I'm not threatening you, only reminding you of the consequences you knew were the inevitable results of gross incompetence."

"Sir, if you would consider waiting until you have gone over our report in full, I think you will see that there was no way we could have brought this operation to a successful conclusion. We know you to be a friend of the people and a fair-minded man. Just read the report, sir, and I believe it will—pardon me, sir," the junior officer muttered. "An urgent message has just come in on my comm screen." As he paused to read it, new hope came into his eyes. "Sir, it may be nothing, but we have combed through the transmitter records and discovered that one of the technicians seems to have made a transmission right before the explosion. An icon . . ."

"And?"

"Well, it's . . ."

"Spit it out!"

"Sir, it appears to be a firecracker!"

"A firecracker."

"Yes, sir, that's what it looks like to me. And a wrench."

The Director's eyes narrowed. "Oh, so that's what it looks like to you, does it? A firecracker and a wrench. Well! There's your trail. Follow it. You may salvage your rank yet. We'll soon get the information we need to break this group and whatever they were up to. Have this technician sent to memory extraction. We'll look into your report later, after we've found what this fellow can tell us about why we were unable to examine whatever was down that shaft before it became an inferno." He waved the young man out of the room while rotating his chair to face the window. "Unity is safety . . ."

"Yes, sir! Fighting for you! Um . . . sir?" The young man had been continuing to scan the communication.

"Yes?" the Director asked without looking back.

"I may have slightly overstated our knowledge to this point about the technician. There is no record on any of the technicians' phones of such a transmission. We only know of it through the relay satellite and the proximity locator. My superior and the technicians were the only people in that window, and my superior is obviously eliminated as a suspect."

"So? Bring the whole technical team in for questioning. Use whatever means to find the rat. Why are you still standing here? Oh . . ." The Director turned back to his desk and scanned up to the top of the report. "Your superior, whom you eliminated is . . . I'm looking for his name . . ."

"Sir, Alex cx94b."

The Director swallowed the rush of anger that welled up with this realization. He took a deep breath and counted slowly backward from ten as he exhaled. The junior officer stared straight ahead, transfixed and terrified.

The Director's knuckles were white as he gripped the edge of his desk and stood up. "Get out," he said, his voice deathly quiet. "Now."

As his face turned pink, the junior officer yelled at his men to return to the site and round up every technician who had participated, even if they had been sent home already.

As he pulled the Director's door closed, the officer glanced back at him and gave the director a bowed-head salute.

❖

THE FRIENDS SPLIT UP

*"I learned that courage was not the absence of fear, but
the triumph over it. The brave man is not he who
does not feel afraid, but he who conquers that fear."*
—Nelson Mandela

The four friends still stood together within their dead
zone, out of sight of the tran they had hoped would take
them to safety, in no danger of electronic detection but
certainly in danger of being overtaken or otherwise accidentally
discovered. They looked one another in the eye and saw a steadfast
determination.

"It looks like we have no choice but to just try to get to the safe
house somehow. That's where Alex will try to join us," Nando said.
"Until we know more, there's no going back to our jobs or our
friends, hoping to resume our old lives. We're probably fugitives,
at the very least wanted for questioning. Girls, leave your packs
here. Madeline and I will steal another vehicle somewhere. She
and I will load up the books and the backups and proceed to make
sure the house has not also been compromised. We'll get coded
word to you in the waterstation classifieds when we know more.
Stand still while I disable our trackers." He went from person to
person with his handheld tool, checking the results with another
device, performing the identical maneuver on himself as well.

Madeline spoke. "There's no way of guessing how much about
each of us is known—no clue as to what they've found out. We
have to split up. Get out your dead zone map, and stay inside those
locations until we can get set up and send for you. You girls will
probably hear from us by nightfall or morning at the latest. If you
don't hear from us, just stay low and maybe try to make it to one of
the fishing villages on the northern coast, though I doubt if they

won't still find you there. Remember what Alex taught us. If you remain in the dead areas when possible and use crowds for cover, you'll be OK. Don't bother with trying to change your appearance beyond sunglasses and a hat."

Nando's face was grim. "There was a sort of sending ceremony I read about in a story of the ancient Habiru. It spoke to me, and I memorized it. It seems appropriate now. If you would, grab a hand and let me say this over you as they might have done. Ready? Okay, here goes . . ." His voice deepened. "The Lord bless you, the Lord keep you, the Lord make his face to shine upon you and be gracious to you, the Lord turn his countenance toward you and grant you peace."

As he chanted these words, each of the friends experienced something odd. Jill felt ready to run and laugh. The others felt curiously shy, inexplicably encouraged, and mysteriously calmed. It reminded Meg of her beloved sponsors. It had a ring of authority that she recognized. The words had a weight to them, a sense of solidity that made her feel like they had always existed, even before the invention of language. What a funny thought that was! She looked up shyly.

They set their shoulder packs and beltpacks in the collection area and waited, though not for long, to see Nando and Madeline return with a "borrowed" bi. In a wink, those two were loaded up and ready to head to the safe house. And then they were gone.

Jill and Meg stood looking at each other with nervous anticipation. They hugged harder than Meg remembered. Now Meg knew what a friend was, because she felt a piece of her soul was leaving with Jill. "Be good!" Jill admonished, and then a moment later, Meg was alone.

She quickly called up the map of the sector on her implant—not the official one; the one Alex had provided for them. She had no more than turned around when a random patrol wheeled into view, spotted her, and raised their hands to indicate she was to remain in place.

The patrol consisted of three officers, all lower level. Their leader was a little nervous, and to hide that fact, she came across a little stronger than she should have. She stopped directly in front of Meg, legs braced, fingering a stunner on her belt.

"Lingering in an unlit area? Please stand still while we read your information." She paused briefly. "4k6p3. You're a little out of sector, but that's probably OK. Will you tell us what you're up to tonight? There's a general alert for us to be watching for suspicious behavior. Did you know your tracker was malfunctioning? Under the glorious privilege of keeping everyone safe, we need you to answer a few questions. Again, what are you doing here? Where are you going? Who are you meeting?"

Meg's only hope was to occupy the patrol for as long as possible to allow her friends to disappear. Her mind quickly called up a strategy, but she realized was doomed the moment she adopted it. Pretending to be drunk, she swayed and threw an arm around the officer. "I'm sooooooooooo glad you showed up! Showed up with your safe, safe, safe heads. I need to sleep. Sleeeeeeeeepy sleep sleep. Nighty nooty. But I can't find my . . . my livingspace! It's gone. Gone, gone, gone, gone. Can you tell me a story?"

Meg slumped over and lay down on the ground as if to sleep right there. The enforcer pulled out her scanner and set it to read for alcohol. Finding none, she got out the sheep bracelets. They escorted Meg to their vehicle and then took her to the nearest enforcement station, where she was scanned, booked, labeled and put into a cell.

As Meg sat on the bed, she fought down a rising terror. She knew she was under surveillance, so she tried to keep her face passive, but inside she was churning. *Why didn't I say . . . But even now she couldn't think of anything they couldn't have checked. At least I didn't have my pack or one of the backups when they found me. What if they had come five minutes earlier? They would have had us all.*

Meg told herself to buck up, then stood up and walked over to the door of her room. No handle, nothing to show it was a door except for the faint outline. Glancing up, she saw that each corner of the ceiling had a cluster of instruments. *No dead spots in this room*, she thought.

She took stock of what was there. The cell was clean, cleaner than she kept her own livingspace. A screen on one wall turned on as she approached. It was capable of providing eleven channels, all of them government channels, of course. Only a few channels were privately owned. She remembered Nando had once remarked that he doubted if even they were not heavily restricted for content.

Switching off the screen, she moved to the sink. Every item needed for good hygiene was provided, though the toilet had no privacy. She had no sooner decided she would never be able to use that toilet than emptying her bladder became the biggest item on her agenda. The only other item in the room was a small desk with a few books on it. Not books like the library, but books like in school. Books that didn't take readers anywhere, just pushed them around and politely bullied them into thinking the way the book wanted them to think.

Meg thought that sleeping, or at least trying to sleep, would be the best use of her time, but halfway across the room, her bladder sent an urgent message. Heading back to the toilet, she moved so fast she almost lost her balance. Her pants came down no more than was absolutely necessary, and she was sitting on the toilet, covered faster than she could say Jack Robinson. The tenseness of her body made her trip last a little longer than she would have wished, and she was embarrassed that it took so long to relax and accomplish the task on camera. Pulling up her pants in the same swift fashion, she fell onto her bed, completely humiliated.

I can't let their cheap psychology get to me, she thought. Chin up, Meg, old girl. It's going to get more embarrassing before it gets less, and you'd better be on top of your game. What's the good in being among the top two percent of intelligence in your pod class if you can't outsmart a gang of government bullies?

Back at the raid site, Alex was on his communications screen with his immediate superior, who had been summoned out of sleep and was still in his pajamas and bathrobe. The man was going over every detail of the raid with him, checking and re-checking. Alex was remaining calm by counting the number of times he repeated an earlier question and tried to stay focused by playing the game of giving him the same answer while making it sound different.

In his peripheral vision, still keeping his eyes on his superior, Alex discreetly scanned departmental bulletins at the bottom of his screen for anything the news agencies might be reporting about the raid.

Then he saw it.

No! Meg? Detained? He had to help somehow, but he knew that for the moment, his presence with her would hurt more than help, drawing unwanted attention. Out of the corner of his eye, he was able to read the whole dossier while seeming to be attentive to his superior, answering every question and reacting appropriately to every observation. It seemed Meg had been picked up for being found out of sector and unable to answer some simple questions. Thankfully, she was far from the raid when they found her. Unless they had reason to believe she was covering something up, the routine would be to continue to question her and then release her after twenty-four hours.

Alex's heart went out to his friend. *Hang in there, Meg. I'll get to you as soon as I can.*

THE HOUSE IN THE WOODS

"It's a dangerous business, going out your door. You step onto the road, and if you don't keep your feet, there's no knowing where you might be swept off to."
— J.R.R. Tolkien

That night, word came to Jill on the run. It was an advertisement in a corner of the local news brief. It read a little funny, and there seemed to be some misspelled words. "Housewatchers. All others need not apply. G5 r2 Sector map 73 Behind 2 Flr Y Bldg 0700."

The location was not too distant from the city, but she was taking no chances of leading a team of enforcers to her friends. She commandeered a uni, which she ditched at a waterstation even farther from the rendezvous than when she began. Then she helped herself to a tran whose driver was grabbing some coffee and talking to the attendant. She left it running in a dead zone east of the coordinates. From there she hitched a ride, without the driver knowing, on the back of a government produce tran going north of the coordinates to stock some of the pampered getaway cabins of the high officials and their consorts.

Crossing through several belts of trees as the sun was just coming up, she found a bi left running in front of a house while its owner ran back in for a forgotten item. She arrived near the coordinates and left the bi in a lot.

Pulling her cap down lower, and trying not to appear nervous, not walking too slowly nor too fast, she made a circuitous approach to the back of the building. There was no sign of anyone, only a few parked vehicles as the earliest workers arrived to service the small town's shops. But her communicator read "Hello." She glanced around but still saw no one. Then she noticed one tran was running, its steam rising gently into the cool morning air. She approached, and the side door opened. "Jill! Quickly!" Madeline said.

As the door closed behind Jill, it took a moment for her eyes to adjust to the unlit interior. "What's happened?" Jill asked. Nando started off while Madeline filled Jill in.

"After we split up, we drove all over the place, making sure we weren't being followed and also randomizing our route. We had no problems until we arrived in visual proximity to the safe house. We waited and watched, just as Alex trained us. It looked okay until Nando sent in a drone, which promptly disappeared. The last image on our readout was a uniformed man aiming his gun at the drone. Somehow they knew, and they were waiting for us! We still haven't heard from Stan. They must have captured him somehow and emptied his mind with their drugs."

Nando continued, "We left. It seemed hopeless. We wracked our brains for what we could do, and then we thought of Meg's sponsors. They had once told Meg that whatever she did, they were proud of her, and if she ever got in trouble, to come to them for help. I don't know how we thought of them in all the confusion. But, we're going to see what we find. It'll either be the end of us or a chance to drop out of sight for a while."

Jill had a growing fear. "Are we picking up Meg somewhere else, or is she already at the house?"

Madeline moved next to Jill and put a motherly arm around her shoulders.

"Madeline, where's Meg?" Jill asked, alarmed.

Still holding onto Jill, Madeline looked around at each face. "Alex sent us word that Meg has been detained."

"No! What can we do?"

"Alex believes they haven't connected her to the raid yet. Worst luck ever, she bumped into a patrol who were a little hyped up, and she is being held routinely for twenty-four hours. I don't know what we can possibly do, but you know we'll try to think of something. Hopefully she'll be released soon."

They made their way northwest along the river, and soon traffic began to pick up, most of it heading into the city.

Soon they reached the outskirts of the little town of Nedney where the pairing who originated Meg lived. Nando dropped them near a junkyard and paid the proprietor handsomely to recycle their vehicle. Nando never actually said he was part of a ruthless gang, but he couldn't be blamed if the owner got that impression, shuddering and promising again and again to forget the whole transaction.

They shouldered their packs and began to walk the narrow backroads to the house they hoped would shelter them. When they got within a couple of miles of their destination, they noticed that the forests were no longer natural looking but more like crops, with trees the same size growing in rows. Some acres supported trees that were tall and of great girth while in another patch the newly planted saplings were spindly and awkward. In several places, they saw crews working with the trees, but none of the crews were near enough or interested enough to notice them. Eventually, they reached the end of a lane where a gravel drive led up a low hill to a two-story, yellow-and-white slat-board house with a gable roof.

"Look!" Jill whispered to the others, "It's a mailbox!"

Nando examined it. "Looks just like the old icon! So this is what a mailbox was. A postman would leave stamped envelopes and magazines and packages from different stores. Rusted. I doubt if you could open it with a pry bar. Wonder where they found it?"

Pausing for a minute to smile helped ease the tension of their approach. Was this the end of their adventure? Would this couple welcome them? Did they still live there? Or was this a trap? Would they be arrested, questioned, sentenced, perhaps even terminated?

Jill counted the 5,324 steps to the house, just to keep calm. She and Nando stood at the bottom of the steps while Madeline went up to the front door. Turning to look at the others and crossing her fingers behind her back, she knocked. Hardly anyone remembered to breathe. After a brief pause, the door opened, and they all gasped. It looked like Meg had suddenly aged twenty years! Of course it wasn't her, but the likeness was striking.

"Yes? May I help you?" the smallish woman asked with a hint of a smile and her eyebrows raised.

Madeline placed her hand over her heart. "We're friends of Meg. Your Meg. Meg 4k6p3."

"Oh! Since you know her, you obviously know that my pairing mate and I are her sponsors."

"Yes. She speaks very highly of you both. She tells us about her visits here and says that often you would tell her that you would do anything for her if she needed help."

A look of alarm crossed the woman's face. "Where is she? Is she alright?"

"I'm sorry to say she's been arrested and is being held by the authorities. We were with her almost up to the moment she was taken. We ourselves are being sought by those same authorities."

The woman looked each one of them in the eye, assessing them each in turn until her eyes came back to rest on Madeline. She looked down the road and checked the sky overhead.

"Come in please." She touched the comm on her wrist. "Dear, there are people here who claim to be friends of Meg. They say she's in trouble, and they need help . . . good . . . all right. . ." She looked at them closely once again and then made up her mind. "Come with me." She led them through the house and out the back door.

The huge trees came up close to the back of the house, and in no time they were in the forest and climbing the scented forest floor among tall trunks of pine. Sunlight was filtered by the thick canopy of the treetops and only made it to the ground in indistinct patches of dancing color. After hours of hiding in the city and the ride in the tran, it felt wonderful to be crunching through pine needles amid the dark columns of the uplifting outdoor cathedral.

"I'm Hisako," the woman called back over her shoulder. "My pairing mate is Mark. Notice the small triangular rocks as we pass them. They're your only guide. Enter the forest at staggered locations, pick your feet up so you don't disturb the needles, and in general, weave as you walk so as not to leave a plain trail. The triangular rocks are taking us to a place where you can be cared for until we figure out what's going on. In the meantime, I want to hear what you know about Meg. What can you tell me?"

"We don't know much more than what we've already told you," Jill said. "Of course, you don't yet trust us, and we have no reason to trust you either, but someone has to start." She looked at the other two, who motioned for her to continue. "We were caretakers of contraband that the Entente has tried to eradicate. We knew we would suffer the same fate if they caught us with it. We were very careful. Madeline and Nando here used to work in surveillance, and another one of us was a top-level enforcer, so our secrecy was pretty impressive. But a man we rescued from the state may've been captured and inadvertently betrayed us to them. We meant no harm to anyone. We're not breaking any laws instituted for the general welfare. But . . . well, Meg was looking for something more in life than working and eating, sleeping and partying. Actually, we all were, and this particular contraband became a window into a world that made more sense than this one."

Hisako looked thoughtful. "You speak of a restlessness in Meg, something inside her that was unsatisfied with the shallowness of our society. She's always had a generous share of curiosity and spunk, one more thing that Mark and I love about her. And your insightful description seems to demonstrate that you indeed know her well."

"She's one of my two best friends," Jill said, "and I love those things about her too. I believe that my other best friend, the enforcer I told you about, will figure out how to help Meg get away. He's extremely resourceful and totally fearless. If anyone can find and free Meg, it's Alex."

"You say contraband. It's hard for me to believe Meg was involved with illegal drugs."

"Drugs? No! I promise the contraband was not drugs." Jill paused and then tilted her head. "But I guess it was both habit-forming and mind-expanding, now that I think about it. But no, it definitely had nothing to do with chemical agents of any kind."

Hisako turned to scan Jill's face, then turned to resume the climb.

"Are you by any chance Jill?" Hisako called over her shoulder.

"That's me. Has Meg spoken of me?"

"Oh yes, you and Alex. As I listened to you talk, I thought you might be her. Meg said you were the kind of friend who it made sense to trust. She described your face as determined and impish. Minus those sunglasses, I think she nailed you, Jill."

Madeline looked up at the sky. "Do you get patrols often? Or drones?"

Hisako shook her head. "The eagles around here play havoc with drones. Since they're supposedly endangered, the government can't do anything about it. They've tried everything, but the eagles view the drones as a threat to their chicks and destroy them on sight. So now about once a year, they send out a team in a quad, and they ask us things and poke around. Their quad has a sign that claims its occupants are with the geological survey, but we know they're enforcers, and they know we know it, so we all just smile and do the dance. Now we have the same team coming each year because of my cookies. Quite often they'll send the rookie around to inspect while the other three sit on the back porch with Mark and me around a hot plate of snickerdoodles and a cold jar of whole milk. Of course, the rookie hasn't been a rookie for three years now, but he remains lowest in the pecking order. He finishes up his inspections quicker and quicker each year and joins us after about twenty minutes!"

The companions felt their hearts lighten, hearing that they might have dropped off the map. As a rule, the Entente didn't look too hard for missing people, for no reason beyond incompetency and laziness. Missing people were an embarrassment to a utopian society, a reminder that perhaps everyone wasn't supremely happy. Files were shuffled from irresponsible departments down to even more irresponsible departments until they ended up in a general slush of unsolved cases. The less said about such cases, the better.

Hisako led them up and up, zig-zagging across the steep, forested slope until they came to a stone outcropping with a view of the countryside. She paused as whistles of delight came from her three guests. "Not bad, huh?" she exclaimed. "Mark and I love it up here. It's as good a tonic for troubled souls as you could find, don't you think?" As the friends murmured their agreement, she turned back to the mountainside. Leading the way around a final switchback, Hisako suddenly ducked in between outcrops of weathered grey limestone. Following her into the dimly lit area, it looked like a dead end, but pivoting, they saw a door on the back side of the rock wall on the right. It would be invisible to anyone who did not actually enter the small space enclosed by the walls of rock and look up the slope. The trees sheltered any view of the door from above.

"We believe this cave has been in use for many hundreds of years but was abandoned for a long time until we found it on a hike. It's surprising how deep the cave goes, and at some point, although the technology is dated, it was made comfortable and modernized. There's something about the deposits in the rock that make scanning for heat signatures nearly impossible. You should be safe here. Solar power, running water, mattresses on the floor. No cyberweb, but there's a wonderful immersionfield with tons of the classics—some of them banned."

"Do you mind if I fool with the electronics?" Nando asked. "I can probably update and secure whatever is in there."

"Not a bit. Go in and get settled. I'll meet Mark at the house, and we'll be back with supplies. Then I want a good long talk to get this all straight."

Madeline stepped forward. "Do you mind if I give you a hug?" In answer, Hisako held her arms out, and the two women embraced. "Thank you," Madeline said, and then Hisako left them.

The companions pushed open the door and filed in. Nando found the controls for the lights and air and began to fiddle with them. Madeline found the kitchen and looked for coffee. Jill explored several of the hallways leading back into the hillside and discovered that the caves were extensive, but the modern parts were mostly to be found near the door. Sometimes doors opened onto what looked like the original tunnels of dry, cool, unlit natural rock.

The main cave was where they would sleep. There was a reasonably serviceable bathroom, old but complete. Nando found the solar batteries were fully charged and turned on the water heater. Madeline found towels, sheets, plates, cups, flatware, and foodstuffs, such as dried and cured meats (fish and beef), flour, dried beans, bags of long-grain rice, nuts, dried herbs, salt, dried red peppers, honey, and other canned and dried foodstuffs. The water from the faucets was not only clear, it tasted wonderful. There were even some kegs and bottles in a cool room down some stone steps from the kitchen.

Madeline filled a glass pitcher with the cold water from the tap, grabbed some glasses, and called everyone around the table.

HOW THE LIBRARY BEGAN

*"One has a moral responsibility
to disobey unjust laws."*
—*Martin Luther King, Jr.*

Madeline looked at the other two. "It's possible Hisako has gone for the enforcers. Apparently, she's on very good terms with them. But I don't think so. I think we've been unspeakably fortunate in coming to this place. The safe house would have been discovered at some point, or we might have been picked out as suspicious by the locals. But there are no locals here except for Mark and Hisako. And blessedly, they're going to hide us at present. I don't know if we could have found a better situation." She poured cold water and handed around the glasses

Jill licked her lips after the first sip and looked in surprise at her glass. "They could sell this with a designer label for a lot of money. Delicious! I'm with you, Madeline. I can't imagine a better spot for us to be in. I can't wait to learn more about our hosts. She sure made her mind up fast. We went from strangers on the porch to honored guests in the blink of an eye."

Nando nodded in agreement. "Remarkable. Just remarkable. Looking over some of the stuff in boxes and at the tools kept here, I believe I can set up a workspace and begin to get us some eyes and ears on the world. I want some news. And I want to talk to Alex if he hasn't been arrested yet. But first, these mattresses look good. After the shock we've all endured, I'm going to try to close my eyes a little until our hosts return. For good or for harm, at least I can face the next thing with a little peaceful rest!"

He actually got a good nap in as the women quietly took inventory of provisions. An hour and a half had passed when they heard Mark and Hisako at the door. Everyone helped unload their antigravity sled. Mark was small, like Hisako, and they both had short gray hair. Mark had a short beard as well. Though he wasn't big, he looked tough. Years of outdoor work had left his skin weathered and his muscles lean and strong. Everyone made four or five trips, and they got the supplies in: fresh vegetables and fruits and perishable foods like bread and meat, all stowed in the cool room off the kitchen. Mark also went from person to person, taking each of their arms and retuning the frequencies in their comms. "You can reach us anytime day or night now. You're on our local network. It's encrypted. We can't have you at the house, but we hope to make it back here at least every few days or so."

As he walked past with a bundle of beef and some bags of onions and carrots, Nando offered to fabricate some virtual simulations of Mark and Hisako. The two men quickly began exchanging ideas for implementation, each finding the other delightfully knowledgeable. There was an immediate connection.

Hisako and Madeline made a giant pot of honey-lemon tea. Soon everyone was gathered around the big table in the common area. The friends asked if the news had reported anything new about Meg, but were told that all there was on the news was that she had been detained the night of a raid and there was footage of her in which she looked drunk. There had been no news of her possible release. Mark looked at Hisako, laid a gentle hand on her shoulder, and turned to the other three.

"We can only wait for what the day will bring. Our hearts are anxious for that girl. Nevertheless, though you are all strangers to Hisako and to me, you have crossed our threshold and have become our guests," he said. "For the sake of our Meg, the gift to us for which we're so grateful, we welcome you. Whatever we promised to do for her, we will do for you. This means we place our lives in your hands because of the love we share for Meg. Hisako and I will feed and house you for as long as it takes to plan your next move. We have talked it over, and we commit ourselves to you in this."

Nando rose to his feet with watery eyes. "We don't know what to say. We were desperate and didn't know what to do until we remembered Meg talking about the two of you and how kind you are. We had no idea how kind. I . . . as I said, I don't know how to thank you." The others rose with Nando in agreement.

Hisako nodded and motioned to the chairs. "You're welcome. Please sit and tell us all you can about our Meg!"

The companions sat and looked at one other, unsure where to begin. Jill tried to say something, but it was Madeline who replied. "The last we heard, she'd been caught out of sector with a disabled tracker. This is all we know, and it comes from our friend, the enforcer. Where she is being held and what she may be charged with or when she might be released . . ." She looked down and shook her head. Suddenly, she looked up at the others with a determined light in her eye. "If there's any reason we cannot let these good people know the real danger to her now, I don't know what it could be. These two have risked their lives to take us in, unknown, sight unseen. We can only reciprocate by telling them exactly what precipitated our situation." Jill nodded in unison with Nando.

"Tell 'em, Linny," he urged.

Madeline took a big sip of tea, followed by a deep breath, and began.

"Some years ago, and quite by accident, Nando and I discovered an old elevator shaft in our livingspace. The space was the one that Nando's sponsor's sponsor—we call him his grandfather—had owned in the first apartments in the city. They were some of the first to come to Netopia and to the new city of Chaldea. Back during the purge. The discovery came about by what I think is a rather humorous incident."

"You don't have to include that part," Nando protested.

"Nando had been fooling around with holography, and after a frustrating dead end, he picked up his heavy office chair and threw it against the wall."

"Not particularly proud of that," Nando muttered. Mark laughed appreciatively. Madeline ignored them both.

"It took out a section of wall. And it echoed. Pulling the chair out of the way, Nando shone a light into the hole and found that the area was fairly large. He called me, and together we removed sections of the wall and found we were looking at a shaft like our elevator, but it went both up and down. Since we were on the ground floor, and there was no basement, we couldn't guess what was down there that needed an elevator. Nando went down on a knotted rope. He reached the elevator car stranded below, opened the access panel on top, let himself inside, and soon brought the car up to our apartment level. I stepped in, and we decided to try up first. We soon found ourselves on the roof. There was a little shed."

"Neither of us knew why that shed was there!" Nando said. "We didn't have a key to go in . . ."

"I'm telling this, dear," Madeline said. "They don't care about the shed. I didn't either, if you remember. It looked like it had been a bird feeding station. But the shocker was when we started down. We went down and down, and then it stopped at the bottom, and there was this room, maybe twenty by twenty. Full of . . ."

Nando, unable to stay silent, burst in. "Old books!"

"Books!" Hisako blurted, wide-eyed. "Black market reading! You involved Meg with illegal books?"

"It was my fault," Jill interjected. "I loved the books, and I loved Meg, and I was the one who brought them together."

Mark waved his hand. "Hisako's tone is not one of indignation; it's one of great relief. We had hoped Meg had not been arrested for anything like stealing or sedition. It is an honor to be branded undesirable because of books. We ourselves have some. We've never shown them to her or even spoken of them. We too have found so much joy in these ancient writings, these supposed dangers to society! Perhaps through being overly cautious, we didn't let Meg know about our secret sin of having them. We don't know what becomes of those who are caught, for we never hear from them again. We suspect they're sent to a place where no word ever returns, a prison for those suspected of carrying the Sickness."

Their eyes moved around the circle with fresh sight, and each one could feel it—the wonder of a very deeply shared experience. Nando whistled. "You guys too, huh?"

Madeline took up the story again. "Nando's grandfather had hidden them from the state, hoping they would be legal again one day. But the secret of his library died with him. Until the day Nando threw the chair."

"Now dear . . ." Nando said.

Mark laughed. "Hisako throws things too. I've become very good at ducking!"

"Nando only throws things that most people can't pick up, and never at me," Madeline said quickly. "And that's the story of how we found the library. We felt it was wrong to keep such a room to ourselves, and it seems like fate brought our little group together. We tried to be as discreet as we could, but we all spent a lot of time there." Then anger rose in her voice. "Until yesterday when Alex sent word that we had been discovered. If he hadn't been on duty when the call came in on the raid, you may never have heard from any of us again."

Madeline's voice choked, and she took a sip of water. Laying a hand on her arm, Nando took up the rest of the tale. "So we had enough time to grab some of the books . . ."

"You've got books?" Mark asked excitedly.

"Right in our backpacks, and our backup scan of every book in our collection."

Mark and Hisako looked at each other in wide-eyed delight.

Nando continued, "And we've been on the run ever since. We've had some narrow escapes, but here we are. We're sorry to put you in this kind of danger."

Mark shook his head with a smile. "We like to avoid hacking off the Entente whenever we can, but there are times when some civil disobedience is necessary to truly live the lives we've been given. One has a moral responsibility to disobey unjust laws . . ."

"Martin Luther!" Madeline exclaimed.

"Martin Luther King, actually," Nando gently corrected her. "Although Martin Luther did some disobeying himself!"

"Those who would give up essential liberty to purchase a little temporary safety deserve neither liberty nor safety," Jill said with a laugh.

"Benjamin Franklin!" three voices said at once.

Everyone pitched in as they prepared and ate their first supper in the cave. They continued to talk about their favorite books late into the night.

The previous thirty-six hours had been full of frustration for Director Phelps. The botched raid was not just a mark on his record, the first ever hint at a failure, but whatever that thing was inside of Goff still haunted him. He could still feel the bone-chilling waves of dead air coming from the creature that sat in his desk chair. He had called in some specialists to deep clean it. He was continuing to read and evaluate reports, aware to some extent of Meg's detainment, but as yet, he hadn't focused on her name, and her face was not familiar.

There were bigger fish to fry before he got down to sorting through the scraps of the evening.

MEG VS. GOFF, FINAL ROUND

*"The difference between a rebel and a patriot
depends upon who is in power at the moment."*
— *Sidney Sheldon*

The morning after the raid, Goff received news of Meg's arrest attached to the morning lab report of missing workers. Apparently, two had not shown up for work, Meg and someone named Jill 89k3g. The report said Meg was being held for further questioning and would not be routinely released. He felt an immediate urge to go see her at the station. Though he knew his recent activity had placed him on probation, and he could ill afford any more black marks, he also reasoned that it would look screwy if he didn't check on one of his workers who was in the unusual position of being held by the authorities. He could send someone, but for some reason, he vetoed that and decided to go himself. Arriving at the station, he was told the chief was out on patrol. It was a time when all hands were on deck and out policing the streets.

"Of course. But one of your new arrivals works for me. Here are my credentials. I would like to see her. Immediately."

A momentary glance was enough. "Of course, sir." And then turning, "Here! You there! Take this man to room B15."

Of all the people Meg expected to walk through her cell door, Mr. Goff was the last. "Help me," she whispered, wondering who she expected to hear her plea.

That same morning, Stan was seated comfortably in the Director's office with a nice single malt scotch and they were discussing yesterday's raid. "So turtle.376 is not yet closed, huh, sir? It wasn't my fault the raid netted a big nothing burger, was it? Sir?" He hoped his smile would convey a light, humorous tone, but the director never let him read his face, standing with his back to Stan, looking out the window. His glass of scotch was untouched on the edge of his desk where both drinks had been poured.

"Oh, you did a superb job, Stan. It's just possible that when we've brought this mess to a successful conclusion, you'll be given an island of your own in the tropics. We'll make you mayor and put some beautiful girls there and fill up the lakes with fat fish, and you can run a banana plantation. But right now, I need you to focus and tell me everything you know about the group."

Stan sipped his scotch. "I'm guessing everything but your last sentence was heavy sarcasm, sir. You have the download from my implant with my notes. I know the first thing you saw: Alex cx94b. Isn't he one of those big, fat fish?"

The Director continued to look out the window. "Sure. Alex is special. It was horrible luck that he was the officer on duty when the raid was given the green light." *How could that happen?* He wondered. *I wish like hell we'd caught that sooner.* "Now the mission is ongoing, we need to watch him like a hawk. He seems to have done everything by the book, and for the life of me, I can't find a single thing that wasn't exactly in line with policy. Nothing to arrest him for. Clever. Of course, I would have had him detained immediately if I didn't know right where he is and how fast we can grab him when the time comes. He's being watched round the clock. At the moment, I'm guessing he must be reading the report we circulated of your dying before any information could be extracted from you. I imagine he feels safe for now. And to think, he was one of the force's brightest rising stars. This is going to be a major shakeup among their ranks. There's gonna be a lot of looking into his associates up and down the line, especially on the force."

"Sir, don't underestimate that guy. He's . . . well, he knows his way around. The sooner you take him off the board, the better for this operation, I would think."

The Director turned to look at Stan. He had done the Entente a great service. And yet, look at him lounging there. A disloyal piece of dirt who had turned on the people who'd been kind to him. A despicable excuse for a human being. Sitting on the couch like a rock star, sipping private-stock liquor, relaxed in his off-duty clothes and flapping his mouth as if his opinion of how the operation should proceed mattered a hill of beans.

The Director despised him. But for the present, he would humor him—up to a point.

The reorienting of Stan's mental capabilities could be accomplished when his brain was wiped.

"Actually, son, that's one way of thinking. I believe in waiting 'til we're good and ready. Waiting until the operation we found going on at that location has been dissected from top to bottom, with every player known and surrounded. We botched the raid, probably due to Alex. We won't get another chance on this mission. Patience. Believe me when I say there's nothing more important to me at this moment than the successful conclusion of this affair."

Stan swirled the contents of his glass. "I heard you picked up Meg 4k6p3."

"What about her? I don't see her name on the report" the Director replied sharply.

"She was picked up in another sector."

The Director tried not to let his surprise show. "Yes, of course."

"Did I not include her in my reports? She's definitely one of the fish."

"Tell me more."

"Well, sir, you can ask her yourself. I imagine she knows codes and names and . . . well, everything."

The Director scanned the arrest. "Hmmm. It says here she bumped into a random patrol who brought her in for questioning and that she's being held in solitary. What's this? Her tracker had been disabled. Hah! Let's talk about how to approach her. Maybe you should be the one to try to break her. She might open up to you. She probably has no idea that you're still alive or that you betrayed her and her friends."

Stan caught the tone Director Phelps used when saying the word "betrayed," and he tightened up, but it seemed the director was still going over the report. *Betrayed, huh?* This was the first warning Stan got that, though his service to the Entente on this mission may have been worthy of praise and even worthy of a glass of the best scotch, still, no one was above the system. No one was safe. He also realized that, deep down, Director Phelps hated him.

"Betrayed, sir?" He tried to keep the question light and casual.

"You know what I meant by that—from her perspective. Of course, from the perspective of the people, it was brilliant work. Just like that English folk hero Ward Bond."

"I believe you mean James Bond, sir, and thank you."

"Yes, James. And soon we will discover every secret and every hiding hole of this group, whatever and wherever they are, and we will turn the embarrassment of this feckless night into a triumph. For the people, of course."

"Yes, sir! My money is on your brains and ability to outfox those seditionists."

"We'll see, won't we, Stan? I have to leave, but you can stay. Refill? Help yourself."

"Absolutely, yes sir."

Alex answered his wrist comm. "Fighting for you. Alex speaking."

"Alex, it's Stan."

"Ah, my old pal, Stan the rat. The guy who grew up with Jill and who she trusted. The guy we thought we were saving from prison and torture. The guy we took in and protected. The guy whose face somehow appeared in a communication from Phelps last night, smiling behind the Director's desk!"

Stan didn't miss a beat. "So you already know, huh? Well yeah, make of that what you will. I don't know how they know what they know, but they seem to have the best information around, and the only way I could see to save my friends and our library was to play along with them."

"I see. They have the best information around, huh? Like from the horse's mouth? Or in this case, an ass. Let me hear you say hee-haw, you donkey's rear end."

"Listen, Alex, I know it looks bad, and maybe you'll never trust me again, but I'm scared and confused with a foot in both worlds. I'm terrified of what may happen to me if they find out I've been talking to you, and I'm devastated that you and the others might never think of me as your friend again. I just left old Phelpsie, and he's as hacked off as I've ever seen him."

"Well let me get a box of Kleenex. You've got me crying alligator tears, Stan."

"Oh, cut it out. I'd like to see what you would have done in my place. Still, I need you to listen. They haven't picked you up yet because they think they can grab you at any time. They hope you'll lead them to the others and that they can find the books that were in my report."

"I'm hanging up, Stan."

"No, Alex, please! I'm telling you to clear out. My report covered everything I knew. It had to. This is Director Conrad Marion Phelps we're dealing with."

"There is no we, pal."

"What I'm saying is, this guy is the best there is. He has never missed on a mission and, for some reason I don't know about, he seems scared out of his pants to fail on this one. You don't have to believe me or trust me. I'm not even sure I believe or trust myself. I'm pretty sure Phelps is going to have me knocked off. And one last thing, Alex. Believe it or not as you wish, but I'm a broken man, used and abused by a system that has me terrified. I'm grateful for what you and Jill and the others have done, and that's really why I called—to say thanks and to try to get you to not completely hate me. Sure, I'm ashamed of the part I've played in these events, but I was only trying to save myself. You know what these people are capable of. I hope you can forgive a man who isn't gifted with courage like you or loyalty like Jill or even brains and beauty in one neat package like Meg. Oh, yeah, Meg! Alex! Mr. Goff knows Meg's being held in a cell. Phelpsie doesn't want her visited until he can get a comprehensive plan together to capture you and the books and everyone and everything with a nice bow, all gift-wrapped for his superiors. But Goff is different. He may pay her a visit as her supervisor at any time. He's, well he's dangerous. And you know how he is about Meg. You've got to do something! I'm hanging up. May the stars of the eternal Plasm favor you—"

"Wait, Stan!" But the connection was gone.

Alex dashed back to his livingspace and gathered the few books out of the wood stove and a few items he could not leave behind, mostly weapons, including a high-powered stunner and his emergency riot bag with first-aid gear. Dimming the lights and quickly arranging some blankets under the bed covers, he hoped this ancient ruse would satisfy a visual scan from the station that he was grabbing a nap after an exhausting night. One of the perks of being an enforcer meant he had an "off" switch on his locator that was part of his implant's software. Actually, he seldom had his locator on, except when he wanted to leave a trail to cover for wherever else he had gone.

He had been trying to figure out what he could do about Meg when Stan's call had come in. Stan didn't tell him anything he didn't know or suspect already, but news of Goff set off an alarm in his head. He knew it was time to act. He knew where Meg was being held, and he brought that location up on his screen. He also knew all about the two agents assigned to shadow him. They never saw him coming.

Navigating the city with speed and anonymity was something he had been doing for a living. His cycle fairly screamed through the city Arriving at the station where Meg was being held, Alex knew it was time to burn bridges. The enforcer on duty might or might not know that Alex was now a criminal awaiting detainment, but it didn't matter.

True to his nature, Alex was going to make the first move.

JASON RETURNS TO EARTH

"An appeaser is one who feeds a crocodile,
hoping it will eat him last."
—*Winston Churchill*

As it turned out, on the very same morning after the raid on Earth, Jason awoke to the dull horn and the flashing lights that signaled they were very shortly to arrive back on Earth. After a quick inspection to see that everything was straightened up, he bid goodbye to the space he had lived in for over a year. It had become his new home, and he reflected that he was coming back a slightly different man. He had dug his cadet uniform out of a deep drawer and had tried to get the wrinkles to lay flat. He smoothed his red hair down as much as possible and pulled on his cap. Izgad supplied some suitable remarks such as, "Missed a spot!" but as Jason could not get him to specify whether it was a spot on the silo or in his personal cleanliness, Jason just smiled and ignored him as much as possible. After a few adjustments to the controls, he stood by the console, waiting to hear from the launch pad crew. He didn't have to wait long.

"Jase!" Max shouted excitedly over his system. "Ya made it back in one piece! You are in one piece, aren't you? Are you inhabited by a space worm that will grow to gigantic size and eat half the city before we can shoot you down? Let me see your foul face!"

Jason sat down in front of the screen and grinned. "I'm back with tales of adventure, Max. Are you bringing a cheeseburger and fries, or do I have to pull my weapon and vaporize you?"

"We brought you burgers and fries from five different eateries just to be sure you got your fave. And a strawberry shake from Rays, just like you like it, man!"

"OK! Great! Get me outta this tin can!"

"Patience, my boy. You've been gone for so long, you can wait a few minutes more. . ."

There was a problem with the cradle, and the door wouldn't open, so they had to get a crane to reposition the silo. But it wasn't long before the door opened, depressurizing with a loud sigh, and Jason stepped out into the sunlight of the planet where he had been born. Harry scooted out and sat, wagging his tail.

Just as Jason told Izgad to expect, the launch site was crawling with dignitaries and reporters. Max was waiting when he opened the door and sidestepped several people who went straight into the collection that Jason had brought back. He and Jason shook hands warmly.

"Man, Jase! You won't believe what's happening! I told you! Look at this! For some reason, they've decided to make YOU the face of our entire space effort! I mean, they're going to make you a star! The stories are already being written about you." He looked down at the dog. "And about Harry, of course!" he added, giving Harry a brisk rub on the top of his head.

"Hand me those bags," Jason said. "The burgers smell great. Is that table over there a place we can sit down? Did you say stories? What sort of stories?" Jason set one of the bags down in front of Harry, who followed the bag all the way to the floor as if the bag were iron and his nose were a magnet. Soon the rustle of paper and the squishing sound of chewing came from inside the bag, which now contained not only the burger and fries but Harry's head as well.

"Yeah, you know, stories about how brave, trustworthy, clean you are, and well––how you're fighting for the people, you know?"

"I'm clean?" Jason took a huge bite out of the cheeseburger he had just unwrapped and sighed all the way down to his boots as he chewed. "What unholy hell have you got waiting for me with all this publicity and coverage?"

"Don't worry, Jase," Max reassured him. "You'll have to catch up on some reading, of course, so you can talk intelligently about the bio we've constructed for you. You were near the top of your pod class—"

"But I wasn't!"

"You are now, which means you were then! Don't worry; just roll with it. It's a cinch. We'll do most of the talking out there today.

Later on it'll be all you. We'll have writers for your appearances, and you'll just say what they put on your prompter. And then party your rear end off the rest of the time! I can't believe your good luck!"

Jason smiled but shook his head. "I don't get it. What's this all about, Max?"

Max clapped him on the back. "Like I said, they've decided you're to be the face of our space program. Don't ask me why. It may have something to do with your red hair and how your ugly Everyman mug will look on screen . . ."

"Oh, shut up! I'm serious. I don't understand. I was hoping you'd let me unload the silo and have some time off." So why did Meg just show up in your brain, pal?

"Time off? Didn't you hear what I just said? You're going to be living the life of an absolute prince! A couple of appearances a day, saying what we tell you to and waving at the crowds. Having your pick of nighttime companions and daytime menus. You'll have a valet and a masseuse and a makeup artist, all beautiful girls. You'll never have to drive yourself anywhere again. You're what people will think of when they think of our department. You'll boost recruiting and community goodwill and put a personal touch on the awkward acronyms we go by. One thing though . . ."

"What's that?"

"Your advertising endorsement money still belongs to the state. Sorry."

"Endorsement . . ."

"Don't get upset, now, Jase . . ."

"I'm not upset. I'm flabbergasted! Disgusted! I don't want endorsements or to be the face of the acronyms or boost goodwill! I just want to take a break and then go back to work!"

"Sorry again, buddy, but that's not the life that has been chosen for you. There are worse fates than being made into a hero of the people! I wish I were in your place. You'll be requested on all the news shows and bachelor parties. I know you don't like immmersionfields, but there have been some major upgrades this year, some of which are sexually intriguing. Oh, another thing, speaking of sex: they say you must never pair. From now on it's strictly spins for you, and the state is gonna pick those girls carefully. If you want a girl a night, that's fine, but no pictures or stories except for the approved ones."

"Oh, shut up, Max—sir!" Jason added hastily. "Give me a second to walk old terra firma, will ya? I'm not the guy you want for this assignment."

"It's not what I want. The whole thing comes from high up. I've heard it's from the Elders."

"I really don't care who it's from."

"Shhh!" Max's face darkened in a flash. "Don't let those thoughts even form in your head. And Jason, never speak such thoughts out loud. You're a hero now, but they can make up a story about your accidental death in a skinny minute and have it broadcast to every station in the city. You've been alone and without anyone for a while . . ."

"Forgetting Harry?"

"You're not hearing me! I don't care what independent track your mind has formed on those godforsaken gravity-conglomerated rocks out there in space. You're not there anymore, chief. I say this as your friend and as your superior in the fight for everyone. Knock it off about wanting anything but what you're told to want. This is serious stuff. I've heard that sometimes guys come back from space, and they're completely off their nut. Minds have to be wiped and replaced. Of course they won't kill you; they'll just clamp you into one of their machines and reprogram your brain. Smile and nod, Jase. Smile and nod. Anything else, and you'll be a walking vegetable."

Jason looked at the floor. After a moment, he looked up and reflexively saluted, fist to chest. "I hear you, sir. And Max," he added in a lower voice, "Thanks. You've always looked out for me. I guess you were the one who got me my job in the first place."

"And don't you forget it. A bunch of the guys were mad as hell at me for doing it."

"I won't forget it. And you're right, I've been away by myself, and I have to get my game back as far as all the stuff you're saying. Thanks. I appreciate it. I won't let you down."

A noise came from Harry, and Max looked down at him. Slobber-infused paper was plastered all over his mouth, even with his tongue continuing to lick his jaws repeatedly. Jason let him sniff the other four paper bags, now empty. After Harry had checked each one to be absolutely sure they no longer contained anything remotely edible, he circled three times and then flopped on the ground with his eyes closed.

After gathering his personal belongings from the silo, Jason was motorcaded to his new high-dollar government penthouse. It had to be a penthouse because of the helos that would be constantly coming and going, carrying him and others back and forth. Jason and Harry were left alone in their new digs after the beautiful schedule girl had given Jason a calendar download on his wrist comm implant that contained his life for the next three years. Jason didn't glance at it or even protest. What's the use? They're going to impose whatever control on my life they want, and it's all "for the people."

"The room is bugged," Izgad whispered, "so refrain from talking to me unless you make it sound like you are talking to Harry."

Jason looked down at him. "What a good dog you are!"

Jason swept the apartment and found that the only room that did not have ears was the bedroom. "And if we turn on the view screen at a moderate level, none of our conversations in here will be known. I think I'll program it to come on when I enter, so I won't forget."

For an answer, Harry hopped up on the bed.

"No, no, no! Down, boy! My bed! That ain't happenin', pal!" But no amount of protest would dislodge the faithful mutt.

"He seems determined," Izgad whispered. "He says he is overly clean because of his daily baths for the camera."

Jason laughed, shrugged, and initiated the viewer, tuning it to a symphonic radio station. He wanted Izgad to understand the world to which he had returned. To explain why they were being bugged. "The Entente thinks nothing of looking in on anything, with the exception of our bedrooms. For some reason, they think bedrooms are off limits."

"The reason is obvious."

"Not to me."

"They are ashamed of their perversions, which is the only shame they still feel. Shame should be a guardrail, but instead, they wrongly believe it is proof that the Maker is cruel. I cannot understand thinking that the Maker would want anything but the best for his creatures, but that is one way they choose to misunderstand Him."

"I never made a conscious choice to misunderstand," Jason observed.

"That is because you never had an encounter with Truth. When a person has that encounter, it is a moment of decision. Many choose to ignore Truth. At that moment, the likelihood of eventually aligning with Truth drops in probability. How much depends on how confident they are that Truth does not exist."

"Why would anyone choose to ignore truth?"

"I am not talking about a concept. I am talking about a person."

"What person?"

"Truth."

"Truth isn't a person, Izgad, it's . . . well . . . all I can say is you know it when you hear it."

"That is exactly why Truth is a person. Ideas come and go. Dictionary definitions change. Truth is a person who never changes, and that is why he is able to be recognized through the ages of your planet."

Jason looked at Izgad in silence. A minute passed. Then he spoke. "So, what do I do with this person?"

"You believe."

"In what?"

"In him."

Silence again. A long silence. And then...

"I think I do believe already, but I can't explain why."

"It is not a process that will fit in an explanation. It is deeper than that. It involves the core of your being."

Jason turned and walked to the window. The afternoon sun was silhouetting the buildings, and its rays danced as they scattered through the cityscape in front of him.

So, truth. It not only existed, something he had often wondered, but it, no, he . . . was a person. Jason didn't understand, and he was aware that not only did he not understand, he was totally convinced. Something had happened to him in these moments that he realized had been building. It was a step out of one thing and into something else.

He knew he was leaving behind uncertainty, instability, and a sense of being untethered. Discarding an empty feeling of fear that life had no existential meaning. He remembered an old nursery rhyme that proclaimed that meaninglessness openly: "

Row, row, row your boat gently down the stream,

merrily, merrily, merrily, merrily, life is but a dream."

Funny how a child's playground song should be so terrifying.

But in sharp contrast, he now held to a lifeline of hope.

No, it was beyond hope. Jason realized that he now knew, to an unshakable certainty, that a person existed who embodied truth and that his allegiance had shifted wholeheartedly to whatever that person was doing.

This was by no means Jason's first epiphany, for though he was a simple guy, he thought deeply to achieve that simplicity, and his life was marked by great realizations that were the fruit of taking things apart and looking at them as he would a repair on his silo. This was like those realizations, but the difference was that it contained all of them. Every time he had a major breakthrough in understanding the world around him, in plumbing the depths of human nature, of unpacking his own soul, it had been a small step toward this moment.

It all overtook him in an instant, and Jason realized he was stepping irrevocably away from his old self and inexorably toward the new.

Izgad waited patiently until Jason turned back around to look at him. Then Izgad broke his silence. "There are elevations in your endorphins, and your pupils are dilated. If I hadn't been constantly with you for the last hour or so, I would have said you were on drugs."

"Well, I guess I've found the drug that all other drugs try to imitate--and can't! Izzie . . ."

"My name does not rhyme with fizzy!"

"Izzie, I want to dance!" Grabbing the dog in his arms, Jason leaped around the room in absolute joy.

"Harry . . . says he is getting . . . dizzy, which, oddly enough, rhymes with Izzie and fizzy . . . but . . . that . . . he likes it!"

Jason ended the romp by tossing Harry halfway across the room to a safe landing on the bed. Harry wagged his tail furiously and barked in utter happiness.

"Harry has longed for the day you would know Truth. His tail is saying 'Congratulations, Slowpoke.'"

"Harry knows this person?" Jason asked as he continued to dance.

"Naturally creation would know its Maker," Izgad explained.

Jason danced over to the bed and flopped down in exhaustion. "Does this truth person like to dance?"

"The one who causes the giant heavenly bodies to dance in orbits and the tiny molecules and atoms to dance in miniature loves to dance. He invented the dance."

ALEX TO THE RESCUE

*"Everybody has a plan until they get
punched in the mouth."*
— Mike Tyson

Alex entered the building cool and calm, as relaxed as if he were watching a sports match with friends. He placed his hand on the doorframe as he walked in, casually affixing the sticky disruptor button in his palm. He went straight to the desk, pretending to be in communication with one of his superiors.

When the man on duty at the station looked up, Alex nodded, held up a finger, and looked away as if trying to hear better, but in actuality, he was assessing the situation as presented. He calculated that three items needed to be dealt with: 1) the officer, who may already know about Alex being a wanted man and who might be at that moment reaching for a weapon; 2) the surveillance array in each corner of the room; and 3) the wildcard of Goff in Meg's cell. Alex quickly determined the order of importance: array, officer, Goff. There was a high probability that more officers were around and just as high a probability that more might come into the station just as he had done, but the risk would not be reduced by waiting.

He clicked the detonator in his pocket. The disruptor began pouring out noxious smoke and producing believable sounds of a full-scale assault, complete with gunfire. Alex pointed to the door. "Look out!" he screamed and then leaped for the desk. "Get down!" As the clouds of fumes obscured all visibility in the room, Alex disabled the officer with a perfectly placed blow to the head as he slid over the desktop. The officer crumpled behind the desk with a soft thud.

Alex believed he now had no more than ten minutes before someone at the monitors woke up and saw the mayhem on screen. He scanned the desk viewer and noticed that Meg was detained in cell B15. He cut all the camera feeds on site.

Racing down the hall, Alex presented his credentials to the guard at the door and ordered the man to cover him, saying the station was under attack. Over his shoulder, he barked that he would prepare the prisoner for transport and that the guard should take a defensive position and hold off the attack for as long as he could. As the guard called out to explain there was someone who should not be moved in that cell, Alex nodded and commanded him to sell his life dearly for the people. He smiled as he heard the first arriving officers yelling in the front. Let them shoot at each other until they figure it out. Not daring to look back, Alex burst into cell B15.

As the door slammed behind him Alex saw that the room was a mess. Traces of blood and signs of a struggle were everywhere. Goff was at the sink looking at the scratch marks on his face and dabbing at them with a wet cloth. Meg was standing resolutely in a corner, only partially clothed.

No time for thinking, only reflex. In a split second, Alex crossed the room and slammed Goff's head on the sink. While that would have been followed by a long nap for a human being, the monster in Goff was unfazed. With blood streaming from an open wound on his forehead, Goff stood up and eyed Alex. "Oh, yes! The mighty Alex cx94 BEEEE. Not superhuman. Merely human. I will crush you and watch you die, you pathetic—"

Alex never got to hear the end of the sentence because his handheld sent an electric shock through Goff's body. The creature could not make specific muscles tighten to move or even talk since they had all cramped at the same time. Goff lay flat where he fell, and Alex grabbed his credentials.

Turning to Meg, he saw that she had fainted. Taking a glass of water, he threw it at her face and looked around for the rest of her clothes.

"Alex?" she murmured. "Is it really you? How in the world . . ."

"Save it, Meg. Put these back on. Your other shoe is around here somewhere. We've got to go! Hurry!"

Somehow, Meg roused herself to motion. Pulling her other shoe on as Alex buzzed open the door, she stood up. Alex put a restraining bracelet on her wrists and took her elbow. As they emerged from the cell, Alex spoke quickly to the frightened guard. "They'll never get her. She's ours. Hold them off as long as you can, and then follow me out the back. Do your best; that's all any of us can do. You'll be a hero of the people!"

"You can count on me, sir!" the officer said in a high, shaky voice as smoke strangled the hallway and wild shots from both sides ricocheted everywhere.

Alex led them toward the back door. Meg stumbled, and Alex caught her as she lost her balance. They continued down the hall away from the gun battle as the first responders were trying to come down the hall for the same reason the guard was holding them off. The chaos was just what they needed.

Coming to the motor pool, where the noise of the firefight had not yet reached, Alex showed Goff's credentials to the attendant. "Taking this prisoner north of the city for sexual privileges. Give me your best tran."

The attendant didn't even look at his face as he pushed the correct summons sequence for a vehicle. "Right away, Supervisor Goff . . ."

The Director was livid. How could Goff have gotten in to see the prisoner and then beat her up and made off with her in a tran? He'd have them picked up before they got to the pleasure cabins up north of the city. What had happened to the regulations? What had kept the station from making the simple call to check with his office to make sure it was OK? I can't fight for the people if my authority is going to be circumvented at every turn!

All the officers on duty would be punished with menial jobs with little chance for advancement. The three responders who the hall guard had wounded defending Goff's escape would heal just fine. That dumbkoff at the cell door was so dim that the Director wondered how he had ever passed the requisite exams—until he saw that the man was the only son of a high-ranking government official.

Incompetence! It was the one thing that the Director could not stand. Efficiency required competence, which required training and accomplishment. Without trained and accomplished people, there was no efficiency. And he had written the book on efficiency. Hell, he himself was efficiency personified.

Beyond all that, what was he going to do about Goff? The voice that came out of the man warned him that Goff was possibly beyond his authority to deal with. But surely something could be done. His department couldn't be wrecked by this factory boss with some sort of creepy personality infestation.

The Director remained cool. If yelling at people would have helped, he would have yelled at people. But it wouldn't help, and the Director was a practical man. For the moment, he could see nothing to do but continue to clean up the messes others had made.

He would put out an all-points notice for Goff and the prisoner. He would make a swift example of the officers at the desk and the door. He would bring Goff in and see what could be seen. And he would do what he always did: make order and production out of chaos and ineptitude.

This was not over by a long shot. Perhaps it was time to collect Alex cx94b and put him through the wringer. Find out everything he knew. Not the way I had hoped, but I need a break on this case, he thought. Apparently, Alex was asleep in his livingspace. He enabled the comm link to his secretary and calmly gave instructions for the arrest when Alex emerged.

Within a matter of hours, Alex and Meg were heading out of town in the fourth replacement they had taken. Two of the vehicles were now missing their locators. Two others were in the river while a third was back where it had been lifted. The quad they were in now was the latest model, but to the wide world, it registered as a farm vehicle on the back of a factory trailer.

They drove for thirty minutes in silence, and then Alex, after a brief stop at a waterstation, pulled under a bridge and stopped. Turning to Meg, he applied first aid using the supplies he had picked up. He gently wrapped her bruised ribs in gauze strips for padding and support. Her cuts and bruises got a treatment from a cream that was both antiseptic and anesthetic. Meg's knuckles were raw and bleeding. Alex realized he had underestimated the fight in this girl. The shiner under her left eye got a cold pad. Her teeth, though bloody, were unbroken.

Meg winced as she shifted in her seat. "Alex, how did you . . . how . . . I'm so glad to see you."

Alex continued to check for broken bones. "I'm not so sure you'll say that when you hear we're out of communication with the team. Once I saw Stan's face behind the desk of Director Phelps, who gave the orders for the raid, I knew how we'd been betrayed. At first I didn't understand why I wasn't arrested immediately, but it didn't take a lot of brainpower to figure out what they were waiting for: they would track my movements and my communications and eventually have a dragnet around us all. I haven't dared to communicate with Nando and Madeline or any of the others since leaving the site of the raid, but I couldn't wait any longer to disappear when I saw Goff had gained admission to your cell. So, as long as you're with me, we probably have the whole government looking for us."

Meg closed her eyes. "I think I hurt him. Bad. I've never had combat training, but it just sort of came out of me to aim for weak spots like shins and his crotch and the tops of his feet. I was even able to push him hard enough to bounce his head off the wall one time. But if you hadn't come, there was no way I would have lasted, no way I'd still be alive. He was making weird noises, unearthly noises, while also using his normal voice, reminding me that he could give me privileges that people only dream about if I would only . . . if I would . . . oh, you know. But it felt good to just let go and hit him and kick him with everything I had."

Even with all his trouble weighing on him, Alex couldn't help but smile. "I'm proud of you, Meg. You've got guts and spunk. You would have done well as an enforcer."

"No, let's not make this into more than it was: a desperate girl alone and afraid who decided she'd go down swinging. My ribs remind me that it was only a brief moment of adrenaline and that I was holding the losing end of the stick."

Alex nodded. "Well, here's the deal. We need to drive around long enough to know we're loose, but the longer we drive, the higher the risk of being pinned down and identified or even accidentally running into the people looking for us. So, I'm going to make for the safe house, just not directly. Snacks are in the bag by your left foot."

"I'm starved. Not to be ungrateful, but could you do one more thing? I can't lean forward without hearing my ribs screaming."

"Sorry! Of course," Alex said as he held out the first-aid bag. Meg began to rummage in it for painkillers.

The officer who came into his office to report that Alex cx94B had eluded surveillance and was officially missing wished she had been anywhere else but on duty that day. Director Phelps no longer cared to keep his polished image on top of his personal presentation. He brought his red face within inches of the officer's face as he chewed her down one side and up the other with words his office had never heard him use. White as a sheet, she ran crying from the room upon being dismissed, not just from the room but from her job. The Director slammed the door behind her. How is this thing falling apart at every turn? How could this possibly get any worse?

Failure was a new taste in his mouth. Since he was known and feared for being so successful, the buzz about his newfound flop was instant and merciless. Many jealous hearts rejoiced as golden boy Phelps face-planted in the mud of defeat.

The Director was painfully aware of this, and it galled him all the more. This is not over, he vowed. He would take risks, he would cash in on his years of prestige, of his impeccable record of triumph. He would call in his chips down to the last favor. His perch at the top had been hard won, and he would protect it with every fiber of his being.

Where was that Goff fellow? Obviously, he could be brought in, and voice or no voice, he would be pasted with every scintilla of the blame. That was for starters. I'll hunt down Alex cx94B and make him the poster boy for bad decisions. Meg will be recaptured and drained of every memory of her short life. The fires of government-powered Hades would roast the group responsible, and he, the formidable C. M. Phelps, would light the match.

Setbacks are expected when you're the pack leader. Chin up, chest out. They were messing with the Director.

After a few hours, Alex felt confident that they were as yet undetected, so he drove to within two blocks of the back entrance of the safe house. Instructing Meg to stay put, he crept forward on foot to reconnoiter, keeping to the shadows. It looked all right. Nothing moving. He was about to go get Meg when he heard a whisper from around the corner of the house. "How much longer are we on for this shift? My legs are cramping."

Alarmed, Alex hurried back to the tran. "Have you seen anyone looking at our tran, Meg?"

"Honestly, I've had my eyes closed."

Alex was glad his training made it an involuntary habit to park inconspicuously and in such a manner as to effect a quick getaway. After some miles, and once again believing they were not being followed, he pulled behind a hedge on a road leading into a field.

Meg was asleep. Think, Alex, he told himself. Have our companions already been scooped up? No way of knowing. File it until more information is available. What were he and Meg to do now? They had to get off the grid quickly, which meant leaving the city.

But where? Out of habit, Alex called up the menu from the codes he still had access to and changed the designation of his vehicle from harvester to "other." However, his mind continued to chew on the destination problem. Commandeer a government cabin northeast of Chaldea? No, that would only put off discovery for, at max, a week. But maybe in a week he'd be able to figure out what was going on, get more intel. Oh man, he thought, glancing at Meg, whether people know her or not, she has got to get out of the public eye. Anyone who sees her will wonder why she's not confined to her livingspace under a doctor's care.

His eyes were looking at Meg, but they seemed to be focused at a spot well beyond where she leaned against the door with a bundle of clothes supporting her head. Hadn't Meg talked about her sponsors living nearby? He grasped at this straw of hope.

He gently took Meg's arm and, holding it up to his comm, accessed the program of her personal information. There they were—tree farmers. So far out of the city as to be almost invisible but still part of Chaldea. Nedney, huh? If nothing else, they'd take great care of Meg. He would be free to come and go as needed instead of having to stick close to a government cabin. And Meg was the only person he'd ever heard of who was still in contact with her sponsors. He certainly wasn't with his own. The nerds in Phelps's team would have a hard time with this riddle.

His mind was leading him through these decisions at lightning speed. In no time, he had made his choice. He reached into the bag from the waterstation and pulled out a couple of energy bars and a chocolate milk.

For now, they were still free, still the masters of their own destiny. The future was unknowable. Just take the next step and hope for the best.

FRIENDS AND ENEMIES

"The real powers at play never take center stage.
Don't follow the marionette, follow the strings."
— William Ritter

Midmorning of the day after Alex rescued Meg and two days after the raid, they ditched their vehicle and hitched a ride with a lovely older couple who dropped them off near the town of Nedney.

Meg took the lead now. They had no trouble staying off the main roads, and soon they were walking, slowly because of Meg's painful ribs, on the logging roads near her sponsors, roads she knew well. Alex took deep breaths of the air that came fresh and clean from the giant stands of trees on either side of the dirt road. Even the soil smelled rich and alive. The city of Chaldea was also clean, of course, and in that city, any single room could be made to smell like whatever the occupant dialed in. But out there in the woods, it was a whole other thing to just . . . breathe. Meg noticed and laughed, "Don't hyperventilate! There's plenty of air. It'll still be here tomorrow and the day after that!"

"Meg, we may not be alive tomorrow. I miss Jill, Nando, and Madeline. I almost miss Stan, though when I see him, I want to wring his neck. What a rat. How did I not see right through him? I'm trained to spot anything that's off, even the least little thing, and I missed it with him. He's the best I've ever seen."

"Are you sure you saw him on that visual link?"

"Positive. Plus he called me right before I came to spring you with a sob story that I don't know what to do with. I only wish I'd spotted him before. We might all still be in the library now. I'm partway through a collection of Zane Grey westerns. At least I was."

"I was reading Little Women. I'm pretty sure it was on the list of books we packed out."

Yeah, Alex thought. But Zane Grey wouldn't be part of their greatest hits collection. It was not especially great writing; it just took his mind off the stress. He pointed ahead. "Which way, left or right?"

"Left goes to the road up to my parents' house."

"Your . . . parents?"

"Sponsors, if you like, but you know our sponsors used to be called parents."

"My sponsors came to see me once when I had earned some big award or something, but that's the only time I remember seeing them. It's amazing that you have this relationship with yours. What's it like? I can't imagine."

"It's like a sense of truly belonging. You know the biology of how babies come into the world. Well, this is beyond that. It's almost mystical, and it's comforting and weird. My parents love me."

"Love you?"

"Yes. They've told me, and I've told them that I love them. I'd do anything for them, and I know they'd do anything for me. Absolutely anything. I just hope that when we see them, they can help us find the others. I told you the left way goes to their house, but go right. It goes over the high ground above their house, and that's the safest way for us to approach. Come on."

Meg and Alex turned up the right-hand split and soon were breathing harder as they gained elevation. Alex kept soaking it all in. After her recent horror, Meg was delighted to be so near to her dear sponsors. They would have wise counsel. They would know what to do.

Goff shifted uneasily in the waiting room. He had been treated for a severe concussion and some broken ribs. The open wounds scratched on his arms and neck were covered by his suit, but the stitches across his forehead as well as his black eye and the large bandage on his ear were impossible to conceal.

What was all this? What was going on? He was not used to being summoned, but Director Phelps's authorization stamps were airtight. What was happening to him? He was painfully aware of gaps in his memory, but those gaps all came with nightmares. While he couldn't be sure of what he had been doing during that time, the visuals he did retain of them had to do with screaming, blood, and abuse, some of it of someone else and some of it of himself. Disturbing.

After being ushered into the Director's office, he did not sit, despite the director's invitation. Being seated was not the way to maintain leverage in such situations.

The Director surveyed Goff. "What's the matter with your eye?"

Goff attempted a smile. "A nasty fall on the hoverball court. You think I look bad? You should see the floor."

The Director had not arranged this meeting to be entertained by lame attempts at humor. "I think you got that when you helped a prisoner escape."

"Prisoner . . . escape?"

"You heard me, Goff. How you got clearance to—"

"I'm her boss. I wanted to make sure she was being treated well."

"I'll bet. That's why she beat the crap out of you and ran out of the cell."

"She didn't do this. I told you I was playing hoverball . . ."

The Director picked up an object on his desk, pointed it at Goff, and pushed a button. Instantly, Goff was immobilized. He could blink and swallow, but he could not turn his head or move his arms and legs. However, his voice was free to bellow indignantly. "What the hell? Who do you think you are, blocking me like this? You're gonna be sorry you ever—"

"Aw, shut it, Goff! In just a moment, I'm turning you over to the enforcers, and you'll stand trial, but I wanted first crack at you. Why did you release my prisoner? Where is she now? Are you and Alex cx94b in league? We have footage of him at the building but lost him when the feeds were cut. What do you know about the operation Alex was spearheading? And what was the trick you did the other day in my office of using that godawful voice?"

"I did no such thing. I have no idea what you're talking about. I can admit to you, and off the record, that sometimes I have gaps in my memory, but it's the medication I take for my stomach ulcers. I didn't release your prisoner, and I don't know Alex C whatever you mentioned. You have me confused with someone else. Get me out of this immediately, or you'll be sorry."

The Director looked at Goff as he took a long breath and then blew it out. He was a little taken off guard. He knew when a liar was lying, and while a lot of what Goff just said was a big, fat lie, the man actually believed some of it.

"You know, Goff, I've made a particular study of you since the day you freaked out in my office, and I've got your trail all the way to the station and then later back out of it. It was you all right. You went to the cell block where we were holding a young girl. Once inside, you appear to have gotten into a helluva cage match with a lightweight and lost. Your blood on the sink and the walls and even the floor, as well as some surveillance footage that people would pay a lot of money to see, are rock-solid evidence that you were there. Then you and the prisoner took a tran from the back lot heading north to the cabins. The prisoner now seems to be gone. So, I'm asking you, where is she?"

Goff was confused. He could remember hearing about Meg's arrest and hurriedly making his way to the station that was holding her, but at some point, he had another one of those blackouts. He couldn't remember a thing until he'd come to, staring at the mirror in the holding cell, gripping the sink and watching the blood oozing down his face. The cell door was wide open, Meg was gone, alarms were blaring all over the station, and he had stumbled out in the confusion, found a public transport, and made his way to a clinic where he could bribe the staff to make no record of the wound cleanup they did.

He had barely slept that night. And then, summoned by Director Phelps, he had unsuccessfully tried to convince the enforcers who brought the summons that there was no need for him to go with them. What was happening to him? How had he gone from such a great life with a cushy job and his pick of the new pod class cupcakes to being a savagely scratched and beat-up man with significant memory gaps?

Director Phelps input information on his desk screen, and a recorded scene began playing in the air between the two men. Goff saw a man sitting in Director Phelps's chair but could barely recognize himself because of the horrific change that had come over his face: dead eyes, white skin, slack mouth. He looked like a hand puppet or a marionette, which was an accurate assessment of his condition. He heard the voice coming out of the man's mouth, and it frightened him. *How is this possible?* he wondered. *Is all of my life a nightmare?*

When the scene ended, and the Director switched it off, Goff swallowed. "That was doctored somehow. That couldn't possibly have been me."

The Director eyed him. "You seem to want me to believe you have a split personality. When did you first notice this, ah, condition?"

"I don't know what you're talking about! I told you, it's my medicine!" Goff exclaimed earnestly, his voice rising. The Director said nothing.

"Look," Goff continued in a softer voice, "this is the honest truth. I have these spells where I seem to phase out, and when I phase back in, I'm somewhere doing something I have no idea about. I've been scared, but I thought I was OK, that I could handle it. I'm . . . I'm telling you what I've never told a soul. Can't you take this damn block off me? I'm telling you the truth!"

The Director still said nothing. He crossed his arms and leaned back. The two men looked at each other for a moment, and then Goff dropped his eyes. "Please take the block off," he murmured. "Have a heart."

The Director spoke into his communicator. "Send the four men I requested earlier, and tell them to put their weapons on hyper-stun. I have a prisoner who is ready to be transported to custody."

No sooner had the Director spoken than Goff's eyes rolled back, and one arm came loose from the block and began clawing violently for the Director. The director calmly re-blocked the arm, but when it pulled loose again moments later, it was bloody from the effort, the skin pulled off, exposing the muscle in some places. Then a bloody foot and a leg followed. By the time the enforcers had entered the room and surrounded him, Goff was partway out of the block hold, blood everywhere, and shouting heart-freezing profanities in a deep voice. His free hand made violent contact with one of the enforcers, who screamed in pain.

"Shoot!" the Director yelled, and the three remaining enforcers fired almost simultaneously. Goff's arms and legs slumped, and his voice stopped abruptly, but his face continued to twitch.

The enforcer who had been hit looked surprised. "I think that son of a bitch broke my arm, sir!"

The Director's eyes never left Goff. "Go get that looked at, son. We can handle him." Then he spoke into his communicator. "Get Haley some medical attention. He's on his way out. Oh yes, and bring that body cage." He turned back to the three remaining enforcers. "Weapons at the ready," he cautioned. "I don't know what this thing is."

When the cage came, they snapped Goff into it leg by leg and arm by arm, finally encapsulating his head and neck. They checked his life signs on the monitor at the side of the device and gasped. It looked like he was functioning on pure adrenaline. Elevated everything. Scary. The officer next to the body cage pushed the motion activation so that it lifted off the floor and hovered, awaiting his voice commands. As the cage disappeared out the door, one of Goff's eyes opened and glared at the Director as Goff howled like a wolf. "You've failed, and you will be made to pay the price!" he said in a low, threatening voice said through the closing door.

Failed, my ass, the Director thought. I'll have the whole thing wrapped up soon. Stan must have some ideas about where the perps might be hiding.

At last, Alex and Meg finally stood before the front door of her favorite house. She knocked urgently. The door opened, Hisako gasped, and Meg flew into her arms. Hisako called loudly for Mark as Meg whimpered in pain, "Sorry! Ribs! I think two at least are cracked." Hisako backed up, concerned, but holding Meg by the shoulder.

"May we come in?" Alex asked. "And quickly?"

The two were pulled swiftly inside. Hisako held Meg at arm's length. "You're the most beautiful thing I've seen in a long time! We were so worried!"

Meg smiled weakly and shook her head. "I doubt I'm all that beautiful with these bandages and bruises. This is Alex. He rescued me from . . . well, it's a long story."

"Ah yes," Hisako said, nodding and tilting her head to look him in the eye. "So this is Alex. We've heard a lot about this young man." She looked back at Meg, her voice full of concern. "Those bandages and bruises, I'll take a look at them."

Mark came into the foyer on the run. Alex started to speak, but he raised a hand. "We must get you up the mountain. Come with us. There are some extremely concerned people waiting up there who'll be overjoyed to see you. We'll look you over more closely up there, Meg."

"And," he added, "the sooner we get you two out of sight, the better."

Meg was near total exhaustion. She leaned heavily on Mark as they set off, out the back door of the house.

UNIQUELY POSITIONED

"You put two and two together, sometimes you get four, sometimes you get 22."
—Dashiell Hammett

He'd only arrived that morning, but already Jason was at work as Mister Space Program as Izgad called him in a sarcastic whisper. After the day's convoys and the public appearances, Jason was left alone. He decided to slide by the silo factory where some of his pod mates were working. They had all heard of his being one of the few collectors to make it back home with a full load. They clapped him on the back and gathered around him. The ones who had worked on his silo had become the envy of all their friends. They asked him how he had enjoyed the limousine they had made for him to cruise the star systems, and he made appropriately disparaging remarks. Their shift was nearly over, and when quitting time came, Jason and his mates headed for the closest watering hole for a beer. They asked Jason a thousand questions, and he answered them all with his customary humor.

"What was it like being alone up there in the sky?"

"Alone? Are you forgetting Harry here?" Harry wagged, and Izgad wisely said nothing, having been warned by Jason that talking dogs would be caged and either experimented on or put down.

"I'll bet all the girls are lining up to spin with you," someone else said, "you sly rascal!"

Jason laughed. "Well, it's kinda nice, I mean all the attention." He figured it would now seem natural to ask the question he had been wanting to ask ever since he got back. "Has anyone seen that, uh, what was her name? Meg 4k6 something? We had a fun time together before I climbed into that leaky silo."

Everyone got quiet. Some looked down. One of Jason's friends looked at him intently. "Meg's on the list of people the authorities are looking for, people they want to interrogate . . ."

"What? What're you talking about?"

"There was a subversive group plotting to hurt a lot of people and perhaps start an outbreak. They even had a rogue enforcer with them. Meg was one of those the report mentioned. There's not a lot of detail on the government channels but it's been all over the dark net. There was a raid yesterday and now this afternoon it's turned into a manhunt. It's pretty exciting, even though those guys don't have a chance in hell. They'll probably be apprehended and erased by tomorrow. I could show you some of the comm footage taken by some guys who were on the scene . . ."

"But there must be some mistake. Meg's cool! She's just a researcher, for crying out loud. She's not a threat to anyone! What's she been doing that the Entente thinks is a danger?"

"Look, Jason, we were just as surprised as you to see her name come up."

"Who else are they talking about?" Jason asked, trying to sound unconcerned.

"Do you know Alex cx94b and Jill 89k3g?"

"Well, I think I heard Meg talk about some lady named Jill at work, and of course, everybody's heard of Alex. But what's he doing with Meg and Jill? He's big-time. A legend."

"Yeah, well, he was. Word now is that he may be contagious and at the least, extremely dangerous. Everyone is supposed to keep a sharp eye out for him, make no move to apprehend him, and to call it in if he's sighted anywhere."

"I understand something now," Izgad said quietly. "Change the subject."

"Did you hear a voice?" one of the guys asked.

Jason smiled. "Well, I have a lot of catching up to do, it seems. Has anyone tried the new uni with the twin-coupled snorkels?"

Three of them had taken them up Mount Jackson, and soon everyone was off on the new tangent.

Jason left the gathering as soon as he could make an excuse to do so. When he was alone with Izgad, he looked down at him. "What was that?"

"Absolutely intriguing. Did you sense anything odd in that room?"

"I've been gone a while, Izgad. Every single thing is odd and new after whatever happened to me that you and Harry seem to know all about. I'm getting used to talking with human beings and seeing faces. I could smell what they've been eating. I had forgotten that people smell like stuff. What was odd in the room?"

"Nothing seemed odd?"

"OK. Maybe it was weird to hear that Meg is on the run. She was just a cool, fun-loving person. I liked her. As you know and have remarked, I thought of her a lot while I was out there. I can't imagine what could happen to make her a person of interest to the state. And Alex! He's the poster boy of honesty and integrity as well as cool nerves and smooth operation. I didn't know Jill, but if she's a friend of Meg's, she's got to have something going for her."

"You know, you are a genius, and I am using the form of wit called sarcasm. You missed the most important part. Jason, they all look up to you like they never used to."

"What? No, it's just the novelty. I'm a freak show in the middle of their boring lives."

"Keep telling yourself that. It is probably healthier than thinking what I am thinking."

"What are you thinking?"

"That we could take advantage of your temporary hero status and use that before you become involved and get labeled as an enemy of the state."

"Me? An enemy of the state? Are you nuts? I'm not getting involved. I'm going to enjoy some well-earned rest!"

"With whom?"

"Well, I might look up some old friends, or I might just get away by myself!"

"Sure. Being by yourself would be a real change over your last year and a half . . ."

"You're really something, you know that?"

"Is that a figure of speech? Because it seems a little obvious that I am something."

"I mean you're hard to take sometimes. Why in the world would I get messed up with some people in trouble like those guys? I'm not a halfwit."

"No, but you think like one sometimes."

"How so?"

"What's your evaluation of Meg 4k6p3? It seems you just described her as a cool person, and while I have no idea what her thermal qualities have to do with anything, I understood from what you said that you not only like her, but you admire her for having special and admirable qualities."

"Well, yeah, I guess so."

"You do not guess so; you know so."

"OK, smarty pants. Man, it's tough to take you seriously when you're talking out of Harry's face."

"What has that got to do with it? You think very highly of Meg and her ability to make the right choices."

"It's not that. It's just . . . OK, say you're right."

"I am right."

"No, I mean . . . let's imagine you're correct about this. What does any of this have to do with my hero status?"

"Everything. You are uniquely positioned to help those three people at this very moment. Before you yourself become a target of the powers."

"Me? A target?"

"You heard me."

"I'm not going to do anything to make myself a target. I'm just an . . . an interstellar bag man."

"Exactly. And the one who sent me is in the business of using people who have no idea about their own importance. I just realized that I am starving. At least, Harry is asking me if we can have a couple of raw slab sirloins, whatever those are."

It wasn't long before the aforementioned steaks were delivered and consumed: Jason's medium rare and Harry's raw. Harry was now snoring at Jason's feet as he sat on his new apartment porch within the space-industrial complex building overlooking downtown Chaldea.

Jason was miffed. It was hard to be upset with Izgad. After all, he was just a nearly limitless being inside a dog's body. But it was deeply unsettling to be told he was . . . what was the phrase? Uniquely positioned.

Jason had no worries about being used by great purposes he did not understand. His life was basically one big involvement with some great purpose or other that was nebulous and out of reach. That's what beer and friends were for—to get away from whatever some great purpose was demanding of them all at the moment.

Hold it. Didn't Izgad say he would become an enemy of the state? That's nuts.

But is it? he wondered. Fighting for you! Jason chuckled. For most of his life, the phrase was automatic. No one gave it a second thought. Like saying hello or goodbye. Actually more like sneezing or yawning. It just came out and no one paid particular attention to any content contained in the phrases. Every now and then, someone would wonder about the chatter they all spoke, but when those people became too loud (which wasn't often), they disappeared one day, never to return.

But Jason was not stupid. Whatever ideas he had, he knew that careless thoughts could become crimes if spoken aloud. He was comfortable with examining big ideas without the help of others, since he never knew whom he could trust. And here was a lulu.

Uniquely positioned? For what? By whom? And why? Why was always the biggie.

Accustomed as he was to being a pawn in some grand scheme he did not understand, it didn't stop him from trying to guess what was going on. Why was he the one in this unique position? And who had put him there?

He wasn't anything special. One of Jason's strong suits was his clinical and calculated evaluation of his own talents. He wasn't the brightest, the most athletic, the best looking, or the most connected. He was sort of good at everything, but there were always guys who were better. He laughed at the thought.

The noise made Harry reposition his head to the side away from Jason.

He had no superlative qualities except his inability to stop himself from evaluating large ideas. And he couldn't possibly know if this was unique since he suspected that if anyone else had thoughts similar to his, they would keep them private and not go blabbing around like a moron.

So, he was right back where he started. He dropped the what, why and who questions since he felt powerless to answer them. He was extremely uncomfortable thinking about giving up any part of his newfound popularity to join in some hare-brained adventure with Meg and her friends. It was nuts to think they could be dangerous outlaws. Probably just a misunderstanding. No need to get involved or ask any questions. It would all work out.

In the meantime, he had plans. Plans to enjoy his fame and fortune. To do the public appearances they wanted out of him. That was a good thing. He'd be helping people by doing what was required of him. That's really all anyone could expect from life, right? Just keep your head down and do your best.

And then just be free to sleep and wander and enjoy. Chase rabbit trails in the woods and in his mind.

And hope that Meg was going to be all right.

STAN THE MAN

*"Jerry, just remember,
it's not a lie if you believe it."*
George Costanza

Late that afternoon when the Director got back to his office, he had several messages waiting. He filed them, his mind filled with a new approach to turtle.376 that he should have tried already. He pressed his wrist comm.

"Would you send in some coffee and a tuna fish on sourdough? And tell Stan to come see me. Now."

He had removed his jacket and was standing in front of his huge window with his back to the door. Stan knocked and hearing the Director's invitation, stepped inside and advanced a few steps.

"You sent for me, sir?"

The Director did not turn to face Stan. There was something powerfully assertive in talking to someone with his back to them. As he continued to let his eyes caress the city that he protected, he nodded. "Yes. There's something bothering me." The Director was using a time-honored approach to making his target unsure and uncomfortable. He said no more. The silence grew.

"Sir?" Stan prompted with what he hoped was a casual smile in his tone.

Still silence. And then, "I'm not convinced you've told me everything about Jill 89k3g. Before running into her during your escape, how often had you two connected?"

"Sir, it's all there in my report. I hadn't seen her for probably ten... maybe ten years or so."

"Do you honestly expect me to believe that?"

"Sir, it's true."

"Describe her to me."

"Slender. Blonde. Athletic. Ponytail."

"Does she ever wear a ball cap and sunglasses?"

"Sir?"

The time of maximum impact for his pivot had arrived. The Director wheeled to face Stan, leaning forward on his desk with both fists supporting his large frame that had seemed to grow even larger and staring icicles straight at his victim. "Where is she now, Stan?"

Stan made himself look as calm and composed as could be expected, but at the same time, tried not to overdo it. "I lost track of her on the night of the raid. When I left to get recaptured, she was still in the target building. There was no way I could keep track of her. She was supposed to get picked up at the tran I left. Did she not?"

The Director shook his head. "You're a horrible liar, Stan."

"Sir?" Stan's heart skipped a beat.

"You heard me. You think I don't know what was going on with your secret little group?"

"I . . . I don't follow you, Director, sir."

"You read those books. Contraband books. Books that infect and weaken our people. Books that spread the Sickness. Books we learned since the Reorganization were just . . . not meant to be read."

"I? Read the books? Sir?"

"Stan, I know you have a high opinion of your intellectual capabilities. That's healthy in someone who works for me. But I wonder sometimes if you are aware of my own."

"I'm not sure I understand what we're—"

The Director exploded, and the room rang with the roar of his voice. "You're playing your own little game of hide-and-seek in your reports, but I KNOW how involved you were within this group of yours, especially with your slender blonde!! She recruited you to their perverted views!! The two of you have actually been seeing a lot of each other for a long time, and both of you are up to your damn eyeballs in these disgusting books!!!"

The Director came slowly around the desk to stand towering above Stan, his words steady and soft. "But it's over. You either tell me where they are, or so help me I will take your brain apart like it was a Reorganization turkey being cut up for leftovers and soup."

Stan did a quick calculation. His internal alarms were firing. He had to play this right. People who messed with the state disappeared. Dead or imprisoned, it didn't matter since no one came back from either. He made a supreme effort to derail every other thought except for the innocent surprise he hoped showed on his face. "You're concerned about the impact of those books on me? Sir, if the books were getting to me, I would have put that in my reports! And I sure as hell wouldn't have shown up at the recapture coordinates! You're just messing with me, aren't you, sir?"

Twenty long seconds went by in which the Director locked eyes with Stan. No words were spoken.

Stan knew that his guess had been correct as he read his boss's face while divesting himself of every other assumed personality identifier but a trusted soldier being unfairly accused by his beloved commander.

As for the Director, he was so sure he had been right, but Stan couldn't possibly be this good a liar. Nobody could be taken by surprise and so easily hide their fear of discovery. The Director didn't move a facial muscle as he pondered his situation. Oh well, it was worth a shot in the dark. His recovery smile began at one corner of his mouth, and his eyes turned into twinkly slits. He was accustomed to being thought of as the funniest man in the world, and he knew why that was. Fear. Stan was afraid of him, and that was good.

His test was at an end. To all appearances, Stan was telling him the truth. *I had to check*, he told himself, while out loud he said, "Sit down, Stan. Take a load off."

He returned to his desk and sat, a fatherly smile on his face. Leaning back, arms crossed. "Next assignment. I want you to take the point with one of the groups that's trying to locate where these clowns have vanished to. As you know, I've kept your reports to a bare minimum with my team so that they stay objective and uninvolved with you personally. They know you were picked up in the raid. I'll bet some of your colleagues will be mighty glad to see you again, and a couple may have some questions for you. What are you hungry for?"

As he said these words, the Director touched his communicator. Stan considered. "Shaved beef submarine with horseradish and a lemonade tea." The Director made sure Stan's sandwich was on its way.

Crossing one leg on the couch by the wall, Stan relaxed slowly without appearing to have any need to relax and soon realized he no longer had to fake normal breathing. He was holding his arms just far enough away from his body so the sweat didn't leak on his shirt.

The sandwiches came, and the Director once again turned to the window. As they ate in silence, Stan had time to wonder. Facing his own mortality just now, he realized that his survival instinct far outweighed his suicidal flights of fancy. He was a survivor. He was still alive.

The only reason he wasn't shaking and crying was his ability to deceive himself that he honestly was unaffiliated to either side of the present conflict. If there were no personal danger, he would gladly throw in with the book-club idealists. But the risk was too great, the nearness of death too close. He would continue as long as he could, the pet monkey of the state, all the while imagining himself as the hero of Jack and the Beanstalk, playing his dangerous game in the very house of the giants.

The Director chewed loudly while talking to someone on his wrist comm, rocking back and forth while gazing out the window.

Stan kept one eye on him. *What do I think I'm doing?* he wondered. Whose side am I on? And how did I get myself into this mess? It's just a matter of time before Jill and the others are caught, and when they are, I'll undoubtedly be brought in to testify against them. What will I say? How will I be able to look them in the eye? Am I so cynical that I think I can stiff-arm the whole world and play this crazy charade of actually caring about either side? I can't see paying a visit to the Termination Center for a stack of stupid old books, and I can't see buying all this "Everything is unity" crap.

His thoughts raced back and forth between trying not to get himself killed and wondering if there was anything worth dying for. Girls were pretty cool, beer was fun, joyriding and racing on a bi were dangerous but still a kick every once in a while. What was life about? What was worth waking up for every day? Was it just to find the next thrill?

He was about done with thrills, and he was definitely done with great causes. Perhaps he was smart enough to wonder if the Director was just a stooge for an over-reaching government monster that wanted to crush the last particle of independence from it's citizens, but he knew he wasn't dumb enough to put himself in harm's way for any romantic drivel either.

Death was one thing he couldn't wiggle his way out of. He was, inevitably, going to die. And what was death, exactly? The last thrill? Or was it just a nothingness? Get hold of yourself! You sound like some of your pretentious friends back in philosophy class. Keep breathing!

The Director swiveled around and looked at Stan. "That was delicious," he said, the last bite of his lunch visible between his excellent teeth. "I've got two more swallows of coffee, and then let's head back to the gang. Oh, and I still don't want the team to have your intel about what the contraband actually was. You're aware of what might unavoidably happen to you if that becomes known. Plus, it's important to keep them objective and open-minded, searching under every rock. OK? Ready?"

Stan crammed his last bite into his mouth (it was actually three last bites) before answering. "Ready, sir!"

It wasn't far down the hall to the meeting theater. The Director told Stan to wait behind his private entryway until called for. With a pat on Stan's shoulder, he took a big breath and then slipped through the door into the room as a hush settled.

With a raised hand in greeting, his polished voice addressed his team. "Does anyone remember the day we started turtle.376? There was someone with us then who we sent forth from our ranks."

"Stan!" came the resounding reply.

"Righto!" the Director replied, beaming. "Well, we've got a surprise visitor here. Won't you join us . . . Stan?!"

As of this minute, you're a loyal subject of the state, Stan told himself as he popped out of the entryway with a convincingly shy smile. He stood shoulder to shoulder with Director Phelps and surveyed the wildly clapping group. He heard his name shouted by many in heroic admiration, and he waved with an expression he hoped was perceived as not only intrepid but also modest.

"As you no doubt remember, we sent this man to infiltrate this group we've had our eye on," the Director said as the applause died down. "He was able to fill in our outline of this little group. Our raid produced all the success we could wish for. But there's still a lot to be done. We need to root out the infection and clean this thing up. Let's have questions for Stan now. Type them in on the big board, and he'll answer them from up front."

There was a momentary pause, and then three questions flashed on the big board from three committee members. The first: "What was the nature of the gatherings?" The second: "Who was the leader of the group?" And the third: "Where is the group now?"

The Director sidestepped with raised eyebrows, motioning Stan to the spot where he had been standing.

"Well," Stan began, "I was honored to be chosen for this mission. The staged chase and arrest came off with near perfection...except for one thing. I guess it was just a bad break, but an enforcer who was not part of the operation got involved. He knew how to disable my locator in a way that none of you would like to experience. I thought my stomach was going to pop out of my mouth." Nervous laughter quickly died off. "When I got my bearings, I realized that an old friend, Jill 89k3g, was with the enforcer. You tracked her side business of pushing illegal books. I hadn't seen her in years, but it was just like we never lost touch. She immediately found me an alternate identity. They really believed giving me a beard and glasses would keep me under the radar from you guys!" More laughter. "But it wasn't all rainbows and unicorns. I woke up every morning wondering if I could maintain the deception. It's lonely out in the field. You feel like you'd give your right arm for someone to talk to and tell all the crazy stuff going around in your head."

"The name of the enforcer who disabled your locator?" someone asked.

"You know him already from the arrest report, Clay: Alex cx94b." Excited murmurings went around the room.

"You know Alex cx94b, Stan?" another committee member asked.

"Well, Alicia, I got to know him fairly well during that time. I saw him every so often, and we talked some. He's a scary dude. Believe the reports on some of the stuff they say he's done. He's an average-sized guy, but you just know he's the real deal. He was actually one of the more exciting parts of the mission."

"And now he's gone dark," a committee member said. "You say this Jill was your friend? Also missing. Do we know where she worked?"

Director Phelps stepped in to answer. "Check your blue folder for Jill's bio, Mark." Then he stepped back.

"No idea what exactly the group was into? Or for that matter where they are now?" a female committee member asked. "Really? That seems pretty lame for such an important mission, Stan."

Stan looked out at the woman who had fired the accusation. It was Eve kk6dt. Stan had taken a spin with her once, but she was not his type. She had wanted to do some pretty kinky stuff, and he had taken to avoiding her. It had developed into a fairly strained work situation.

He forced a smile. "I would definitely agree with you, Ellen," he said, deliberately botching her name. "I should have dug up more, and that's a weak showing on my part. But I was part of setting up the raid, and I was certain we were going to get a big score. Of course, I knew what Alex cx94b is capable of, but I didn't guess that the underground room was wired to blow sky-high. I came close to being erased myself, you know. You almost didn't get a chance to have my appearance here today, so you almost missed your opportunity to state the painfully obvious fact that we still haven't brought this thing home even after over four months of infiltration."

"The name's Eve," she replied sharply. The room became deathly quiet, so much so that the barely perceptible hum of the support tech in the room could be heard. "So how did it happen that you didn't prevent Alex from being in charge of the raid? Didn't he mess the whole thing up singlehandedly? Wasn't that complete ineptitude from you?"

Before Stan could stammer out a non-answer, the Director stepped in with his reassuring baritone. "It was vitally important that Stan make every effort not to get too close to Alex during the operation. As a master interrogator, Alex would have smelled us a mile away, and that would have blown the whole thing from the start. It was just unfortunate that he was the officer on duty when the op was downloaded that night."

The room nodded in unison. Eve's question may have been justified, but this room was not the place for disunity or negativity. She should know that. The Director was doing his best, and his best was better than anyone else's by a mile. The Director swept the room with determined eyes, speaking slowly in a measured and commanding voice. "Everything was on a hair trigger. Alex just got lucky. But his luck is running out. And the people in this room are going to track him down. We *will* find whatever hole he and that bunch have dived into. Then we'll wrap this whole sorry tangle into a nice neat ball and hang it on the wall of victory, right next to all of our other successes!"

The group was well aware that applause was called for at that point, and they supplied it. As the room filled with the sound of their clapping, the Director smiled and put his arm around Stan. "We'll get these guys!" he shouted over the roar of approval. "Everyone! Back to your posts! Fighting for you!"

"Everything is unity!" came the enthused response. The noise died down as they went back to work.

As he followed the Director out of the room, Stan glanced out at the team. Eve was staring bullets.

AVOIDING CAPTURE

The trouble is not in dying for a friend,
but in finding a friend worth dying for.
—Mark Twain

The days flew by as Alex anxiously tried to figure out how to escape, though he knew there was probably nowhere to go. At least Meg had been healing nicely. The seven of them had time to talk and get to know each other well, often sharing meals. Mark and Nando spent a lot of time fiddling with the electronics and made a serious dent in the beer supply. Madeline and Hisako also became very close and, over numerous pots of tea, admired each other's wisdom and courage. Alex taught Jill and Meg Canasta, Bridge and Poker.

None of the companions could envision what escape might look like or how it could be accomplished. They thought about trying to leave the city and head up high into the mountains or even head for the small coastal towns in the northwest of Neotropa or to another continent, but it was a small planet. The Entente could find anyone they really wanted to.

Alex knew this respite would be short lived. Sooner or later—and sooner was more likely because it was only a matter of time—Meg's sponsors would be visited by an interrogation squad, and although he had been comprehensively training Mark and Hisako, he could see they wouldn't hold up long. It wasn't their fault; they were honest through and through, and couldn't be reasonably expected to misdirect forever. Plus, he decided he didn't want them in any more trouble than necessary and told them that if they could only stall a few minutes by simply pretending to be bewildered, that might give he and his friends enough time to make a break for it. But that was hopeless too. He didn't want to leave Mark and Hisako to suffer whatever the state dealt out for harboring fugitives, and he didn't see a way the five friends could evade capture when the search got around to focus on Nedney.

The day Mark and Hisako's names became the focus of the post-raid operation, it was game over. The techniques at the disposal of the state for harvesting information from citizens were too effective.

Alex doubted if even he could hold out for long.

But no regrets. He would rather have had this experience than never to have read a dangerous book or had the chance to enjoy friendship like this. To be part of whatever this was. When he joined the enforcers, he had hoped for a sense of great purpose, but the deeper he went, the shallower it got and the greater his disillusionment. Meeting Jill that day had opened a door out of the crush of conformity.

Alex knew now why the state wanted these books destroyed. He knew that the Sickness wasn't something someone got when someone accidentally sneezed on them; it was something people could only contract by being exposed to the kind of outlook that these books contained. There was . . . light in them. Hope, a sense that there actually was right and wrong, that morality was not just an arbitrary construct.

There was something real, unchangeable. Alex hadn't gotten farther than that, but that was enough for now: to know that this life was more than what it seemed on the surface.

They shared the daily chores. Whatever needed doing, they pulled together and got it done. There was no automation, no AI, no mechanical servants. Whatever the task, there were always plenty of volunteers.

Meg was peeling carrots and potatoes, and as she worked, she discovered an odd condition of her heart. Gratitude had become a large part of her awareness. This was an emotion she had often experienced during the joy of a particularly engaging passage in her favorite books. And there was something troubling about it: she felt as if it should be directed somewhere. She wondered about this yearning to have a locus for her newfound appreciation. Could the universe possibly fill this void?

Something was worth gratitude. Something deserved a word of thanks. Maybe that "something" didn't exist. Maybe the cosmos, as she had often suspected, was a riddle that would cheat an honest enquirer in the end. All this stuff that seemed to point to design and purpose was probably illusory.

Jill wanted to know more about Meg's long-standing relationship with her sponsors. She made several clandestine trips to the house, where she and Hisako would talk quietly together in the unfinished attic where Hisako kept her colorful keepsakes. As well as being a medical professional, Hisako had spent a lot of time in the theater, and the trunks were full of costumes, props, and makeup. The wondrous and surreal room itself seemed part of the mysterious world where progeny and progenitors developed attachments and wished to remain together until the progeny was ready to begin to raise their own brood.

She felt her understanding of the world was being pulled up by the roots and was amazed at how easy it was to rip up her former perception of reality and how firmly it was being replaced by this newly discovered one.

Because of drone surveillance, the companions seldom went out without concealing their faces, even at night. They never knew when an eye in the sky would appear out of nowhere and ID them. Trips were brief. They even kept their visits to the house brief and felt like the fewer the visits, the less the danger for Mark and Hisako.

Hisako bought lots of fresh produce for everyone to supplement their diet of stored food. By the most wonderful of coincidences, the local community center was offering an ancient civilizations class in which time-honored methods of food preservation were an elective badge. The grocers thought she was pickling, brining, drying, and salting the large quantity of food, which she was actually smuggling up the hill to her charges.

Meg couldn't help but notice all the fanfare around Jason and his return. She had no idea she had spun with a future "hero of the people." She laughed. Though not bad looking, he was not all that photogenic, but his dog sure was. What an expression that animal wore! Almost as if a great intelligence lay behind its eyes . . .

The friends had their smuggled books to read and the radio to listen to, but they had precious little else to while away the time. They studied maps of the land to the west over the mountains. Perhaps they might even find a spot on one of the thousands of newly ice-free tropical islands floating in the center sea of Neotropa, anywhere that wasn't densely populated and monitored.

Mark and Hisako would often join them, using the holograms that Nando constructed for them.

Time and time again, their searches came up empty, and they all came to realize that as much as they might wish to begin a secret new colony where they would be left alone, there was slim to no hope, and slim was barely hanging on.

"Listen, you guys," Alex told them one day. "Here's what it boils down to. We must get the Entente to presume we're dead to get them to stop looking for us. I've been giving this a lot of thought. To convince them, we'll need them to find our corpses. And to trick them into thinking they've found our corpses, we'll need some actual dead people. Did you know the city morgue is just southwest of Nedney? If we get our hands on the cremation schedule, we can pick a day when they have a lot of business and maybe pull a switch. There's usually only one furnace operator. We'll make him wonder why he's missing a day in his life and suspect it was something he drank, which will be true. We can put some farm animals in the furnace instead of human cadavers. Then we can steal a quad, crash it somewhere with the bodies in it, and leave some signs that indicate a strong possibility that we were in that quad. Not too obvious but not too hard to discover. The crash will be analyzed; the furnace will not."

Jill laughed. "So, all we've got to do is approach a couple of large and dangerous farm creatures we know nothing about, persuade them to ride with us, surprise the furnace attendant at the morgue and, after surprising him or her, get him or her to drink something oddly suspicious without triggering an alarm, cremate the animals instead of the people, grab the human bodies, secretly stage a deadly crash after defeating all vehicular safety and tracking programs—"

Hisako jumped in via her hologram. "Convincingly stage a fake scene that will flummox the highly trained and presumably intelligent government technicians, make a water-powered vehicle explode for some unknown reason, and then all return undetected to this cave. Piece of cake!"

Alex smiled, joining in their amusement. He looked around at the group, nodding. "Sure, it's nutty. More than that, it's desperate, insane. But I've been going over and over in my mind what's next for us, as I'm sure you all have. Have you guys come up with anything workable?"

His question was met by silence as heads shook in a circular roll call of negatives.

"Well, we've got to do something," Alex continued, "and soon. I agree that my plan is loopy, and if any of you guys don't want to join me, I totally understand that. We've all taken so many chances, and I know you're thinking that sooner or later the odds will catch up with us. And they will. If we can't get them to stop looking for us, they're sure to eventually run us to ground."

He turned to Jill and Hisako. "Since you so perceptively nailed my plan, you probably realize that you correctly identified the greatest challenge to it: figuring out how to convince the Entente's foremost experts in criminal detection that they're looking at the final resting place of our incinerated bodies. That won't be easy, especially once they begin to examine the crash site in depth."

Nando spoke, "I'd put our chances at one in a couple hundred. Sounds like child's play. So!" A broad grin stretched across his face. "Shall we?"

Jill cleared her throat. "After sitting around here with no hope for a lasting future, it actually...sounds like a lot of fun!"

Madeline agreed. "We could either cower in fear in this cave until they find us, or we could try to alter the inevitability of our recapture. Staying here has an expiration date. I want to seize the hope we were given by coming to this blessed place."

Meg laughed. "Sounds to me like one of those impetuous and impossible prayers from the Book of Esaias!"

Mark offered support. "If you decide to try this, we'll gladly do our part. I wish there were an approach that involved less risk. But just sitting here waiting is getting on my nerves too."

No one could think of an alternative. They all knew Alex's plan probably had as good a chance as any, and there was no way they could stay in the cave forever. They might as well try a plan that barely had a chance rather than know their recapture was guaranteed if they could not disappear soon.

They all voted to try Alex's plan. Time was the most precious thing in their lives at the moment, and they wanted to buy as much of it as possible. Meg remembered a history book she'd read in the library. "To quote old Titus Livius, 'There is nothing man will not attempt when great enterprises hold out the promise of great rewards!'"

"My sponsors used to say, 'No risk it no biscuit,'" Nando muttered. It's not Livius, but it works."

They wholeheartedly threw themselves into planning their own destruction, at least, the appearance of it.

THE BEST-LAID PLANS

*"Every man's life ends the same way. It is only
the details of how he lived and how he died
that distinguish one man from another."*
—Ernest Hemingway

The companions were grateful to have something to do, something to push the worry of being caught to the back of their minds. It was the first time they had a chance to act as a unit, as a team. They valued each other and began to realize that they were all made of tougher stuff than might have been evident previously.

If they could avoid capture for a little longer, Jill told them over supper one night, they might have time to explore the cave behind them, see how far it went, and determine how it might aid them in the future as far as coming and going unseen. But still, they'd have to make risky trips for food and supplies. Not a permanent solution.

Nando explained that he was working on a holographic program that might cloak their location, but so far, the rocks of the mountain themselves were their greatest ally in that regard. But even if he could write such a program, he admitted it would require massive amounts of power for the illusion to work, which would be self-defeating.

Time and time again, they were forced to realize that dropping off the map could probably only happen if the authorities could be convinced of their deaths.

To that end, Alex located a pig farm near the morgue. It had several trailers that would be suitable for the beasts. Security was lax, and they doubted if the record-keeping was tight enough to trigger an alarm if their numbers were off one day.

They needed to tell the tale of five deaths, so their visit to the morgue had to be on a day when a lot of bodies were scheduled for the furnace.

Adding to their growing feeling of vulnerability was the unnerving fact that so many things had to line up for the plan to work. They wondered if they were helping or hurting by drawing attention to their disappearance. But it was an unavoidable conclusion that at some point, they had to try to change their odds. And they were amazed that, so far, their efforts at evading the enforcers—from the early warning of the library raid until Alex and Meg's arrival—had bordered on the supernatural.

Alex felt the burden more keenly perhaps than the others. He had a clearer idea than they did what the state was capable of and the muscle it could bring to bear on a problem. He also knew that Director Phelps's committee would not stop looking under every rock to find and make an example of them. To the people on the committee, it was a game, but to the Director and the powers behind the state, incidents like the botched raid at the library threatened their authority to rule as well as their ability to control. One might think that the Entente could misplace a few citizens every now and then, and the less said the better, but that was not their way. They keenly felt how tenuous was the coefficient of fear that held their society together. The state needed to make examples of troublemakers or else risk losing hold of the puppet strings.

Dominion, cradle to grave. The benevolent state claimed to exist for the common good, at least, the common good as they defined it. *Our values* was the way they put it, because *our values* had no specific meaning. In other words, since it could mean anything, it meant nothing. It became the perfect justification for any behavior whatsoever. Want to do something? Want to neglect something? Want to destroy something or support something or acquire more of something? Just announce it's got to be done or neglected or destroyed or supported or acquired because of...our values.

And besides bypassing ancient moral constraints on their way to controlling a population, the state knew there was an indispensable key to producing a progressive society--the nebulous and mythical promise of safety and security.

To access this promise by the state, the citizenry must relinquish all personal responsibility for taking risks. What was required in exchange for safety was, in effect, freedom. Freedom to fail but also freedom to succeed. Freedom to tempt death, but also freedom to discover life, for only the man prepared to die can ever truly be said to have lived.

Only those who momentarily undervalued freedom would ever trade it for the empty promise of safety and security. And so in all of human history, it was in moments of crises when governments were able to annex the self-determination of the individual and transfer that as sovereignty to itself. Such a crisis was the rotational shift. Such a crisis was the resulting destabilization. Such a crisis was the Reorganization and the birth of the Entente.

So the pledge to provide safety and security was the bait the totalitarian state offered to its subjects, the lure by which the population was ensnared. For that promise to have teeth, the state required absolute control over all variables. It was easier to manage docile cows in a fenced area than wild horses on the free range. Herding cows from place to place was child's play. In fact, it was precisely the children in times past who were the ones used as cowherds. Sure, occasionally some cows were unruly, but they were usually the first to disappear on a night when meat was served at the table.

Having gotten a consensus on his project, Alex began to plan in earnest. Locating a hog farmer with sloppy record keeping was child's play. Finding out when a bunch of bodies were being incinerated at the morgue was nothing. Even stealing a couple of quads and a trailer would merely require seconds for someone with his training. But doing all of this under the radar and without attracting attention would be nearly impossible.

The quad would have to be stolen from a satellite lot to minimize correlation. Perhaps the lot attendant would write it off as a stunt by local kids. The pigs would most likely never be missed. The mortician's lost day would be too embarrassing to report.

But Alex knew there were teams using computer algorithms that could flag all kinds of seemingly unrelated anomalies. He worried that when the reports of illegal activity were entered into the system, someone might put some of the disjointed pieces together.

With any luck at all, he thought, we'll be long gone from here by then.

He knew the most challenging job by far would be to fool the crash scene processors. While they would rarely if ever suspect that someone was faking their own death, the tricky part would be to burn the bodies so much that identification would be impossible while still leaving enough residue to make them suspect it was the fugitives. He instructed his friends to gather anything that had their DNA—hair brushes, plastic bottles they had handled, traceable personal items—to be left at the crash site.

The crash also had to happen in a sector far from their present location. That would make for more travel, and all travel was risky. The most dangerous thing was probably a drone spotting a vehicle out of sector.

He sighed, tensed and relaxed his shoulders, and began again to work through the operation in his mind.

Madeline would stay at the cave to monitor official activity. Hisako would stay put too. In the early morning darkness, long before sunrise, Mark would drive them to one of several remote vehicle storage lots in the area. He would stop momentarily undercover to let them out and continue to a nearby twenty-four-hour waterstation to pick up some snacks to ensure he could easily explain his nocturnal trip. Then he would return home.

At the lot, they'd nab two vehicles and destroy their trackers. Nando would take one of the vehicles the long way to the crash site and wait to pick up the trio. Using the other quad, Jill, Meg, and Alex would raid the pig farm and take temporary charge of a trailer, to be returned the next night. The farmers probably had a better idea of the number of trailers they had than the number of pigs.

From there they'd proceed to the mortuary and then to a distant site southeast of the city to stage the crash.

As it turned out, their opportunity came almost immediately. A report came over the radio about a boat accident involving several locals. It was easy for Alex to discover when their bodies would be processed.

He was glad for the accelerated schedule. He knew that waiting too long would give the others too much time to think, too much time to fight against their natural fear.

Operation Fake Death was a go.

Hisako gave Alex a realistic beard and a pot belly. Jill got a large pair of glasses and a red wig. Nando sported a chest-length beard and bushy eyebrows. Meg went with pigtails and tight-fitting clothes that gave her youthful features the look of a sixteen-year-old. A bit of dark foundation transformed her complexion into a beautiful dark walnut. Alex laughed. "You look like someone from my branch of the family tree!"

Mark drove the quartet to the storage lot gate and was gone. Entering the well-lit building, they approached the sleepy night watchman. As they'd rehearsed, Meg explained that she'd left something important in her impounded quad that was now somewhere on the lot and had no problem charming the guy into getting him to bring a second and third quad out to the front for her to look through. The fellow probably wasn't awake enough to realize that the first quad was gone when he brought out the second, nor did he miss the second when he went to get the third, but on returning, he did wonder where the girl had gone. Whatever. He got paid by the hour, not by the number of transportation devices on the lot.

Nando was already off for his meandering trip to the crash site, and soon the trio had arrived at the hog farm, where all was dark and quiet. Without lights, it was a tense time of driving nearly blind across a couple of fields and through a number of gates to the sleeping herd. Jill had a wonderful memory of some fabulous sausages she'd discovered at a party and was appalled that something that tasted so delicious could smell so bad on the hoof.

Alex knew that attempting to round up a couple of large, active sows would be nearly impossible, so he had brought along his stun gun from his riot bag, a handy tool that no enforcer was ever without. He dialed the effect back after the first pig dropped to the ground like a stone. Obviously, a lighter setting was needed if he wanted the pigs to be able to walk. Working quickly, they separated three large and wobbly specimens, who allowed themselves to be prodded into the trailer.

They were out of the field and on the open road as the sun was coming up. As Meg looked in the mirror by the early morning light, she saw the first pig they'd knocked down struggling to stand, legs waving wildly in the air. "Sorry," she muttered, "but your day will be better than your friends in the trailer."

Their next stop was the mortuary. They pulled around back under some trees for cover from drones. They pulled on gloves so they wouldn't have to wipe afterwards. Jill swapped out her clear glasses for a pair of dark sunglasses and palmed a small capsule containing a liquid that Meg had concocted: triazlamine. It was a tasteless, quick-dissolving, fast-acting, long-lasting drug so long out of use that it might not even be in the diagnostic system if the poor mortician had himself examined after losing a day of his life.

With a last reassuring look from the other two, Jill breezed around front, pushed open the door, and was met by the one employee on duty who, without bothering to look up, told her she was lost and asked if he could redirect her.

Jill looked her target up and down, a hand on her tilted hip. "My! If I had known you were here, I would have made sure my quad had broken down in front of your building long before this."

The mortician, not used to being given a second glance from a woman, looked up in surprise. "You've . . . you broke down? May . . . may I be of service?"

Jill took a few suggestive steps forward. "Excuse me for staring, but I thought all the truly *delicious* men were taken. Are you spinning anyone currently? Of course not. Who'd leave you just lying around? You think they'd mind if we tried a few things? You look like you stay in great shape. You must be very experienced." She lightly bit her lower lip.

The poor mortician didn't stand a chance. "Well, I . . . I . . . I am in a r-r-relationship . . . I mean I sort of . . ." he replied as Jill's index finger motioned him to come around the counter and stand in front of her.

"I can just imagine a man like you would have to fight them off. Say, are you a Pisces? I noticed that poster on your wall."

The amount of time it took for him to look behind him at the abstract poster of a fish was just enough for Jill to drop her triazlamine into the cup of coffee he was holding in front of his pudgy middle. He turned back to her.

"Nope. L-L-Leo," he lied. "Some call me the . . . lion," he added with a weak smile. He moved closer to Jill. "In just a little bit, I'll have a . . . break, and I'll have some free time. What's on your m-m-mind, you . . . you gorgeous thing?"

Jill reached slowly for his cup. "I hope you don't mind me taking a drink of your coffee. Sharing coffee really turns me on."

She pretended to take a sip. "I've had to put up with synthetic for so long," she said in a baby voice. "Is this Arabica?"

The man shook his head. "I . . . really don't . . . I guess . . . I don't really know." He laughed. "But . . . um . . ."

Jill didn't wait for the silence to get awkward. "Would you like to see what my lipstick tastes like?" She pretended to swallow her sip, generously smudging her lipstick on the edge of the cup. "Mmmm . . ." she purred, then turned the cup and seductively held it up to his mouth with both hands.

He took the cup and tilted it to his mouth, taking a large swallow while watching her over the rim. Attempting, but horribly failing, to be sexually provocative, he stuck his tongue far into the coffee and drained the cup. Setting the cup on the counter, his roaming hands were just about to make contact with Jill when his eyes glazed over and rolled back into his head. Jill grabbed his hands and lowered him to the floor. Then she ran to the back and unlocked the door for her friends.

The pigs had regained their wits after the drive from the farm, so Alex took the edge off them again, careful to give them just enough juice to keep them workable. While he went to the front to deal with the sleeping mortician, Jill and Meg herded the pigs into the building and from there into the furnace room, then crowded them into the incinerator.

Before shutting the door, the girls mercifully gave the pigs the full force of the stun gun. The animals dropped in their tracks, never knowing the terror of being transformed into ash or, like their buddies back on the farm, breakfast. The controls were no problem, and soon the smell of burning flesh began rolling out of the smokestack above the facility, and the pigs were roasting at 900 degrees Celsius. Their ashes would be a good match for human ashes.

The bodies of the five unfortunate boaters were waiting in bags on their respective dollies and were wheeled out to the trailer.

In the front, Alex, though smaller than the sleeping mortician, easily deadlifted the man and took him to his office, then dropped him on a couch. Searching the lower-right desk drawer (*Why is this stuff always there?* he wondered), he grabbed a couple of lurid magazines and a bottle of scotch. He left the magazines strewn at the base of the couch with one open on the mortician's chest. He poured part of the liquid on the man's shirt and pants and some of it into an empty coffee mug on his desk. After placing the bottle in the man's hand several times to get a randomized set of prints, he let the bottle roll across the rug, spilling the rest. He had already noticed that there were no security cameras when he entered the building. Of course, he thought, who wants to see what happens at a morgue? Probably the less known, the better.

Heading back to the rear of the building, he double-checked the pig roast. The girls had rolled the bodies out on their carts, sliding them into the trailer—Meg couldn't help but whisper *I'm sorry!* every time—and had just returned to leave the carts where they got them. They all took one last look around for any traces of their visit as they prepared to leave.

"We've been lucky so far," Alex said. "We should be at the crash site early this afternoon."

At that moment, the back door banged open.

A NASTY SURPRISE

"The best thing you can give is the gift of possibility. And the best thing you can give each other is the pledge to go on protecting that gift in each other as long as you live."
—Paul Newman

The friends turned as they heard the sound of the back door slam wide open. They stood transfixed as the mortuary supervisor came barreling in, shouting angrily. "What's a frickin' cow trailer doing parked out back? We're not running a frickin' slaughterhouse here!" He stopped in his tracks when he saw the three friends. "What the frickin' hell? Who authorized you to be back here? This is the last straw for that no-good, lazy bum, Roger! No one should frickin' be back here! Are those today's bakings? They should have gone in separately! We don't frickin' burn people in groups. We need to give people their frickin' loved ones back with no frickin' intermingling! Show me some identification! I'm phoning this in! I'm not going to be reported for this man's frickin' incompetence!" He moved through the room as he was talking. A moment later, another angry cry came from Roger's office.

Alex had followed the man down the hall and, placing him in a standard hold, put him to sleep. "His memories are going to be a problem. I don't have the equipment to replace or remove them like I would if I were on a sanctioned operation. Do you have any more of the triazlamine? Could we get some of that into him and hope he's too embarrassed from waking up with his drunk employee to remember seeing us?"

"What if he suspects we stole some bodies and runs some tests on the ashes in the oven?" Meg wondered.

"Did he strike you as someone who would be sharp enough to frickin' do that?" Jill replied.

"I have three more capsules here in my frickin' pocket," Meg said, chuckling at their lame imitations.

Alex sighed in relief. "Great. Jill, watch the supervisor and yell if you see him twitch. I'll grab some fire accelerant from the back room and pull the quad and trailer up to the back door while Meg deals with this guy."

"You got it. If he so much as flares his nostrils, I'll know."

Alex wondered what the supervisor was doing there on a day when there was always only the one worker. Unusual behavior was what enforcers were trained to spot and suspect. It felt wrong. People in such jobs did not go above and beyond but instead could be counted upon to mail in the bare minimum, especially supervisors. "We need to leave!" he called from the back door. "Soon!"

"How do we get this into him?" Meg asked Jill.

"Give it here. My neighbor used to own a cat, and I had to poke medicine down his throat. Help me pry his mouth open. There." Jill made a face as she took Meg's capsule on the tip of her finger and forced it as far down the supervisor's throat as she could reach. "He should wake up about the same time as old Roger here, or whatever his frickin' name is."

"Now! Come now!" Alex called.

The girls ran out the back door. The three of them piled into the quad and were back on the road, heading around the outskirts of the city to avoid cameras and enforcers.

Alex was still turning the appearance of the supervisor over in his mind but soon gave up. Human behavior was unpredictable. They had accomplished two of their missions so far and were still alive and free. He was proud of the girls. For brainiacs, they had for sure shown their guts and coolness under fire.

The staged crash was the last part of the plan. It had been Meg who thought of picking up the fire accelerant from the incinerator supply room. She thought the team that processed the crash would hopefully be led to believe that they were building some weapon or other with the accelerant.

Alex contacted Nando to let him know they were on the way to the site. Every moment they were away, they were sitting ducks for any citizen who happened to notice them. Calm down, he told himself, slowing his breathing. If we make it undetected, you're worrying for nothing, and if we're spotted, being rattled won't help.

"Is there anything we should say to each other before we die?" Meg deadpanned from the back seat of the quad. She passed around the lunch they had packed. "I mean, if we're about to be cremated by accident on the side of the road, any last words, my friends?"

"Sure," Jill mumbled, her mouth full of food. "You owe me for that bet we made when we started at the plant. I said, with your looks, you'd be the first girl or boy molested by upper management. I wish I had been wrong, and I'm sorry you went through it, but I did win the bet."

"I meant anything mushy or sappy," Meg replied. "I'm fishing for sentiment here."

"As far as I'm concerned—" Alex began, but just then, two things happened. Meg began to cry, and Alex noticed a drone overhead. It seemed to be keeping pace with them.

"What's wrong, Meg?" Jill asked.

"The families of those folks in back are going to believe the ashes they receive from the morgue are their loved ones. I hate that we made it so they're going to get urns of pig ashes."

"Meg," Alex said as he watched the drone buzz out of sight, "There are only so many atoms on the surface of the planet, and we've been sharing those with everything that has ever lived and moved for some time. A little extra molecular swap is not going to upset any cosmological applecart!"

"Do you . . ." Meg started and then fell silent.

"What?" Jill asked.

"Nothing."

"Nothing?"

"I was just going to ask if you guys believe in the Plasm."

Jill shrugged, "It's either that or believe in some voodoo religious stuff. Mythology. Nursery stories."

Meg stared out the window. "But don't the nursery stories . . . I mean, don't they stir something in you?"

"They stir my imagination," Alex replied. "Sometimes I like the nursery stuff better than the stuff we know that's true. You can look at the passage of billions of years inevitably producing life on each planet, and it's kind of like knowing that if you let go of an object your holding, it will inevitably fall toward the center of the Earth. But to think of a super being just speaking the whole shooting match into existence is more exciting for me. If that had happened —and I know it didn't, but if it had—I would have loved to have been there to see it! What a show!"

Meg gazed out the window. "But that's just it. You say we know it couldn't have happened that way, but what if it . . . oh, never mind."

Alex and Jill glanced at their friend. Though a few months ago they might have been alarmed by such questions, she was giving voice to a growing unrest they felt in themselves. Old explanations were not wearing well.

They continued down the mostly deserted highway. Alex guessed the site was about thirty minutes away. Meg and Jill were talking to each other, and he was not needed in their conversation for the moment.

His mind went back to the drone. Was it on a standard patrol route? He didn't know what was normal in that sector. If the drone was tracking them, why? What had attracted its attention? The trailer? Could the hog farm have noticed something missing? Had they tripped a wire at the morgue? Had the supervisor phoned in something before he burst through that door?

Then another explanation came to mind. He glanced up again, but the drone was still gone. He hoped he was wrong. What if the drone had picked them up near Mark and Hisako's and had tracked them all through the day?

What if a surveillance team had been watching and reporting the entire time? What if this was all for nothing, and the desperate play they had made to stop all pursuit was the very act that would betray them, just as Stan had done at the library? The strange feeling was like having a tiny rock in his shoe while he was running. It was irritating but not enough for him to stop running and shake it out. He decided to say nothing of the drone to the others.

They met no one else along the road. Alex was still uneasy because they had probably dropped several clues behind them just waiting for some hyperactive data comber to discover and to trace their trail of activities through the day. If their luck held, they would be presumed dead before any of the pieces fell into place.

Meg noticed the concern on Alex's face. "Something worrying you? Me too. I'm going to ask the Plasm to get us safely back to the cave."

"You're what?" Jill sputtered.

"You heard me." Meg was resolute. "It's a matter of logic. If the Plasm's not real, what could it hurt? But if the Plasm exists, perhaps it doesn't mind people asking it for help. Now shut up. Dear Plasm, I don't know what you are, but if you're there, we need help. We just want to read our books in peace. We're not trying to overthrow the government—well, not much. And we're not hurting anyone. Will you help us? Thank you . . . um, yours truly. Meg."

Jill shook her head. "You're nuts, Meg, but I suppose you're right. It couldn't hurt, and it might help."

Worry won't change a thing, Alex told himself. We can only meet the moments as they come.

They arrived at the "crash" site without further incident. Nando was waiting. They unloaded the bodies from the trailer and somehow packed them into their quad, along with the accelerant and all the hair, spit, tissues, lipstick tubes, paper coffee cups, clothes from the hamper, and any other items they could collect that contained their skin, hair, or bodily fluids. Alex affixed some prints from Madeline and Nando to likely surface locations on the quad. Then they hitched the trailer to Nando's van.

While the others kept a lookout up by the road, Alex climbed in and started through the field toward a nearby grove of trees. He had no trouble letting the clue items drop randomly along the route in the rutted grass, tossing them out the window every so often. Stopping out of sight from the road, he tugged one of the corpses into the driver's seat and then used his knife to rip the bags off the bodies. It was disgusting work.

Finally, leaning in front of the cadaver in the driver's seat, he started the quad, engaged the autopilot, set the igniter to forty seconds, and pressed "Autopilot." He stepped away from the quad as it sped straight ahead for maybe a hundred yards, then burst into an orange-white ball of flames and slammed into a large tree, which also burst into flames.

In no time, a merry blaze was burning, which was visible from a little-used road in the southeast of Chaldea. Alex, Meg, and Jill had climbed in with Nando, and the four of them were heading back north.

They left the trailer on the road near the hog farm.

As the sun was setting, they paid a last visit to the storage lot, leaving Nando's quad behind, and took the glorious walk back to Mark and Hisako's in the starlit night.

As they drew near their house, the four of them still found it hard to believe they had navigated successfully through that anxious day, but it was becoming more of a reality in their minds with every step. Alex even forgot about the troublesome drone. They would pick up Madeline from the house and then head out back to the cave to celebrate.

As they gathered on the steps by the front door, they felt an inexpressible sense of relief. Perhaps now they would be forgotten.

"Made it!" Jill said, smiling.

Meg nodded in agreement. "Home sweet home."

Alex reached forward to knock, "Can't wait to tell them all the crazy stuff that happened today!"

To his surprise, the door opened before his knuckles could make contact.

"Welcome home," growled a smiling Director Phelps. "We've missed you. You've led us on quite the merry chase."

A CITIZEN'S RIGHTS

*"For the thing which I greatly feared
is come upon me."*
—Job

It had happened. The moment they had all lived in their nightmares. They were caught. It was over. Their minds were blank.

The Director's frame filled the doorway to Mark and Hisako's house. He stepped forward, and in an instant, the four were overwhelmed by enforcers. Mark, Hisako and Madelyn were brought out, and each was placed in a hovering containment frame that immobilized their arms, legs, torso and neck. They could have screamed—in fact, the Director had hoped they would for the sake of the night vision news cameras that were rolling—but they had seen this coming for too long to give him the pleasure of more than widened eyes.

The Director looked them over and then stopped in front of Alex. He shook his head with an air of fatherly disappointment. "Hello, son." Alex said nothing in reply.

Then the Director nodded with admiration to Meg. "This must be the little girl Goff couldn't handle. There's more spunk in you than most." Jill and Nando got nothing more than a glance. After a few pictures had been taken to complete the report, the Director gave a curt order. "Bring 'em!"

The captives were pushed into a waiting van where their containment frames were strapped to the walls. The Director stepped into the van and drew a stool up in front of Alex.

"You know, I may be gloating here, but it's because of my profound admiration for you. You now hold the all-time record for evading my team, my young friend. You're an amazing guy. You and I would have been great friends if we had met in better circumstances. I'll try to get some leniency for you and your friends if you can give me any help. The public sees you as a renegade group of domestic terrorists, exposing them to dangerous and explosive materials with the potential for an outbreak of the Sickness." His face softened. "But you know how that is. I can make a new story that will swallow that story up. I have no desire to put any of you through the wringer. What do you say? You're too smart not to see that I'm the only one who can help you now. For the sake of your friends. You have the power to save them or condemn them. Where have you hid your cache of books?"

Alex knew the director was lying to his face. This was a standard tactic he himself had often used to fish for information: a seemingly friendly approach that would be dropped the moment it was no longer needed. A slight shake of his head as he looked at the others let them know this offer was not what it seemed to be.

Alex maintained an unreadable expression.

The Director's smile vanished. "OK, have it your way, punk," he snapped. "I thought you might want to be helpful. The enforcers can ill afford to lose someone of your talents, but I imagine we'll make out somehow. I will definitely enjoy testifying against you at the hearing."

Alex had read about court cases in the past where these hearings were known as trials, but there was nothing to be tried anymore. People were simply brought before a callous magistrate and a bloodthirsty jury who did nothing more than decide what kind of punishment fit the accusation made by the state. There was not much presentation of evidence, and whatever was presented was totally one-sided. No arguments from a lawyer could change any verdict. People were considered guilty when arrested. Otherwise, why would they have been arrested in the first place?

The Director squared his shoulders, stood up, and stepped out of the van, leaving the door open as an impressive backdrop to the swarming press, who had been held back until his little talk with Alex was complete. This would be incredible breaking news in a few hours as a sleepy Chaldea awoke to a brilliant final chapter of another of the Director's sting operations. What a scoop! As their lights turned on to showcase his smiling, chiseled face, he began answering their questions.

"What? Yes, these are the last of the criminal group we have been seeking. We've already taken into custody three other members of the group. They're in the van with this last batch. . ."

"Yes, we believe they were involved in terrorist activities. . ."

"No, I assure you the movement is now finally contained, and in record time, I may add. We managed to plant a heroic citizen in their midst, and with his information and at the direction of my office, we were able to mortally cripple their organization in the initial raid that shut down their base of operations. Since then, it has been mostly mop up and analysis of the threat. These are the last. No citizens were hurt during this undertaking. . ."

"The nature of their activities? That's classified, but I'm sure it will come out in the hearing.. . . No, we're still deciding whether the hearing will be broadcast or whether we'll even allow news teams into the venue, but rest assured, justice will be served. These and the others we have corralled will be fairly convicted and justly sentenced. . ."

"Yes, we expect to conclude this matter quickly and add it to the string of recent successes our group has had in the last several years. Then it's on to the next threat. Fighting for you! Everything is unity!"

The Director held up two fists in the air for these last slogans and then waved a grand goodbye to the cameras and swung back into the vehicle with the prisoners and their guards. As the door closed, he strove to conceal his immense pleasure at the successful conclusion to yet another operation.

Of course, teasing the press that they might be kept out of the coming spectacle was just to whet their appetites. The Director was not a retiring personality, and there was no question of whether or not to broadcast the sentencing. No glory, no promotion, and no promotion, no power. He had already shot some of the flattering broadcast he had planned since Eve's group had first hit upon the idea of surveilling Meg's sponsors.

As they rode to the interrogation center downtown, the Director surveyed the four prisoners. So this was the enforcer he had heard so much about. Nothing physically commanding about him. Skin the color of dark coffee. Eyes quick and penetrating, concealing a mind that was obviously undaunted by his and his companions' situation. The Director wondered if he could be reclaimed chemically and given a new memory and identity but realized that re-braining science was still in its infancy. There were always test subjects, and perhaps Alex could be worked on. Sadly, the results of past experiments were not just disappointing––the screams, destructive behavior, and ceaseless bodily shakes and jerks of the poor subjects had necessitated termination after a few days of observation.

Eh! It was worth a try anyway. It was always good to have friends in Experimentation who owed him favors. The two older couples could be given to medical teams for vivisection. And the girls? With their youth and looks, they could be high-level servants for the northern pleasure houses. Nothing need be wasted. All of it would add to his already considerable cachet.

Suddenly Alex's voice sounded clearly and distinctly in the van, easily heard and recorded by every enforcer's body cam and sent on a live feed to the main building of records downtown. "As a citizen of Chaldea. I request an audio and visual record of my words to be made. I take full responsibility for the actions of these other prisoners, including the three citizens previously gathered, and request their immediate release. If not released, we may not be separated. I demand a public trial with a jury made up of citizens of my pod class. I further..."

The Director quickly made an adjustment on his communicator, and Alex's restriction included an inability to speak. Nevertheless, he knew Alex's words were accessible as a feed. He also knew that since being shooed away from the departing vehicle, every reporter would be glued to any feed from the general data servers.

How could he have been so careless? Why had he not ensured the prisoners were gagged after initial interrogation, as he had ordered? Someone would pay dearly for this oversight.

He sighed inwardly. This new development would be a pain. It wouldn't change the outcome, but it would prolong the process. The laws concerning Alex's maneuver were screwy, and he made a note: *needs to be updated.* A citizen of Chaldea had certain rights, and Alex had just deftly brought them into play. Now the seven prisoners could not be isolated in separate cells to be dealt with one by one, but must be housed together awaiting their trial. The trial would not necessarily end differently, but the jury would be an extra complication. He would have less control over the whole thing than he wished, and that introduced new variables.

Director Phelps hated variables.

The public would be entertained by the spectacle, and a few copycat clubs would form to mimic their sedition. Of course, they too would have to be smoked out and dealt with.

His triumphant smile gone, the Director began to put together a script for the trial that would be overwhelmingly one-sided and entertainingly decisive.

He grimly thought of the higher-ups in the Entente. They would be made cognizant of the glitch immediately, but they would not be concerned in the least about the volcanic potential of a looming public trial. If it went poorly, they would hang it all on him. If it were a success, they would step in and appropriate it.

Damn. Damn, damn, damn!

When the prisoner transport arrived at the massive downtown Chaldean Office of Domestic Equilibrium, the reporters were camped and waiting. They fired questions like shotgun blasts, but the Director just smiled and waved as he hurried the prisoners and their guards into the restricted quiet of the lobby leading to the containment cells on the basement access side of the building. The press was made to wait outside as officers began to process the new arrivals.

When the outside door had clicked, and the windows were made opaque, the Director wheeled on the nearest enforcer. "Who was in charge of the prisoner transport?"

"Um, sir, it was Officer xd435."

"Where is he?"

"Um, that's him over there with the captured enforcer, Alex."

"Thank you. Bring him to me."

"Sir? Um, yes, sir."

Officer Brian xd435 had been trying to get Alex to open up, but Alex had already said all he intended to say. Brian had been hoping that his failure to gag the prisoners electronically would be forgotten now they were in their block without further incident, but apparently, that was not to be. He held his head high with his chin up and covered the distance between himself and Director Phelps in what he hoped was a confident and competent stride. "Sir, you sent for me?"

"How long have you been out of school?"

"I don't understand, sir."

"Were you taught that prisoners should be allowed to blab away without restraint?"

"No, of course not, sir."

"Then why in the bloody hell did Alex get to request a trial by his pod class while riding to the CODE building? Do you realize the expense and the adverse publicity this trial will cost the citizens of Chaldea? Are you an incompetent doofus or just an ignorant imbecile?"

"Sir, I can explain, you see—"

The Director did not let him finish. The chewing out continued unabated, to the delight of all those within earshot. Blank expressions hid their exultation at overhearing such a delicious dressing down of their fellow. It was a rare spectacle, and they could each imagine themselves for many weeks to come being the center of attention at every party and bar as they told the story of "Brian the Incompetent Doofus" being sliced and diced.

Alex could no longer speak, but he could still hear. As they were being ushered into their cell, he smiled inwardly even as the thought of the next battle loomed. Alex was not one to passively accept fate if there was anything to be faced and fought. Although they would certainly not receive justice at the trial, every moment of exposure gave them a chance of somehow making it through this. He did not want to think about what awaited them if the trial went badly.

Even as he turned these things over in his mind, he marveled at their fortune, both bad and good. So many things had gone right. He suspected they must have had help of some kind—from what sector he could not imagine—or they would have been caught long ago. He remembered some of the odd thoughts Meg had been voicing lately and decided he'd sound her out further when he got the chance.

He was in awe not just at how everything was crashing down but at how long they had been able to escape detection before it all came apart at the seams. The surprising thing wasn't being caught; it was not being caught instantly.

Just to consider another bit of good fortune, Alex knew that, instead of being arrested and taken into custody, they could have been shot on sight and the whole thing staged to look as if there had been a firefight and the arresting officers had no choice but to shoot to kill.

Even though they were now incarcerated and awaiting almost certain death, Alex did not give in to despair. He wondered at his own state of mind.

Strangely, he felt a sense of relief at finally having reached the end of their race. There was no running from the Entente on this planet, but some sort of outside power was still rooting for them.

Wait, what was that thought?

No running from the Entente on this planet. On this planet. A light went off in his head, but he said nothing to anyone about his thoughts—not that he could.

The friends were reunited and mostly left to themselves in their cell, their restraints removed.

"If you look at the cameras, they're all turned off," Nando said. "We can speak openly. They're so afraid of catching the Sickness that we can count on a great deal of privacy in our high-class accommodations here!"

It was a kind of emotional release to be able to fill in gaps and tell the stories of that last day. Jill told their tale: the lot attendant's gullibility, the poor pig who went down like a stone before the stun level was reset, the mortician and the supervisor, the drone, and the scene at the door that night.

"I don't think they know about the cave," Madeline mouthed quietly facing away from the camera. "None of us were arrested anywhere near it."

"Although I don't see how that will help, I think it was wise to try to keep them from it," Alex said. "Perhaps one day someone will find that place and our books."

Madeline said she doubted anyone could stumble upon the cave. Or if they did, they probably would never find the books. She and Nando had done some of their best work concealing them in one of the large closets.

Alex told her she was probably right and then turned to Meg.

"In the quad this afternoon, you were talking about stuff you called bedtime stories. I've been wondering, not about our bad luck but about our extremely good luck through all this. It got me thinking about all the lessons we were taught in school. Gravity, electromagnetism, relativity, and quantum physics. Those things are all demonstrable, and above all, objective and dispassionate. But I don't understand why it follows that the Plasm has to be the only explanation for the universe. I mean, is it actually an explanation, or is it an inoculation?"

Jill laughed. "Inoculation?"

Alex nodded. "An inoculation to prevent us from catching a healthy case of curiosity. Not an answer but something to prevent us from seeking one. What if . . . I mean . . ." He paused and frowned in thought. "What if there is no impersonal guiding force? Or to put it differently, what if the Plasm is actually a mind?"

"Do you understand what you're saying?" Nando asked.

Alex was earnest. "I think I do. My impending death and all of us perhaps, coming to the end of our race. Well, it finds me fairly introspective. At least, I don't believe we've been given all the reasons why we were taught the things we were. I have a gnawing idea in the back of my mind that I believe was planted there by the books. It could be that the universe bears the marks of something we're missing, something like us but not like us. A Plasm with preferences. A Plasm . . ." He smiled at Jill who involuntarily blushed. ". . . that appreciates beauty. A Plasm that appreciates mind over muscle. Rational over irrational. Design over chaos. It may even have an unalterable morality. Unchangeable preferences for right over wrong."

"It sounds like we're going to have a philosophical party in here," Meg observed with a laugh. "Good. If we're going to be put on trial for our lives because we've been reading books that produce treacherous ideas, we should at least *enjoy* our treacherous ideas."

The friends sat close to one other and talked deeply about the troubling inconsistencies and the unexpected epiphanies they were encountering from their reading. The cell walls seemed less restrictive as their conversation let them wander freely and fearlessly through the delightful pages of those books, which were the root of their troubles and the buttress of their mutual strength.

As the trial began, a seemingly unrelated item hit the news wires. A quad accident with fatalities south of the city had been discovered.

Interestingly enough, the dead people from the crash seemed to also be on trial in the center of the city.

JASON'S EPIPHANY

On the day of the trial, Jason found it hard to find anything else on his screen. He had no calls to appear anywhere that day, his handlers having surrendered to the popularity of the hearing. They couldn't afford to have Jason's adoring crowd dwindle in the face of the competing spectacle of the terrorists. Of course, his handlers could do what they often did —hire a group to show up—but why spend money on an event that no one would be watching anyway?

As the pre-trial news documentaries on Director Phelps's brilliant team aired, Jason watched with interest in his bedroom, searching for the face that he had daydreamed about for over a year. Izgad and Harry were having a mid-morning snack in the kitchen.

There she was. Hmm. Yeah. Definitely pretty, but underneath? What did he actually know?

He began to struggle with his thoughts, and as he wrestled to make sense of it all, he became increasingly confused, anxious and alarmed.

What to think of Meg? Did he honestly know her? Had he fallen for a girl who wasn't at all the way he remembered? Had she deceived him? Was this beautiful, brainy lab chemist nothing more really than a petty criminal, a radical, an enemy of the people?

The room felt chilly. He began to think that maybe his newfound popularity could be used to really fight for the people in Chaldea. It was too precious to throw away on this bunch of antisocial rabble-rousers. Whatever they had done, they knew the risks.

Don't get involved, you chump, he advised himself. You have a nice position now and real power. You can finally make a difference in the world like no one else can. You're basically a good person, and the citizens need the comfort you can now give them.

Go along with these government people who are treating you so well. All they want is unity and peace for the good of everyone. What a great opportunity you've been handed on a silver platter. And you even get to keep the platter!

You deserve it too, pal. You've worked hard to get here. This Izgad fellow: how well do you know him? If you listen to him, you'll just get in trouble. He says he's a good guy, but of course he would say that.

He's dangerous. A spoilsport. A killjoy, and maybe he's been sent by sinister forces to drag you down and ruin you and all the good you're doing. You should tell him to leave. You should stand up to him. You should . . ."

At that moment, Harry walked into the bedroom. "Whatever thoughts you're thinking, they're not your thoughts, you know," Izgad said. "If you had my eyes, you could see that you, me, and Harry have been joined by a being of my kind. I have fought in battles against many of them. Was he telling you to take it easy and not make waves? To get along with your handlers and just enjoy the ride? To compromise your beliefs for the greater good you can do because of your power and prestige? Standard stuff. I have no idea why it almost always works on humans. Sex, possessions and pride are the weak points of your species, according to my training. But check your mind right now. Are you still befuddled? I mean more than usual. I'll bet not. That guy left not long after I entered the room..."

Jason wondered at his recent thoughts. "How do you know what I was thinking?"

"You weren't thinking; you were listening. He was doing your thinking for you, something I know you don't like and one of the reasons I respect you. You're your own man."

"I was thinking that maybe I don't know you."

"Were you?"

"I just told you I was."

"I know, but my question is, were you thinking that or was he doing your thinking for you?"

"Who's he?"

"I just told you, a being of my order. He was here when I walked in, but he left as soon as he saw me."

"There was someone else in the room? I didn't see anyone."

"If Harry wasn't giving me a ride, you would not see me either."

"So you're invisible?"

"No, I am extremely visible, but your eyes are not tuned to my frequency."

Jason smiled. "But what about the part where I was thinking that I don't know you?"

"How long have we known each other?"

"I don't know. Weeks."

"Fifty-five days. In all that time, is today the first time you have wondered if I was a . . . well, I have a choice of words here: a charlatan, quack, mountebank, sham, fraud, humbug, impostor, pretender, masquerader, hoodwinker, hoaxer, cheater, deceiver, dissembler . . ."

Jason laughed. "Stop! I get the idea. And, well . . . yeah, today is the first time I wondered about you."

"Do you think of yourself as slow on the uptake?"

"No, I don't."

"Would I not have alarmed you long ago if I were a threat? Would you not have sensed something off about me?"

"Um . . . I guess so." Another smile. "And all the time I was, as you say, listening to someone else talk before you came into the room, I sensed a kind of, well, a kind of cold darkness, if that makes sense."

"It does. The temperature of the room has actually dropped several degrees."

"Now that you mention it, it is a little chilly in here. Plus, I'm coming out of a weird mood. I had begun to think of myself quite highly. It was like the time when I was very young, and I ate every bit of my friend's birthday cake in the kitchen before the party even started and while his mom was welcoming the other kids. I felt like the world was all about me and getting whatever I wanted."

"Yes. That is the way the darkness thinks. Forget it. Or better yet, remember it and recognize when that other being is

264

whispering in your ear. So tell me, how soon before they start the proceedings?"

"A couple of hours. It's still early. I'm tired, and I wish I could go back to bed, but I need to fight through it. I haven't adjusted to this planet's time. We're not in solar rhythm yet, and sleeping while the sun is on the other side of the planet hasn't become normal. But if I go to sleep now, I won't ever adjust."

"Speaking of sleep, Harry tells me he needs to check on the bed in the kitchen. He thought it had a lump in it that you should mention to your staff."

Jason chuckled and then went to put on his exercise gear. He used to go for long bike rides early in the morning quite often. In his helmet and goggles, no one would recognize him. He needed to burn off some energy, and he had time before the hearing began. He checked himself out with his handler and then went down to the street.

As he pedaled furiously, Jason thought about the charges being brought against Meg and her friends: defiance of the government. He knew he was playing around with defiance himself, that his mind was rejecting his old understanding of how the world worked, that the things he had always believed were being examined and found wanting, and they had been doing so long before he met Izgad.

The thing that was sticking in his mind was the universe itself. He had been taught that it obeyed laws, which it did. Without those laws, there would be bedlam.

What if you were pouring milk on your cereal, and the stream of the milk went up instead of down or in any direction it chose?

What if gravity was seasonal or totally capricious?

Why was there such a force as gravity in the universe anyway?

Were there parallel universes where there was no gravity, as I was taught in physics classes?

The road sped by as he went faster and faster.

What about language? Why can I utter sounds with my tongue and oral cavity and vocal cords that excite a tympanic membrane in another person's aural canal? Why does everyone else have vocal cords and tympanic membranes, and how do they result in communication?

Why do the complex sounds we make and that others hear elicit meaning to that person?

How is language possible in an impersonal universe that built itself by chance from inert compounds into complex organisms by seemingly random actions operating over untold expanses of time?

His pedals were a blur, and the wind whistled in his ears . . .

Perhaps it's possible to make sounds that signal other organisms, but how am I able to think about these things? Where did my mind come from?

Jason came to a stop so fast that the gravel under his tires went flying into a nearby hedge. Looking down, he picked up a rock. It was wet from the sprinkler system of the perfect green lawn beyond the hedge. Beyond the hedge was a massive building of concrete, steel, and glass. He squinted at it.

Could that building have been built by chance acting over immense spans of time?

Is it conceivable that the walkway accidentally led to the door, when it could have led anywhere else?

Why does it lead specifically to the door?

Is it possible that the door accidentally has a hinged slab that allows a person to enter, that the floor inside is perfectly flat, that the ceiling is the exact height needed to allow human beings to walk upright and not feel claustrophobic?

Is it a coincidence that there's an exchange of air at a comfortable temperature in that lobby circulated by machines that came together haphazardly from the action of the sun's rays?

Is it an accident there's an elevator that can be used by human beings to travel upwards at great speed and with pinpoint accuracy take them to any of the floors above? Lifted by a cable fortuitously attached at one end to the car and also fortuitously at the other end to a spindle that is the perfect size and strength to wrap and lift the cable without breaking to bits? And that the spindle is operated by a powerful motor that appeared by mutations and attached itself to the spindle while allowing itself to be controlled by buttons within the elevator car by human beings who have fingers that perfectly fit the buttons?

As he continued to pile absurdity upon absurdity, Jason laughed out loud. How could so many bright people be duped with this dispassionate undirected universe nonsense?

He knew in his own case it was because he had never actually thought it through. He had simply trusted that his instructors wouldn't teach him anything that wasn't so, and then he realized they were paid to teach, not think!

That's why intelligent people believed this stuff; it was what they were taught.

Why were they taught things that weren't true? Something else had to be at work. Maybe he had experienced it that morning in his bedroom. If Izgad hadn't told him that his thoughts could come from somewhere besides his own brain, he'd never have guessed on his own.

So, how had he broken free of the flow? How did he find himself doubting the disinformation that made up the bedrock of the new society? What had allowed him to question the doctrinal tyranny of the people who claimed there was no doctrine?

Then he saw it.

He was seeing the universe through his own eyes for the first time. He was not being given the explanation of the universe in a classroom setting. He was dealing with the outside world *prima facie*, firsthand, without the baggage of his educational upbringing.

The universe itself had a voice, a voice of truth, reason, and it spoke volumes. It proclaimed a spectacular wonder that could not be accidental or impersonal. The very heavens were proclaiming the truth of the cosmos, putting the lie to those who said the cosmos had no purpose, no hope, and no Maker.

As Izgad might say, absolutely intriguing.

Jason realized that the building in front of him was the handiwork of intelligence. Therefore, the universe––infinitely more complicated and of inconceivable complexity and wondrous design––was also the handiwork of intelligence. And apparently, this intelligence was okay with Jason knowing that this intelligence was there, for the announcement was everywhere to be found now that he knew how to look for it. Now that his eyes were open.

Jason stooped down to pick up one of the chunks of gravel and pursed his lips in a grim smile. Hummingbirds and high-rises were not the result of sun rays on rocks in hot water. There was no Plasm. There was something or someone else. Bigger. Wilder. Creative. And with a mind.

He no longer bought the company line about the cosmos composing itself by accidental laws of physics, and this knowledge both delighted and alarmed him.

After all, when he last met this intelligence face-to-face back at the penthouse, he had been unable to stop himself from dancing for sheer joy.

THE SUPREME ARBITER

*"The past was erased, the erasure was forgotten,
the lie became the truth."*
—George Orwell

All viewing devices in the city were tuned to the government channels. Their immersionfields let the viewers experience the spectacle as if they were really there: all the tiniest noises, scents, and sights present and enhanced. The channels whose format did not carry the trial—the ones themed with sex, propaganda, vacation destinations, food, spinning games, exercise, horoscopes, violence, and gambling—were bleeding money left and right, but they didn't care. They would be subsidized for their losses, and they knew when the trial was over, their viewership would be right back.

For the moment, the people's eyes were on the hearing taking place in the heart of the city.

Jason couldn't miss it. He almost wished he could. He sat and watched the pre-roll of background information as the news teams unloaded all they had rooted out concerning the arrest so far. It wasn't much, but it was amazing to see how far they could stretch a few items of fact with flashy graphics, quasi-related history, wild hypothesizing, and simply interviewing each other. The latter involved lots of offhand jokes, comments on each other's outfits, and kiss-up strokes for the great cause of the Entente. In their eyes, the apprehended citizens weren't actual people but simply convenient tools through which they could catch and hold viewers. They didn't care what became of them as long as they made for exciting coverage.

In his imagination, Meg's face kept crowding out the optics on the screen in front of him. How could he ever have thought she was terrific? Here she was, a hardened criminal attempting the vicious and unthinkable. She had seemed so sweet and . . . well, pure. So much for perception, he thought.

Izgad parked himself in front of the screen. "This is a big thing," he said. "This is very much a part of my mission. Do you mind moving my bed over here? Harry wants to lie down where I can watch."

Meg's face dissolved. "Tell Harry the rug's good enough," Jason growled.

"And also the food and water bowls?" Izgad continued as if Jason had not spoken.

Jason rolled his eyes and then, shaking his head, got up and pulled over the items Izgad had requested.

Harry circled his standard three times and plopped down.

The Supreme Arbiter entered the court as a Roman conquerer might have entered a vanquished city. She was a high-ranking member of the Guard, and she wore a white wig, a black robe, and a gilded headdress. Her face and hands were painted blue. Her eyes flashed. Everyone stood as she climbed the stairs to the high seat. Turning to face the room, she grasped the heavy bronze labarum bearing the emblem of the Entente from its stand. Slowly lowering herself, she sat straight upright, surveying the room with a sour eye. Three echoing, well-spaced thumps of the labarum signaled that the others present were permitted to sit, and there was a moment of rustling and creaking as the crowded room did so.

The Supreme Arbiter had decided in a preparatory meeting with the Director to come down hard on the prisoners, as a stark warning to anyone thinking about violating what the Entente—their compassionate, watchful, and wise government—had determined was best for everyone. After sentencing, they would be put on display for the public until time to send them to the Termination Center.

Director Phelps, the chiseled and kindly face of the prosecution, looked every inch the part of the dauntless defender of the people, which he naturally considered himself to be. His lighting was spectacular, heroic.

Not so the prisoners housed in their dark cages, one to a cage, to announce their menacing instability. They were of course fitted with appropriate restraints on their movements and their mouths. The drone cameras carefully scanned each one, zooming in on each face. In their ultra-closeups, they looked rough. Dangerous. Unhinged. Dirty faces, greasy hair, blackened eye sockets.

The makeup crew had done a superb job. Not too theatrical. Nothing obviously overdone. Simple and suggestive.

"Impressive cosmetics," Izgad muttered. "Especially on your friends. And the blue lady looks spectacular, doesn't she?"

"They're not my friends."

"Oh really? Why does your heart rate increase when you look at the dark-haired girl?"

"You're monitoring my heart rate?" Jason exclaimed. "In what pod class were you selected for the study of medicine?"

"And now the volume of your voice is rising," Izgad continued, his eyes on the screen.

"Oh, have it your way! All I'm saying is those people are no friends of mine. Yes, I sort of know Meg, and everybody knows Alex, but we're not friends by any stretch. And the blonde is a girl I barely know from the spin with Meg. I think they worked at the same lab. I have no idea who the older couples are. But Izgad, they were caught red-handed doing something terrible. Are you saying we should be OK with that?"

"Oh, I didn't realize it was terrible. Whatever it was. We are fighting for something . . ." came the sing-song reply.

"What? No!" Jason laughed. "Fighting for you. And . . . well . . ." He noticed how hollow the words sounded. "Everything is unity. Kinda, I guess. Those are the watchwords of our civilization. They bind us together for a common purpose. We used to struggle and claw for what we wanted, and now we have peace and safety. Everyone has everything they need."

"Everything except freedom. And truth. And..."

"...and what's wrong with you?" Jason broke in. "Of course we still have freedom. Well, within certain boundaries..."

"Who gets to draw those boundaries?"

"And we've got plenty of truth," Jason continued, ignoring him. "All kinds of truth. And anyway, they say truth is just an arbitrary construct to quiet primitive minds."

"Good! Quote from your indoctrination classes."

"Those classes give us the structure we need to form an efficient, functioning society!"

"Those classes have gummed up your mind. You're not letting your recent revelations affect the rest of your thinking. You have roped off access to those places where you still have blind spots. Do you know what a cliché is?"

"Haven't we talked about this before?"

Harry's head turned to Jason. "I wanted to nod just now, but Harry said animals don't nod. Still, the answer is yes, we have discussed this several times. Do you remember what we said?"

"Sure. If I remember, you said . . ." Jason closed his eyes and thought. "That clichés were gravel caught in the gears of a mind. They don't belong, and they don't help. They only keep us from moving forward."

"That is acceptably close. If you remember, I also talked about a veil."

"Oh, right. The veil. The veil is . . . it's . . . tell me again."

"The veil is a condition imposed on those who have rejected truth. People's cognitive abilities become hardened. The word *seared* comes to mind. They are unable to recognize truth because they have chosen a truism instead."

"But those truisms are just a way to remember something important, right?"

"No! Those truisms are inoculations. Small dosages of partial truth that prevent you from being able to access the larger, universal, absolute truths. The clichés insulate you from reality by giving you a truth that has no foundation. Take 'Fighting for you.' Who are you fighting? What are you fighting for? When will the fight end? What will the victor receive as a reward?"

Jason looked at the floor, holding his chin in one hand and rubbing his index finger against his cheek. "You say these phrases obscure the truth because they give us a truth that is not grounded in . . . what?"

"Reality."

Jason shook his head. "I don't understand."

"They make a little prison for your mind. In that prison, you may feel secure. In that prison, no disturbing new thoughts can penetrate. Only one thing can reach you."

What is it? What could it be? Jason wondered, but at the moment that he wondered, he found that he was surrounded. Not by a new thought, viewpoint, or perspective but by a Presence. He had no name for it, but as soon as he realized it was there, he also realized it was within him, saturating him, overwhelming him. It was not he himself, and just as clearly, *it* was not an *it*. It was a person, a Presence. The Presence was bigger and wilder than anything that could fit in his brain, and the overwhelming otherness and inarguable realness of this being made him forget the room, Izgad, what they were talking about, everything. Nothing mattered but the Presence. All his questions disappeared into it. All his fears melted into the joy that filled him. All his anxious thoughts about what might happen in the future were calmed and quieted as he swam in the liquid light of the Presence.

Seconds after he experienced all this, it was gone, but there was no doubt in Jason's mind that Someone unseen was yet still with him. Somewhere inside. And that was a deep comfort.

Harry got up, sank his teeth in his bed, and dragged it closer to the screen. "There you go, my friend," Izgad mumbled, his voice muffled by the corner of the bed clenched between Harry's teeth, "I think you've just met the only One who can ever truly reach anyone and set them free."

The Supreme Arbiter addressed the prisoners. "You have been dredged up, ferreted out, pursued, and captured by the vigilance of Director Phelps and his courageous team. You have been brought here by force after attempting to subvert the good people of this city and the Global Entente. The charges against you will now be read."

She lifted a comm pad from her desk and peered at it as she continued. "Illegal and clandestine gathering for the purposes of sedition and treason. Attempting to harm the general public through spreading lies, disseminating contraband, and calling for the worship of ancient evils. Organizing the downfall of our orderly and protected community well-being to bring about conditions ripe for the spread of the Sickness. Representing an existential threat to Chaldea and certainly all of Neotropa." At this charge, the Supreme Arbiter gurgled a chuckle and looked up. "Though to look at you now, really not much of a threat here!"

Uproarious laughter broke out throughout the room. When the Supreme Arbiter felt they had fully appreciated her bit of humor, she raised her hand for silence, and her solemn countenance returned.

"And finally, the thought crimes, which are the worst of all. You have imagined a world where everyone is not safe, not fought for, and not unified. You have permitted these thoughts to fester even though you knew they were horribly and unconscionably destructive. Your very thoughts brand you as unfit to continue to live among our glorious and enlightened society on this or any other planet. Let the accusations now be buttressed. I call for Director Conrad Marion Phelps and his team to come forward, bringing their presentation of these accusations in specificity."

Viewers watched in rapt attention as Director Phelps and his team ran a video displaying the serpentine trail they had pieced together. Records were produced, surveillance revealed, witnesses interviewed, and guesses confirmed. Each new revelation adding its weight to their damning accusations.

All across the city, those who could not get tickets to attend in person gasped in unison as the violent explosion at the site of the raid, captured on body cams, powerfully shook the screen. The cowardly and treacherous act intended to kill and maim their pursuers was simply one more proof of their guilt, piled high on top of all the other proofs. The dirtbags had tried to murder the team that had smoked them out of their rathole. Without the swift actions of the brave men and women on the scene, there might have been massive deaths of innocent citizens.

Director Phelps's team had supplied the jury with all the incriminating proof any reasonable person might wish for. No stone was left unturned, digging all the way back into their first days at school, playing footage of the obvious roots of their depravity, clawing their way into their progenitors' dirty habits and failings.

At the conclusion of the team's presentation, gasps of horrified surprise broke out from the gallery as the Supreme Arbiter called, "Silence!" A deep quiet fell. Not a soul could doubt that these seven were depraved savages indeed.

Starting from the premise of guilt, an efficient government could bring a lot of pressure to bear in order to validate that assumption.

Eve kk6dt produced a long litany of incriminating evidence against the two sponsors of the dark-haired female prisoner, who she said were not fit to even be present in the proceedings but she pointed them out anyway. Eve was wearing an eye-catching outfit, that showed her fine qualities to best advantage, and from that moment, she became something of a cult figure in Chaldea, popular and in demand with both men and women.

Director Phelps now brought the prisoners out of their cages to be paraded in front of the courtroom, still shackled and silenced, looking apelike and vicious. They were finally each positioned directly beneath the Supreme Arbiter high above.

He planted himself before them, fixing them with a long and withering stare before turning to the camera, shaking his head as if to say, I'm sorry we must all share a space with these degenerates.

Then he spoke, lines that he had lovingly rehearsed, and his loud voice rang in the viewers' ears to which the audio technicians added a small amount of reverb and a touch of bass frequencies.

"We will no longer let you mock this courtroom or this city with your brazen attack on our values! No more will we stand by as you spit on our society. Or threaten our sacred unity! In your attempt to pull out the foundation of our culture, you have surely pulled down the righteous anger of all virtuous citizens upon your own heads! You have failed, and you will pay the price of that failure!" His upraised hand brought a halt to an outbreak of applause. In the hush, his voice assumed a quiet intensity for maximum impact, "And so, in the end, you are revealed to be exactly what you're charged with being: enemies of the greater good, destroyers of the lasting peace, abominations and blights on all we hold dear. By your unconscionable actions, you have condemned yourselves, and in light of that, I will demand the most severe sentence to be pronounced. May the heavens have mercy upon you, for we surely will not."

The script now called for the grand finale. Here was the undercover agent who, at great personal risk, had infiltrated the subversives and supplied enough detail to trigger the raid. Stan was called to the Director's side and asked to give his testimony as a final nail in the coffin. His likeness was now seen suspended in the courtroom, along with background footage of his staged release and recapture that had its own stirring theme music. When it ended, the drone cameras all hovered in front of Stan. Applause was called for, and it was enthusiastically given.

As the clapping was drawing to a close, Stan, at a nod from the Director, began his tale. They hung spellbound on every exciting word. He described his assignment in detail, often referring to maps and other visuals. There was a tour of the house where he stayed and often received visits from the conspirators. They had recently shot some auxiliary video of Stan, sitting on the actual bed there in his bedroom, recording the day's observations secretly into his wrist com. It was dramatic and effective.

And then, warming to his tale and a little too eager to embellish his part in the performance, it slipped. "I never actually *saw* the library, but I sure was able to document a ton of books that ostensibly came from it, and I..."

The Director abruptly shoved him aside, "Thank you Stan! Let's hear it for this man!" A few people who had not been paying attention began to clap, but their neighbors immediately stopped them.

The Director bowed and addressed the Supreme Arbiter. "I apologize for this man's imaginative testimony, your Excellence, and may I add, you know, we were never able to confidently confirm the existence of any sort of..."

He himself was cut off as the Supreme Arbiter stood, cold with rage. "What is *this*?! Why is this the first reference to any library?! A *library*! Here in our city! How *ever* did you believe you could *conceal* this from us?! Silence all!" She pounded the labarum repeatedly on the floor as the buzz running through the crowd was abruptly choked off. Leaning forward to glare down at the Director, she bit her words out in acid tones. "We will look carefully into this matter, Conrad. You will need to provide us with convincing reasons to justify your judgment in concealing this terrible contagion. It seems reckless in the extreme, and you and I will speak of this later. Nevertheless, and especially in light of this news, I am ready to pronounce the verdict. I ask the jury to accompany me to my chambers. Let no one speak a single word until we return."

With a great deal less pomp than she entered, she whirled down the stairs and swept out of the room through her chamber door and the jury filed in after her. No one looked at their neighbor or uttered a syllable. The sound of the drones was all that could be heard along with the livid tirade of unintelligible words coming from the the Supreme Arbiter's chambers.

The networks' ratings were through the roof. This was a great show! Emanating undetected from the viewing devices and from tiny vents inside the courtroom itself was an invisible cloud of a vaporized drug that targeted the fight-or-flight response in the viewers' cerebral cortexes, producing an even more intense feeling of anxiety and fear. *What might have happened had your government not exercised sleepless vigilance?* was one of the chyron graphics that scrolled across their viewfields.

It was as if someone had pressed a pause button on the world and the progress of time was frozen, rooted to the spot.

Thankfully, it was not long until the chamber door slammed open and the Supreme Arbiter led the jury out. Ascending rapidly once again to her authoritative heights, she held her labarum horizontally above her head with both uplifted hands as an offering to the skies before throwing it to the floor of her platform with a resounding boom. Seven smartly uniformed officers forced the prisoners to kneel. In a loud, commanding voice, she pronounced their doom, to the approval of all.

"Your very lives are forfeit. I pronounce you carriers of the Sickness. You are a material danger to us all, and your miserable existence will no longer be permitted to continue. Tomorrow, you will be terminated for the world to see and applaud. Now! Take these repulsive and nauseating obscenities out of our sight!"

Harry looked up at Jason. "Tomorrow, Jason. There is not much time," Izgad said, his voice tingling with urgency.

THE MOMENT ARRIVES

*"War is when the government tells you
who the bad guy is. Revolution is
when you decide that for yourself."*
—Benjamin Franklin

Jason turned off the screen as Izgad continued to speak. "She said they'll be executed."

Jason nodded. "I heard."

"Tomorrow."

"Yeah, that's the day after today."

"There is not much time."

Jason's thoughts had been centered on Meg and her face and voice in his memory, but he came out of this reverie in an instant. "What do you mean? Time for what?'"

"To rescue them, of course."

"Resc . . . rescue them? Are you nuts? I can't rescue them any more than I can fly to the moon by flapping my arms! And why would I want to anyway?"

"Because you are the only one who can."

"But they're enemies of the state!"

"So are you."

Jason opened his mouth to reply, but the words caught in his throat. The enormity of this accusation repulsed him, and at the same time, he realized it was true. His mind was newly free from the Entente's clutches. He guessed he actually had become just such a threat, though the state didn't know it yet. *Wow,* Jason thought, *I'm sorta just now finding out about it myself.*

He had wondered about this subconsciously for a long time, but now . . . well, here it was. All of his unconnected thoughts about the Plasm and the purpose of his life had hovered in his mind in a shapeless mass, but at last, they had come together to form a solid object.

Jason remembered one of his classmates who wrote a paper on a story he heard about rainbows being a promise from a god of some kind. He was a kid who was always asking big questions and being unsatisfied with the answers. One day he just disappeared. No one knew where or why. And then without fanfare, he returned, a blank smile on his face. He couldn't remember any of them anymore, and he seemed hollowed out. What was his name? Greg 304b8. So sad. It could have been him, Jason realized with alarm.

He thought of the times he'd marveled at the delicate and detailed designs of leaves and insects, impossibly complex, bearing the undeniable trademarks of planning and purpose.

He had reveled in the beauty of the dazzling stars and had been enthralled by the glory of deep space, frozen and limitless. Marveled that his wounds would heal and grow new skin, eventually erasing all evidence of the injury. Laughed every time Harry did that goofy dance waiting for his food, wholehearted, refreshing laughter. Stared all through class at the face of a pretty schoolgirl simply because she was a joy to look at. Happily lost himself inside the haunting symphonies of a Russian composer from the 1800s. Felt the tickle of a raindrop. The delight of a dark beer. The thrill of a mystery movie. The dance of flame in a wood fire. The smell of an early morning.

He had so many experiences that warned him there was more to existence than simply being part of a safe and efficient society. Things he couldn't deny, things he couldn't turn his back on. Things he was grateful for, and his gratitude wanted to be expressed. Expressed he now knew where—expressed to that Presence.

He realized that the trial he just witnessed could easily have been his own. He presented the same sort of danger those seven presented.

Maybe he was an enemy of the state...

Such thoughts take time to write and time to read, but they took no time flashing through his mind. He patted Harry on the head, causing the dog's tail to sweep back and forth across the floor.

"Look, Izgad," he began, still trying to put the burden of action on someone else, anyone else. "I'm nobody. All this pomp and ceremony about my being one of the first in a while to complete my stupid mission with a completely full silo has nothing to do with my abilities. It was luck. I'm not as hot as they say. I'm actually pretty worthless. But there's you. You're apparently well-connected, and you've got real power. Plus, you have this ability to inhabit other bodies. Why not just take over some guard's body? Heck, why not that Phelps character? You could make him turn Meg and the others loose."

"Turn them loose to where? Where could they go? Where would they be safe?" Izgad asked while Harry began licking a paw. "And anyway, it does not work like that. You have an odd sense of power, my friend. It would be nothing for me to unmake a large part of your planet. And as you say, I have the ability to take up residence inside a creature of flesh, but we cannot use our power without approval from the Maker, nor can we invade a body without permission."

"I don't understand why you can't just hop into somebody's body. It was nothing for you to share Harry's body."

"Harry invited me. It is a kind of courtesy that is baked into the universe. Fascinating! Listen to me use a metaphor! I am getting the hang of this . . . ooh another metaphor . . ."

"So you can't just zap yourself into these people?"

"I have no idea what you mean by 'zap.' I am not allowed to go where I have no legal right. That is one of the biggest differences between my order and the other side. There are creatures like me who care nothing for legal rights when they take possession of reckless humans."

"I don't understand, but I think you're telling me you can't possess Director Phelps."

"Right."

"OK."

"What is the problem?" Izgad asked.

"Well, I'm confused. Apparently, you can't do anything. Even the stuff you can do is forbidden. I thought you were here to help me."

"I am. But not that way. And do not write off my abilities so easily: there are things I will be allowed to do. I have an idea for a plan of action. Would you like to hear it?"

"Shoot."

"The first thing we must do is to pick up their library."

Jason stared at Harry in shock. "What? What are you talking about? What library? Doesn't the state have it? And isn't that the thing that got them in trouble in the first place?"

"You are so perceptive. Again, I say we must pick up the library. It is near the residence where your friends were apprehended."

"Right. Except they're not my friends."

"The residence of the sponsors of one of the prisoners."

"Meg."

"The one who makes your serotonin levels rise."

"So you say."

"The authorities were kept from discovering a cave behind the house."

"How on earth do you know that?"

"I have sources. If you want to know, I am not the only high heteroclite present on the planet at this moment, and I am in contact with several of my kind. They let me know that your friends—"

"Oh, c'mon! They're not my friends."

"—had concealed their books and other storage devices in a cave behind the house."

"Why didn't Phelps's people find them?"

"They were kept from discovery."

"How?"

"The right question is 'By whom?', but I am not allowed to disclose that information."

"Oh, have it your way. You said, 'books and other storage devices.' You think of a book as a storage device?"

"What do you think of it as?"

"I guess I never thought of it like that . . ."

"So, before anything else, you and I must get that library and put it in your silo."

"My silo is on display in the park."

"Perfect. I couldn't figure out how to free your ship and the prisoners without having a whole planet full of law enforcement come down on us. But being on display in the park is perfect. This just might work. Call your friends at the news bureau, and get them to meet you at the Termination Center with them bringing your vessel. Use them as a foil to keep the Terminal Center staff on its best behavior. Show up with me looking like Harry—"

"You *do* look like Harry. And... the Terminal Center?!"

"—and you can escape from this planet in your government-issued molybdenum ride."

"Are you actually using ghetto vernacular from the early two-thousands?"

"Have you got any more of that leftover ribeye? Harry is not looking forward to eating a bunch of rubberized pellets again."

Jason laughed. "Sure. But as far as rubber pellets, tell him not to worry. The silo has been restocked with high-class provisions, tools, and toys. Every current refinement and a couple of brand-new ones. They let people walk through it like a museum, and the recruiters want everyone to think we live like kings and queens out there in space. Every luxury is on that contraption as we speak. Harry won't be eating rubber pellets, at least not right away!"

Harry got up and danced in a circle, chasing his tail. "Stop, Harry!" Izgad pleaded. "I cannot think!"

Fifteen minutes later, after getting a clearer idea of the scheme from Izgad, Jason lifted his wrist comm and told it to call the lead producer at the newsroom.

"Hello! Can you see me on your screen? Good. Guess who this is? That's right; it's Jason t4... Aw, thanks, I really don't understand the fuss, but I was glad to do it. Thank... thank you... Hey, hate to interrupt, but I'm in sort of a hurry, and I need a favor. Can you grab my silo and meet me at the Termination Center when the prisoners who are now on display arrive there? Yeah, that silo, the one in the park. We need to use it for a prop... Yes, a prop for an exclusive interview. I've got some ideas... yes, now, right now... No, no, of course I have permission. I mean, if I didn't have the OK, we might be doing something illegal!" Jason muted his comm and looked at Izgad. "They're laughing like that's the funniest thing they've ever heard." He unmuted it again. "What? Hello? No, that's all right, no offense taken. Sure, that was funny... Yeah. No, no, not at all. Listen, um, what did you say your name was? Right. I've got some ideas to goose the whole event up a notch or two. I'll tell you when I see you. And after the interview, let's maybe do lunch. In the silo itself. Maybe ten of you. Could you have that ready to go as well? Right... Oh, hot subs and chips and maybe pies or something sweet... Uh, Director Phelps might be there, and he asked for a large tub of that Karmelpop popcorn... I think so! Yup... Sure... Yes, just get the boys there to strap my silo onto a trailer, and you can bring it with you to the center. My promoters think this little event will give you guys one more shot to boost your ratings. Why, I don't really know because they must already be in record territory, right?... Yeah, I thought so... and afterward, we could go kinda in-depth as we eat our lunch in the Silo itself. Heck, you can keep your recorders rolling while I show you around the ship. Well, I gotta go... Uh-huh... Yeah, I'm fighting for you too."

Jason hung up and looked at Harry in amazement. "It's gonna happen. They're gonna bring the silo and meet us there. Right now. I have to say, I'm astounded at what you can get away with when you're famous!"

THE TERMINATION CENTER

"If a thing is worth doing, it is worth doing well.
If it is worth having, it is worth waiting for.
If it is worth attaining, it is worth fighting for."
—*Oscar Wilde*

Bots were cleaning the empty courtroom. The show was over, the cameras turned off, the people having left to crowd into nearby eateries for lunch. All that was left were the prisoners in their cages with one guard who must have drawn the short straw. Soon the people would return to see them on display outside the building. Alex looked out from behind the carbon-steel bars, unable to move, still held immobile in a containment frame, while his mind was racing.

He knew there had never been any ultimate hope of escape, that they would eventually, at some point, be captured and condemned. He wondered why he had even attempted to evade arrest as desperately as he had.

He was not an emotional guy. He was a thinker, cool under fire, unflappable. That's why he was so good at his job. But at some point, his outlook on life must have changed. How else to explain this—convicted of being involved in illegal activities, associating with criminals, thinking and acting in ways that landed him in a cage and a containment frame?

What happened to him? How had he arrived here?

It wasn't hard to find an answer when he observed the way the Entente stomped on anyone who came between them and their absolute control of the citizens' lives. He thought of Phelps and the Supreme Arbiter, the toadies who testified against his friends, the jury, and the courtroom gallery—their faces had an opaque sameness, their voices betraying an emptiness, all seeming like the bloodthirsty Roman circus crowds he had read about in Ben Hur. His focussed skipped, and he wondered: did that book make it into the cache of books we're going to be killed for having?

He closed his eyes and pictured his new friends, thinking of the simple meals they shared where they talked with one another about the magical worlds coming from their beloved books written so long ago. Worlds of adventure, of uncomplicated values and genuine companionship, desperate struggle, and ultimate rescue. Worlds of pirates and giants, dark lords and knights in armor, Native Americans stalking quietly through the trunks of a great forest, gumshoe detectives and the first men on the moon, and children visiting magical lands via wardrobes. Worlds of shipwrecks and tropical islands, paper-and-wood airplanes dropping primitive bombs on enemy soldiers, marching armies, talking dragons, and magical leprechauns with their pots of gold. Worlds of explorers in wooden sailing ships, cowboys and rustlers, mountain climbers, and hot-air balloons that took people around the planet in eighty days. Worlds where great civilizations sprang up from one person's vision and where those same civilizations collapsed because their citizens forgot what was important, seeking only safety and security.

There it was. That was what had happened to his cool, collected mind. He'd gotten a taste of a world that was not at all secure and definitely not safe. And he preferred that world to this one with every fiber of his being.

He saw that his sensibility rebelled at the terrible cost of being protected, not only from disease and violence but also from upsetting ideas.

And he saw that the only way for anyone to get safety and security was to give up their liberty, their uniqueness, their humanity, and everything that made life meaningful.

Alex knew he and his friends were going to die. But as a famous Scottish warrior had said, the one who defied the English conquest of his land, "Everyone dies. Not everyone lives."

His thoughts were interrupted by the guards pushing their floating frames down the hall to the viewing stage. He shut his eyes and tried not to hear the insults and taunts or notice the heartless animosity of the crowds that shuffled past them, wanting one last look at the condemned. After what seemed like an eternity, their guards pushed them into the back of a prison vehicle that would take them to the antechambers of the Termination Center.

Alex was not one to give up, but he couldn't imagine how this vehicle might be taking them anywhere but to the final chapter of his life. Annihilation. Obliteration. Total destruction. And then nothingness. Ceasing to be.

The weight of his own end closing in on him, he recoiled at the helplessness of their situation.

The prisoners were not secured to the walls or anything else. With a callous disregard, the guards simply tossed them into the back, closed the door, and laughed their way to the front cab. These prisoners wouldn't be alive much longer; it was time to have a little fun. Starting the engine, the driver floored it and took every turn as sharply as he could while he and his companion doubled over in hysterics as they heard the muffled thumps from the cargo section.

And "cargo" was too nice a word for what the prisoners had now become. Immobilized in their containment frames in the darkness in the back of the vehicle, they bounced wildly around and were soon bruised and bleeding and throwing up on one another, scared and disoriented. The thirty-minute ride was a nightmare.

When they arrived at the Termination Center, the guards, still chuckling, brought a hose around to the back of the transport. As soon as they opened the doors, they turned the water on full force. Pinned at the back, the prisoners endured the outrage, thankful at least to be rid of the vomit and some of the makeup. As much as the water stung Meg's face and her wounds, even the sharp pain was, in a way, refreshing to her battered body.

Jill realized they would soon get their final chance to see the sky before being locked in a holding cell to await their public demise.

But Alex's mind was off again—alert, watchful, probing, still searching for any chance to break free, however brief that freedom might be. He had no idea how irrepressible his own survival instinct actually was.

At that moment, the doors of the Termination Center opened, and out came the most unlikely group imaginable. Of all the people in the world to be waiting inside the execution reception area, through the doors came the governmental posse of the hero of the moment, freshly returned from his successful exploration of deep space, the man who was now the toast of Chaldea. The guards were so flustered that they dropped their hoses, which skipped wildly around until they stepped on the nozzles and turned the water off. They saluted at attention, although it was not their superior officer, standing together in a futile attempt to hide their grisly handiwork, which was plainly visible through the transport's open doors.

It was, in fact, Jason. *The* Jason. Jason t43p7. And, of course, his famous black-and-white mutt named Harry, who had been Jason's furry fellow traveler in his glorious exploits. Jason was wearing his most impressive governmental uniform: gold and silver gleaming from every metal fitting, the dark black-and-royal-blue silk and satin cloth providing the gravitas of an emperor and his jaunty black leather cap matching his calf-high black leather boots with their permanent wax shine.

His unruly red hair set off his oddly handsome face as he acknowledged the guards, clapping them on the shoulder. "At ease, gentlemen. I'm just a dude like you!" The guards looked with awe as they saw the silo set up right there in the parking lot. "Yup, boys." Jason winked at them. "That's exactly what you think it is!"

Accompanied by all manner of city officials in their finest suits and dresses, and with the large news team intermingled among them, it was quite the reception. Talk about pomp and circumstance. The prisoners didn't see it very well, since their frames had tumbled into heaped disarray on the floor as the water pressure let up and abruptly dropped them. But they heard what was being said, and they wondered what could possibly be happening.

"Will you make room for our news friends?" Jason asked. "Would you mind moving back there so the camera people can record this? Yes, you. Excuse me, that's my dog. Thanks. OK, on me in three, two one . . ." The cameras captured every angle and nuance of the scene.

"First, I would like to commend these two brave men who, at great risk to themselves have brought us these justly condemned traitors from their sentencing before the Supreme Arbiter. You guys are amazing!" He grabbed them around the neck, one in each arm, in a friendly but excruciating headlock and gave them a hard and horrifically painful squeeze, smiling the entire time. "Great job, you two!" With the cameras on their faces, the guards did not dare show the agony Jason was putting them through, and they tried to smile through their torment. Giving the cameras plenty of time to get some good shots from several angles, and to give the guards a taste of the suffering to which the prisoners had been subjected, Jason released his hold and gave their heads a congratulatory rub that knocked their hats off. The cameras reflexively closed in on the guards' rear ends as they bent over to retrieve their hats.

Jason motioned the audience to walk with him to the open doors at the back of the transit. His expression became serious. He dropped his chin and crossed his arms impressively. "Harry and I were watching the proceedings with intense interest, just as you, my fellow citizens, were. It was an honor to see the Supreme Arbiter and Director Phelps and his entire team expose this treachery. I was outraged that in our time there might still exist people so vile and perverse that they'd have no thought for how they were endangering us all. These prisoners deserve the death they will most certainly be given as a warning to all who would do us harm and a reminder to all the good folks . . ." He paused and turned to the closest camera. ". . . like you . . ." He tilted his head slightly with the most sincere look he could muster and held up a finger. ". . . that our government will never forget that we're all in this thing together, fighting for you . . ."

Back in the heart of the city, Director Phelps's secretary burst through his door, "Sir! You have to see this!"

"See what?"

"Jason t43p7 and his dog, Harry, are at the Termination Center! It's so exciting! And his silo is there too!"

"He's . . . he's *where?*" the Director roared. "I didn't hear about any plans for this! What the hell?"

In his hands, he held his team's in-depth report on Meg 4k6p3, which had revealed a crazy coincidence: she and Jason t43p7 had had a spin. He had no time to figure out that connection because here was an emergency of the first order.

He stabbed his finger at his wrist comm, and a rectangle appeared on top of his desk. He pulled up the news channel, and there was Jason t43p7, front and center, making a speech!

Who did this yahoo think he was? This was supposed to be *his* moment, *his* supreme triumph on *his* pristine record. A conquest that might finally propel him to a seat among the Elders. First that idiot Stan had tried to bungle away his triumph. Now this red-headed, country-fried space freak was stealing *his* glory! And look at the toad-eating press and those crap-for-brains city officials! Suck-ups! Butt-kissers!

Furious, the Director rang the headquarters of the enforcers. "Yes. Phelps. I said, *Phelps*! Shut up and give me the chief... Hello, Chief? Who's this? Huh? It's *not*? Oh? Where the hell *is* he? He's at the event? Of all the... Oh, he left *you* to take the heat for this, huh? Well, holy heat is what you're about to get! Who gave the OK to have our damned little pompous redbird lead the parade to the Termination Center? Huh? *No*! I'm talking about that damned Jason t43p7, you moron!... You didn't know either? How could you *not* know?... Of course I didn't give the OK! Do I look like a complete fool? Is that what he said? You incompetent, oafish, overpaid, underworked, figurehead of a jackass idiot! I want your precious chief to call me *immediately*, or I'll send him before the Supreme Arbiter, and he'll be washing toilets at some waterstation out of town before you can blink! He's not taking calls? Just who is in charge over there? God*dammit*!" The Director cut the connection abruptly and began kicking furniture and shouting obscenities at the walls.

At the Termination Center, the news event of the decade was rolling right along. In several preplanned tight camera angles, Jason had reamed the prisoners and branded them every odious and traitorous label in the book. Viewers who were watching the live feed were treated to his righteous indignation on full display, complete with close-ups that showed the spittle coming from his exalted mouth while artfully interspersing beauty shots of the approving important personages, fully aware of the value of being on-site for this historic meeting of the man of the moment and the condemned insurrectionists.

Jason called to the guards, who had been glaring at him from behind the crowd, to gather the prisoners in their containment frames and follow him for some picture-taking in front of the silo. As the cameras pivoted to put them once again in the public eye, one would have thought they were the founders of the Jason t43p7 fan club. They were caught up in the moment, and all indignation was forgotten. Reveling in their new importance, with thoughts and fantasies of how their friends were enviously watching them perform their enormously consequential jobs, working hand in hand with Chaldea's favorite son, they snapped into action with practiced efficiency; heads held high.

As soon as the shot was composed, with the gleaming molybdenum walls of the silo behind and the prisoners and guards displayed in the middle ground, Jason faced the cameras and paused for effect. As he cleared his throat, there was complete silence, and he addressed the cameras. "You and I will be watching when these blights on humanity get what's coming to them, and we'll be stronger together for having weathered this attack on our values and on the cherished safety and security of every citizen. This is a grand day for people everywhere in Chaldea, Neotropa, and the world! Fighting for you!" he shouted, pumping his fist.

Every voice on site, including the cynical, hard-bitten camera crew, and every person in the viewing audience thundered back with answering fists on chests, "Everything is unity!"

The glorious event over, Jason waved to several of the dignitaries, thanked them for coming, patted some on the back, and shook hands. Completely disregarding all protocols, the guards were signing autographs, glad to talk to anyone and everyone who wanted to know what it was like to hang out with Jason t43p7. There was a kind of afterglow, and the news hounds made sure the cameras kept rolling, most of them following Jason through the tangle.

It was now or never.

Jason took a deep breath and then stood in front of the frame that held Meg and almost imperceptibly shook his head, but it was enough to translate what he was feeling to the cameras. He held his pose for a moment and then spoke. "Meg? Meg, you sly fox. You still look so innocent, you beautiful snake in the grass. Remember me? We had a spin once long ago, before I left to do my duty to this great city of ours. Do you now carry the Sickness? I wonder if you had it back then. I remember how I enjoyed being with you and thought you were just like me. You can only imagine what I felt when I discovered your true nature . . ."

While every eye in Chaldea was watching this unexpected soap opera with great interest, Alex stared in surprise as Harry stood up on his frame and pressed the release button. Falling free of the restraining field, Alex felt a rush of adrenaline. Not wasting a moment, he knocked the guard closest to him unconscious with a practiced double blow to the body and head. So intense was the tableau with Jason and Meg that no one but a few people nearby even noticed that Alex was loose. He was about to free the others, but Harry was already standing on the next frame, Nando's. Alex pulled the weapons belt off the fallen guard and used the stun gun on the back of the remaining guard. In a flash, the crowd became aware of the new situation.

"He's got a blaster!" Jason yelled. "He'll kill us all! Run! Run for your lives!" Alex aimed his stun gun at Jason. *Well, at least I'll send some volts through this paper-diaper prince before we're recaptured,* he thought with grim satisfaction.

At that moment, the dog put his paw on Alex's leg.

"Stop. Put that down," it said. "Are you able to understand that Jason and I are rescuing you people? I will free the others while you pretend to take Jason hostage. We must get into the truck and get that silo to the portal and be gone before the authorities catch on. This plan seems impossible, but we will dare to hope that the Maker will find a way for us. Alex. You need to both breathe and blink."

Alex shook himself and pushed the incongruity of a talking dog to the back of his awareness. He would sort that out later. Even if this was delirium, it was something to *attempt.* He was trained to act instinctively, and he grasped the possibilities of the situation in an instant. "Do whatever the dog says!" he whispered to his companions, who were in various states of confinement and newfound freedom.

The smile of a man of action spread across Alex's face.

ORGANIZED CHAOS

*"The longer I live, the more convinced am I that this
planet is used by other planets as a lunatic asylum."*
—*George Bernard Shaw*

As the crowd scrambled for the safety of the Termination
Center, Alex sprang to Jason. Jason realized that, even if
he hadn't been play-acting, he had no chance against
him, though he outweighed Alex by twenty pounds. Maybe more
since I've been stuffing my face recently, he thought. Alex had
already pinned him in a hold.

"You need to act more frightened," Alex muttered in his ear.
"And struggle a little harder."

Jason tried not to laugh, "You kidding me? Can you let up a
little? I can barely breathe let alone make this look hard for you."

Alex forgot that his nerves were over the top. "Sorry," he
whispered. "Try that."

With a herculean jerk, Jason nearly twisted out of Alex's hold.

"Pretend to fall," Alex said. Jason felt Alex's weapon graze his
head as he dropped on cue. "Stay down!" Alex ordered.

Alex strapped on the weapons belt he had taken from the
officer as he called to Nando to grab the other guard's belt. After
attaching an anti-gravity band to Jason's manacled wrists, Alex
pretended to look around for an escape, made a little sort of
theatrical epiphany as he saw the others getting into the vehicle,
and began to float Jason's crumpled form toward the transport.

"Hi, I'm Jason," Jason muttered under his breath. "Of course I
know who you are. I have no idea if this will even work, but I hope
you can get us to the launch site before the authorities realize I'm
not a hostage."

"The launch site? So we're going to get off the planet?" Alex replied. "I never ever thought we'd get the chance. We may be dead in an hour, but thanks for giving us a straw of hope to clutch at. What's with the dog?"

"I've been wondering that myself."

"Huh?"

Jason laughed. "I'll explain later. Make this look good. Maybe pretend to hit me again, and yell something about taking me as a hostage for insurance, if you don't mind . . ."

Alex performed another believable fake punch to Jason's stomach, doubling him over, and then steered him towards the cab. Turning to the abandoned drone cams floating in the air above them, snapped, "We'll just take Mister Garbage Collector here along with us for insurance!"

Nando had used his blaster to fry the tracker under the hood. "Everybody in? Let's get outta here!"

The cab was crowded, with all eight in the front section. Nando had taken the wheel, and Alex had jumped in beside Jason, who sat up and gave directions. "We gotta get to the launch site fast. There's a . . . what's your name? Nando? Hi. Jason. There's an entrance to the site where they know me and where there's no surveillance. It's how all the big names keep from getting spotted by the press when they come to the site. Turn at the next intersection, and go west. Any chance you might be able to go a whole lot faster?"

In answer, Nando floored it, and the vehicle jumped into top speed.

"Turn here again," Jason instructed. "We're heading roughly for the surplus store in sector seven near the giant waterstation there. Do you know it?"

"Sure do," Nando said with a grin. "And I know a faster way there. Cuts 15 minutes off. Is the silo secure? The road I'm thinking of is a little rough."

Jason held up his wrists for Alex to remove the cuffs, confessing, "I don't know whether it is or not! I had the folks from the press get this thing from the park! But the techs know their stuff, and this particular truck is made specifically for my silo. We should be fine."

"Should be?" Madeline exclaimed.

Jason shrugged. "Yeah, it looked all right to me at the event. Hey! This is cool, I've never been in a desperate escape from a planetary government before. Izgad said our chances were about one in a hundred."

"What?" Jill, Meg, and Hisako cried in unison.

"Perhaps the time has come to introduce myself," Izgad.

"Hold on to your hats!" Nando yelled as he spun the controls to head off the road on a dirt track that looked as if only all-terrain cycles had ever dared attempt it.

"Are you *nuts*?" Alex shouted.

"Maybe! But what the heck!" Nando sang over his shoulder, smiling.

"We're all gonna die!" Hisako screamed.

"This is *great*!" crowed Jason.

"This is *crazy*!" the girls howled.

"Crazy enough to work perhaps. But as I was saying . . ." Izgad attempted yet again.

"Nando, you'd better be right!" Madeline warned.

"Now, Linny," Nando replied soothingly, "I only—"

"Watch out!" every other person in the transport bellowed as Nando barely skirted a boulder that seemed to appear suddenly in front of them. He had not slowed down a bit when he turned onto the path.

"How are we not dead?" Hisako moaned as the boulder receded behind them.

"Absolutely *fascinating*. Perhaps I should introduce myself at a less stressful moment," Izgad offered.

It wasn't until then that the others realized the dog had actually been speaking.

The vehicle roared as Nando coaxed it faster and faster along the dirt track.

THE RACE TO ESCAPE

"Who would not, finding a way, break loose
from hell, and boldly venture to
whatever place, farthest from pain?"
—John Milton

Director Phelps stopped storming around his office and pulled himself up straight with a deep breath, dropping the lamp he had been about to hurl through the window.

As he surveyed the wreckage—broken furniture, dented walls, shards of glass, and general havoc—he realized he could not just straighten the mess up. Neither the mess in his office nor the mess of this whole operation.

If I don't get on top of this, he thought, *I won't have to worry about straightening up the office because it will be the next director's problem. Think, Phelps. You can do this!*

Informed by his people that the event at the Termination Center had devolved into a crisis, the Director recognized it as a new path to glory. Every disaster is simply a new opportunity to shine, he reminded himself. After tracking the criminal ring and bringing them to justice the first time, he'd soon be the one to thwart their second escape.

He brought up and studied the initial reports coming in from the scene. Perfect! The renegades had taken that little usurper, Jason t43p7, hostage. Maybe they would kill him during recapture, and if they failed, he himself would make sure the little twit caught a bullet in the crossfire. This was splendid. Better than he had hoped.

Calling for his chauffeur to bring his quad around, he hoped the news cameras at the Termination Center would still be rolling.

The vehicle with the escaped terrorists had dropped off surveillance somewhere west of town and vanished like a ghost. The department in charge of tracking it was embarrassed and decided to report an equipment malfunction instead of admitting their unhappy reality.

The Director arrived at the Termination Center at top speed, imagining there would be a crowd stunned into confusion and uncertainty. He knew his arrival would be welcome. Everyone was always more at ease with him around. They knew him for what he was—a rare man, a swift and capable leader—and the impression he gave of competence and confidence was no illusion. He had a broad smile on his face as his detail swept into the lot in front of the Termination Center.

But his smile vanished when he saw nothing in the lot but two stunned and disarmed guards lying face down on the pavement while their empty transport lay wide open to the world. Leaping from his vehicle before it had completely stopped, he ran to the back of the transport. Looking inside beyond the swinging doors, he was nearly blinded by startled birds that had been curious to explore the inside of the vehicle.

"What in the name of the almighty Plasm is going on?"

He strode to the building doors and heard the screams of the people inside. He was unable to turn the handle. Reflexively, he dialed one of the proprietary settings on his wrist comm, forcing the lock on the door. When he tore it open, he was instantly walloped off his feet by the simultaneous force of three different stun guns operated by the terrified officials brave enough to protect the rest from the murderous escapees outside. Mistaking Phelps's forceful entry for a bloodthirsty attempt to breach the building's security, they each had let him have the maximum setting on their stunners. With the crowd behind them shrieking in terror, the officials gazed at the unconscious body crumpled at their feet, wondering why Alex looked so much like Director Phelps . . .

❖

Nando had been driving them headlong through a section of undeveloped land known mostly only to trail unis and off-road bis. At length, they returned to a paved road. "Brilliant, Nando!" Jason shouted and then leaned forward. "It is Nando, right?"

"Nailed it."

"Not me, you nailed it! This is less than a mile from the VIP entrance I told you we were shooting for. Pull over, and let me drive from here if you don't mind. And you guys had better get in the silo. I don't think the sentries should see your faces. You're way more famous than I am."

"I think the word you want is 'infamous,'" Meg said, but they quickly obeyed Jason's instructions.

Harry jumped into the front passenger seat. "What is meant by 'shotgun'?" Izgad asked, then turned to Jason. "Harry just called shotgun . . ."

In seemingly no time at all, Jason pulled up to the checkpoint kiosk where the armed sentries kept watch over this private gate. Instantly, they recognized the man of the hour and his faithful dog. They also recognized the silo, which was just as famous as they.

"Hey, guys!" Jason said. "How ya been? I didn't think you two would be on duty today! You, Bert, say, wasn't your pairing mate due to provide this year's pod class with another outstanding student sometime around now?"

Bert leaned out the window to shake Jason's hand and smiled sheepishly. "Sure. But the lab says she's got three more days to go. She's pretty crabby, so I'm pulling some overtime."

Jason knew every moment's delay was critical, but he dared not seem to be in a hurry. "What are you guys watching? Oh, that lady singer/dancer, what's her name . . ."

"Chaldea's Whore!" the other sentry said, leaning past his buddy to shake Jason's hand. "She can really crank it, brother Jason! I'm Doug, remember?"

"Yeah . . . Hi, Doug, good to see you! Of course I remember you," Jason lied. "Um, I thought I would bring the old silo out here and look for some good places to shoot the documentary we've got planned to air later this fall."

"They're gonna do a docular-mentatary?" Bert asked.

"Pretty cool, huh?" Jason beamed, not bothering to correct the total massacre of a perfectly defenseless word. "And I . . . uh . . . I mean, me and the producers talked, and we definitely want you two guys in it, you know . . ."

"Just let me finish my lunch, and I'll be right out!" Doug said, with parts of his lunch clearly visible on his face.

"No need just yet!" Jason laughed, hoping he sounded natural. "I'll just be checking out some angles we might go for. That's why I brought that thing." He motioned behind him without looking back. "We won't be shooting for several weeks, so you have time to drop some pounds, both of you, to look good on camera. Just watch the carbs. Hey! So great to see you guys. You two take care. And Doug?"

"Yes, sir?"

"Maybe shave that beard before the shoot. You want people to be able to recognize you in a cap and sunglasses!"

"I'll do it! How long will you be, sir? I've got to call it in and enter it on the logbooks."

Jason had forgotten about the call-in protocol. He held his voice steady. "Just a couple of hours. Hey. Could you maybe hold off on that call? You know how crazy some people get over being on screen, and if they know I'm here looking at locations for the shoot, they'll pop over and get in the way and want to jabber about all kinds of stuff, and I'll never get any work done."

"Um, it's protocol, sir," Doug said, but Bert waved Jason on.

"You go ahead and get started. We're both on lunch break anyway. No need to rush our call-in. Good to see you again, sir! And you too, Harry," Bert added. "My pairing mate likes you better than Jason!" Harry barked and wagged in reply.

Jason chuckled. "Harry says you guys rock. Thanks a million!"

As the gate opened, Jason drove in. His upper lip was sweating with the strain of every precious second. He was just a collector. How did he ever think he could pull this off? *Help*, he mumbled to the Presence.

Just outside the massive front door to the Termination Center, the Director was slowly regaining consciousness, but it was hard work swimming back up from the depths of confusion. Where he had fallen, he was a mass of bruises, and his wrist comm had smashed against the pavement. Several of his security detail were squatting around him, one administering medical aid. He sat up angrily and pushed them away. "What the hell?" he growled. "What idiot did this to me?"

"It was several of the idiots...I mean, the dignitaries, sir," the sergeant said. "They thought you were Alex cx94b."

"Why the hell would they think I was Alex cx94b?" the Director asked as he stood up to his full height and barely caught himself from going right back down, savagely shaking off the sergeant's steadying arm.

"From what I've been able to gather and from watching the last feeds of the news recorders, Alex cx94b broke free of his containment frame somehow, overpowered both guards and took Jason t43p7 hostage. Then he freed the others and got into the vehicle in which they fled the scene. It shouldn't be hard to locate a vehicle hauling a silo, sir. Do you want me to get the news to put out a general alert?"

"No, you halfwit!" the Director barked. "That'll just bring a lot of vigilantes and fame seekers out of the woodwork, create a traffic problem, muck everything up, and get in our way. And anyway, Alex is too good for any of these bumpkins around here. That's why we have an elite team. No! Don't do anything until I've been able to sit down for a moment and think. And bring me some damn water!"

"You're holding some, sir . . ."

"Shut up! Bring me a damn chair then! Why do I have to do everything around here? Go away! And let me think! Confiscate the recorders from all the news people, and destroy the memory sticks in them. We can still control the narrative if I can just have a moment to think!"

The Director was having a difficult time getting his mind to focus. It had been decades since he had been stunned as part of his training, and he had forgotten how hard it was to pull his thoughts together afterward. What was that name? Andrew? Allen? Alex. Alex was obviously the leader. What was the . . . he shook his head in a vain attempt to clear the cobwebs. What was the objective? What was Alex thinking? Alex had to know there was no way he could evade the authorities for long.

Was he crazy? No. Was he executing a strategy? Impossible.

Was he simply reacting like any other caged animal? Sure. Slowly, a new idea entered the arena of his patchwork of reasoning.

Continuing to wave away questions without even hearing the officers who attempted to get his attention, he grabbed onto this new thread. Did Alex have outside help? One of the guards, maybe? He quickly barked out orders to have the guards drained of every thought they'd ever had and put his team on analyzing the contents of their brains.

"No, they don't have to be able to use their minds when you're done. Just get the information, dammit!" *Get hold of yourself, Phelps,* he told himself. Calm down.

He took a deep breath. Where was I? It was something about . . . Yes. Perhaps the guards or perhaps someone else aided and abetted them. But who?

Stan maybe. Ah! Yes. Stan was hinged both ways. Stan was useful as a spy but unreliable for the same reason. And his nearly disastrous blunder at the hearing, chattering on and leaking the news of a library made him... well, so expendable.

He told the officers nearby to find Stan and put him in a separate room from the guards and give him the same going over. It was imperative to know what Stan had in the innermost recesses of his mind.

"Sure! Chemical, electrical, physical, use it all. It's all authorized. Wring him dry!" he growled impatiently.

OK, he thought. You have a little more time now that your underlings have something to concentrate on. He was liking this new idea. Alex must have had outside help to pull off this seeming masterstroke. He tried to think of anyone else who might have been in a position to . . . what the hell was Jason t43p7 doing out here? How he hated Jason! Flash in the pan. Johnny-come-lately. Carpetbagger. Phelps had worked and sweated and sacrificed his whole life to be where he was, and this unaccomplished trash monkey had, by simply falling back to earth early, stolen all the glory that was rightfully his! Curse him and his stupid dog! That dog . . .

The Director was having one of his famous nudges again.

He turned to the closest man. "You!"

"Sir?"

"Get me Alphaeus Goff."

"On communication?"

"No, not on communication! What good will that do, oaf? Have our people back in town bring him to me. Immediately! I want him yesterday. Understood?"

"Yes, sir! Right away, sir!"

The Director frowned. What was it about the dog? Why was he getting a nudge about the dog . . . and Goff? He observed that Jason t43p7 was never without the dog. Why? The Director seemed to sense that, somehow, Goff was the key to the riddle of the dog.

He set that thread aside and called for a list of the reporters and dignitaries, scanning it for anyone halfway capable of pulling this off. While doing that, he gave instructions for what to say to the calls from every governmental department that had begun pouring in. Some variation of, "We have everything under control, the prisoners will be re-apprehended shortly."

None of the names jumped off the page.

The ones with the brains to pull this off weren't these beat reporters or city dignitaries.

DESPERATE MEASURES

*"I would challenge you to a battle of wits,
but I see you are unarmed."*
—William Shakespeare

Back at the launch site, the guards, per Jason's request, had turned off the interior site cameras, since that would have alerted their superiors that Jason was there, and as Jason had told them, he would join them shortly, and together they would call headquarters and report the access. How cool would that be? Everyone down at the precinct would be jealous that they were hanging out with Jason t43p7 and wish they were the lucky ones keeping secrets with him. As they finished their lunches, they drifted in dreams of fame and envy.

Jason wheeled the silo into position on the launch pad. After completing that operation, he opened the access door, and he and Harry climbed inside.

"Hey, you guys," Jason said, "so far, so good. You may have guessed that we're about to make an attempt to get off this planet. If you have any better ideas, my dog and I are listening. And I know if I were you, I'd want to know a whole lot more about me—and my dog! Unfortunately, the authorities probably won't give us a ton of time for lengthy explanations with flowcharts and diagrams."

"Believe it or not," Alex said, "I've long thought our only hope was to get off this planet. I never in a million years imagined you would be the guy to make it happen. Meg says you're OK, and we all believe her, even though the rest of us only know you from the parades and the bios. So, what are we doing? What's the plan? We can wait to ask why you're doing this, but we seem to owe you our lives. Or at least this last chance to hang on to them. So. Thanks."

Jason looked around at them and smiled before walking over to the launch panels. "Um . . . I'm not entirely sure about this plan myself," he said over his shoulder. "Yesterday, I thought I was going to live the rest of my life as a VIP, find a nice house, and start inviting lots of friends to lots of parties, or maybe just go fishing. But. You see Harry here?"

Harry sat down next to Jason and turned to wag at them. Harry opened his mouth, but Jason clamped a hand over it and, with his other hand, began to pull charts and flip toggles. The others heard a faint humming sound emanating from the silo. "Harry is still inside, but there's someone else inside him too," Jason continued. "A heteroclite."

Again Harry opened his mouth, and again Jason clamped it shut. As simultaneous questions erupted all around him, Jason held up a hand. In the ensuing quiet, the sound of clicks and whirs came from the console. "Yeah, I'd never heard of one either!" He fed numbers from a chart into a keypad on the nav comp. "We're heading for a place that I've explored, actually it was the last place I visited. It's a little . . . ostentatious visually. Lots of bright colors and stuff, but I think it'll do for us."

"Heter-al what?" Jill asked.

"Heteroclite. Not important. For the moment, let's leave it that this heteroclite, named Izgad, is friendly to us humans and is helping us get off the planet, since at this point none of us are safe if we stay on it. You have no reason to trust me, but if you think about it, you really have no choice. The world thinks you've taken me hostage. They're scared of you, and they think I'm great for some reason and probably would want me returned alive from your clutches. But as far as the authorities go—I know them and the way they think all too well—they won't hesitate to blow this silo and me and every one of you to bits if by doing so they can score a publicity point or two."

Jason continued. "If you think about it, trusting or not trusting doesn't matter, since the worst that can happen if you do as I say is that you'll die quickly in this silo instead of over the weeks they'd take to perform your execution. Your long and painful terminations would be good for ratings."

Meg walked toward where he was busy with another segment of the console. "You know I already trust you. How can I help?"

Jason grinned at her. "Thanks." He motioned to a doorway. "Look back there for some more seating. Somewhere there's a first-aid kit. You guys look like you've been run through a stone pulverizer. Speaking of rocks, I'm getting us off this one as soon as I can feed the numbers into the console, so if you could give me a minute of silence to monkey with the auto-nav . . ."

As he continued to work feverishly, Mark, Jill, and Nando went to help Meg while Madeline and Hisako searched for the medical kit. Their experience in eluding the authorities for so long had molded them into a tightly-knit unit that any military commander would have been proud to command.

❖

Goff glared at the Director. "How dare you send your flunkies after me! Manhandling me as if I didn't have important and influential connections in the city! What could possibly justify—"

"Shut up," the Director said quietly. Sometimes he found this more effectively terrifying than yelling. He was in no mood to placate anyone. "I have a feeling you know something about a dog. Jason t43p7's dog. Why is that dog important?"

"His dog?"

"You know what I mean. You know what I'm looking for. I can't ask it any plainer."

"You're crazy; I don't have any idea—"

"Guards!" the Director called. "Apply some persuasion to this man. Use your fists."

Goff screamed as two large men began to pummel his face and body with blows from their gloved knuckles, designed to inflict maximum pain and blood flow. "Stop! Stop! St—"

Suddenly, Goff's voice changed to a deep animal snarl. "Imbeciles!" he said in a completely different tone. "You have no idea who you're dealing with!"

"Ah!" the Director said, smiling. "So there you are—the other Goff. Hold on," he commanded his men. Before he could address whatever was speaking, Goff, with no change in expression, wrenched his arm free from the containment frame with a loud cracking and tearing sound, leaving a bloody hand behind, still imprisoned. Pointing with the stump of his arm, the voice continued. "You! Phelps! You are insignificant, and yet you think you run this city! We see you! We know you! You have failed to deal with these diseased rats, and now you have allowed them to unite with the hero and his animal! You have allowed them to escape!"

The Director was not one to be intimidated, not even by this bloody, handless accuser with the low voice. He grabbed an immobilizer from the belt of the nearest guard and fired point blank into Goff's body, producing more animal roars but pinning Goff's body back into the frame. The Director was not easily impressed, but he watched with amazement as Goff's body, not particularly impressively built, began to warp the frame itself as it strained against its confinement.

"Maximum stun! Fire!" he called as three officers hit Goff with enough voltage to drop a bull. Though Goff's eyes and mouth were closed, the voice continued to use his tongue and vocal cords, speaking in menacing tones.

"The dog is a heteroclite. One of my order. But warped. The heteroclite is helping the vermin escape. They have taken the silo to the launch site and are moments from departure. You have failed us for the last time. You will pay dearly. I will—"

The Director did not wait for whatever vengeance the voice was promising to inflict. He barked into his communicator to get five B9 drones to the launch site immediately. He called for his vehicle and left Goff raging as he jumped inside and bellowed for the driver to pound like hell for the site.

On the way, he called for every available law enforcement unit to block entrances and exits to the launch site. No one in or out. But do not enter the facility. His mind wanted to go back to the word heteroclite, but his disciplined thought processes rejected that for the present, and he kept his focus on the silo.

"Alex!" Jason shouted, having finished his preparations at the console. "Come with me! The last thing we have to do is maneuver the silo into launch position. I don't know how much time we have, but I doubt it's much. You've got to be ready to hold off any attempt to recapture us while I finish this step! Come on! And bring that weapon on the desk over there!" Opening the door and diving through it, he was gone. Alex lost no time in grabbing Jason's firearm and following.

The others were treated once again to the shock of a talking dog. "Do not be worried," Izgad assured them. "I am reasonably sure we are going to make it, as you say. Our chances have risen dramatically to maybe two out of ten."

Outside, there was no sign of Jason, but Alex heard him on the other side of the silo. Alex also checked the guard's belt on his waist for any ordinance other than the stunner, although Jason's imposing sidearm was a step up in armament. He looked around for any possible large-scale weapon he might use.

Think, Alex, he calmly ordered himself. Stop and think. What will they send when they find out where we are and what we're doing? He racked his orderly mind for likely protocol.

No. Forget protocol. Alex knew he would be dealing with Phelps. Phelps cared more about results than protocol. So, what will Phelps do? Call his team of computer nerds? Order an infantry attack?

Then he had it. Drones. It'll be drones because Phelps knows speed will be the deciding factor. "What stops a drone?" he wondered aloud.

"Huh?" Jason shouted from behind the silo.

"How do you stop a drone?" Alex replied.

"You can't! They have evasive software!"

"That's it!" Alex said. "Software! Software is their strength and their weakness!"

"What?" Jason shouted.

"Never mind!" Alex replied. He pulled up the guard's communicator and entered an emergency message that only a prison guard or warden could issue.

His car hurtling toward the site, the Director leaned forward and peered at the news broadcast on his in-vehicle screen. It said someone had reported a full-scale radiation leak and chemical fire panic/evacuation report happening at the Termination Center. The reporter said he had been told a guard was the source of the signal.

The Director swore he would have the man fricasseed because a call like that temporarily halted all official directives, including drone activity, until the situation could be assessed. The override would not be in effect fast enough.

Curse it! Drones are out. What was his move? Nothing was any faster than the ground units already closest to the site. They had their instructions, but what if they were halted too?

He typed in an all-units command for local authorities around the launch site to continue at all speed to apprehend anyone attempting to do anything at the launch site.

His eyes narrowed as he realized he had a worthy opponent. Someone who knew protocol was helping to confound every system that the Director could muster to re-apprehend the prisoners.

Alex. The Director smiled through his rage. This countermove was genius. Brilliant. Praiseworthy.

I'll watch his bloody execution with particular delight.

"How much longer, Jason?" Alex asked when he had located him on the other side of the launch pad.

"I honestly don't know. I've never done this part before. I've always been inside when they did this. I've garbled the transmission of our coordinates—they won't know where we're heading—but I'm kind of stuck on the x-axis command. I did the y and z, but I can't seem to get the thing to jump over to the x-axis angle input. It should have jumped there after I entered the other two. And every second that goes by makes my angles for the other two go out of whack. Earth's rotation scrambles the position needed for the silo to enter the portal."

"When I'm working with stuff like this, and it fritzes on me, I turn it off and back on," Alex offered.

"The startup takes time we don't have," Jason said, "but I think you're probably right."

He reached for the restart sequence. At that moment, a security copter came roaring over the site, and a voice over a bullhorn commanded them to lie face down and await the arrival of the authorities. Alex never even thought; he just sprang away from Jason to draw their attention.

"I'll try to give you all the time I can!" he yelled as he dashed around the silo and up the embankment beside the pad. The chopper followed, just as Alex had hoped it would, and Jason began his desperate reboot while checking for new axis coordinates in his launch codes.

Alex knew the chopper had an immobilizing cannon with a targeting laser. He doubted they would use the laser but guessed they would use the cannon to freeze Alex and his companions, so everything could be sorted out later. They didn't need a clear shot; they just needed to get close.

As he ran at top speed, he counted the seconds in his head for how long it would take their marksman to sight him and fire. He planted a foot on the ground and began running at a right angle to his previous trajectory. He smiled as he saw the air shimmer and heard a low vibration to his left. He had caused the excited marksman to miss. It would take ten seconds for the weapon to recharge, and that would allow him to double back to the control/communications tower, a giant pillar of welded steel. He hoped their training had not included a technical point about firing the immobilizing cannon at an object like the tower.

Dashing around the backside of the spire, he stopped and waited. Looking up, he saw the copter's operator smile and the grim determination on the marksman's face as he pulled the trigger. Alex clamped his hands to the side of his head as an ear-splitting sonic blast filled the air with sparks and fire and rebounded on the copter. The occupants were stunned and immobilized by the weapon's ricochet, and the copter hovered obediently, frozen in place as the autopilot took over.

"Geez! What was that?" Jason yelled as Alex ran back to the silo.

"I can't hear very well right now," Alex replied. "Are you done?"

"Didn't have to reboot. Something happened when the cannon fired the first time that let me add in the third axis."

"What did you say?"

"Tell you later!" Jason shouted through cupped hands.

"Right!" Alex agreed. "If we're done, let's get outta here. Come on!"

They raced back into the silo. While Alex secured the hatch, Jason slid into his nav chair. "Here we go, boys and girls! You'd better strap into your chairs, though you're about to experience the weirdest feeling you've ever felt while sitting in one place. If

308

you'll look around here, I may have some bags for you to throw up in."

He fumbled with the last buttons.

The next few moments were an entirely new sensation for all but Jason and Harry. Their thoughts became slow, as if their perception were running a race with their powers of recognition and losing.

It was an out-of-body experience. Apparently, all motion had a component of inertia, even the mind in motion, and they struggled to reach for thoughts that were both lagging behind and streaking ahead, obviously present but hopelessly out of reach.

The chopper's occupants, unable to move anything but their eyes, saw the silo shimmer like a dissolving seltzer tablet and then vanish out of their peripheral vision.

THE NEW NORMAL

"Let us try to see things from their better side:
You complain about seeing thorny rose bushes;
Me, I rejoice and give thanks to the gods
That thorns have roses."
—Alphonse Karr

The Director roared up to the launch site moments later, bawling at the horrified sentries. "Get those damn gates open now!"

Upon making his furious way through the gates, he found a copter hovering next to the control/comm tower and a truck with no silo anywhere in sight.

"Stop for Plasm's sake!" he bellowed. When the driver had done so, the Director leaped out to see that the prisoners were long gone, his hopes dashed, and his plans ruined.

It rocked his world to the core.

His anger came crashing down all around him in a cold and numbing realization of glory slipping through his fingers. It left him crippled, physically drained, and weak. Bracing himself on the vehicle, he slowly and mechanically spun 360 degrees to survey the scene. The only sound was the drone of the copter blades, and the only sight was the empty truck bed. His stumbling walk to the launch pad seemed like it took years. All emotions were swallowed in a great sense of despair and loss.

Stopping beside the waist-high concrete staging platform upon which the empty truck bed mocked him, he placed his palms on the platform and bowed his head with an infuriated groan. He knew the Elders would demote him to some obscure post like director of mining operations or perhaps a news liaison. He would lose his team, his position, his perks, his reputation, his life's work.

But even as he despaired, his will hardened, and his spine stiffened and straightened. Was he not the great Director Phelps, the most indispensable man in the city? What would this place be without him? Ha! No despair would be countenanced! This would not finish him; he was far too necessary. He would prepare a devastating case against the people in charge of silo transport. And the launch site. And the news teams. And the city officials. And the guards at the Termination Center. And Stan would *definitely* get his share of what was coming.

Oh, and there was one more person to wrap this ball of humiliation up and hang it on–hang it on his goddam nose: Goff!

Yes. Sure. Old Alphaeus Goff, a gift if ever there was one. Wait till they heard him speak!

It would be child's play to shift the blame. They were the ones who had bungled this, not him, and they would be made to bear the brunt of the Elders' displeasure.

He turned to sit on the edge of the launch pad and began making the necessary calls to plant these ideas in the system. Behind him, a useless strap slipped off the cradle with a loud bang. The Director ignored it.

Inside the silo, somewhere in space or perhaps nowhere at all, the friends were safe for the moment but found themselves unable to properly appreciate their rescue. Their first hour or so had been horribly confusing and disorienting, and several of them had used their emergency bags, though there was precious little in their stomachs to contribute. Jason made his way among them, providing blankets, moist towels, and ice cubes as needed. As their systems became more acclimated to the sensation of the portal, they were able to drink some of the strong tea Jason brewed for them and begin to nibble on some dried banana slices and saltines to settle their turbulent insides. Every now and then, they would hug each other and shake their heads in amazement, but conversation was beyond their ability just yet.

A call came in from Max over the emergency system. Jason knew communication was nearly impossible during this phase of the journey, but apparently, *nearly* impossible left room for *remotely* possible. He was surprised, but he saw no reason not to answer.

"Hey, Max! You look a little frazzled."

"Jase! You're free? Excellent! You must've overpowered your kidnappers! Bravo! Way to do it, my brah-thah! Got 'em all in hand, huh?" He chuckled. "Probably in some of those extra-large collection jars of yours or something. I was calling to negotiate for your release, but now you can just turn that silo around and deliver those prisoners right back to the center. And then, my friend, we'll throw you a second welcome home party!"

"Max, you're a good man. It's great to see you, and I'm so glad you called. Actually, the whole escape thing was kind of Harry's idea! I thought these guys needed to be rescued, so me and the dog sorta organized a . . . I guess what you'd call a jailbreak."

"You and Harry—"

"Yeah, it was touch and go for a while there, but here we are, and there you are, and there's no telling how far our here and your there are swiftly getting to be."

Static interrupted the connection momentarily, and then Max's face returned to the screen.

"I think I'm losing you, Jase. It sounded like you said something about you and the dog organizing a jailbreak? Did I hear that right?"

"You did. But feel free to tell any story you like. We don't care."

"Jase! Are you turning around? They say you didn't file a flight plan. How can we find you, my friend? I mean you could end up anywhere in the known universe. Are you turning around? Tell me you're turning around . . ."

"Max, you know I love you, buddy, but this is goodbye for a long time, if not forever. You understand?"

Max leaned in with a sideways glance and lowered his voice. "If I did, you know I couldn't possibly say it. But Jase, champ," he urged, "think of the life you're leaving! I'd trade my left lung and part of my liver for the easy street you were on! How can you just turn your back and walk away?"

"It just got to be impossible to have people fighting for me, and I couldn't believe any longer that everything really was everything.

It got to be a problem, a big problem, and then it became a conundrum, and then it ended up just being funny."

"Jase, this is being recorded!"

"Give our love to Director Phelpsie. And love to you, my old pal. I hope you can someday become unsatisfied with what they're selling you too!"

More static. This time the picture came back sideways, and the sound was nearly unlistenable with a high-pitched hum that made Harry stand up with his front feet on the console.

Max's voice scratched through the speakers. "There's Harry! Good boy, Harry! Hey there, you ol' mutt! Talk some sense into your redheaded master, will ya? Hey Jase, seriously, you can't just —"

"Bye, Max, you're breaking up! There's more than one way to be a prisoner, you know. Get your brain out of their clutches while you still can!"

The signal was deteriorating rapidly, but Jason could still hear Max's voice. "Jase! Stop! Come back! You don't know what you're miss . . ."

The signal went dead.

AFTERMATH

"And they lived happily (aside from a few normal disagreements, misunderstandings, pouts, silent treatments, and unexpected calamities) ever after."
—Jean Ferris

After a few nauseous hours, even Hisako was no longer bothered by the forces that were catapulting them—without a hint of motion—light years upon light years from their own solar system. There were no windows, and for all they knew, the silo could have been still sitting in the cradle on the launch pad.

Jason winced with one eye closed. "Yeah, in the early days, we lost some folks who couldn't believe they really were moving, and they tried to go outside to see. That's why the computer now auto-locks the door."

With their recovering equilibrium, the friends soon realized they had not eaten since the morning of the trial, and they were famished. To their delight, Jason showed them the warmers full of meat-and-cheese subs. They gave the pies and Karmelpop a good run as well.

The shock of the rescue would take longer than the nausea to wear off. As they ate, bits of conversation revolved around the events that had so recently taken place.

When Jason was asked how he had been able to get his silo delivered to the site, he explained that the news crews had a lot of embarrassing information on all the right people, and if they ever needed a prop, even a large prop like the silo, they could usually finagle it without much trouble.

Of course, Izgad had to be reintroduced and explained and then re-explained. They enjoyed hearing Jason and Izgad recall their first meeting and laughed through the stories they told about their time together and their deep and growing friendship. Jill said Izgad reminded her of some of the odd characters in C. S. Lewis's *Space Trilogy*, and Nando said for him it was the mythical world of the Nordic peoples and the Greeks. Hisako said that her sponsors and their sponsors preserved many rituals with long-dead ancestors and that she felt at home with a creature she could not see. Even one inhabiting a dog.

Of course, they all had the wrong impression of Izgad's superhuman abilities as well as his limitations. Jason and Izgad tried to explain that the limits mostly involved not having permission to do stuff as opposed to not having the capacity to do it. The companions could be excused for still not understanding after several attempts.

Soon their conversation returned to their own situation. Harry circled up at his new favorite place: Meg's feet. Jason explained that a priority tomorrow would be to study Izgad's prophetic message. But tonight, that could wait.

As the first stage of their journey wore on, they all knew they had to get to sleep eventually, but for a long time they talked about their future. Where they were going, what they would find there, how they might build their lives. They reasoned that they would be relatively safe from any large-scale attempt to recapture them. They felt sure they would be mostly left alone by the authorities and bid "good riddance."

Periodically, they would run up against the freakishness of sharing the company of a heteroclite speaking through Harry the dog. When one of them remarked on what a bizarre and surreal experience it was, Jason would chuckle, looking directly at Harry and say, "Welcome to my life!"

Their minds were still full of the excitement of the day, but their bodies were worn out, and Nando had already fallen asleep in his chair. Hisako had been straightening up the control room, as she said, "to keep from curling up right there on the floor with Harry." Nearly everyone had yawned at least twice. Since there was only one sleep field on board, Jason suggested that the now-empty collection bays in the next room would make good bunks, especially if they grabbed some of the air-cushioned packing bags for mattresses as well as pillows and blankets. The older ones immediately said goodnight. Madeline woke Nando, and he followed the others out of the room with a husky "Sweet dreams, you crazy people!"

The four younger ones stayed up a little longer on principle. There was so much to plan and dream about. But after a while, Jill excused herself and left for the bunks. In about fifteen minutes, Alex said goodnight too. It was just Jason and Meg. They were sitting next to each other with Harry in between. They were both staring at the floor. Jason broke the silence.

"Would you forgive me for that scene at the Termination Center? You know I was just trying to create a distraction, so Harry could free Alex."

Harry's tail twitched at the mention of his name, but his eyes stayed shut, and nothing else budged.

Meg frowned. "At first I was shocked . . ."

"Yeah, I was right there, remember? You looked like you wanted to strangle me."

"But it's OK," she assured him. "I understand now. And Jason, if you had been able to warn me ahead of time about what you were thinking of doing, I wouldn't have been able to pull off a believable reaction. I bet I did look like I wanted to throttle you, 'cause I felt like it was the crowning insult the wicked world could throw at me, having you show up—the guy I spent so much time wondering about—and having you publicly humiliate me. It was too much!"

Their eyes never left the floor.

"Well, I owe you," Jason said. "And Meg, I mean it when I say I was glad for the containment frame because the ferocity I saw in your eyes was . . . Well, let's just say I'd never want to make you mad unless you were immobilized in one of those frame things!"

"Remember that, Mister!" Meg said and then laughed. They glanced at each other and then looked down again. "But I meant what I said about wondering about you. I just found myself sort of thinking about what you might be doing and maybe when you'd come back. It's not that I was lonely because I had Jill and Alex and the gang at the library. I just—"

"Me too," Jason said.

"No! Let me finish! I just wanted to tell somebody what was happening to me, and you were the one I kept wanting to tell. That time we went out together was really something. I never connected with someone quite like you. And then you were gone. For more than a year. But I never stopped . . . well, I can't think of a better word than *wondering.* I kept wondering about you: where you were, what you were doing, what you were thinking, and if you were also wondering about me . . ."

"Are you done?"

"I just. . ."

"Because I think it's my turn to tell you that I kept thinking about you. It's lonely out there—out here—in space. I was lonely for my livingspace and my friends and my favorite hikes and games and food. Lonely for the hubbub of my collector class at the academy. Lonely for solitude on my home planet, not these far-flung corners of the galaxy. But when I thought of you, all that loneliness took a backseat. With you, it wasn't like any of that loneliness at all. It was something else, it was . . . well, I was just content. You were more than a memory. You were solid, tangible, reassuring."

"Pfft. Yeah, right . . ."

"No, I mean it! I didn't think of you as far away. I thought of you as if I could reach you anytime I wanted. Weird, huh?"

Harry seemed to snort. Meg didn't hear it, and Jason ignored it.

"It is weird," Meg replied. "And it isn't. I can see that we need to discover what we can about what's happening between us."

"Sounds like I'm one of your laboratory experiments."

"So what if you are? I put my heart and soul into those!"

"Then I'll gladly submit to being the subject of your scientific investigation."

They had been talking so plainly that eye contact would have been impossible, but now they both looked up. And both saw there was a bond. Something that would grow into a world as vast and as glorious and as constantly fascinating as the cosmos into which they were hurtling.

After a moment, Meg reached over and laid a hand on Jason's arm. "I wanted so much to see you when you got back, but by then we were on the run. Jason, listen . . . something has happened to me. I'm not the same girl you met that night so long ago. I've been reading, Jason. Reading books! Forbidden books. Seditious books. Dangerous books! They were correct in what they said at the trial! I don't belong in any world that doesn't have books!" Her face melted from serious to joyful, and she spoke more rapidly. "Sublime books, funny books, spellbinding books, transformational books. I've got to tell you about what we were doing and why we were raided and why I think we were such a threat to them." Starting at the beginning, she explained the library and how everyone fit into the story. Neither one of them was the least bit sleepy. As a matter of fact, they were both wide awake, thoroughly happy, glad to finally be together.

Jason listened to Meg's tale with admiration. All that she and her friends had experienced while he had been gathering plants and watching movies and having conversations with a talking dog. He scanned Meg's face, watched her eyes sparkle as they focused on something far away, and listened to her captivating voice as she told her story. She and these people Izgad had gotten him involved with had more raw courage than he could ever hope to possess.

When Meg finished, he shook his head in amazement.

"You guys took incredible risks!"

"Well, it's not so much the risks that were incredible; it was the books. Jason, we never realized when we were growing up how much imagination and truth were taken from us. How much history and wisdom were just wiped away as if they never existed. How huge ideas that seem to fill a hunger in each of us were suppressed and erased from everywhere but our wildest dreams. We were conditioned to feel that life was simply beating out the meaningless time while we were waiting to die. We thought our own pleasure was the only mitigation for the coming mystery of death. But these illegal books are stories about risk, about daring, about rescues, about great friendships and great loves and how these loves and friendships drive people to face challenges that cost them everything. These books inspire us to seek for the simple reason of finding. Finding, Jason! They told us not to look because there was nothing to look for. They lied and said that being safe and hoping for a little happiness is all there is. There has to be more, much more! We each have a hidden gift of curiosity, and with that curiosity comes stepping out without being able to see where we're going. A world without curiosity is a living death. And each of us feels an awakening inside and that nagging curiosity about the deepest and the highest and the lowest levels of the human experience. To earnestly want answers to questions that burn in our hearts, questions we've been inoculated against by shallow non-answers and mindless truth-isms. But these questions and their answers are the great purpose of our being. We were made to explore, to wonder, to marvel. There are always greater and more astounding discoveries out there! And Jason, those people back there can't begin to account for the universe. There's an intellect behind everything, and the intellect is like a personal being. And that? That is the reason for the thirst. That's who the thirst is for! To probe. To uncover what's been hidden. We have to go deeper."

Jason nodded. "I've got a lot to tell you too. Well, Izgad and I do. And Meg, I know exactly what you mean. Because something's happened to me too! It has to do with someone called the Maker and the Primal Story. We should probably get some sleep at some point, but there's so much racing around in my heart that sometimes I feel like I'm gonna explode."

They grew silent. They both knew the other one shared a deep and exciting understanding about life. It was a great comfort.

Though neither felt particularly sleepy, they knew they should probably fall in line with the others.

Meg turned to Jason. "Tomorrow is another day. That's what my parents would always say."

"You call them what?"

"And each day we live is a gift, which is why we call it the present!"

"Very clever."

"Also true."

"Goodnight, Meg."

"Goodnight."

They reluctantly got up to find Meg some packing bags and an unused bunk. Jason walked with her, saying he'd sleep in his chair at the console, just in case something needed attention. He told Meg that he was excited to hear more about her reading.

They paused together in the doorway to the specimen room. "Yeah." Meg sighed and looked at the floor. "We loved our time with those books. I don't know if Phelps ever found the cave behind the house. I guess the books we were able to save are still there. We even moved Mark and Hisako's books up there for safekeeping."

She looked up at Jason, a fierce determination in her eyes. "But they're gone, back on Earth, wherever Earth is." She shook her head. "We'll probably never hold a book again. Or see one on screen. Maybe we can write down passages we remember from them. I'll bet if we take our time and concentrate, we might . . ."

"You don't have to!" Jason broke in, laughing. "I almost forgot! Izgad and I already picked up the library from your cave! It's all back there in the supply closet! If you need some night reading, feel free to go back there and grab one of 'em!"

"What?" six sleepy voices asked together.

"What did you say?" came Hisako's voice through her pillow.

"Did we hear you right?" Mark asked.

"The library?" Nando rumbled.

Madeline gasped. "*Our* library?"

Jill sat up and demanded. "Say it again!"

"You picked it up, and it's here, in the silo?" Alex marveled.

"Jason?" cried Meg looking at him with wide wondering eyes.

Jason smiled at Harry. Harry wagged his tail.

ABOUT THE AUTHOR

Alan Root Robertson is a writer of both books and songs. He has done post-graduate work in geology, has been a college instructor, a watercolorist, a conversationalist, a Nashville writer/producer, a conference headliner and workshop teacher, a children's pastor, and a worship leader. He has done advertising for Wrigleys, Kelloggs, and McDonalds, been on stage with Amy Grant, and sung for 13,000 people at a Billy Graham Children's Crusade. He and his wife, Emily, have two daughters, two sons-in-law, and six grandkids. Alan is theologically a Christian mutt, being at home in all the different flavors of churches as long as they preach the Gospel of the manger, the cross, and the empty tomb.

His love of teaching has made him a lifelong learner. He has a default mode for simplification, encouragement, and a seeming inability to be serious for long stretches of time. He's always had an intense fascination with what might be happening on other planets, especially when things on this present one are not making much sense.

Made in United States
Orlando, FL
02 April 2024

45375530R00193